THE

CROW'S
CALL

Amish Greenhouse Mystery
Book 1

THE
CROW'S
CALL

WANDA &. BRUNSTETTER

SHILOH RUN PRESS
An Imprint of Barbour Publishing, Inc.

© 2020 by Wanda E. Brunstetter

Print ISBN 978-1-64352-021-6

eBook Editions:
Adobe Digital Edition (.epub) 978-1-64352-022-3
Kindle and MobiPocket Edition (.prc) 978-1-64352-023-0

Cover Design: Buffy Cooper
Cover Photography: Richard Brunstetter III

For more information about Wanda E. Brunstetter, please visit the author's website at www.wandabrunstetter.com

Published by Shiloh Run Press, an imprint of Barbour Publishing, Inc., 1810 Barbour Drive, Uhrichsville, OH 44683, www.shilohrunpress.com

Our mission is to inspire the world with the life-changing message of the Bible.

ecpa Member of the
Evangelical Christian
Publishers Association

Printed in the United States of America

Dedication

To my Amish friend, Cindy, who suffered a great
loss but came through victoriously.

What time I am afraid, I will trust in thee.
PSALM 56:3 KJV

Chapter 1

Strasburg, Pennsylvania

An April wind's flurry sent swirls of dust into the air and across the yard. *This isn't a good day for a celebration.* Amy King shielded her eyes for a moment. The current of air rustled her dress as she cradled a basket of spring flowers from her parents' greenhouse up to their home. Amy's sister, Sylvia, and her family would be coming for supper soon to help them celebrate Mom's birthday, and she wanted everything to be perfect.

Amy's brothers Henry and Abe still lived at home, but their older brother, Ezekiel, and his family were now part of an Amish community in New York State. They had hired a driver and planned to join them this afternoon. Amy always looked forward to the times when their whole family could be together.

As the wind calmed down, Amy gazed at the basket of flowers and smiled. She would put the lovely blooms in a glass vase and set it in the center of their dining-room table. Mom had a love for flowers, which was why she'd worked faithfully in the greenhouse with Dad for so many years.

Amy liked flowers too, but there were other things she enjoyed more, such as spending time with her boyfriend, Jared. He'd begun courting her almost a year ago, and Amy figured most any time now Jared would ask for her hand in marriage. She was prepared to say yes, of course, for Jared was all she'd ever wanted in a husband. He was courteous, kind, strong, and gentle, and of course she thought he was the most handsome man she'd ever met.

Amy halted her footsteps when the eerie sound of a crow's call invaded her dreamy thoughts. She'd had an aversion to crows ever since she was a young girl and one had flown over the blanket she'd sat upon, dropping a corncob right on her foot. It had left a nasty bruise, and following the incident, the crow carried on like Amy had done something wrong. It was superstitious of her, but ever since that day, whenever she saw or heard a crow, Amy expected something bad might happen. Today was no exception. The crow, sitting on a fence post and making such a fuss, seemed to be taunting Amy as she stood with goosebumps on her arms and chills tingling her spine.

Refusing to give in to her anxiety, Amy hurried toward the house. *Caw! Caw! Caw!* The crow's foreboding call continued.

Amy shuddered and moved on. It was childish to allow an irrational belief to take over her thoughts, but she couldn't help feeling that something bad was on the horizon. Maybe this time it would be worse than a simple corncob bruising her foot.

She brushed the notion aside and stepped into the house. Amy wanted everything to be special for Mom's birthday, and she wouldn't let a silly old crow and her unfounded trepidation put a damper on this evening's celebration.

"It's so good to see you again!" Amy gave Ezekiel and Michelle a hug and reached her hand out to stroke the top of their little girl's head. "Angela Mary has grown so much since we last saw her. It's hard to believe she's two years old already."

Michelle smiled and placed one hand against her stomach. "I wasn't going to share this till we were all sitting around the supper table tonight, but in about five months our daughter will have a little sister or brother."

Amy clapped her hands and gave Michelle another hug. "Oh, that's *wunderbaar!*"

"What about your big brother? Don't I get another hug?" Ezekiel nudged Amy's arm.

"*Jah*, of course." She gave Ezekiel a second hug.

When Amy stepped back, he looked around the yard. "Where is everyone? Figured when our driver's van pulled in, we'd be greeted by the whole family."

"Henry went out to buy a gift for Mom. Abe's still at work. Dad and Mom are in the greenhouse, getting ready to close up for the day. They might not have heard the van come into the yard."

At that moment, their parents stepped out of greenhouse and headed for Ezekiel and his family. Hugs started all over again.

"It's so good to see you." Mom teared up. "I wasn't sure you could come."

Ezekiel shook his head. "We wouldn't have missed your birthday for anything."

"That's right," Michelle agreed. "Happy birthday, Belinda."

"*Danki*." Mom leaned down and swept Angela Mary into her arms. "How's my precious little granddaughter doing?"

The child giggled when her grandpa reached over and tickled her under the chin.

"She's doing well." Michelle looked over at Ezekiel. "Should we tell them our news now?"

He nodded. "May as well, since you already let Amy know."

"Let her know what?" Mom's eyelids fluttered. "Are you planning to move back to Strasburg?"

"No, it's nothing like that, although we do miss everyone here. My business is doing well, and we're all settled into the community at Clymer." He pointed to Michelle's stomach. "We have another little one on the way."

Dad thumped Ezekiel's back, while Mom handed Angela Mary

to Amy and then gave Michelle another hug. "That's great news. When is the *boppli* due?"

"In about five months." Michelle's blue-green eyes glistened. "Sometimes I have to stop and pinch myself to see if I'm dreaming. Becoming a Christian, joining the Amish church, and marrying Ezekiel were the best things that ever happened to me." She smiled up at him. "I feel like my life is complete."

Amy smiled too. It was a joy to see the radiance on her sister-in-law's face. It was hard in the past when Michelle used to be English and had deceived them into believing she was the Lapp's granddaughter, whom they'd known nothing about for too many years.

Thank the Lord that through the power of God's love and forgiveness, people can change and start fresh with a new life in Him. Amy held her little niece close and said a silent prayer. *Heavenly Father, may this child grow up to be a woman who seeks Your ways and walks the right path that will be pleasing unto You.*

"Well, let's get your suitcases out of the van, and we can all go up to the house." Dad's booming voice ended Amy's prayer.

"Good idea." Ezekiel's head moved quickly up and down. "I'll remind our driver what day to pick us up, and then after we get the luggage out, he can be on his way."

Amy waited beside the van until everything had been taken out. Then she handed Angela Mary to her mother, picked up one of the suitcases, and started for the house. As soon as Sylvia and her family got here, they would get things going for supper.

Everyone sat around the living room and visited until Sylvia and her husband, Toby, arrived with their two-year-old boy, Allen, and four-month-old baby girl, Rachel. Henry returned from shopping about the same time, and Abe, who worked for a local buggy maker, showed up a few minutes later. After greeting everyone, they grabbed some chairs and joined in on the conversation.

Amy smiled, seeing Henry sitting by his twenty-one-year-old brother. He appeared to be attentive as Abe told Dad about his day at work. Henry and Abe were close, despite their six-year age difference.

I wonder if Henry will become a buggy maker as well. Or will he end up helping us full-time in the greenhouse? Amy shifted on her chair.

It wasn't long before Ezekiel announced Michelle's pregnancy to the rest of the family, who were enthusiastic at the news.

Amy thought how much easier it would have been if they'd shared their good news once everyone had arrived. *I suppose it's more exciting to share the news more than once.* Amy rose from her chair. "I believe supper's about ready. If you all want to take seats at the dining-room table, I'll bring everything out."

"I'll help." Mom started to rise from the couch, but Amy shook her head. "Not tonight, Mom. Since it's your birthday, you're the guest of honor."

Mom's brows furrowed. "Now how can I be the guest of honor in my own home?"

"Because we say so." Dad grinned at her and then looked around the room. "Isn't that right, family?"

Everyone nodded.

"I'll help get supper on the table." Michelle gestured to her daughter. "Ezekiel, would you please keep an eye on Angela Mary?"

"Of course, but I doubt I will be the only person watching her." He glanced across the room at their mother and winked. "Right, Mom?"

"Absolutely."

Michelle left the room with Amy. "Your family is so special," she said when they entered the kitchen. "You are blessed to have such loving, caring parents."

"I think so too." Amy grabbed two potholders and opened the oven door. Warm steam escaped along with the tantalizing aroma of ham and baked potatoes. She placed the ham and potatoes on the kitchen table and asked Michelle to dish up the green beans on the stove, while she took sour cream, butter, and freshly cut chives from the refrigerator.

"When I was growing up, I would have given anything to have parents like yours." Michelle frowned as she placed the green beans in a serving bowl.

"I'm sorry you had such a difficult childhood."

Her sister-in-law shrugged. "It's in the past. I had to move on with my life."

Ezekiel had told Amy about the abuse Michelle and her two younger brothers, Ernie and Jack, had suffered at the hands of their parents. She couldn't imagine how hard it must have been for Michelle to endure such a thing, or to be taken from her parents and put in foster care with people she didn't even know. What made it worse was that Michelle and her brothers had all gone to different homes and never saw each other again until the day of Michelle and Ezekiel's wedding. What a wonderful surprise it was when Mary Ruth's granddaughter Sara located Ernie and Jack and brought them to meet her.

So many good things had happened in her family. Amy knew folks who had dealt with worry, fear, and even tragedy, but things had been going along quite well for her family. The greenhouse ran smoothly, providing for them financially, but since Sylvia was a full-time wife and mother and no longer worked for their folks, Amy had left her job at a dry goods store to help in the greenhouse full-time. Dad took care of advertising, billing, and making sure everything ran smoothly, while Amy and her mother were responsible for the plants and flowers they sold to the public, as well as providing a few florists in the area with flowers to make their floral arrangements. It was a good life, and Amy felt content. The only thing that would make it better would be if Jared proposed marriage to her soon.

Michelle tapped Amy's shoulder. "You look like you're a hundred miles from here. Didn't you hear what I said?"

Amy shook her head. "Sorry. I was deep in thought. What did you say to me?"

"I was wondering if you're ready to take the food items out to the dining room yet. I'm sure our hungry family is waiting eagerly."

She laughed. "Of course they are, and I'm eager to join them."

Amy picked up the platter of ham and was about to leave the kitchen when Abe stepped in.

"Hey, Sister, what's taking so long? Don't you know we're starvin' in there?"

She rolled her eyes. "Well, if you're starving, grab a couple of dishes and take them in."

Thank You, God, once again for my family. Amy glanced around the table at the smiling faces looking back at her as they all enjoyed the tasty meal.

Mom was in especially good spirits this evening, laughing and enjoying the antics of her three grandchildren. It wouldn't be long before she'd be blessed with four little ones to dote on.

Amy thought of Jared, wishing he could be here with them as part of the family. But since they were only courting and not an engaged couple, she felt it wouldn't have been right to ask him to join them. She would be seeing Jared tomorrow night anyway, when they went out for their evening meal at the Bird-in-Hand Family Restaurant.

"Let's not worry about doing the supper dishes right now," Sylvia said when the meal ended. "We can just put them in the sink till after Mom opens her presents and we've had cake and ice cream."

Amy thumped the side of her head. "Oh, no. When I went shopping yesterday, I forgot to get some ice cream."

"That's okay." Mom flapped her hand. "We can get by without it."

"No, we can't." Dad shook his head. "It wouldn't seem like a birthday celebration if there wasn't cake and ice cream."

"We could crank out some homemade if we had all the ingredients." Amy leaned her elbows on the table. "Trouble is, we don't have any heavy whipping cream and maybe not enough eggs. Even if we did, it would take too much time to mix it all, crank till it froze, and then let it set until we could eat it." She looked over at Mom. "So, I agree. . . . We should settle for just cake."

Dad shook his head again—this time with a determined set of

his jaw. "I'll hitch my horse to one of our carriages and head for the grocery store." He glanced around the table. "Anyone wanna come along for the ride and to keep me company?"

"I'll go." Toby pushed his chair away from the table.

"Me too." Abe also left his seat.

"Okay, guess I'll take the two-seater. Anybody else want to join us?" The others, including Amy, shook their heads.

"After that good meal, plus the long ride down here from New York, think I will try to catch a few winks while you're gone." Ezekiel yawned and stretched his arms over his head.

Mom rose to her feet. "Well, if we're going to wait on ice cream to have our dessert, we may as well do the dishes." She reached for her plate, but Michelle grabbed it out from under her.

"This celebration is in honor of you, so you ought to go relax in the living room. Amy, Sylvia, and I will take care of the dishes. Right, ladies?"

"Absolutely," Amy and Sylvia said in unison.

"All right." Mom heaved a sigh. "I can see I'm outnumbered."

Amy got up right away and started clearing dishes. Sylvia and Michelle did the same. Mom led Angela Mary and Allen to the living room, and when Amy glanced over her shoulder, she saw her mother peek at baby Rachel, where she lay sleeping in the playpen.

Dad, Toby, and Abe said their goodbyes, put on their straw hats, and went out the back door.

A short time later, as Amy began filling the sink with warm, soapy water, she saw her father's horse and buggy go down the driveway at a steady pace. She placed all the silverware into the sink and glanced out the window again in time to see Dad's rig ease out onto the road. The horse and carriage had gone only a short distance, when a semitruck came out of nowhere. Amy clutched her throat and screamed as the semi rammed the back of Dad's buggy. For a few seconds, her mind went blank, as if her brain had stopped working. Then, just as quickly, Amy screamed for the rest of the family to come, before she raced out the back door.

Chapter 2

Amy's chin trembled as a wave of grief threatened to consume her. *Lord, I don't understand at all. . . .* Through blurry eyes, she saw Henry sitting alone on the sofa. His collapsed body posture and distant, empty stare revealed that his heart was also breaking. Amy worried about him not having Abe and Dad around anymore.

She sniffed and blotted her tears. A funeral service for three family members on the same day was unimaginable. But that's exactly what would happen tomorrow. The caskets of her father, brother, and brother-in-law had been placed in this room for the viewing that had occurred a few hours ago.

Nothing about today seemed real, and tomorrow would be worse. Relatives and friends from their community as well as other areas would be here for the funeral service and to say their final goodbyes. People would speak kind words and offer comfort, but nothing in the King family would ever be the same. When that semitruck hit her father's buggy, three men's lives had been snuffed out. Dad's horse had also been killed, but the animal could be replaced. No one could replace Dad, Abe, or Toby. And nobody but God could heal the rest of the family's broken hearts as they continued living without their loved ones.

Amy swiped again at the tears rolling down her cheeks. *Poor Sylvia. She's taken her husband's death so hard, I don't know how she's ever going to cope. With two small children to raise and no financial support, she'll have no choice but to move in with us.*

During the last three days, Amy's older sister had spent most of her time tucked away in her room, hardly eating or talking to anyone. Sylvia's children were too young to grasp the reality of the tragedy, which in some ways made the situation that much more difficult.

Amy struggled to accept and deal with the tragedy that had befallen her family. She continued to stand in the living room, contemplating whether to go out to the mailbox. After what had happened, it was hard to go out there. The sight of a semitruck passing their place caused her to relive the accident, and she dreaded going anywhere in the buggy. Thankfully, their friends had offered meals as well as comforting words, so she could avoid making a trip to the store for now.

Caw! Caw! Caw! A crow calling from the yard sent chills up Amy's spine, and she glanced toward the window. She had never been one to believe in superstitions or omens but couldn't help thinking about the crow she'd spotted in the yard three days ago, before their company arrived for Mom's birthday party. Had the black bird with its raucous-sounding cry tried to warn them of impending doom?

Amy shivered and rubbed her arms. It wasn't cold in the house, yet she felt chilled to the bone.

Maybe it's warm, but I don't feel it because my body and soul have been numb ever since that horrible accident took away three important men from our family.

"It's hard to believe they're gone, isn't it?" Ezekiel's deep voice drove Amy's thoughts aside.

She blinked. "How long have you been standing here?"

"Just came into the room a moment ago." He glanced in Henry's direction. "Let's go sit with him."

Amy followed Ezekiel over to the sofa, but Henry remained quiet as he scooted over, barely glancing at them.

"I keep wishing I was caught in the middle of a nightmare and would wake tomorrow morning and find out Dad, Abe, and Toby are still here and everything's as it should be."

"I know." Ezekiel groaned. "If only Dad hadn't been so determined to go for ice cream. If the three of them had just stayed home...." His voice trailed off. "Guess there's no point in rehashing all of this. We can't bring 'em back by wishing."

"That's for sure." Henry's voice sounded strained.

"No, but if we could, I'd wish upon a star, toss a penny in a wishing well, and put candles in Mom's birthday cake that none of us ate, and then make a mighty big wish." Ezekiel slipped one arm around Amy's shoulder and the other around Henry's. It was a comfort to have her big brother here and know he would take care of them. She felt certain that under the circumstances, Ezekiel and Michelle would move back to Strasburg to help in the greenhouse and offer emotional support to her, Mom, Sylvia, and Henry during this most difficult time. *Of course, Ezekiel's grieving too,* she reminded herself. *He's bound to realize that his place is here with us now, not in Clymer, New York.*

Ezekiel turned toward Amy with glassy eyes. "We need to get the funeral behind us and let things settle down a bit before we talk about plans for the future and let you in on what Michelle and I have decided."

"What's that?"

"Jah, what's your idea?" Henry leaned forward.

"Okay, guess I'll tell you now rather than waiting. I'm going to give up my business and sell our home so we can move back here and help run the greenhouse." Ezekiel's hands and arms hung limp at his sides. "It's either that or Mom will have to sell this place and you'll all have to move to Clymer to be with us."

"I don't wanna move." Henry shook his head. "Let's not talk about this right now."

"I don't think Mom will go for that idea, Ezekiel. She was born and raised in Strasburg, and this is her home." Amy motioned toward the window, where the crow still carried on. "Besides, she enjoys working in the greenhouse and would not want to sit around while you try to support us all financially."

"I wouldn't be carrying the whole load. Mom would have money from the sale of this home and the greenhouse."

Amy rose from the couch and shook her head. "Your house isn't big enough for all of us. The best thing would be for you to sell your place and move back here."

"Nobody is selling or moving anywhere."

Amy whirled around when Mom stepped into the room. "You heard our conversation?"

Mom gave a quick nod. Her pained expression and unsteady voice said it all. "This is not the time to be discussing our future, but since the topic has been brought up, you may as well know that I am not going to sell my home or the greenhouse your *daed* and I worked so hard to establish and keep going." She pointed a trembling finger at Ezekiel. "As far as you and your family moving back here, that's not going to happen either."

He touched the base of his neck as deep wrinkles formed across his forehead. "Why not, Mom? You can't run the business by yourself, and it's only logical for me to. . ."

Tears sprang into Mom's eyes, and she dabbed at them with the handkerchief in her hand. "It's not logical at all, Son. You've made a new life for yourself there in New York, and you're happy making bee supplies." Mom kept her gaze fixed on Ezekiel as she spoke in short, strong sentences. "You were never happy working in the greenhouse. You found satisfaction in working with the bees and selling honey." She paused. "Amy, Sylvia, and Henry will be here to help, so let's not talk about this anymore."

When Mom moved to stand beside Dad's casket, Ezekiel shrugged his broad shoulders and shuffled out of the room.

Henry got up and joined Mom. He stayed there a few minutes then turned aside. "I'm goin' out to the barn and check on the horse. It's feeding time anyways. The mare seems to be missing Dad's horse that died."

"I'm sure she is lonely out there all by herself and also with none of us using her for several days. Your daed and I. . ." Mom choked up, looking back at Dad's coffin. "We bought those two horses at the same time. It's been almost ten years ago now." Using her handkerchief, she blew her nose.

"I'll go get on my shoes and take care of the horse now. Maybe I'll even do some brushing while she eats." Henry's bare feet padded across the floor to the hallway, where he disappeared.

Amy was tempted to try and talk some sense into her mother, but it would be better to wait a few days for that. She felt certain that Mom was riding an emotional roller coaster right now, which made sense under the circumstances. So instead of voicing her thoughts, Amy walked up to Mom and slipped an arm around her waist.

No words were spoken between them, but she could almost read her mother's thoughts. Mom was wishing that she could ask Dad what to do. As head of the house, he'd been the one to make final decisions. Now Mom felt that the burden of providing for the family fell on her slender shoulders. Well, that wouldn't be fair, and Amy was not going to let it happen. If she had any say in this at all, she'd do all she could to talk her determined mother into letting Ezekiel move back home. At a time like this, living close by the family was exactly where he belonged. If she could not get through to Mom, the burden of helping to run the greenhouse would fall on Amy. Mom had made many sacrifices for her children over the years, so taking charge of the greenhouse was the least Amy could do.

Belinda took little comfort in Amy's presence. Truth was, she preferred to be alone as she stared at her husband's lifeless form.

Oh Vernon, I miss you so much. How can I go on without you? If only you could tell me what to do about the greenhouse. She touched the side of the casket. *Ezekiel thinks I should either sell it and move to New York or allow him to move back here and run the business. I don't want to move, and I don't want him to give up what he has there. The question is, Do I have enough strength and wisdom to run the greenhouse without you?*

Will our children who live here be willing to help?

Her gaze came to rest on Toby's coffin. *Sylvia's in a bad way right now and probably won't be up to helping for some time, if at all. Even if she felt able, what about her* kinner? *Who's going to take care of them while their mother is busy working? It wouldn't be practical to bring them out to the greenhouse during business hours. It would be a distraction for Sylvia and most likely the customers too.*

She looked at the casket where her son lay and blinked back the stinging tears almost clouding her vision. Abe had a girlfriend, and they'd been talking about marriage. But now Sue Ellen had no future with him.

And I've lost one of my kinner so dear to me. Belinda pressed her lips tightly together. It was hard to accept that even one of these special men were gone, let alone all three. She lowered her head. *If only they had listened to me and not left the house for something as unimportant as ice cream.*

"Mom, we're going to make it through this; I promise you that." Amy's sweet voice broke through Belinda's troubling thoughts.

She swallowed hard, nearly choking on the sob in her throat. "Jah, we need to believe that God will be with us every step of the way."

🐦

Weeping continued as Sylvia spoke above a whisper. "How can I be of any help to myself or anyone else without Toby?" Nothing seemed right with her husband, father, and brother gone. Less than a week ago, everything was perfectly fine, but today, like yesterday and the day before, was too painful to bear.

Sylvia lay in a fetal position on her bed in the room that used to be hers before she married Toby and left home. Her two children lay next to her, oblivious to the fact that their father, uncle, and grandfather had died. All Sylvia had told Allen was that these three special men had gone to heaven to live with Jesus. At his young age, she wasn't sure how much he comprehended. Baby Rachel was too little to understand anything at all about this sad situation. Poor little girl would never have any recollections of her daddy. As time moved on, Allen quite likely would not remember Toby either.

Tears slipped from Sylvia's eyes and rolled down her hot cheeks. *Oh Lord, how could You have taken my dear husband from me? Don't You know or even care how very much I loved and needed Toby?*

Ever since they'd been given the grave news that Toby, Dad, and Abe had died in the accident, Sylvia had barely been able to function. She couldn't imagine trying to get through the funeral service tomorrow.

I didn't just lose my precious husband either. Sylvia moaned and covered her mouth with her hand when both little ones began to stir. *I lost my daed and oldest* brieder *all at the same time. Oh, how could God be so cruel?*

Sylvia's conscience pricked. She wasn't the only one hurting right now. Mom had lost a husband and a son. She couldn't imagine how hurt her mother must be from losing those who'd been so dear to her. She and Dad had been married a good many years. Sylvia hadn't been with Toby nearly as long, yet she felt broken to the core.

Sylvia looked at her sweet, sleeping children. *I don't know how anyone gets through losing their child. I can't imagine how I'd feel if one of my precious little ones were taken from me.* She rolled over onto her back and reached out to touch each of her children. *Lord, please protect them.*

Sylvia's mind wandered as she thought about her siblings. Amy, Ezekiel, and Henry had also lost three people they cared about. And of course Toby's parents had lost their only son. They, along with Toby's three sisters, had been devastated and were struggling to deal with their loss.

If only the men had listened to Mom and been satisfied with just cake for dessert, they'd be here with us right now, and none of us would be grieving. Mom would be enjoying her birthday presents—none of which she opened—and Ezekiel and Michelle would be on their way home after a satisfying, enjoyable visit with our family.

Sylvia sniffed and swiped at the fresh onset of tears that had escaped under her lashes. *I don't know how I'm going to provide for or do right by my children. Nothing in my life will ever be the same.*

Chapter 3

As Belinda stood at the kitchen window, her knuckles turned white while she held on to the rim of the sink, watching Amy and Henry's rigid forms in the yard. Their raised voices and body language alerted her to the fact that an argument had ensued. She couldn't imagine what their disagreement might be about.

My children should be getting along better than this especially now, when we ought to all be pulling together. Her eyes closed tight. *Oh Husband, how I am missing you. My heart feels as though it's been torn asunder.*

Things were different now, dealing with everyday life—even something simple like her kids not getting along. Belinda couldn't talk things over with Vernon anymore or be consoled by him when things went wrong. All she had now were friends and family to offer support. And the news that the investigation had found her loved ones had truly died in an accident—the semi driver had been blinded by the setting sun—hadn't provided any comfort.

Belinda wanted to be strong for her family, but it took a lot of energy to keep it going. She hadn't a clue how to work through losing three people so dear to her. She couldn't think of another person in their community who'd dealt with anything like this. It was true that some had lost a family member because of an accident, but not three—maybe in other Amish communities, but not here. Theirs was the first that she knew of.

Yesterday during the funeral, graveside service, and even the meal afterward, Henry had barely spoken to anyone. She understood his grief, but shutting oneself off and refusing to communicate with anyone would not help the grieving process. Belinda felt it best to talk about her feelings—reflect on the love she felt for all three men who'd been buried yesterday and let the tears flow.

With everything else on her mind, Belinda was most worried about her fifteen-year-old son. He hadn't been to school since the accident but would start back Monday morning. She hoped he could deal with things well enough to get through the next couple of weeks leading up to his graduation, after having completed his required eight grades.

Maybe I should go out there and find out what's going on between Henry and his sister. The last thing we need is for them to be at odds with one another.

Belinda moved away from the window and went out the back door. Stepping between her son and daughter, she placed a hand on each of their shoulders. "What's going on? From what I saw out the window, it appeared as if you two were quarreling."

With furrowed brows, Amy turned to look at her. "I just asked him a simple question, but he refused to answer. Then when I asked again, he snapped at me."

"Everyone's emotions are high right now." Belinda spoke softly. "We need to be patient with each other." She patted her son's shoulder. "This is a difficult time for all of us, but with God's help, we'll get through it."

Henry shrugged her hand away. "Where was God when he took Dad, Abe, and Toby from us? He could have prevented that accident." Before Belinda could form a response, Henry ran off toward the barn.

A lump formed in her throat, and she swallowed hard, trying not to break down. Tears were cleansing, but she wouldn't give in to them at the moment. Belinda had to be strong for the rest of the family. She felt sure that was what Vernon would want her to do.

Amy came alongside her mother and slipped an arm around her waist. "Ezekiel asked me to talk to you about him and Michelle moving back to Strasburg."

"Forever more! Why doesn't your *bruder* talk to me himself instead of sending you to speak on his behalf?" Mom cheeks darkened.

Amy cringed. She'd figured it wouldn't go over well if she tried to play go-between, but she hadn't wanted to deny his request. "I guess Ezekiel assumed since he'd already brought up the subject and his idea was rejected, you might change your mind if I mentioned it and—"

"And tried to talk some sense into me?" The ties on Mom's white, heart-shaped *kapp* swished back and forth as she shook her head forcefully. "When he brought up the subject to me again last night, I thought I'd made it perfectly clear that I don't want him making such a sacrifice—especially since he was recently chosen by lots to take the place of a deceased minister in their church district."

"What? This is the first I knew of this happening. How long ago did it occur, and why didn't he say something sooner?"

"I'm not certain, but I assume he didn't want us to know because it would be one more reason I would use to try to talk him out of moving back here to help in the greenhouse—which is exactly what I did last night."

"Did you get anywhere?"

Mom shook her head. "He said he was tired and headed for the guest room before I could say another word."

"Wow! I'm stunned by this news. I never imagined that my big brother would become a minister." Amy's thoughts swirled so quickly it was hard to follow them.

"It's an honor to be chosen, although it means a lot of responsibility in addition to Ezekiel's full-time job." Mom pursed her lips as she clasped Amy's arm. "I can't, and won't, ask him to leave his home in New York and move back here. Can you help me run the greenhouse until Sylvia's up to helping?"

"That could be awhile, and besides, with her two little ones to care for, I don't see how she could work in the greenhouse too."

"Maybe Henry could watch the kinner. He'll be out of school soon."

Amy lifted her gaze toward the sky. "I hardly think my teenage brother would make a good babysitter for any child, Mom. You know how impatient and sometimes forgetful he can be. Henry would probably become preoccupied with something and wander off, leaving little Allen and baby Rachel by themselves."

Mom's head moved slowly up and down. "Good point. There are many other chores for Henry to do around here, as well as helping us with some things in the greenhouse. I guess once Sylvia feels up to working, we'll have to hire someone responsible who can come to our house and take care of the kinner." As though the matter was settled, Mom turned and headed in the direction of the barn.

"Where are you going?" Amy called to her retreating form.

"To talk to Ezekiel. He went to the barn a while ago to let our horses into the corral. I need to make it clear to him once and for all that we can make it without his help, and he's staying put at his place in New York."

"Good luck with that," Amy whispered as she turned and headed for the house. Her padded steps moved through the grass until she halted in thought. *It would be nice if Henry could do more around here, despite his mood. Mom wants to show Ezekiel that he isn't needed, which I don't understand. I still feel like he should move back with the family to help out.*

Something hit her face, and Amy realized a honeybee had flown into her. It was on the ground now, buzzing and whirling around. "That was weird. I've never had that kind of thing happen before." She rubbed the spot where the flying insect had hit her. "Sure hope there's not a mark on my face."

Amy watched the bee right itself and disappear on the breeze, and then she headed inside and looked in the bathroom mirror. Leaning in close, Amy couldn't see anything but the small, nearly invisible mole on her right cheek. She felt thankful she hadn't been stung.

After Amy left the bathroom, she found Michelle in the living room, wearing a different dress than she'd seen her in earlier today. "Did you have to change your *frack*?" Her voice was nearly a whisper.

Michelle nodded as she sat in the rocking chair, holding her little girl, who'd obviously fallen asleep. "I did have to change my dress." She looked down at Angela Mary. "My messy little girl ate a brownie with chocolate frosting, and she managed to get some on me."

"Sorry about that." Amy took a seat on the couch.

"How are you doing?" Michelle turned her head to look at Amy.

"As well as can be expected, I suppose. But I'm kind of in shock right now."

"Because of the buggy accident, you mean?"

Amy shook her head. "I'm still sad about that, but the shock has worn off, replaced with deep sorrow and concern for all our family members."

"It's a rough time for everyone." Michelle stroked the top of her daughter's head. "Angela Mary has been kind of fussy today. I'm sure she senses my stress and maybe everyone else's around her as well."

"That could be." Amy sighed. "What shocked me is hearing that Ezekiel is now a minister in your church. Mom told me a few minutes ago that he'd given her the news. Now we are both wondering why he didn't speak up and say something about it sooner."

"We were going to tell everyone the night of your *mamm*'s birthday supper, but after the accident occurred, our thoughts were consumed by what had happened." Michelle heaved a sigh. "The lot falling on my husband doesn't seem so important anymore."

"It is important, Michelle." Amy crossed her legs. "It's one of the reasons Mom doesn't want you and Ezekiel to move back here. You've established a new life there, and things are going well. Mom knows how important Ezekiel's business is too." She glanced at one of the barn cats that had snuck into the house and sat on the other side of the room, licking its paws. Then she looked back at Michelle. "Can't you convince your husband to abide by Mom's wishes and stay put in Clymer?"

When Angela Mary stirred, Michelle got the rocking chair moving at a steady pace. "When we first moved to New York, I didn't like it at all. It was hard to make new friends, and I struggled with depression because I missed everyone here so much. But now, things are different. Ezekiel and I both have a bond of friendship with several other young couples in our community. It also brings me joy to see how happy he is with his beekeeping supply business."

"How do you feel about his new ministerial position?"

"At first I felt nervous, wondering what expectations there might be of me as his *fraa*. But after I prayed about it, God gave me a sense of peace." Michelle pushed her shoulders against the back of the chair as she continued to rock. "I miss everyone here, but whether Ezekiel decides our place is in Strasburg or Clymer, I will go along with his decision."

"I guess we'll know what he decides soon, because Mom is in the barn talking to him right now."

Ezekiel grabbed a curry comb and started working on Dad's buggy horse. His thoughts and emotions had been running amuck ever since the tragic accident. Through all the years of working in the greenhouse, all he'd been able to think about was his desire to do something else. When the opportunity to move to a fairly new Amish community in New York was offered to him, he'd jumped at the chance. He remembered when he told his folks about his plans, Dad had said that Ezekiel had a right to live where he wanted and work at the job of his choosing. He'd reminded Mom that they could not stand in the way of that.

Ezekiel never had been as happy as he had been the last two years, and the idea of leaving the new life they'd established and returning to Strasburg to run the greenhouse held no appeal. Now that he was a minister, he had a new obligation in Clymer, but he had one here too.

He paused from his chore to reflect further on the matter. *It would be selfish to stay in Clymer when my family here needs my help right now.*

Just dealing with the trauma of losing Dad, Abe, and Toby will be difficult enough for Mom and the rest of our family, not to mention trying to run the greenhouse by themselves.

Ezekiel thought about Sylvia and how he'd seen her last night, sitting in the rocking chair holding her baby girl. She hadn't said a word to anyone else in the room—just sat there, staring off into space. There was no way in her condition that she'd be able to help out in the greenhouse. He shook his head. *No way at all. It'll be all my sister can do to take care of her two kinner. And Mom, well, she's grieving deeply too, and so are Amy and Henry. They all need my support.*

Ezekiel also grieved for his father, brother, and brother-in-law. Who wouldn't be deeply saddened when they'd lost three family members?

After Ezekiel and Michelle had retired to the guest room last night, she'd mentioned that he should pray about the matter. He'd agreed, but as far as Ezekiel was concerned, there really wasn't much to pray about. His presence was needed here more than in Clymer; it was just that simple.

When Mom entered the barn and called out to him, Ezekiel pushed his thoughts aside.

"I'm back here in your horse's stall."

She walked toward him and leaned on the stall door, looking at him with her chin held high. "I am well aware that you are determined to move back here, but I have a proposition for you."

He set the curry comb aside. "What proposition did you have in mind?"

"How about giving me, along with your sisters and younger brother, a chance to prove ourselves?"

His brows furrowed. "What do you mean?"

"You and your family can return to Clymer to take care of your job and duties as the new minister."

"Huh-uh."

She held up her hand. "Please, hear me out."

Ezekiel remained silent.

"Give us, say, six months to see if we can make a go of things on our own, and if we succeed, you remain in New York." His mother stood tall with her shoulders back. "If we can't make it, you can choose to move back here if you want."

Ezekiel rolled his neck from side to side as he contemplated her suggestion. "How 'bout three months instead of six?"

"Let's make it four. How does that sound?"

The whole thing sounded impossible, and he felt sure they wouldn't succeed, but Ezekiel nodded slowly. "Agreed."

Chapter 4

For almost two weeks, the greenhouse had been closed for business, and Henry had finished his schooling. Ezekiel and his family had returned to Clymer a week ago. It was time to get things up and running again so they would have some money coming in. The one thing that hadn't been settled yet was which of them would be in charge of what tasks.

"If we're opening the greenhouse today, shouldn't we come up with a plan for who will be responsible for that?" Amy asked her mother as they prepared breakfast on Monday morning.

Mom continued stirring pancake batter, giving Amy a sidelong glance. "I suppose you're right. You and Henry will need to make sure that the plants are arranged properly and that the watering system is working as it should." She paused long enough to add a few sprinkles of cinnamon to the batter. "And of course we'll need to take turns waiting on customers."

"Who will be responsible for placing orders and tallying up the expenses as well as the items sold each day?" Amy placed silverware on the table. "Since Dad used to do that, and now he's not here..."

"I didn't need that reminder, Daughter." Mom's jaw clenched as she tapped her foot, the way she often did when she was annoyed.

"Sorry, Mom. I just meant..."

"I know what you meant, and I apologize for overreacting. The agony of losing three members of our family is still raw, and it's hard to control my emotions." Mom teared up. "We're taking on a daunting job, especially without Sylvia's help."

"Maybe you should have accepted Ezekiel's offer to move back here."

"No! I will not ask him to make that sacrifice."

Amy could see by the stubborn set of her mother's jaw that she was not going to change her mind, so she decided to drop the subject, at least for now. Perhaps once they got the greenhouse going and Mom saw what a chore it was, she would come to her senses and call for Ezekiel. In the meantime, Amy would do all she could to keep the greenhouse open for business, because they certainly needed some money coming in.

"Sylvia could do the books and place orders if she were feeling better," Mom said. "But right now, she's barely able to take care of herself and the kinner. Losing Toby has been the most difficult thing she's ever faced, not to mention losing her father and brother in the same accident." She moved over to the stove with the pancake batter. "Your sister has always been the sensitive type and doesn't adjust to change easily. And losing one's mate is a terrible thing for anyone. I had no idea how difficult it would be until it happened to me." Her voice faltered. "I am still struggling to comprehend how I could have lost my husband and son the same day. Abe was in the prime of his young adult life, and so was Sylvia's husband."

"It was a terrible tragedy, and I doubt any of us will ever fully recover." Amy's lips trembled, and she pressed them together.

Mom turned and placed one hand against her chest. "We will always miss them, but we must find the strength to go on. As our bishop said when he and his wife stopped by the other day: 'In time, the pain will lessen.'"

Amy wasn't sure that was true, but it was obvious that Mom was trying to set an example for the rest of the family. She would persevere despite her grief and their current situation.

Amy went to the cupboard and took out the glasses. *If only there was something I could do to lighten Mom's load.*

In frustration, Amy marched toward the outbuilding where her brother had gone. It was time to eat, and she'd been asked to go get him. She and Henry weren't getting along these days.

I sure miss the old Henry. Before the accident, her little brother had usually been in good spirits and often told goofy stories or jokes that made others laughed. Now all he did was sulk, complain, or say curt things that hurt Amy's feelings. She wished there was a way to reach him, but she had no idea what to do.

Amy opened the barn door and poked her head inside. Looking around the dimly lit area, she spotted Henry seated on a bale of straw with his head down. Amy understood they were all trying to get through their grief, but Henry dealt with it in such a negative way. At least Sylvia, who was almost drowning in sorrow, didn't say snappish things or gripe about every little thing.

How can I talk to my brother without him getting temperamental or defensive? Amy collected herself the best she could. *Okay, here goes.*

"Mom sent me out here to tell you that breakfast is ready." Amy moved closer to him. "I assume your chores in here are done, or you wouldn't be sitting there doing nothing."

"I ain't doin' nothin'." He lifted his head and crossed his arms.

"Looks like it to me."

Henry's eyes narrowed as he stared at her with a look of defiance. "I'm thinkin' on things—trying to figure out what all's expected of me now that Dad and Abe are gone."

"I thought Mom made it clear what chores she'd like you to do around here this summer."

"She did, but I'm wondering how I'm gonna get 'em all done with no help from anyone. Mom will probably come up with some other things she wants me to do—stuff in the greenhouse."

"We will need help in there because Mom and I can't do it alone."

"If Sylvia helped out, I'd be free to look for some other kind of work—something I'd like to do rather than a job that's expected of me." He looked at Amy with a glassy stare. "Ezekiel oughta be here doin' his fair share, even if he doesn't like working in the greenhouse. He may be livin' someplace else, but he's still part of this family, ya know."

Amy placed both hands behind her back, gripping one wrist with the other hand. "Our brother has responsibilities in his church district now that he's a minister. He also has a business to run."

"I don't care. If I have to do a bunch of things I'd rather not do, then he should too."

Amy realized she wasn't going to get through to Henry—at least not today. He needed time to mature and come to grips with the way things were. "Let's go inside. Breakfast is ready."

"You go ahead. I ain't hungry."

This isn't good. Now look what I've done. I don't want to be the reason my brother isn't cooperating again. Amy drew a quick breath and released it before speaking. "You'll have more energy to get your work done today if you eat, but it's your choice." She whirled around and tromped out the door. Things were bad enough with everyone attempting to deal with their loss. Did her little brother have to make it worse by being so uncooperative and martyring himself?

Sylvia sat at the breakfast table, forcing herself to eat one of her mother's banana-flavored pancakes. Allen sat in his highchair beside her, enjoying the breakfast treat with his sticky fingers full of maple syrup. *He's lucky to be young and carefree—barely noticing that his* daadi *is missing.*

Sylvia wondered what the future held for her and the children. It would be difficult for them to grow up without a father. Some widows her age might hope for remarriage but not Sylvia. She could never love another man the way she loved Toby. She would not get married again for the sake of providing Allen and Rachel with a father either. The children's uncles would have to be their father figures. Of course, with Ezekiel living several hundred miles away and Henry taking no interest in the children whatsoever, it wasn't likely they would have much "uncle time" either. They still had one grandfather left. It was too bad Toby's parents didn't live closer.

"Would you like a cup of tea, Sylvia?"

Mom's question pulled Sylvia out of her musings.

"Uh, no thanks. I'm fine with my glass of *millich*."

"Okay." Mom looked over at Amy. "I wish you could have talked your brother into eating breakfast. He's gonna turn into a twig if he doesn't eat more."

"His appetite will come back in time. And if I know Henry, he probably has a stash of candy bars to snack on."

"Puh!" Mom wrinkled her nose. "I taught all my kinner that too much *zucker* isn't good for them."

"Right now, I'm afraid my little brother doesn't know what is good for him."

Sylvia tuned out their conversation as she put all her energies into finishing the pancake that seemed to have no flavor at all. Nothing tasted good to her these days, but at least she was forcing herself to eat.

About the time they finished eating, Sylvia heard the baby crying. "I'd better feed Rachel and change her *windel*. I'll wash the dishes after I'm done."

"If you're not up to it, I can do them," Amy said.

"No, you and Mom need to get the greenhouse opened."

Sylvia pushed back her chair and was about to take Allen from the highchair when Mom said, "I'll take care of getting the boy cleaned up. You go ahead and tend to the baby's needs."

Sylvia gave a quick nod and hurried from the room. This was only the beginning of another long day—a day when she would only be going through the motions of trying to take care of her children's needs. Truthfully, she wished there was someone who could provide for her needs right now. She blinked back tears of frustration. *It would help if I had someone to watch Allen and Rachel for a while so I could lie on my bed and let the tears flow all day.*

When Belinda stepped into the greenhouse and saw all the plants waiting to be sold, a flood of emotions threatened to overpower her. *Oh Vernon, how can I do this without you by my side? If only you were still alive and could be here right now.* Nothing about the greenhouse held any appeal for Belinda anymore. Yet this was their livelihood and the only way she knew of to make a living for her family. Even if they closed the doors on the business permanently and she and Amy found other jobs, they would never make enough money between the two of them to equal what they could make here in the greenhouse. In addition to their returning customers, as well as new ones, they earned a decent amount selling flowers to some of the florists in the area. Those businesses counted on them.

The first thing Belinda did was put the OPEN sign in the window. Then she checked a row of plants to be sure they'd been getting enough water. Next, she got out a dust rag to clean off the counter where they waited on customers. She'd just finished cleaning it when Amy came in.

"I finished the dishes and checked on Sylvia and the kinner."

"Are they doing all right?"

Amy nodded. "Sylvia's in the rocking chair with the baby, and Allen's stacking wooden blocks on the living-room floor."

"Did you by any chance think about going out to the phone shed to check for messages?"

Amy shook her head. "No, but I can do that now since we have no customers yet. I'll see if the mail's come too."

"Danki." Belinda heaved a sigh. "If you see Henry, would you please tell him there are a few chores in here I'd like him to do?"

"Sure, Mom." Amy opened the door and stepped outside.

Belinda took a seat on the tall wooden stool behind the counter. *I probably should pick some dead blossoms off some of the flowers, but I honestly don't feel like it.* She really didn't feel like doing anything at all. Everything about the greenhouse seemed so overwhelming. Things she used to take for granted that had once seemed like simple chores now felt like heavy burdens she could hardly bear. As time passed, she hoped they would settle into a routine and things would become easier.

The bell attached to the main door at the front of the greenhouse jingled, and Belinda turned her head. She was surprised to see Mary Ruth Lapp enter the building, since she'd been under the weather recently with sinus issues. Mary Ruth was such a dear, sweet woman—always helpful and putting others needs ahead of her own.

"Guder mariye." The elderly woman smiled as she approached the counter. "I came by to see if there was anything I could do to make your load a bit lighter."

Tears gathered in the corners of Belinda's eyes, and she was powerless to stop them from spilling over. "Bless you, Mary Ruth. I appreciate the offer so much, but I really don't know what you can do. Besides, from what I understand, you haven't been feeling well lately, so you should probably be home resting."

"I'm doing much better since the antibiotics the doctor gave me did their work on my sinus infection. It's not easy having such horrible face pain and pressure, but I was able to get through it."

Belinda patted her friend's arm. "Glad you're doing better."

"Danki. Now back to what I'm here for. . . . What can I help you with?" She set her purse on the counter. "If not out here in the greenhouse then how about inside the house? I'm sure there are plenty of things I can do there."

Belinda couldn't deny it as she slowly nodded. "Sylvia's in the house with her children, but I doubt she'll get any housework done. She's taken Toby's death really hard and can barely function."

"It's understandable. It was difficult for me when Willis passed, but keeping busy helped."

"Busyness is a good antidote for depression. However, Sylvia hasn't realized that yet."

Mary Ruth stepped around the counter, put her hands on Belinda's shoulders, and massaged them. "I don't have a lot to do these days except dote on my great-grandchildren, so feel free to let me know whenever you need anything done in the way of housecleaning, pulling weeds in the garden, cooking, or even babysitting the little ones."

"That is so kind of you, Mary Ruth."

"So, what should I start on today?"

"The kitchen may need some tidying. Amy did the dishes, but she probably didn't take time to do much else."

"I'll take care of it. Anything else?"

"Maybe sweeping the front and back porches."

"Consider it done." Mary Ruth stepped back around to the other side of the counter. "I'll check in with you after those chores are done and see what you all might like for lunch." She ambled out the door before Belinda could respond.

How nice it was to have friends willing to help in a time of need. Several other women from their Amish community had come by these past two weeks with food and offers of help. Belinda didn't know how anyone could get through something like this without family and friends.

A few minutes later, Amy came back in and handed her mother a stack of mail.

"Did you see Henry and give him my message?"

"No, Mom. I didn't see him."

Belinda lifted her gaze to the ceiling. *Oh, great! This is certainly not what I need today.*

Chapter 5

With her last bit of energy, Amy yanked on the green hose and turned on the water to reach some thirsty flowers on display. She gently sprayed them and rearranged the whole group after removing some of the empty trays the plants sat on and placing them on the concrete floor. They'd sold quite a few bedding flowers, and it seemed the bright yellow ones were the most popular.

When Amy finished her chore, she coiled the hose back in its spot. Then she picked up the wooden trays and stacked them near the rear of the greenhouse. Mom had said she would do it, but Amy was more than willing to take care of the task.

She wiped her forehead with the back of her hand and reached for a bottle of water she'd left sitting on a shelf. Taking a needed break felt good, and the cool drink relieved her parched throat.

It was almost time to close the greenhouse, and Amy's feet hurt so bad she couldn't wait to soak them. She'd been busy all day walking up and down the plant aisles either pruning, repotting, or repositioning to make some of them more noticeable. When she wasn't doing that, Amy answered customers' questions and directed them to various plants, seed packets, and other gardening items. Mom had spent the day behind the counter, waiting on a steady stream of customers.

Amy didn't know if the larger-than-usual number of people who came into the greenhouse today was because most folks in the area knew about their tragic loss and wanted to help out financially or if it was simply a matter of the greenhouse having been closed for two weeks and so many were in need of things for their garden. Either way, she felt thankful for the money that came in and also the offer by some to help out with chores or whatever Amy's family needed to have done.

Jared, who'd arrived a short time ago, was one of those people, and he stood beside Amy now. She couldn't help her attraction to him, and his tender smile made her heart melt. Jared had a sweet way about him, but Amy wouldn't allow her feelings to undo a thing. Her mind was centered around the work that needed to be done at the business and the support her family required at home. The combination was proving to be exhausting.

Jared shifted as he stood looking at Amy. *What a pretty color his brown eyes are. And that genuine smile nearly melts my heart. Oh, I wish things could be different, but they're not, and I must accept it.* Amy blinked away her thoughts.

"If your stables need cleaning, I can do that now for you," he said.

"The offer's appreciated, but Henry should have done it this morning."

"Are there any other chores I can do?" Jared's words were rushed as he rubbed his hands down the sides of his trousers.

"I can't think of anything, but you may want to check with my brother. Mom and I have been in here most of the day, so Henry would be the one to know if there were any chores left undone." Amy swiped a hand across her sweaty forehead as she offered him a tired smile.

"Okay, I'll do that in a few minutes, but first, I wanted to ask if you'd like to go out to supper with me this evening. It's been a while since we spent any time together, and I've missed you so much."

"I've missed you too, but I'm too tired to go anywhere this evening. We had a very full day here, with so many people coming in. We barely had time to eat the lunch Mary Ruth brought out to us."

"Glad to hear you had lots of customers, but sorry to hear you're too *mied* to go out for supper. I was looking forward to us being together for a few hours."

She drew in a weary breath. "Maybe some other time, Jared, when things slow down and Mom and I get more organized."

"How long do you think it'll be?"

She shrugged. "I have no idea. With only the two of us working here right now and Henry running a few errands for us, it could be some time before I'm free to go anywhere just for fun."

Jared's shoulders slumped, and he lowered his head. Just as quickly, he looked up at her, and his brown eyes softened. "I understand, and I want you to know that I'm not being selfish wanting to take you out." Jared gestured to the array of plants nearby. "Just figured it would be good for you to get away from all this for a while and do something fun and relaxing."

Amy didn't want to hurt Jared's feelings, but her grief over losing Dad and the others was still too raw to consider doing anything for fun, not to mention her lack of free time. It also wouldn't be right to take off for the evening and leave Mom, Sylvia, and Henry home alone. They might think she was insensitive to their needs, and indeed, she would be. At least that's how she felt about it.

Bumping Jared's arm lightly with her elbow, Amy looked up at him and offered another smile, more heartfelt than the last one. "Things will get better in time, and then we can begin courting again." *If only Jared could help my brother somehow. Or maybe he could fill in here at the greenhouse temporarily until Sylvia can help out.* Amy rubbed away the dirt smudges from her hand. *But I won't ask because he's too busy with his roofing business, and that's his livelihood, so it should come first.*

He shuffled his feet a few times and gave a quick nod. "I'll go see if I can find Henry now. If he has more chores to do, I'll help out before heading home."

"Okay, Jared. Danki."

"Sure, no problem. Take care, Amy, and I hope things go better for you soon." Jared gave her arm a gentle squeeze and hurried from the building.

Amy looked at her mother, still sitting behind the counter with a slumped posture and shear exhaustion clearly written on her face. *I could never have gone out with Jared this evening and left cooking supper up to Mom. She looks like she's almost ready to collapse. Her needs come before mine even if it means I have to sacrifice my relationship with Jared. The next time he comes around, I should tell him that he should look for someone else to court, because it doesn't look like I'll be free for that anytime soon. It wouldn't be fair to expect him to wait for something that may never occur. Mom will always need my help to keep the greenhouse running. And for sure, Sylvia—and even Henry—need me right now.*

As Jared headed for home that afternoon, all he could think about was Amy. If they couldn't spend time together, their relationship would suffer.

He had courted two other young women before he met Amy, but neither of them stole his heart the way she had. Thoughts of her were never far from his mind. It wasn't Amy's pretty face, shiny brown hair, or soft brown eyes that attracted him—it was her gentle, sweet spirit and concern for others.

Jared remembered the first day he'd met Amy and seen her consoling her little brother after his dog had run away. She'd not only given him a pep talk but had also combed the neighborhood, helping him search for the dog. There was no doubt about it: Amy would make a good wife and mother.

His thoughts went to Henry. Things weren't right with him. Henry had taken his father and brother's deaths really hard. Jared had a feeling the boy was full of pent-up anger that would not be resolved until he gave it over to God. During his visit at the Kings' today, Jared had found Amy's brother leaning against the corral gate. Henry's drooping shoulders and negative comments told Jared the trauma of losing three family members must be burning inside the young man. He'd asked Henry about helping in some way today, but his efforts had been squashed. Amy's kid brother was either too proud or too stubborn to accept Jared's help.

As Jared's horse and buggy rounded a bend in the road, he kept a firm grip on the reins. *Since Amy doesn't have time to go out anywhere with me, maybe I should go over to her place some evenings and we could play a few games. No doubt there would be other family members hanging around, but at least we could see each other and have a little fun. Think I'll drop by the greenhouse in a few days and mention the idea to her.*

Amy watched her sister out of the corner of her eye. Sylvia hadn't said a word during supper, and now, as she sat holding her baby in the living room, she remained quiet. Two weeks wasn't enough time to heal her broken heart, but holding everything inside and refusing to talk about it wasn't good for her either.

Henry had talked some while they ate, but it was mostly complaints. He'd gone outside as soon as they'd finished the meal. *If only there was someone he could talk to, he might feel better.* Henry looked up to Ezekiel, so he should be the one. But what were the chances of Henry going out to the phone shed and calling his big brother? Slim to none.

Amy rubbed her hands down the front of her apron as she continued to fret and seek answers. *Maybe I should give Ezekiel a call in the morning and ask him to phone here and leave a message for Henry, saying he'd like to talk to him and asking him to call. If anyone could get through to our younger brother, it would be Ezekiel.*

Amy remembered how when Henry was a boy, he used to follow Ezekiel around, asking all kinds of questions and seeking his attention.

She glanced over at Mom, seated in Dad's favorite chair with her eyes closed. Today had been exhausting for her mother, even though she had been sitting most of the time. The last thing she needed was to deal with Henry's complaints and angry attitude. All of them were sad about what had happened to Dad, Abe, and Toby, but getting mad and taking it out on the others didn't make things better.

Yes, she told herself, *I'm definitely going to call Ezekiel again in the morning. He has the right to know what's going on with Henry and be updated on how the rest of us are doing.*

Clymer, New York

"Have you heard anything from your mamm in the last few days?" Michelle asked as Ezekiel sat beside her on the sofa that evening.

"No, but Amy left a message this morning, saying they would be opening the greenhouse for the first time since the accident. She asked for our prayers that everything would go well and lots of customers would come in." With a grimace, he set the newspaper he held aside. "I can't help but worry about them. How are two grieving women and a troubled teenage boy supposed to take over a business that did so well with my daed in charge?" Ezekiel rushed on before Michelle could respond. "Dad knew everything about running the greenhouse, and he had a certain way of doing things. I don't think it'll be long before Mom comes to her senses and realizes they can't do it without my help."

"Your mother and Amy may be stronger than you think."

He shook his head. "This is not just about being strong or full of determination. Running a business is a lot of work, and it takes a person with a business head to make it succeed." Ezekiel touched his chest. "Just ask me. I had no idea when I took over my beekeeping supply business what all was involved."

"But you have done well and are making a decent living to provide for our little family."

"True, but it hasn't come easy. I'm still learning new ways of doing things almost every day. I can't help worrying about them."

Michelle placed her hand on his arm. "I'm gonna give you the same piece of advice that you offered during the message you gave to our church members last week on the topic of worry." Michelle stood and got the Bible from the side table nearest the couch. She opened it to the book of Matthew and read from chapter 6, verse 27: "'Which of you by taking thought can add one cubit unto his stature?' You explained that the verse means we can't add a single hour to our life by worrying. Remember?"

"Jah." Ezekiel took the Bible from Michelle and held it against his chest. "If I can't even practice what I preach, then how am I ever gonna be a good minister?"

"You'll get there, dear husband. Just remember to trust God in all things."

"You're right. That's what I promised myself I would do if the lot ever fell on me."

Ezekiel reflected on the recent event of choosing a new minister for their church district and how he'd received enough votes from the congregation to be nominated as a candidate for ministry. Ezekiel had broken out in a cold sweat as he and the other men who had also received more than three votes chose a hymnal. He, like the others, was well aware that one of the songbooks held a slip of paper with a scripture verse written on it. He couldn't help holding his breath as the bishop inspected each of the books to see which one the lot had fallen upon. When Ezekiel's hymnal was opened and the verse was found inside, he nearly collapsed from the emotion and realization of what it meant.

Becoming a minister in the Amish church was not viewed as an honor, as some might believe. Rather it was a serious, heavy responsibility. Ministers usually served in their position for life and received no salary. But that wasn't what bothered Ezekiel. His greatest concern was whether he was spiritually and emotionally up to the task. His duties as the new minister included studying the scriptures in preparation for preaching a sermon on Sundays and at other church-related functions; assisting the bishop in administering church discipline when necessary; baptizing; and helping to regulate any new changes within the church district. Each Saturday, Ezekiel would need to spend a good amount of time preparing for their biweekly Sunday services, where he could be expected to preach an hour-long sermon.

The worst part was that he was supposed to preach without any notes.

The first week Ezekiel had preached was the Sunday before he and his family had gone to Strasburg to celebrate his mother's birthday. Never in a million years had he expected such a tragedy would occur. It was proof that people should live each day as if it were their last for no one but God knew when a person's life would come to an end.

Ezekiel bowed his head and closed his eyes. *Heavenly Father, please guide and direct me in the days ahead. Give me the wisdom to make good decisions and deliver messages to the people in our congregation that we all need to hear. And please be with my mother, sisters, and brother. Let them feel Your presence, and help each of us as we deal with the grieving process. Amen.*

Chapter 6

Strasburg

Amy stepped into the phone shed and took a seat on the wooden stool. She dialed Ezekiel's number, hoping he or Michelle might be nearby and would hear the phone ring. No such luck; she had to leave a message. "Hi, it's me, Amy. Just wanted to give you an update on things. We opened the greenhouse yesterday and were busy the whole day. So many people came to buy plants and other things, and Mom feels hopeful that it'll be full of activity throughout the spring and summer months. Sylvia's not up to helping us yet, but Mom and I did okay by ourselves. Henry popped in a few times and did some things to help, but he mostly kept busy with other chores outside the greenhouse."

Amy paused when she heard that irritating crow creating a ruckus somewhere in the yard. Refocusing, she said, "Henry has an attitude problem, and I was wondering if you could call or write to him and say something that might help him deal with our family's loss. He won't talk about his feelings to anyone, and holding them in is not good. Danki, Ezekiel. I love you, Brother."

When Amy hung up the phone, she checked for messages and found one from Sara, asking if they had any carnations they could sell to her flower shop. With many English young people graduating from high school in June, Sara stated that she had several orders already for floral bouquets, corsages, and boutonnieres.

Figuring it would be best to return Sara's call right away, Amy picked up the phone again and dialed the number. She didn't want to miss this opportunity for more business.

After she made the call and wrote down the number of flowers Sara needed, Amy left the phone shed and went to the end of the driveway to check for mail.

Once Amy opened the mailbox and retrieved a stack of mail, she turned toward the road and was surprised to see two men standing in the yard across the street. The home there had recently come on the market and had a FOR SALE sign on the lawn near the edge of the property. One man, who appeared to be asking the other man questions, was quite tall and dressed in blue jeans and a beige jacket. The older man wore dark gray dress slacks and a white shirt. Could they be father and son? Or might one of them be a Realtor?

Amy didn't want to appear snoopy, so she started back up the driveway toward the house. An elderly English couple used to live in that home across from them, but they couldn't keep it up anymore and ended up moving in with their daughter, who lived in Lancaster. Amy missed seeing them sitting on their front porch, always offering a friendly wave. Mr. and Mrs. Benson had come over to the greenhouse a few times, and Mom offered them produce from her garden on several occasions. It was nice to have good neighbors, and Amy hoped whoever moved into the vacant house would be friendly too. It didn't matter whether they were Amish or English as long as they were good neighbors.

Sighing, Amy came up to the checkout counter where her mother stood. "Can I help in some way?"

"Jah, this customer is waiting for some assistance with a tree," Mom replied.

An elderly English woman stood at the register with her cane. She was the last patron for the day. "I would like to buy one of your small ornamental trees back there along the greenhouse wall." She pointed her walking stick in that direction.

"Did you have a particular one in mind?" Amy looked at the woman and smiled. "I can go get one for you."

"I know exactly which one. I'll come with you, dear." The woman pulled a tissue from her sleeve and blotted her damp forehead with it.

Amy felt tired and sleepy in the unrelenting heat. She walked ahead of the lady and visited with her until they stood next to the trees.

The older woman looked over the selection while Amy waited for her to pick out the one she wanted. However, all the woman did was look back and forth with furrowed brows. "Thought I knew what my choice would be, but now I can't decide. They're all so lovely."

Maybe I should give her some input about the trees and see if that would help. Amy touched the slender trunk of the closest tree. "This one is the smallest and will bloom white flowers in the spring. Those two next to it have pink blooms, but all of them will need pruning during their growing season."

"Good to know." The woman moved toward the pink variety. "I'd like this one—the largest tree."

"Okay, I'll get my brother's assistance to bring it up to the register and then take it out to your vehicle." Amy plucked the price tag off and handed it to the lady. "You can take this up to the checkout counter; I'll meet you there soon."

"Thank you." The woman turned and ambled along, using her cane.

Amy left the greenhouse and hurried outside, where she found her brother playing fetch with his dog. "Hey, Henry, I need your help inside."

With a shake of his head, Henry frowned and said, "I'm done for the day."

"I just need you to do one more thing. Our last customer wants an ornamental tree, and she is paying for it right now."

Henry's frown deepened. "If Dad was here, he'd be the one doin' it. Now I'm stuck doing everything."

Amy brought a hand to her waist. "Not everything, Henry. I just need your help for this last person, and then you can do whatever you want."

Groaning, he made his way to the greenhouse with Amy following. Her brother's attitude was getting old, and she bit her tongue to keep from saying anything more. If she said what was really on her mind, Henry would end up getting mad and might not help her at all.

When they got to the trees, Amy showed Henry which one they needed to lift and set in the wagon. His face reddened as he struggled to put the tree in the four-wheeled cart, but he wouldn't allow Amy to help. Then with an extra loud huff, Henry wheeled the plant up to the register, where Mom and the elderly lady waited. Soon, they headed out to the parking lot and loaded it into her small pickup truck.

"Thank you both for helping me with my purchase." She teared up. "My children are going to help me plant this tree in my yard in tribute to my late husband. He passed away a few months ago."

Henry remained silent while Amy felt led to say something. It was a bit awkward, but she went ahead and spoke up. "We understand your grief, for my brother and I lost our father, older brother, and a brother-in-law. They were killed in an accident."

"I'm so sorry to hear that."

"What you are planning to do with this tree is a wonderful thing in remembrance of him." Amy teared up too but somehow managed not to fall apart.

"Thank you both again." The woman turned away and got into her vehicle.

Henry was already on his way back to the yard when Amy caught up to him. "Henry, wait! I want to thank you for helping me back there."

"No problem," he mumbled with his head down. "When will the pain go away, Sister? Did you hear what that woman said? She's hurting too."

"Yes, losing a loved one is painful, and it takes some time to come to grips with it all."

"Yeah, well things keep reminding me of my hurt, and I don't need some stranger opening up my wounds again."

"Henry, she didn't mean to hurt us. Besides, she said she was sorry about our loss."

He leveled Amy with a frown that went even deeper this time. "You shouldn't have said anything about us losing Dad, Abe, and Toby. It was none of that woman's business."

Amy placed a hand on his arm. "There is no reason we shouldn't talk about it. Discussing the way we feel can actually help in the healing process."

He shrugged her hand aside. "Let's drop this topic. I've gotta finish something Mom asked me to do earlier." Henry sauntered off in the direction of the barn.

Amy lingered for a moment and then headed back to the greenhouse, where she found her mother counting out money from the cash register.

"How'd it go?" Mom asked.

Amy told her what the elderly woman had said and what had transpired between her and Henry.

Mom shook her head. "Your brother is a challenge, but we need to be patient and keep showing him love."

"You're right." Amy came around and gave her mother a hug. Then she helped her count out the rest of the money. Henry popped in to flip over the sign on the door so it read CLOSED. Then he left just as quickly without saying a word to either of them.

That evening, shortly after they'd closed the greenhouse for the day, Jared showed up. Before Amy had a chance to say anything, Mom invited him to stay for supper.

He gave her a bright-eyed smile. "Danki, Belinda, I'd be happy to join you. My folks are eating out this evening, so I would have been at home by myself with a boring sandwich."

"Well, you certainly won't have to do that tonight, so why don't you come on in with us?" Mom gestured to the house.

Jared nodded then turned to Amy with another pleasant smile. "Sure am glad for the opportunity to spend some time with you and your family."

You might not be when you hear what I have to say. Amy kept her thoughts to herself and forced herself to offer him a brief smile. She wouldn't say anything to Jared about her decision unless they had a few minutes alone. No point in telling anyone in her family right now that she planned to break things off with Jared. Mom liked Jared and would probably try to talk her out of it. She'd no doubt feel guilty for keeping Amy from marrying the man she loved all because of her duties at the greenhouse. One thing was certain: Mom couldn't run the business by herself, so Amy needed to give it her full attention. The only logical thing to do was release Jared of his obligation to court her. Of course, he may not see it as an obligation, but in the long run this was the best thing for both of them.

Jared's mouth watered as he smelled the enticing aroma from the meal being cooked in the next room. So far he hadn't had a chance to be alone with Amy, since she was in the kitchen with her mother and sister while he sat in the living room alone. Henry had come in briefly but barely mumbled a hello before heading down the hall to take a shower.

Jared shifted on the sofa and picked up a copy of *The Budget* from the coffee table. He browsed a few pages then set the newspaper aside. *Sure wish Amy would come out here and talk to me. Maybe I should go into the kitchen and see if there's anything I can do to help.* Jared massaged the bridge of his nose. *That may not be a good idea. The women might think I'm impatient about waiting for supper.*

Jared got up and went to look out the window. The wind had picked up, and he noticed several blossoms had blown off some of the trees and were scattered about the yard. Wind and rain were typical weather for spring, and he'd be glad when the warmer days of summer swept in. Of course, summer heat usually brought humidity, which made roofing or any other kind of strenuous outdoor work a challenge.

Jared heard footsteps, and he turned around. Seeing Henry had returned to the room, he smiled and said, "How'd things go in the *griehaus* today?"

Henry shrugged and flopped into an overstuffed chair. "Don't really know. I didn't work in the greenhouse that much."

"Really? I thought—"

"I've been stuck doin' a bunch of outside chores this week, and I also have to make deliveries when one of the flower shops in our area places an order." Henry's facial features sagged, and he dropped his gaze to the floor. "Ezekiel used to do most of that stuff before he moved away, and then Abe took some of it over when he wasn't helpin' out at the buggy shop."

"Do you have to hire a driver to take you around for the deliveries?"

"Only when there are more plants and flowers than will fit in the back of our market buggy. Otherwise, I deliver 'em myself. That ain't all I have to do either. Now that Abe's gone, I'm stuck takin' care of the bees and trying to sell off the honey."

Jared was about to comment when Amy entered and announced that supper was on the dining-room table. Henry and Jared got up at the same time and headed in that direction.

After everyone was seated, all heads bowed for silent prayer. When Jared heard the rustle of napkins, he opened his eyes and looked up.

Belinda ladled some stew into a bowl and handed it to Jared.

"Danki." He smiled and sniffed deeply of the savory aroma. Then Amy passed him a basket full of fluffy biscuits. He took two and passed it to Henry.

As they began eating the meal, Jared noticed that Sylvia, whose face looked pasty white, said very little and ate even less. Dark circles rimmed the poor woman's puffy eyes. No doubt she hadn't been getting enough sleep.

None of the others were saying much either, so Jared decided to break the silence. "I was talking to the people I was working for today, and the husband mentioned that he heard a new greenhouse is going to be built on a stretch of land between Strasburg and Paradise." He looked at Belinda. "So, it looks like you may have some competition."

Amy's forehead wrinkled as she glanced at her mother. "If that's the case, we're gonna have to work even harder to encourage customers to come here for their gardening needs."

"You're right. This news worries me a bit." Belinda pinched the skin on her throat.

"I wouldn't worry too much about it." Jared reached for another biscuit. "It'll probably be a while before the other greenhouse is up and running. Besides, your business is already established, and you have a lot of repeat and steady customers." He hoped his confident tone would put their minds at ease.

Everyone fell silent again. Jared saw the women's tight facial muscles and the scowl on Henry's face. Now he wished he'd never brought up the topic of the new greenhouse.

After supper, Jared decided it was time to go home. He'd resigned himself to the fact that he and Amy would not get any time alone. Truth was he still felt bad about blurting the news concerning another greenhouse and thought it best if he took his leave now, before he said something else that might upset this nice family.

He grabbed his straw hat and was almost to the door when Amy called, "I'll walk you out to your buggy."

"Sure. . .okay." *Maybe Amy's not put out with me after all. She must want us to spend a few minutes in private conversation.*

As they approached his horse and buggy at the hitching rail, Amy offered Jared a flash of a smile, but it disappeared quickly. "Umm. . ." She twisted the ties on her head covering around her fingers. "There's something I need to tell you."

"Oh?" He leaned in closer and felt disappointed when she took a step back.

"Is there something wrong, Amy?"

She moved her head slowly up and down. "I'm sorry, Jared, but we can no longer court."

"Huh?" Jared reached under his hat and scratched his head. "Why would you say something like that?"

"Because I don't have time for courting anymore. I have too many responsibilities at home and in the greenhouse."

"I understand that, and I'm willing to wait until things slow down and level out for you and your family."

Amy shook her head vigorously. "It's over between us, Jared. It has to be. Mom needs me now, and she may need me indefinitely. You and I have no future together."

"You can't mean that, Amy. I love you, and I want to make you my—"

She held up her hand. "Please don't say anything more. I'm sorry, but I've made up my mind. I care about you too much to have you waiting around for something that may never happen. You need to find someone else—someone who can make you happy."

"No one can make me as happy as you do, Amy."

Tears welled in her pretty brown eyes, but she said not a word. Instead, Amy whirled around and bounded off toward the house.

Jared stood with his mouth slightly open and both arms hanging loosely at his sides. He felt like someone had punched him in the stomach and taken away his ability to breathe. He'd been on the verge of asking Amy to marry him, but she didn't want to hear it. Now it looked like that may never happen.

What should I do? Jared asked himself as he undid his horse and climbed in the buggy. *Should I accept her decision or try to make Amy change her mind?* Jared would never be happy without her, so he'd make every effort to say and do the right things. Maybe he would enlist the help of Amy's best friend, Lydia Petersheim. If she couldn't get through to his girlfriend, no one could.

Chapter 7

Clymer

Before Ezekiel headed out to work, he went to the phone shed to check for messages and make a few calls. One of them was to leave a message, asking Henry to give him a call.

Ezekiel had thought about writing Henry a letter but decided it would be best if he could talk to his brother man to man. A letter would be too impersonal, and he might not put down the right words or say something that could be taken wrong.

Ezekiel punched in his mother's number, and when the voice mail came on, he spoke the words he'd wanted to say. He ended his message by reminding Mom that if she needed him, he'd come home.

Ezekiel left the phone shed and headed off toward his shop. He enjoyed his work here so much, and it would be hard to go back to working in the greenhouse and making honey to sell, but he'd do it if it came to that.

Strasburg

Belinda entered their phone shed, and seeing a green light blinking, she clicked the button on their answering machine. She was pleased that the first message was from Ezekiel. She settled herself on the stool to listen.

"Hi, Mom. I'm calling to see how you're all doing, and also, I'd like to talk to Henry. Would you please ask him to call me at noon today? I'll be sitting by the phone at that time, waiting to hear from him."

Belinda smiled. It was nice that Ezekiel was taking an interest in his younger brother. Henry needed to know that his brother cared about him, not to mention be exposed to Ezekiel's positive influence, which Henry was lacking right now. Belinda had little influence on her teenage son these days. She could also see that Amy spent more time butting heads with Henry than getting along. Belinda kept praying for her family because each of their lives needed the Lord's mending.

Soon, she found herself staring out the open door of the little shed toward a tree line on the property next door. Somehow the swaying of their branches on the breeze made her feel at ease. A few minutes passed, as she felt herself melt and relax in the quiet solitude, but just as suddenly, it was over when the telephone rang.

"Ach!" Belinda jumped. She drew in a deep breath to calm herself and picked up the receiver. A man who was obviously hard of hearing asked for the address of their business. It became a bit frustrating when she had to keep repeating herself. Belinda tried to be patient with him and felt relief when the conversation ended. She could only imagine what his family must go through each day, probably repeating a good deal of their dialog. Did he have hearing aids, or was he like Belinda's father, who had refused to admit his hearing was diminished or to have his hearing tested?

Belinda drew a sharp intake of breath. *Well, if the man does show up at the greenhouse, I shouldn't have a hard time picking him out.*

Most of the rest of the messages were from other prospective customers, asking questions about what was available in the greenhouse right now. A few of their family's friends had called to check on them, which was most appreciated. Dear Mary Ruth had been back a few times to offer her help wherever it was needed.

Belinda wrote down all the messages and stepped out of the small wooden building, already stuffy from the sun beating down with not much ventilation inside.

A crow cawed repeatedly from a tree in their yard as Belinda headed for the greenhouse.

She found Henry outside the building wearing his beekeeping gear. It hadn't been long since his brother had been the one out collecting honey. *Oh, how Henry reminds me of Abe in that getup.*

"Came to tell ya that I'm goin' out to check for honey," Henry mumbled. "Sure hope I don't cook in this outfit, since it's already heating up outside."

"You'll be okay. Your brother did all right wearing that gear, and you'll do the same. Oh, and before you go, I need to tell you something."

Henry stood with his legs slightly apart and one hand against his hip. "What do ya need me to do now?"

"Nothing at the moment, but there was a message from Ezekiel. He wants you to call him at noon."

"How come?"

"He'd like to talk to you."

"About what?"

"Your brother did not give any specifics—just asked you to call and said he'd be waiting in his phone shed at twelve o'clock."

"Okay, whatever." Henry turned and sauntered off in the direction of the beehives.

Belinda grasped the doorknob and stepped into the greenhouse. If things weren't too busy close to noon, she'd remind Henry to make the call.

Amy smiled when Mary Ruth came into the greenhouse with her granddaughter Lenore. Lenore carried her two-month old son, Noah, in her arms, while Mary Ruth held the hand of Lenore's three-year-old stepdaughter, Cindy. Both children were adorable, and Amy felt a pang of regret. With all her responsibilities here, it was doubtful that she'd ever get married and have a family of her own.

"What can I do for you ladies?" she asked, trying not to stare at the dark-haired baby, sleeping contentedly in his mother's arms.

"We came by to see if you have any radish seeds," Lenore replied. "I planted some last month but would like to plant more."

"We'd also like some plants for ground cover if you have them." Mary Ruth smiled. "Lenore's husband, Jesse, created a few more flowerbeds in our yard the later part of March, so now they need to be filled with color."

"I'm sure we have some flowers and plants to your liking." Amy thought it was nice that Lenore's husband had been willing to move into Mary Ruth's house after he and Lenore got married. It gave them a place to call home that was big enough to raise a family, and it allowed Mary Ruth to remain in her home. Otherwise, she'd have felt the need to sell and move to Paradise to live with her son and his wife.

Amy led the way to the aisle where several multicolored ground covers sat in pots.

"These are so *schee*." Lenore pointed to a vivid pink plant.

"Jah." Mary Ruth gave a nod. "They are all quite pretty."

"I'll let you two do your choosing." Amy pulled a metal wagon over beside the women. "You can put whatever you decide on in here and pull it around until you're ready to check out at the counter."

"Danki." Mary Ruth placed a hand on Amy's shoulder. "When I was here the other day, I didn't get to talk to you much. Just wondering how you're holding up with all your responsibilities."

Amy couldn't hold back a sigh. "I have a lot more responsibility now, but so far, I'm managing."

"Your mamm really appreciates the way you've pitched in. She told me that when I was here."

"She's a good *mudder*, and there isn't anything I wouldn't do for her." *Including setting aside my plans for marriage.* Amy didn't voice her thoughts.

"I've known Belinda a good many years, and she's made plenty of sacrifices for her family. Guess it's her turn to be on the receiving end and accept help from you and your sister and brother."

Amy nodded. No way would she admit to Mary Ruth that Sylvia

could barely help herself, much less anyone else, or that Henry was being so difficult and hard to live with since the accident.

"We'll see you in a bit," the dear woman said.

Lenore laughed. "I'm sure by the time we're ready to check out, we'll have a whole wagon full of plants."

Amy smiled. As she moved back up the aisle, she overheard Marilyn Yoder, who was married to one of their ministers, talking to Mom at the counter.

"Say, I heard from Monroe Esh's sister the other day. She said he's bought a business in the area and plans to move back here soon. He's been away a long time, so it'll be kind of strange having him living here again."

"That's interesting." Mom continued to ring up Marilyn's purchases. "I'm sure his family is happy about that."

"I would think so." Marilyn spoke quietly but not so much that Amy couldn't hear what she said. "As I recall, Monroe left Lancaster County soon after you broke up with him."

Broke up with him? Amy had never heard her mother mention a man named Monroe Esh. She assumed Mom must have been courted by him before she met Dad.

She reached behind her back and tightened her apron ties. *Maybe someday when I'm Mom's age, I'll look back and think about Jared and how it was when we courted and had to break up. Only I may not be married to anyone by then. I may still be an old maid.*

Sometime later, when it was close to noon, Amy heard her mother remind Henry that he needed to go out to the phone shed and call Ezekiel.

"Jah, okay." With his shoulders curled forward, he slumped out the door.

Mom looked over at Amy and shook her head. "You'd think he'd be eager to talk to his bruder."

Amy swatted at an irksome fly. "My brother's not eager about anything these days."

Clymer

Ezekiel stepped into the phone shed and took a seat. Hopefully, Henry had gotten his message and would call him on time. With all the work that needed to be done in his shop, he couldn't afford to sit here all day waiting. *Sure hope I can reason with my brother enough for him to change his negative attitude. This has to be wearing on my mother and sisters' nerves.*

Since he'd been asked to speak to his brother, Ezekiel wanted to help fix this problem. He pulled his fingers through the back of his thick hair. *Henry is a lot like our daed—not too good with change.* Ezekiel's father was the last one to agree to the idea of replacing their old horse and letting the old gelding live out his days in the pasture. He wouldn't throw away his old straw hat either, no matter how much Mom had pestered him about it. She'd bought Dad a new one, but he still wore the old hat most of the time when around home or if he went fishing.

I sure miss you, Dad. Ezekiel let his head fall forward into his outstretched hands. *It's strange to be seeing so much of you in my little brother.*

There were moments, like now, when Ezekiel still wondered if he should pack up his family and go back to help Mom and the rest of the family. It was overwhelming to feel helpless and unsure of what to say to his brother. *Dad, if you were still alive, I wouldn't be faced with this matter right now. But you, Toby, and Abe were called home. Guess it was your time to leave us and join others who died in the faith.*

Ezekiel remained in thought for a while then closed his eyes and prayed for his family. He asked the Lord to give him the right words to say to Henry and that whatever was said on the phone today would help somehow. Even if it didn't go the way he hoped, Ezekiel would put his trust in the Lord. He had a lot on his mind and much to learn as a new minister. Ezekiel remembered how Mom had often stressed the importance of being patient and showing love to those who were hurting.

A few minutes later, the telephone rang. Ezekiel opened his eyes and picked up the receiver. "Hello."

"It's me, Henry."

"Hi, buddy. It's good to hear from you. How are you doing?" Ezekiel kept his tone on the cheerful side, although it was hard to be upbeat these days.

"My name ain't Buddy."

Ezekiel frowned. "Don't get *umgerennt*. It was only a figure of speech."

"Who says I'm upset, and why'd ya want me to call ya?"

"I wanted to see how things are going."

"You coulda called Mom and asked her that."

Ezekiel shifted the receiver to his other ear. "I wanted to talk to you and find out how you are getting along."

"How do ya think? Dad's gone; Abe's gone; and I'm stuck doin' all their chores." Henry's voice cracked. "I—I wouldn't mind doin' any amount of chores if they were here with me right now."

At least he is venting on me instead of Mom or one of our sisters. I'm certain that my brother needs to say it again and again, but how many more times will it be needed? This is agonizing for all of us. Ezekiel's eyes stung as he listened to the raw pain in his brother's voice. "I miss them too, Henry."

"Then you oughta be here with us to help us get through."

A deep sense of remorse settled over Ezekiel like a heavy blanket of fog. "I told Mom I'd move back to help out, but she wouldn't hear of it."

"Since when did you ever do what our mamm said? You ran around with Michelle when she was English, even though Mom didn't approve."

"That was different. I was in love with Michelle. And eventually, Mom and Dad came to love and accept her." Ezekiel didn't know why he felt the need to defend himself. This phone call wasn't about him—it was about Henry and his attitude.

"If things don't go well and Mom needs me, I won't hesitate to come back to Strasburg, even if it's not a permanent move."

"So, you'd just come for a visit and then go back to New York?"

"Jah, unless Mom decided she needed us there permanently."

Henry grunted. "Like that's ever gonna happen. She's got it in her head that she can make it without your help, which means I'll never have a life of my own."

"Sure you will, Henry. Someday Mom might get married again, and then. . ."

"She'd never do that. Mom loved Dad too much, and nobody could ever replace him." Ezekiel held the phone away from his ear. His brother was practically shouting.

"I don't believe you have to worry about anything like that happening anytime soon, if ever. The main thing is, you need to be supportive of her and help out wherever you can." When Henry didn't comment, Ezekiel added, "I'll be in touch again soon, and we can talk some more."

"Okay, sure, whatever. I've gotta go now, big brother. Mom's probably got lunch on the table." Before Ezekiel could say goodbye, Henry hung up.

Ezekiel rubbed his forehead and moaned. *Sure hope something I said got through to him. It's hard enough for Mom to deal with Dad and Abe's death without having to put up with my little brother's negative attitude and self-centeredness. It's not like he's the only one struggling with grief and unpredictable emotions right now. We all need to lean on God so we can get through this with a stronger faith and greater reliance on Him.*

Chapter 8

Strasburg

Jared had been so busy with roofing jobs, he hadn't found the time to visit Amy's friend and try to enlist her help. Since today was Saturday and his work week had come to an end, he was heading to see Lydia now.

"Sure hope she's willing to help me with this." Jared held tight to the reins as his horse picked up speed. "I can't let Amy go. I'll do whatever it takes to change her mind about breaking up with me."

When Jared turned up the driveway leading to the home of Lydia's parents, he spotted her sitting on the front porch with her mother. *Not good. I can't talk to Lydia about Amy in front of her mother. Darlene is a gossip. She's sure to repeat whatever is said to Amy or someone else.*

It was too late to turn his horse and buggy around; the women had seen him, and both had waved. He guided his horse to the hitching rail and climbed out of his rig. After securing the horse, Jared headed to the house and joined the women on the porch.

"Hello, Jared. It's nice to see you. Are you heading over to see Amy, or have you already been there?" Lydia tipped her head, and in doing so, a wisp of blond hair escaped her kapp.

"No, I. . .uh. . .haven't been over there for a few days." Jared shifted his weight and leaned against the porch railing.

"I'm surprised to hear that," Darlene spoke up. "Since you and Lydia's friend are courting, I figured you'd be over there every day. I'm sure with the recent death of her father and brother, Amy needs your support and probably some help with chores around the place."

Jared moistened his parched lips and moved away from the railing. "I have offered my help, and I was going over there often until Amy broke up with me." His teeth clenched so hard his jaw ached. *Now why'd I go and blurt that out in front of Lydia's mamm? By Monday, if not sooner, our whole community will know about the breakup.*

Lydia's eyes widened, and her lips parted slightly, but before she could comment, her mother spoke again. "Oh, my. . .I had no idea. What happened?"

Jared's fingers curled into the palms of his hands. He'd already said more than he should have. *How do I get out of this? Is it too late to ask if I can speak to Lydia alone?*

He cleared his throat a couple of times, and without answering Darlene's question, Jared looked at Lydia. "Could I speak to you alone for a few minutes?"

"Of course you may." Darlene jumped up. "I'll go in the house, and you can have my seat." She smiled at Jared. "It will give you two some time to talk, and then I'll bring out some millich and *kichlin*."

"I appreciate the offer, but I won't be here long enough for milk and cookies. I have something I need to ask your daughter, and then I need to be on my way."

Darlene's shoulders slumped a bit, but her countenance brightened as a smile took over. "Maybe the next time you come calling you can stay long enough for a treat. For now though, I'll leave you two alone to talk."

Jared wasn't sure what the woman meant about the next time he came calling, but he simply nodded and sat in the chair beside Lydia.

She looked over at him with wrinkled brows. "Did Amy really break things off with you, or was it the other way around?"

"She broke up with me." He heaved a heavy sigh. "With all her responsibilities at the greenhouse, plus trying to cope with her father, brother, and brother-in-law's deaths, while offering support to her mother and siblings, Amy said she has no time for courting."

"But she will someday, right?" Lydia looked steadily at Jared.

He shrugged. "I don't know. She wants me to move on without her."

"I'm so sorry, Jared." Lydia placed her hand on his arm and gave it a few gentle pats. Her sympathy made him choke up.

"I came over here to see if you'd be willing to have a talk with Amy—try to make her see that she doesn't need to end our relationship. I realize she won't have time for social events and long buggy rides, but I'm more than willing to court her by simply going over to the house and helping out wherever I'm needed. Eventually things should get better for Amy and her family, and then we can start doing some fun things together again."

"But your job keeps you so busy. Would you have time to do extra chores over there?"

"I'll make the time." He leaned over slightly with both hands on his knees. "I would do most anything for the woman I love."

"Jah, I'm sure of that."

"So would you speak to Amy on my behalf—make her see that, despite the trial she and her family are facing right now, we can have a future together?"

Lydia slowly nodded. "I can't promise how Amy will respond, but I'll do my best to get through to her. In fact, I'll go over there on Monday."

"Danki." He rose from his chair. "I'll come by again sometime next week and see how things went."

"Keep the faith, Jared. Keep the faith," Lydia called as he stepped off the porch.

"I will." Jared turned and looked over his shoulder as a sense of hope welled in his soul. Amy and Lydia had been close friends since they were children. Surely Amy would listen to her.

"Hey, Daughter, could you please give me a hand? I'm losing my grip here." Mom nearly dropped the load in her hands.

Amy intercepted her mother carrying two large flowering plants. Then she set them down on a table that was nearby.

"Danki. Guess I shouldn't have tried to carry both plants at once, but I was too impatient and didn't want to make two trips." Mom massaged one arm and then the other before pointing to a large sealed cardboard box setting on the floor.

"What's in there?" Amy asked.

"You remember I ordered those shallow hanging pots awhile back. Well, they finally showed up, and we're going to arrange each one with starter plants to sell."

"Okay, but I'm not the best at arranging different flowers that are intended to go into baskets that hang."

"I'll see if I can talk Sylvia into coming out to the greenhouse for a little while and putting some together for us. Of course, it means I will need to go in and watch the kinner while she's in here."

"Do you think my sister will be up for it?"

"I'm hoping she might like to get out of the house and do something creative with these baskets." Mom gestured to the box again.

"Hanging baskets are a nice and easy way to spruce up a spot around the outside of one's house—maybe hanging from a porch or on a shepherd's hook in the yard."

"Jah, and the fuchsia starts are also ready to plant, so those will make a nice addition. We have a few different color variances, and of course some other flowers that can be included in the baskets." Mom smiled. "You know, Sylvia enjoyed doing this kind of work in the past. I'm hoping this idea might draw her out. It's not good to stay in the house so much of the time."

Amy touched one of the lovely plants. "I've always thought fuchsias look so pretty in full bloom—especially the red ones."

"They seem to be a favorite with folks to dress up a front porch or deck. A lot of customers like to give hanging baskets as gifts for different occasions."

"I agree. As summer continues, we'll probably sell out our supply like we did last year."

Mom nodded and stood there quietly for a moment as though in thought. "You know what I'd like to make for supper soon?"

"What?"

"Stuffed cabbage rolls."

"Those do sound good. We haven't had them in a while."

"They were one of your daed's favorite meals, and he liked creamy mashed potatoes to go with them." Mom rubbed a spot on her apron where a blob of dirt had attached itself. "Maybe we could invite our bishop and his wife for supper one night."

"That would be nice but also a lot of work. I'm not sure either of us would have time for that, and it's doubtful Sylvia would feel up to having company for a meal." Amy leaned against the stacked bags full of potting soil.

"You're probably right." Mom touched Amy's arm. "You could invite Jared, though. That would be only one extra person at our table."

Amy remained silent. *I was hoping this topic wouldn't come up so soon. Guess it was only a matter of time until Mom mentioned him.*

"It's strange, you know, but Jared hasn't been around lately." Mom reached under her head covering and pushed an errant piece of her mostly brown hair back in place. "I wonder if his workload has him tied down."

Mom gave Amy's arm a little nudge. "Daughter, did you hear what I said?"

"Jah." Amy tilted her head from side to side, weighing her choices. She could either go along with what Mom said about Jared working long hours or tell her the truth. She opted for the latter, figuring she may as well get it over with before someone else came into the greenhouse and blurted it out. No doubt Jared had at least told his parents by now.

"Jared won't be coming over to see me any longer." Amy lowered her gaze.

"How come?"

"When he was here for supper the last time, I told him we wouldn't be courting anymore." She lifted her head to see Mom's reaction.

Her mother's dark brows shot up. "For goodness' sakes, Amy, why would you do that?"

"Because with all my responsibilities here, I don't have time to be courted by anyone now."

"That's nonsense. You should make time for something as important as spending time with the man you love."

Amy shook her head determinedly. "Our days are long here in the greenhouse, not to mention all my other chores in the house. If Sylvia was up to helping more it might be different, but under the circumstances. . . Well, it's just better this way."

"Better for who?"

"For Jared. He deserves the chance to be happy. He's a wonderful man, and I'm sure it won't take him long to find a more suitable wife."

"But Jared loves you. I've seen his expression when the two of you are together, and I've heard the tender words he's spoken to you." Mom clasped Amy's arm. "Don't throw your chance at happiness away because of your duties here. Things won't always be so hectic, and there has to be a way for you and Jared to work things out."

"There isn't, and my mind's made up." Amy pushed up her dress sleeves. "Now, please, let's not talk about this anymore. There's work to be done."

Sylvia's head throbbed as she struggled to diaper the baby. Allen sat on the floor not far away, beating on a kettle he'd found in one of the kitchen's lower cupboards and dragged into the living room, where a portable crib had been set up.

The baby howled and kicked her chubby feet, making Sylvia's chore even more difficult while increasing the pain in her head. Every chore, no matter how simple, seemed insurmountable. She couldn't fathom how Mom and Amy managed to work in the greenhouse six days a week, dealing with customers and making sure everything from the watering system to proper ventilation worked as it should.

Don't think I could last even an hour out there, she told herself. *I'd cave in if one person even looked at me and asked how I was doing.*

Sylvia set the baby lotion back on the stand with the diaper wipes. She wanted to lie down on the bed and close her eyes. *If I could only get in a nap somehow, maybe that would lessen the pain in my head.*

Now that the diapering was done, Sylvia picked her daughter up and carried her to the rocking chair. She paused and looked back at her bedroom door. *Why does my head have to hurt like this? I've got household chores as well as my kinner to take care of, and I'm barely able to cope.*

Taking a seat, she got it moving at a steady pace. The only time she felt a moment's peace was when she sat here with her eyes closed, holding her precious child. Rachel burrowed her head against Sylvia's shoulder, as if trying to get comfortable. Sylvia patted the baby's back. *Too bad your daadi will never hold you again.*

Thoughts of Toby were never far from Sylvia's mind, which only added to her depression. She had a recurring dream about him that happened again last night. Toby was home with her and the children like he'd never left. It had seemed so real until she'd awakened to Rachel's crying. Sylvia wished she could simply will herself to stop hurting, but it was impossible.

She'd gone back to her own home only once since Toby's death and then only to get more clothes for her and the children as well as some of Allen's favorite toys. When she'd entered the bedroom she used to share with her husband, Sylvia had thrown herself on the bed and sobbed for hours. She didn't think she'd ever be able to move back there, but she didn't have the energy to begin thinking about all that was necessary to sell the house. How thankful she was that Mom didn't mind having her and the little ones living here. At this point, Sylvia didn't think she'd ever be able to leave.

She opened her eyes and glanced across the room. Her gaze came to rest on the coffee table, where her father's Bible lay. *Dad was a good Christian man, and so were Toby and Abe. Why would God take them from us when we needed them so?*

Allen began pounding on the kettle even harder, until she thought she would scream. How was she supposed to be a kind, patient mother when she needed mothering of her own? Sylvia wished she was a little girl again, cradled in the safety of her mother's arms.

Rachel squirmed as the noise continued. *I can't let Allen keep making that racket. His sister will never be able to sleep, and my nerves need a break.*

Sylvia rose with the baby and placed her in the crib, and then she sauntered into the kitchen to get her son something to drink. She returned shortly and removed the noisemakers, replacing them with a sippy cup full of diluted grape juice. The room fell silent while Allen sipped his beverage and his baby sister's eyelids closed in slumber.

Sylvia felt like she'd won this battle as she took a seat in the chair again. Releasing a lingering breath, she felt the same awful feeling creep back into her soul. *Toby. . .Toby. . .I miss you more than I ever thought possible. It grieves me to know that our sweet children will grow up without you.*

She swallowed hard, trying to push down the lump that had formed in her throat. *It's best that none of us can look into the future and see what's coming. If I'd known that after only a few years of marriage, I would lose my husband, I'd never have gotten married at all.*

Chapter 9

Monday morning, Belinda had begun drying the breakfast dishes when she saw Amy sprinting across the yard. A few minutes later, she dashed into the kitchen with a reddened face and eyes wide. "What's wrong, Daughter? You look umgerennt."

"I am quite upset, and you will be too when you hear what I found."

"What was it?" Belinda placed the dish towel on the counter.

"I went out to the barn to remind Henry about the deliveries he has to make to Sara's flower shop today." Amy paused and wiped a trickle of sweat off her forehead. "On my way back to the house, I noticed water seeping out of the potting shed. So, I went inside to see where it was coming from and discovered a broken pipe. Water was leaking out everywhere."

Belinda put a hand to her mouth. "Oh dear. Were you able to get the valve turned off that supplies water to the shed and greenhouse?"

Amy shook her head. "Not by myself. I ran back to the barn to get Henry. He's out there now, looking for one of Dad's wrenches."

"They're in the toolshed." Belinda frowned. "He ought to know that."

"I'll run out and tell him." Amy turned and rushed out the door.

Belinda stood at the window, watching her daughter enter the barn. A few minutes later, Amy and Henry emerged and headed for the toolshed.

Belinda drew a deep breath to calm herself. They couldn't be without water in either the greenhouse or the potting shed, and she didn't like the idea of spending money to have the pipe repaired or replaced, but there was no other choice. They had to take care of the problem, no matter what it cost.

Belinda put her head down. "I'm trying the best I can to hold things together, but it's ever so hard."

"What was that, Mom?" Sylvia spoke quietly as she came into the room.

"Oh, I'm just fretting out loud. We have a water leak in the potting shed that needs to be dealt with right away. Your brother went out to the toolshed for a wrench so he can shut off the water. Amy is with him."

"That's sure not what we need." Sylvia sucked in her bottom lip. "I don't know how you three manage to endure all of this."

"When problems arise it's not fun, but we have to expect that things don't always go as we would like them to." Belinda looked toward the doorway. "I assume my sweet grandchildren are resting?"

"Jah." Sylvia yawned. "Is there anything you need me to do right now?"

"I'll need the phone book to find a number to call a plumber."

"No problem. I'll get the spare one sitting on Dad's desk." Sylvia left the kitchen and returned almost immediately with the phone book.

"Danki." Belinda began turning the pages. "Here we go. I've found the page I need, and it looks like your daed circled the one he liked to use. What a blessing this is. I wouldn't have known who to call."

"Sure hope you can get someone out here soon. You need water for all the plants that are for sale in the greenhouse."

"How well I know. We sure don't want to lose any of our flowers and other items in stock." Belinda reached for a pen and paper then jotted down the phone number. She hoped they would get prompt service so things could move forward.

"I'll be back soon." Setting the pen down and getting up from the kitchen chair, she went outside and began the trek to the phone shed.

Plodding along, her mind drifted to her dear husband. *Oh Vernon, I never had to worry about such things when you were here. You always kept our business running so smoothly. I'm juggling what I used to do with all of the new responsibilities you cared for in the past.* Her vision blurred. *If you were here right now, you'd tell me: "Belinda, I've got this covered. I'll have it fixed in no time at all."* She wiped at the tears dribbling down her cheeks.

When Belinda reached the phone shed, she opened the door and stepped inside. The blinking light on the answering machine flashed, but she had something more important to do before she would check messages. Belinda wiped her eyes and tried to calm down. She grabbed the slip of paper with the number on it and dialed the plumber. The phone rang a few times until a man answered: "Hello. Bailey's Plumbing. How can I help you?"

Once Belinda explained what had happened, the man said he could be out in an hour or so. She hung up, relieved that they'd soon have the problem fixed.

Belinda listened to the messages then. The first one turned out to be from Jared. "Hi, Amy, it's me." His voice sounded strained. "I wanted to let you know that I'd still like to remain friends. And if there's anything I can do for you or your family, don't hesitate to let me know." There was a pause, and then he hung up. By the tone of his voice, Belinda knew the man had been terribly hurt by Amy's rejection. She rubbed her temples. "Oh Amy, I wish you'd reconsider your decision to cut Jared out of your life. You're being so foolish, Daughter. Can't you see that?" She closed her eyes as more tears came. *Heavenly Father, my family is in need of Your help. I'm struggling to hold things together, and I need Your wisdom and guidance with everything.*

"You do realize this is only the beginning of our problems, don't ya?" From his kneeling position in the potting shed, Henry looked up at Amy and scowled.

"You're being negative, little brother. Something like this may never happen again."

"Yeah, right." He cranked on the wrench until the water shut off. "These old buildings have been around for a while, and there's no telling what else might go wrong."

"Well, if it does, we'll take care of it. Also, with your negative attitude, you're not helping things around here. Our mamm doesn't need this extra stress right now."

Henry stood. "Well, I've got the perfect solution to that."

"Oh? And what would that be?"

"Mom oughta close the greenhouse, and we can all get other jobs doing something we like."

"Mom enjoys working here, and so do I."

"Are you sure about that, Sister?"

She nodded.

"Yeah, well, Sylvia doesn't want to work here, and neither do I."

Her brother's caustic tone caused Amy to bristle. "You know perfectly well why Sylvia isn't helping in the greenhouse right now, and it has nothing to do with whether she likes it or not."

"I bet she feels guilty 'cause the three of us are doin' all the work."

"I can't say for sure if she does or not, but emotionally and physically, our sister is not up to helping, so we need to do the best that we can."

Henry glared at Amy as he stood with folded arms. "I hate working here—hate everything about my life right now."

The anger he obviously felt lingered in his eyes as he stared hard at her. That look frightened Amy, and she clenched her fingers. It was all she could do to keep from giving her brother a strong lecture. But what good would it do? She'd already tried to talk to him about his attitude, and according to Mom, so had Ezekiel. If Henry wouldn't listen to their big brother, he sure wouldn't listen to her. Even so, she felt compelled to say one more thing.

Her brother crouched again, putting a hand at the area where the pipe leaked. With his less defensive form, it gave Amy the opportunity she needed to say what else was on her mind.

"Hate is a strong word, Henry, and whether you like working here or not, you are able-bodied and part of this family." She pointed at him. "Your duty is to help out, so please, stop complaining." Amy swung her body around and tromped out of the potting shed. *Doesn't my brother realize his uncooperative, angry attitude is only making things worse?*

A plumber came shortly after noon and replaced the broken pipe. The man showed Henry another pipe that could likely give them issues in the future and said they should keep an eye on it.

Amy's brother seemed disinterested in what the repairman had to say, which to Amy was not a surprise. She watched in irritation as Henry rolled his eyes after the plumber turned his back and picked up his tools. *My brother sure is disapproving. Why can't he snap out of this?*

Amy chose to step outside for some cooler air, putting some space between herself and Henry. *If Dad could see this side of Henry, he'd give him a stern lecture.* She picked at a hangnail on her thumb. *Henry is so off-putting these days. If he doesn't shape up, he will never find a girlfriend when he reaches courting age. Of course, like me, he probably won't have time for courting.*

Amy looked up when the potting shed door opened. "I'll send you a bill," the plumber said before getting into his work van.

He'd just pulled out when Amy's friend Lydia showed up. The cheerful smile on her pretty face as she came toward Amy was a welcome contrast to Henry's unpleasant frown. *I wish it were possible to trade Lydia for Henry right now.*

"Do you have some time to talk?" her friend asked, stepping up to Amy.

"Maybe a few minutes. Mom's at the house checking on Sylvia and the kinner, so I'm by myself until she comes back—which won't be till she's fixed herself a bite to eat."

"There's only one person browsing around right now, and I doubt she's here to buy anything. I think I saw her walking along the road toward town about a week ago." Lydia gestured to the stringy-haired elderly English woman wearing a tattered dress and a faded pair of sneakers that looked like they should have been thrown away months ago. "I believe she resides in that abandoned old shack about a mile from here."

"It's so sad. That poor woman comes in here at least once a week," Amy whispered. "She never buys anything—just looks at all the pretty flowers and sometimes comments on how nice they smell." Her voice lowered even more. "I think she might not have a real home of her own and maybe no family either."

"That's a shame." Lydia turned her head as though unable to look at the woman anymore. "I can't imagine how it must be for people who have no place to go or money to buy things."

Amy nodded. She too felt sorry for the woman who had never given them her last name. Just said one time when they'd asked that her name was Maude. "Mom sometimes brings out a sandwich or some apple slices and cheese to share with the poor lady."

"That's very kind of her; it's the charitable thing to do. I have a few extra dollars on me. Maybe I'll buy a couple of those flowers from the table she's looking at and give them to her."

"Are you sure you want to do that?"

"Your mamm has been nice to her, and I'd like to do the same." Lydia handed Amy the money and headed over to the table where the woman looked intently at the petunias.

Amy watched as the bedraggled lady brushed aside a strand of gray hair and then touching the red flower, she glanced at Lydia.

"These are sure pretty, aren't they?"

"Yeah." The old woman moved on but didn't look at the plants anymore before she ambled toward the exit.

Amy saw Lydia pick out two of the red petunias and walk up behind the elderly woman. "Ma'am, I want you to have these."

The woman's brows furrowed. "Are. . .are you sure?"

"Yes. I've already paid for them."

A faint smile formed on the woman's face. "Thank you."

"You're welcome. Have a good day," Lydia called as the lady ambled out the door with the flowers.

"She looked happy. That was a nice act of kindness." Amy moved to the other side of the counter and motioned for Lydia to join her. "Did you come by for anything specific or just to chat?"

"I came here to see how you all are doing, and—"

"It's difficult, but we're getting by and keeping plenty busy."

"Is Sylvia doing any better?"

Amy shook her head. "She's still too distraught to work in the greenhouse. It's all she can do to take care of Allen and the boppli."

"That's too bad. If she could help out here, it might take her mind off her situation and help relieve some of the depression she feels."

Amy nodded. "Keeping busy has helped my mamm and me from falling apart. By the time we're done for the day, we are both so tired, we just fall into bed at night in dire need of sleep." Amy's forehead wrinkled as she slumped on the stool. "Of course, we still have plenty of moments when we give in to our tears."

Lydia gave Amy's shoulder a comforting squeeze. "I heard about you breaking up with Jared."

Wouldn't you know it? Amy's muscles tightened as she sat up straight on the stool. "Who told you?"

"He did. Came by my house the other day and asked if I would talk to you."

"Really?"

"Jah. He wanted me to speak on his behalf and try to convince you to let him continue courting you."

Amy's jaw clenched as she picked up a pencil and tapped it against the counter. "He had no right to do that."

"Jared loves you, Amy."

"I care about him too, but it's not going to work out for us." She made a sweeping gesture with her hand. "I am responsible for a good many things here and will be for a very long time."

"Is there any reason Jared can't share in your responsibilities?"

"Jah, he has his own business to run, and I could never ask him to give up what he enjoys doing to help run the greenhouse." Amy shook her head. "I don't have time for courting anymore. So, when you see Jared again, please tell him for me that he may as well accept the fact that our relationship is over."

Lydia looked at Amy with a pinched, tension-filled expression. "I'll give him your message, but I think you'll end up regretting that decision."

"I probably will, but I have no choice in the matter." Amy turned her attention to the door when a group of English people entered the greenhouse. "Please excuse me, Lydia, but I need to see if my customers need any assistance."

"Of course. Take care, my dear friend. I hope to see you again soon." Lydia hurried out of the building, and Amy set her mind on business and hopefully making at least one sale.

Chapter 10

Two more weeks went by, and soon it was the last Monday of June. Every day seemed to blend into the next. Amy had gotten into the routine and did her best to keep things running smoothly. She'd been happy a week ago when Mom talked Sylvia into helping them out. Amy had hoped her sister would come to the greenhouse to fill the hanging baskets, but Sylvia had been adamant about not having to speak to the public or be around too many people at once. Mom had been considerate and asked Henry and Amy to bring the baskets and needed supplies over to the house, where Sylvia could arrange them.

With Michelle's baby due in three weeks, Amy hoped Sylvia would be up to helping in the greenhouse so Mom could go to Ezekiel and Michelle's home in New York to help for a few weeks. Ezekiel had been so busy, and Michelle's back bothered her, so they hadn't made a trip to Strasburg since their stay after the funerals. They both called often though to see how everyone was doing. Mom always returned their calls, and Amy was sure nothing was ever said to give Ezekiel the impression that things weren't going well. She knew without question that her mother wanted to be independent and did not want Ezekiel to give up his new life and ministry in Clymer.

As Amy headed down the driveway to get the mail Monday morning, she saw a moving van parked in the driveway at the home across the road. Apparently, someone had bought the house. It would be nice to have new neighbors. The home had been sitting empty too long.

She kept watching as a middle-aged English couple got out of the older-model car parked behind the moving van. Amy was pretty sure the tall man was the same person she'd seen with the Realtor a few weeks ago. The woman appeared to be at least a foot shorter than he was. Her red hair was styled in a short cut, and she walked with a slight limp. They stood on the overgrown lawn, talking with the two men who'd gotten out of the van, and then they all went inside the house.

Amy glanced at the area out front, where the FOR SALE sign used to be, and noticed that it had been taken down. *I wonder if it's just the two of them moving into the house, or if there are other family members joining them.* They looked too old to have young children, but she supposed they could still have teenagers or college-age children who might live at home.

Well, it's none of my business, and I need to get back to the greenhouse before customers start coming in.

Remembering the reason she'd walked down the driveway, Amy opened the mailbox and removed a stack of envelopes. Thumbing through them quickly, she saw that most were advertisements, with just a few bills.

"That's good," Amy said aloud as she headed back up the driveway. The bill from the plumber they'd hired to fix the broken pipe had been high enough, and they didn't need any other large bills to pay right now.

"Are you sure you can handle things while I'm gone?" Belinda asked Amy at two o'clock. "My dental appointment is in half an hour, and afterward I want to go to the bank and stop by the grocery store. My driver should be here soon, but I wanted to make sure you're okay with me being gone that long."

"It's fine, Mom." Amy, although she looked tired, offered Belinda a smile. "I've already alerted Henry to the fact that I'll most likely need his help in here."

Belinda gave her daughter's arm a tender squeeze. Henry had become so moody, and Sylvia was still despondent. It was a comfort to be able to count on Amy.

The crunch of gravel could be heard outside the greenhouse, followed by the tooting of a horn.

"That must be my driver, Sandy." Belinda gave Amy a hug. "I'll see you in a few hours and will be praying that all goes well here for the remaining hours you are open."

"Danki, Mom. I'm sure everything will go fine, and I hope things go well at your dental appointment."

Belinda gave a nod, grabbed her purse from behind the counter, and hurried out the door.

Things became busy that afternoon, and Amy felt thankful for Henry's help, even though he walked around with a scowl on his face. Hopefully, none of their customers had noticed.

Amy looked toward the door when some English people came in and headed over to the area where a few gift items were located. It wasn't uncommon for tourists to check out the items for sale in the Amish-run greenhouse. Before Amy's father died, her parents had decided to carry some lawn decor, such as solar-lighted animal figurines, garden signs, wind chimes, and a few small fountains and birdbaths. All those things helped bring in more income.

While the place became busier, Amy found herself needing to leave the register more often to assist a couple patrons, but she didn't feel right doing that. A gray-haired man approached her and reached into his pocket to retrieve a slip of paper. Then he asked Amy for some help finding a certain plant. Amy assumed he must be hard of hearing because she had to repeat herself a lot. She glanced back at the checkout counter and saw a line of people beginning to form. Seeing her brother on one side of the greenhouse, she called: "Henry, could you please come over here?"

He took his sweet time and sauntered up to her with a disgruntled expression. "What do ya need?"

"This gentleman here needs some help, and as you can see, I should be up at the register where customers are waiting for assistance."

Henry looked around. "Where's Mom? Why isn't she helping people up there?"

"She went to the dentist, remember?"

"Oh, yeah, that's right." Henry motioned for the man to follow him down the aisle, while Amy made her way back to the counter. She hoped her brother wouldn't be too upset with her when he discovered that the man she'd asked him to wait on had trouble hearing.

Pulling her attention back to the immediate need, Amy smiled at the woman who'd picked out two sets of wind chimes. She wrapped each one in bubble wrap and placed them in a box. Amy hadn't expected things to be so busy while Mom was away, but at least with Henry's help, they'd managed so far.

She'd finished waiting on the woman when a tall, beardless Amish man entered the greenhouse and approached the counter. She didn't recognize him and figured he must be from a neighboring community.

He smiled and removed his straw hat, revealing a thick crop of brown hair with a few touches of gray here and there. "Hello." He extended his hand. "My name is Monroe Esh, and I was told that Belinda King owns this greenhouse."

Amy reached out a hand tentatively and shook his large hand. "Jah, Belinda is my mamm." She hoped he wasn't here to try and sell them something.

"Is she here?" Monroe glanced around as though expecting Amy to point out her mother among some of the Amish women looking at the plants.

"No, she's in town right now."

"Aw, I see. Do you know what time she'll be back? I'd like to talk to her."

"No, I don't. She probably won't return for a while yet."

"I see." His lips pressed tight into a grimace.

"Can I give my mother a message, or is there something I can help you with?"

"No message." He looked at Amy with a strange expression. "You remind me of Belinda when she was about your age—same color hair, same pretty face."

Amy's cheeks warmed as she looked up at him. "Did you know my mamm when she was my age?"

He gave a quick nod. "I not only knew her, but we were a courting couple. At least we were up until Vernon King came along and stole her from me." His brown eyes darkened further, and a muscle on the side of his neck quivered. "She ended up marrying him, and when that happened, I quit my job and left the area."

Unsure of what to say and unable to hold the man's steady gaze, Amy lowered her head to look at the floor.

"I heard about Vernon's passing, and I'd like to offer my condolences. Would you please tell Belinda I came by and that I'll return in a few days to see how she's doing?"

Amy lifted her head. "I will give her your message."

"Danki." He plopped his hat back on his head and strolled out the door.

Amy sank to the stool as an uncomfortable feeling settled over her. The fact that Monroe was clean-shaven meant he was obviously not married. She hoped he didn't have any ideas about getting back with her mother. It was way too soon for Mom to even be thinking of remarriage, and for that matter, Amy felt sure her mother would never get married again. The love she had for Amy's father went deep, and Amy felt certain that Mom would never love another man the way she had Dad.

Jared had only been home from work a short time when a horse and open buggy pulled into the yard. He walked out to the hitching rail as Lydia pulled up to it, and then he secured her chestnut-colored horse.

"I spoke to Amy on your behalf, and I'm sorry for not coming by sooner, but my parents and I had to go out of town due to a death in my dad's family."

"Sorry to hear that. Was it someone you were close to?" Jared asked.

"It was my great-aunt Matilda. She lived in Tennessee, but I didn't know her well. Even so, I wanted to attend the funeral in support of my daed."

"I understand." Jared waited until Lydia stepped down from the buggy. "So, what did Amy have to say when you spoke to her?"

Lydia slowly shook her head. "I'm sorry, Jared, but she wouldn't change her mind about the two of you courting."

He bent his head forward, releasing a heavy sigh. This was not the news he had hoped for. If Lydia couldn't get through to Amy, then what chance did he have?

"Danki for trying," Jared mumbled. "Guess I'll have to accept Amy's decision—at least for now."

Lydia patted his arm. "Maybe in a few months she will change her mind."

Jared wanted to believe Amy's friend, but he had a sick feeling in the pit of his stomach. As much as he hated to admit it, no matter how many times he went over and tried to talk Amy into letting him court her, her answer might always be no.

That evening, while Amy and Belinda fixed supper, Amy brought up a subject that sent a ripple of shock through Belinda.

"A man named Monroe Esh came by to see you this afternoon, Mom. He seemed disappointed that you weren't here and said he'd be back in a few days to talk to you."

A flush of heat erupted on Belinda's cheeks as she touched her parted lips. "I. . .I heard he was moving back here, but I had no idea he'd come to our place to see me. Did he say what he wanted to talk to me about?"

"Said he'd heard about Dad's passing and wanted to offer his condolences." Amy reached into the refrigerator for a slab of bacon. Tonight they'd decided to keep supper simple by fixing BLTs. "Monroe seemed eager to see you, and he looked disappointed when I told him you weren't here."

"I see."

"Monroe also mentioned that he used to court you. Is that true, Mom?"

Belinda nodded slowly, and her thoughts wandered as she leaned against the counter. She hadn't thought about it for a long time, but hearing that Monroe had been here took her mind back to the day she'd broken things off with him. She could still visualize his look of rejection when she'd informed him that she thought of him only as a friend and had agreed to be courted by Vernon. Monroe's eyes had appeared so dark and serious, and there'd been a grim twist to his mouth. "If you felt no love for me, Belinda, it was wrong to lead me on," he'd muttered.

Did I lead Monroe on? Belinda asked herself now. *During the brief time he'd courted me, did I give the impression that I'd fallen in love with him? If so, I hadn't meant to. I just assumed Monroe knew I wasn't serious about him.*

Pushing her memories aside, Belinda took out a loaf of bread and removed the plastic wrapping around it. *What will I say to Monroe if he does come back to the greenhouse to speak to me? I hope he's not harboring ill feelings.*

Chapter 11

When Virginia Martin woke up the following day, her whole body ached. She wished she knew of a good massage therapist in the area and could get in with them today. Virginia had overdone it by trying to move some of the boxes the movers had set in the wrong spots. Earl had caught her trying to move one of them and took it to the place she wanted in the dining room. With the exception of a quick trip to the grocery store yesterday before the movers arrived, she and Earl had spent most of the day unpacking boxes and putting things away. By the time they were ready for bed last night, she'd barely had the strength to put sheets on the bed. Fortunately, her husband didn't have to start his new job until tomorrow, which gave them today to do more unpacking. Virginia couldn't wait to be settled in—it sure was a draining process. She wanted to have everything where it needed to be.

Right now though, as Virginia sat on the front porch with a cup of coffee in her hand, all she wanted to do was relax. Her gaze trailed to the overgrown yard of their new residence, desperately in need of being cut. She could see that the previous owners had fallen behind on a good many things around the place. Either that or the place had sat empty too long.

Virginia sipped on her steaming beverage. *Too bad I couldn't get all the work done by simply snapping my fingers.*

One idea she'd been kicking around in her head since they'd

moved here was having a garden. With the amount of property they now owned, it was a no-brainer. Virginia had only grown a few tomato plants in a pot and some herbs in smaller containers when she and Earl had lived in the city. The idea of a full-blown plot of land growing an edible array of food seemed inviting. Maybe Earl could rent a tiller, and they could purchase some seeds or plants to get started.

It was so quiet here in the country. Virginia was used to city sights, noises, and odors. Birds chirping, cows mooing, and the smell of new-mown hay would take some getting used to.

Maybe it's a good thing, she mused. *I could use some relaxing days and quiet times in my life.* Being married to Earl for the last three years had brought many changes for Virginia, and this move was yet another one. Her husband had given hints of discontent about living in the big city, sometimes mentioning the growing traffic and the huge number of people in Chicago.

Virginia could see Earl gravitating to the country life. He'd even mentioned wanting to take up fishing. She figured he'd put a lot of thought into what he wanted to get out of this move. He said the change of pace and country living might do them both some good and could even add a few more years to their lives.

Virginia wrinkled her nose. *Now that I doubt.*

At the sound of a steady *clippity-clop, clippity-clop,* she glanced up the road. Here came not one but two horses and buggies. They slowed down and turned up the driveway leading to the house across from them. Or maybe it was the building on the left side of their property where those people were headed.

She craned her neck a bit and continued to watch. Sure enough, the rigs headed to the parking lot where the greenhouse stood.

"I hope there's not a steady traffic of buggies or cars all day," Virginia muttered.

"Were you speaking to me?" Earl asked, joining her on the porch.

"No, I was talking to myself." Virginia pointed across the road. "It's only 9 a.m. and there's buggy traffic." She looked up at him and scowled. "You never told me we'd be living in Amish country."

Earl lowered himself into the chair beside her. "Didn't think I had to say anything. Figured you knew there were Amish communities in Lancaster County."

She folded her arms and grunted. "Now how would I know that? I'm no expert on the Amish or where they live."

"For crying out loud, Virginia, information about the Amish is everywhere these days—in the paper, on TV, and even bookshelves in places like Walmart and Sam's Club."

"Doesn't mean I knew they'd be here where you bought this house without me even seeing it."

"Let's not go down that road again. You were sick with the flu when I came to Lancaster to interview for the job at the car dealership, and after I called and told you I'd gotten the position and wanted to look at some houses in the country, you said you would trust my judgment."

"You're right. Just didn't realize you'd end up picking a home way out in the boonies or that there'd be a place of business so close to us." Virginia pulled her fingers through the strands of her slightly damp hair. She'd been so tired when they went to bed last night that she hadn't bothered taking a shower until this morning.

"Now don't forget, I took plenty of pictures of this house." He reached into his pants pocket and pulled out his cell phone.

"Yeah, but those were of the inside of the house, not what we would see from our yard."

He shrugged. "Didn't think it was that important."

"It is to me." She gestured to another Amish buggy approaching. "I don't care for the road this house is on. With that greenhouse across from us, there's bound to be steady traffic most of the day."

"So what? You're used to all that traffic we had in Chicago."

"Yeah, but this is different. Instead of horns honking and exhaust fumes from cars, trucks, and buses, we now have to put up with smelly horses and the irritating sound of their feet clomping along the pavement." She stood up and pointed to the road. "And just look at all those ruts out there—no doubt from the buggy wheels."

"You'll get used to it, just like you did when we first moved to Chicago."

"I doubt it." She lifted her gaze toward the sky. "If I'd come here and seen the place before you signed your name on the dotted line, I would have told you I'm not a country kind of gal."

Earl said nothing. All Virginia heard was the slamming of the screen door.

She flopped back into her chair. *Earl doesn't understand my needs any more than my first husband did.* She sat for a while, watching the goings-on at her Amish neighbors' property.

Yesterday, after she and Earl had gone to buy a used pickup at the place where he'd be working, Virginia had planted herself at the living-room window and observed the quaint way those Amish people dressed—so old-fashioned. She hadn't seen any men around though—just a lanky-looking teenage boy and two women. She'd noticed one of them watering some flowerbeds in the yard. *Surely there's a man about the place, especially with a business on that property to run and all the outbuildings to keep up.*

She stood for another moment and then retreated inside to put her empty cup in the sink. *I'm not sure about those Amish across the street. They seem so odd and unconventional.*

"Would you like a second cup of *kaffi*, Son?" Jared's mother moved toward him with the coffeepot in her hand.

He shook his head and grabbed his lunch pail from the counter. "I don't have time for more coffee, Mom. I'm already running behind this morning and need to get out the door and head to my first job. By the time I get there, my newest employee, Sam, will probably be up on the roof of the grocery store that hired us, tearing off the old shingles."

"Can't you spare a few minutes to talk to your mamm? There's something I want to discuss with you."

"Can't it wait till this evening?"

"It could, but if your daed's around, which I'm sure he will be, he'll probably accuse me of *neimische*."

Then maybe you shouldn't say it, because if Dad thinks you're meddling, no doubt I will too. Jared didn't voice his thoughts. Instead, he turned to face her and said, "What is it you want to say, Mom?"

"It's about you and Amy."

Jared clenched his lunchbox handle. "She broke up with me. I told you about it and explained her reason right after it happened."

She gave a nod. "You've been upset about the breakup, jah?"

"Of course I'm upset. I love Amy and was hoping she'd be willing to marry me."

Mom took a few steps closer to Jared. "I've been thinking things over since this all happened."

"Oh?"

"It came to me last night that maybe her breaking things off was for the best."

Jared poked his tongue into the side of his cheek and inhaled a long breath. "How can it be for the best?"

"Amy's an independent, stubborn woman, so maybe she wouldn't make you a good fraa."

Jared tensed as heat coursed through his body. "Amy may be independent and perhaps even a bit stubborn, but I love her with all my heart. She's everything I've ever wanted in a wife."

"But if she doesn't want you to court her anymore, maybe it's time to move on."

Jared had heard more than he wanted to, and if he didn't leave now, he was likely to say some hurtful things to his mother. "I've gotta go, Mom. I'm even later now than before." Before she could utter another word, he headed out the back door. This was not a good way to start the day. He wished his father hadn't already left for his booth at the farmers' market, because he would have been an ally. For sure, Dad would have put Mom in her place. *My mamm has no idea how deep my feelings for Amy go.* He shook his head. *I'm not ready to give up on our relationship yet. I just need to be patient.*

"When I went up to the house to eat my lunch, I discovered that Sylvia had set out a container of vanishing oatmeal raisin cookies for us," Amy announced when she returned to the greenhouse. "She was also in the process of preparing to make some double-fudge brownies." Amy set the plastic container on the counter in front of her mother.

Mom smiled. "That's *wunderbaar*. If your sister has been in the kitchen baking, it must mean she is coping a bit better now."

"That's what I thought too until Allen said the word *Daadi* and Sylvia burst into tears."

Mom rested her elbows on the counter and folded her hands as though praying. "It's understandable. I have to blink back tears every time I hear someone mention your daed's name."

"Me too, and the same goes for whenever anyone talks about Abe." Amy swallowed hard. "I miss them both so much as well as Toby. He was a good brother-in-law—always so kind and helpful."

"Jah, but they will all live in our minds and hearts." Mom touched her forehead and then her chest.

"You're so right. We will never forget any of them and the good times we used to have."

Mom tapped the top of the cookie container. "I hope you didn't bring all these kichlin out here for us to eat."

Amy laughed. "Not hardly. Thought I'd take 'em across the road as a welcome gift to our new neighbors."

"That's a good idea. We need to introduce ourselves and let them know we're glad they have chosen to live in this area." Mom pointed to the closest aisle where a variety of potted plants had been displayed. "Why don't you take them something nice from our greenhouse as well?"

"Okay." Amy headed down the aisle and returned to the counter a short time later with a pot of miniature roses. She noticed that the lid on the cookie container was off. She assumed her mother had opened it and eaten a few, until she glanced to her left and saw the elderly homeless woman with a cookie in each hand. Mom was in the next aisle over, talking to an Amish couple from their church district.

Amy was on the verge of saying something to Maude about helping herself to the cookies but changed her mind. The poor woman was probably hungry. Maybe she even believed that the cookies had been placed on the counter for the customers to help themselves.

Amy set the roses down and closed the lid on the cookies before the rest of them vanished. As soon as Mom came back, she picked them both up. "If you think you can manage things on your own for a short time, I'll go over to the neighbors' right now. Otherwise, I could wait until we close the greenhouse for the day."

Mom shook her head. "No, you go ahead. There are only three customers right now, so I'm sure I can manage. And if it gets busy while you're gone, I'll call for Henry to come help. Oh, and please let the neighbors know that I'll come by to welcome them myself as soon as I can."

"Okay." Amy chose not to mention that the elderly woman had taken two cookies, although she felt sure Mom would have understood.

Amy left the greenhouse and started down the driveway. The place across the road still looked the same, except for the two vehicles parked in the driveway. The moving crew that had worked steadily was gone. It was sad that the older couple who'd lived there so many years had moved away. But Amy could see the house and yard were in need of new people who could handle the amount of care it required. *I wonder what these folks will do with this place.*

She crossed the road and walked up their driveway. While eager to meet the new neighbors, she felt a bit nervous as well. What if the man and woman she'd seen previously didn't welcome strangers or weren't friendly people? They might not answer the door or could even slam it in her face.

I'm worried for nothing, she reprimanded herself. *Hopefully, once they see that I come bearing gifts, they'll welcome me into their home.*

Chapter 12

Amy looked both ways before crossing the road. After the accident that had taken three of her precious family members, she'd been watchful and more cautious, whether on foot or with the horse and buggy.

Stepping onto the neighbors' porch, Amy set the miniature roses on a small table positioned between two chairs and rapped on the door. After waiting for a couple of minutes, she knocked again. Since two vehicles were parked in the driveway, someone had to be home.

A few seconds later, the door swung open. "Whatever you're selling, I'm not interested." The woman with short red hair scowled at Amy.

"I'm not here to sell you anything. My name is Amy King. My family and I live across the street." Amy paused and drew a quick breath. "I brought some oatmeal-raisin cookies and a plant from our greenhouse to welcome you into our neighborhood." Her lips formed into what she hoped was a pleasant smile.

The woman stepped back, eyeing the offerings. "Oh, I see."

"Who is it, Virginia?" A tall man wearing shorts and a cotton T-shirt came to the door.

"My name is Amy King and—"

"She lives over there." The woman pointed across the road. "Said she came over to welcome us into the neighborhood with a plant and some cookies."

"Well, that's sure a nice gesture." The man extended his hand. "I'm

Earl Martin, and this is my wife, Virginia."

Amy shook his hand and then Virginia's. "It's nice to meet you both." She handed the cookies to his wife, and then picked up the plant and gave it to him. "My mother is busy in our greenhouse right now, or she would have come over to meet you too. One of these days soon, while I'm keeping an eye on things there, I'm sure she'll be over to say hello and get acquainted."

A sheen of perspiration erupted on Virginia's forehead. "That place keeps you pretty busy, I'll bet."

"It can at certain times of the year. We close up a few weeks before Christmas, after many of our poinsettias and Christmas cactus plants have sold. Then we open up again in early spring."

Virginia's lips parted, like she was on the verge of saying something, but Earl spoke first. "I imagine running a greenhouse is a lot of work. Are both of your parents involved in the business?"

"My father died several weeks ago, so it's just me and Mom in the greenhouse full-time. My younger brother, Henry, helps some there too."

"Sorry for your loss," Earl said. As he spoke, his wife gave a brief nod.

Amy didn't feel led to explain the details of her father's death or to mention that her brother and brother-in-law had also died the same day as Dad. She also said nothing about Sylvia. As they became more acquainted with the neighbors, more details about her family would likely come out. Perhaps Mom would tell them when she came over for a visit.

Fiddling with the ties on her covering, Amy said, "Well, I'd better let you two get back to whatever you were doing when I showed up on your doorstep. I'm sure you still have unpacking to do, and I really should get back to the greenhouse."

"Thank you for coming over, Amy." Earl's smile stretched wide. "The cookies and plant you brought us are appreciated." He bumped his wife's arm with his elbow. "Isn't that right, Virginia?"

With lips pressed together, she nodded slowly.

"All right then, I hope you both have a good day."

When Amy turned and started down the stairs, Earl called, "After the cookies are gone, we'll bring the empty container back to you."

She lifted a hand in a backward wave. "No hurry."

As Amy made her way back across the street, she thought about the reception she'd received. While Earl had appeared friendly enough, his wife seemed kind of aloof and distant.

Amy gave a quick shake of her head. *They didn't even invite me inside or engage in much conversation. I wonder if Virginia is just an unfriendly person, or is there something about me she didn't like?*

Pushing her troubling thoughts to the back of her mind, Amy went to the mailbox. When she'd checked earlier this morning, it had been empty, but now when she pulled the flap open, several envelopes waited for her. Amy took them all out and walked on, stopping at the phone shed. *I may as well check for messages while I'm out here.*

She stepped inside, placed the mail on the wooden counter, and listened to the first message. There were several others, and while she was listening to them and writing things down, she heard the awful racket of a crow in the yard. *I wonder if it's the same one that's been in our yard before.*

A few seconds later, Amy saw and heard a horse and buggy come up the driveway. No doubt it was another customer coming to the greenhouse.

After Earl closed the door, he smiled at Virginia. "Wasn't that a nice surprise, receiving the plant and cookies from our neighbors?" He gestured to the container Virginia still held in her hand.

She passed it to him. "Those people aren't right. They live in the past." Virginia gave her earlobe a tug. "What was that gal's name again?"

"Amy King, and before you go ranting, would you like a cookie?" Earl opened the container.

"No thanks, and I'm not ranting."

He popped a cookie into his mouth. "Mmm. . . this is sure good. You should try one, honey."

"Enough about the cookies. Did you hear what Amy said about her mother planning to come over to meet us?"

"Yeah, but if it bothers you, then don't answer the door. You don't have to get to know her or become friends. It's all up to you."

"That'll work out fine, unless you're the one who answers the door."

"What's that supposed to mean?"

"You'd probably end up flapping your lips, and soon the woman would know our whole life's story."

Earl shook his head, "Oh, come on. I'm not like that, and you know it." He grabbed another cookie and bit into it. "I do admit though certain people can engage me in conversation."

Virginia rolled her eyes. "And when have you ever needed encouragement?" She rescued the container and snapped the lid on. "I'd better take these to kitchen and put them away before you end up eating all of them."

Her husband mumbled something as she left the room. Virginia sometimes felt like she was living with a child. She placed the container on a shelf in the pantry and took out her grocery list. She needed to come up with something for lunch this afternoon but wasn't in the mood to make anything. *Maybe we'll go out to one of the restaurants in town. That way, if the neighbor lady stops by to meet us, we won't be home.*

The bell on the door jingled, and Belinda turned in time to see a tall, cleanly shaven Amish man enter the greenhouse. His dark brown hair had a bit of gray in it, and a few wrinkles showed on his face. Even after all these years, she knew he was Monroe Esh. At the same moment she spoke his name, he said hers.

"Belinda, you've hardly changed a bit." Monroe removed his straw hat and stood looking at her from his side of the counter with a wide smile.

Her cheeks warmed, and she reached up to touch them with her suddenly cold hands. Monroe was every bit as good looking as she remembered him. Only now, much older and hopefully wiser, he was no longer a young man full of adventure and flirtation; Monroe was a mature-looking man in his midfifties. It was surprising that he sported no beard—a sign that he was not married. Either that or he'd been unable, like a few other men she'd met, to grow any substantial hair on his face.

"Did your daughter tell you I was here the other day?" he asked, leaning on the counter.

"Jah, she did."

"I wanted to let you know I was sorry to hear about Vernon."

"Danki. It's been most difficult to accept that he's gone." Belinda's throat felt swollen, and her eyes burned with unshed tears.

"My folks told me all about the tragic accident that took three of your family's lives."

Monroe's sympathetic expression was almost Belinda's undoing. Talking or even thinking about the accident was still very raw. The last thing she wanted to do was break down here in front of Monroe or any of the other customers in the greenhouse.

"I understand you're running the place by yourself." Monroe's tone was soothing.

"Amy and Henry—he's my youngest son—help out here, and we're managing."

"Do you have other children?"

"Jah. Sylvia, my oldest daughter, has been living with us, along with her two small children, ever since her husband was killed in the accident." Belinda shifted on the stool she sat upon. "I also have a son who lives in a small Amish community in New York."

"I'm sure it's a comfort for you to have family during this time of grief."

She gave a nod. "Do you have your own family, Monroe?"

"Just my folks and siblings." He reached up with one hand and rubbed the back of his neck. "I've never married, so. . ." Monroe's words trailed off when Amy entered the store and stepped behind the counter next to Belinda.

"I see you came back empty-handed. Guess that means the neighbors must have been home?" Belinda tipped her head in Amy's direction.

"Yes, they were. The man thanked us, and I told them you'd be over to meet them soon." Amy glanced at Monroe then looked away. Belinda couldn't read her daughter's thoughts.

"Well, I should get going." Monroe placed his hat back on his head. "I'll drop by again sometime to see how you're doing. No doubt you could use an extra pair of hands around here from time to time."

Belinda could barely find her voice as she said quietly, "It's kind of you to offer, but we're getting along okay."

"Even so, it's not good for you to be here without a man." Monroe's forehead wrinkled. "You never know what might happen." He tipped his hat, said it was nice seeing her again, and went out the door.

Amy looked at Belinda with furrowed brows. "I hope that man doesn't have any ideas about courting you again, Mom."

Belinda lifted her gaze toward the ceiling. "Of course he doesn't. I chose your daed over Monroe, remember?"

"Jah, but. . ."

Belinda put a finger against her lips. "Let's not talk about this right now. There are other people here in the building."

"Sorry, you're right." Amy stepped out from behind the counter. "I'll go see if I can help any of them find what they need."

As her daughter walked away, Belinda's thoughts returned to her conversation with Monroe. *I surely hope he doesn't have any idea about us getting together again, because that's never going to happen. I loved Vernon with all my heart, and no one will ever replace him.*

Amy needed to talk to someone about Monroe Esh. She was concerned about the way he'd looked at her mother this afternoon. Didn't the man have work of his own to do or something else to keep him busy? Why would he want to come here and help out?

Who could I discuss this with? Amy asked herself as she closed things up in the greenhouse. Mom had already gone up to the house to rest awhile before it was time to start supper. Poor thing looked exhausted at the end of their workday, and she hadn't said much after Monroe left the greenhouse.

I wonder if seeing her old boyfriend upset my mamm. It sure upset me. It's way too soon for my mother to even be thinking about a suitor, and I have a feeling that's what Monroe has in mind.

Amy walked up and down the aisles, making sure everything was in place and all the hoses for watering were turned off. *I could call Ezekiel and leave a message, letting him know what happened here today. But if I do that, my brother will make a call to Mom right away, and then she'll be upset with me for alarming Ezekiel for what she would refer to as "nothing to worry about."*

But Amy was worried. She flexed her fingers, and then pulled them into the palms of her hands. *Oh Dad, if you hadn't been so determined to get ice cream, none of this would be a problem. Mom and I wouldn't be working so hard in the greenhouse; Henry would be in better spirits; and Sylvia could be at her own home with her children, living happily as Toby's wife.*

Amy had gone over all of this so many times, and the same words would pop into her mind. Of course, it did no good to rehash the past that couldn't be altered, but it helped to release some of her tension and the emotions she kept bottled up most of the time. She would like to talk to Sylvia about her concerns, but that would upset her sister even more. For now, at least, Amy would keep her thoughts and concerns to herself. She would, however, keep a close watch on things, and if Monroe kept coming around, acting all friendly and nice toward Mom, she might have to put the man in his place.

Chapter 13

When Belinda opened the front door and screen door to the greenhouse the following morning, a swarm of honeybees headed right for her. She ducked, nearly hitting her head on a shelf full of vegetable plants. Looking up, she watched as the flying insects made a hasty exit out the open door and into the yard. She hadn't yet opened the door at the other end of the building, which they usually kept open during business hours for cross-ventilation.

Oh, dear. . . That was too close for my comfort. It's a good thing I'm not allergic to bees. Belinda's skin prickled as she straightened to her full height. "Henry King, where are you, young man?" she shouted as she hurried out the door.

"What are ya yelling about, Mom?" Henry stepped out of the barn, his straw hat askew.

Belinda pointed in the direction of the bees circling the yard. "How did those *ieme* get into the greenhouse?"

With open palms, Henry gave a brief shrug.

"Did you go back in after Amy locked up last evening?"

"Nope." He rubbed at the red blotch on his left cheek. "Well, come to think of it, guess I did."

"How come?"

"I remembered that I'd left my can of soda pop in the greenhouse, so I went back to fetch it." He dropped his gaze. "When I couldn't find the can, I stepped outside and looked around, thinking I might have gotten it earlier and forgot where I set it."

"Did you find it?"

Henry shook his head. "I left the door open a ways, and the screen door may have blown open in the wind when I went lookin' for it, but I wasn't gone long and I did eventually close and lock both doors."

"Apparently, while you were out looking for the soda can, a swarm of the honeybees got into the greenhouse. They almost hit me in the face when I opened the door a short time ago. What if it had happened when we had customers? Someone could have gotten stung. And no doubt it would have frightened them to see all those bees flying around." She tapped her foot, trying not to give in to the anger she felt.

"Sorry, Mom."

"Jah, well, the next time you come into the greenhouse for anything, be sure you shut all the doors, even if you're planning to come right back."

Henry dug the toe of his boot into the ground. "Ya know, if we didn't have those stupid bees, they wouldn't be flyin' all over the place. When Ezekiel moved, he shoulda sold the bees to someone else in Lancaster County who raises them for *hunnich*."

"He could have done that all right, but Abe agreed to take care of them."

Henry scrunched up his face. "Jah, Abe—not me. I hate takin' care of those *ieme*."

"They don't demand much of your time, Son. And the extra money we earn from the honey sales helps out."

Henry's arms hung at his sides as he stared at the ground. "Jah, okay. . .whatever. Nobody in this family cares about me and my needs anyway." He tromped off before Belinda could respond.

She gave a frustrated shake of her head. *Henry should set his own needs aside and realize that we all need to pull together right now.* Belinda understood that her son was still young and often acted impulsively. But he had to grow up sometime and learn to be more responsible. She couldn't think of a better time for that to happen than now.

"I'll join you in the greenhouse as soon as I get the mail," Amy called to Mom when she stepped out the front door. She'd left Sylvia in the kitchen to do the dishes by herself, since she and Mom were running behind and needed to get the business opened before any customers showed up.

Sylvia had said she didn't mind. With the exception of going to church every other Sunday, Amy's dear sister hardly went anywhere these days. Amy didn't think it was good for Sylvia to stay cooped up in the house so much, but she tried not to be pushy or pressure her about it. It was best to let Sylvia deal with things in her own way. Amy hoped that eventually her sister would come through this crisis stronger and better able to serve the Lord.

Amy hadn't admitted it to Mom or anyone else, but she too was having a difficult time coping. The loss of Dad, Abe, and Toby was never far from her mind or the fact that she'd also lost Jared by breaking up with him. The thing that helped her the most, however, was staying busy and concentrating on her duties in the greenhouse rather than focusing on all that she'd lost or given up. Amy felt thankful for every day she worked there and had the chance to talk to their customers about flowers and plants and answer all kinds of gardening questions. In addition to taking her mind off the grief she felt each and every day, Amy enjoyed being able to share her knowledge of gardening with others. She knew without reservation that Mom did too. It gave Amy a sense of satisfaction to be able to work alongside her mother to keep their business running and money coming in.

She'd heard a little more the other day about the new greenhouse that was in the process of being built. She'd read about it in the local paper, and it stated there would be three large buildings that would house nearly everything related to gardening. Amy hoped it wouldn't hurt their business, because it was a much smaller operation.

We might need to think of adding on and for sure offering more items for people to buy that would be related to gardening. It's important that we stay up with things so we don't lose customers to the new greenhouse when it opens.

As Amy drew close to the end of their driveway, her mouth gaped open when the mailbox came in sight. The sides and top of it had been smashed in so badly, Amy wasn't sure she could even get the flap open in order to retrieve the mail.

Her forehead creased. *Who would do such a thing?*

Amy looked at the mailbox next to theirs. It belonged to the neighbors across the street, but it had not been vandalized, nor had the ones up the road. For some reason only theirs had been singled out. Why? Could someone be angry or unhappy with them? Amy wondered what Mom would have to say about this. No doubt she'd be upset.

Amy grabbed the handle on the mailbox and gave it a tug, but it had been so badly bent, it wouldn't budge. She gave it another hard yank, but it still didn't move. She'd have to go get Henry and see if he could get the mailbox unbent enough to at least open the flap.

Amy ran back toward the greenhouse, but spotted her brother coming out of the barn. "Henry, I need to talk to you," she called.

He put both hands on his hips. "What do ya want now?"

"Our mailbox has been vandalized."

"Are you kidding?" He scratched under his straw hat.

She shook her head. "It's all bent up, and the door won't open. I tried to wrench on it, but with no luck."

Henry groaned. "I'd better go take a look. But first, I'll see what I can find in the toolshed to pop the lid free."

"Okay. I'd better get to the greenhouse now and tell Mom what happened."

"I'm so tired of bein' stuck here at this stupid greenhouse all the time." Henry turned and headed for the shed.

Amy chose to let his comment go. She was about to enter the greenhouse when their first customer arrived by horse and buggy. It was their bishop and his wife. She waved at them and stepped inside, where she found Mom sweeping around the checkout counter.

"What took you so long getting the mail?" Mom paused from her work.

Amy was about to respond when the bishop and his wife entered the building. Everyone exchanged greetings, and as Mom continued talking to the elderly couple, Amy picked up the broom and finished cleaning the floor. While their customers began browsing through the plants, Mom returned to Amy and asked a second time about the mail.

In a hushed tone, Amy explained about the mailbox.

Mom's eyes widened. "I can't believe anyone would do such a thing."

"It seems we were singled out for some reason, but I don't understand why someone would do this to us." Amy gave her mother a hug. "I told Henry about it, and he's going out to see if he can get the mail out of the box."

Mom leaned against the register. "This was not a good way to start our morning. We'll need to get the mailbox replaced."

Amy figured one of them, probably Henry, would have to go to the hardware store in town and buy a new mailbox. Perhaps it would be good to get a larger, stronger one this time—maybe the kind that locked. If someone was mean enough to ruin their mailbox, she wouldn't put it past them to steal the mail inside the box either.

That evening, after the little ones had been put to bed, Amy sat in the living room with her mother and Sylvia. After only a few minutes of idle conversation, Mom mentioned the vandalized mailbox as well as all the bees that had gotten into the greenhouse.

She stopped rocking in her chair and looked at Amy and Sylvia, sitting beside each other on the couch. "I waited until Henry went out to the barn to check on the animals before I brought this topic up, because I didn't want him to know what I've been thinking." She paused and pushed her reading glasses firmly on the bridge of her nose. "I'm deeply concerned about what happened today."

"Henry knows about the mailbox." Amy's lips pressed together in a slight grimace. "After all, he's the one who got the mail out of the box, and he also went to the hardware store to get a new mailbox. So why would you want to keep him in the dark about our conversation?"

"I am well aware of what your bruder knows." Mom leaned forward in her chair. "He also knows about the honeybees that got into the greenhouse, but I am equally sure he has no idea that I suspect he's the one who did both of those things."

Sylvia's eyes widened, and Amy shook her head in denial. Although Henry had a bad attitude these days, she felt sure he would not be capable of doing either one of those things.

"You're both aware that your brother is full of anger, and on top of that, he does not want to take care of the bees or help in the greenhouse. He may be looking for ways to vent that aggravation."

Amy sighed. "If it actually was our own brother who bashed in the mailbox, he may have gotten up early this morning and done it or even snuck out of the house sometime during the night. But do you really think our little brother would go to such lengths as to release the bees into the greenhouse and damage our mailbox?"

"I hope not, but it is a possibility that we can't ignore." Mom pinched the skin at her throat, as she often did when she was worried.

"Maybe Henry needs another phone call from Ezekiel," Sylvia suggested.

Mom shook her head vigorously. "If Ezekiel even thinks things are not going well for us, he might change his mind and decide to move back here." Her gaze traveled from Sylvia to Amy. "I don't want him to know anything about this."

"We could ask one of our ministers to talk with Henry." Amy pointed to the Bible on the end table closest to Mom's chair. "They're full of wisdom and know the Bible so well. Maybe it would help."

"Just having a little talk with him about facing his responsibilities without grumbling might improve things," Sylvia added.

"That's a good idea. I'll speak with one of the preachers sometime tomorrow. I'm sure he'll be willing to come over and talk to Henry." Mom gave a nod. "I'll go as soon as the greenhouse closes for the day."

Chapter 14

"Hang on!" Breaking hard, Amy's driver, Pauline, gripped the steering wheel so tightly that the veins on her hands protruded.

The van stopped and things were quiet, except for the steady idle of the engine.

Amy slowly opened her eyes. Even though a dog had run out in front of them, they'd avoided a bad outcome. "That was close." She drew in a shaky breath as she watched the pooch wander off the street and into a nearby yard.

Pauline drummed the steering wheel. "I wish owners would keep a better watch on their pets."

"Henry has a dog, but he keeps the mutt penned up when he's not able to keep an eye on him." Amy pulled on the seatbelt to get some slack again, as it felt like it was cutting into her neck. She hoped the flowers in the back of the vehicle weren't disturbed from the force it took to stop. She looked straight ahead while her driver resumed the proper speed.

It wasn't long before they pulled into a space in front of Sara's flower shop. Amy got out of the van and went inside.

"It's good to see you. How have you and your family been?" Sara asked when Amy stepped up to the counter.

"Not the best, but we're getting by." Amy was tempted to mention what had happened with their mailbox, but since it had been replaced with a larger, stronger one that locked, she saw no reason to bring the topic up. Lenore's husband, Jesse, had come over to help Henry erect the new mailbox, so everything was as it should be, at least for the time being.

Amy had suggested to her mother that they call the sheriff's office to report the incident, but Mom said it wasn't necessary since they had no evidence or even a clue as to who had done it. Amy figured if her brother was guilty of the vandalism, Mom wouldn't want the law involved.

Amy gestured toward the window, where her driver's van sat in front of the building. "I came with the cut flowers you ordered yesterday. I wanted to get them to you early in case you needed them for any orders you might have for today."

"I appreciate it because we got several new orders yesterday before closing time." Sara glanced out the window. "If you'll ask your driver to pull around to the back of the store, we can get them unloaded."

"Sure, no problem." Amy went out the door and gave directions to Pauline. This was the first time Amy had been the one to deliver flowers to Sara's shop and the first time she'd called upon their new driver.

While the van pulled around back, Amy returned to the flower shop. "Pauline should be at the back door soon," she announced to Sara.

"Okay, I'll let my designer, Misty, know. She and my new assistant, Stephanie, will unload the flowers and bring them into the back room." Sara disappeared into the other room and returned a few minutes later. "I spoke to your driver. She said she'd pick you up out front."

"Okay."

Sara moved over to front counter. "While they're unloading, I'll write you a check for the flowers."

"Thank you."

While Sara took care of that, Amy meandered around the floral shop, observing the lovely way Sara had decorated the place. She paused to admire a glass cross and several other pretty trinkets that adorned the table. She moved around the store, soaking it all in. The window display and every table and shelf in this room had something unique and attractive to look at in addition to some of the bouquets and houseplants Sara offered her customers.

Amy's excitement overflowed as an idea popped into her head. "If you have some free time some evening, Sara, if you wouldn't mind, maybe you could come by the greenhouse and offer us some suggestions as to how we might display the items we have for sale in a more appealing way. Once that new greenhouse we've heard about opens for business, we're going to have some competition, so we need to make an effort to keep up with them."

"One thing you must keep in mind, Amy, is that tourists seem to be attracted to the Amish way of life. And since your place is owned and run by Plain People, it is, and will continue to be, a tourist attraction. That is one key thing the new business probably won't have." Sara handed Amy a check. "Now, as for me coming over and giving you some suggestions, I'd be happy to drop by. If Brad isn't busy, maybe he'd like to come with me."

Amy smiled. "That would be nice. Maybe he'd be willing to have a talk with my brother. He needs cheering up and some guidance these days." She hoped she hadn't said too much or that her mother wouldn't get upset about it. Sara wasn't a family member or the first person Mom would turn to for advice about personal matters.

"I've suspected as much. Henry's the one who has been making deliveries since the deaths of your family members, and I've noticed a deep sadness in his eyes."

"It's not just his sadness, for we all have that. It's his angry, defiant attitude I'm most worried about." Amy's facial muscles tightened. "Mom's going to ask one of our preachers to speak with Henry, but it wouldn't hurt if Brad spoke to him too."

"When I go home this evening, I'll bring up the topic." Sara touched Amy's arm. "I'll also be praying for Henry as well as you and the rest of your family."

"Thank you." Amy caught sight of her driver's van out front, so she turned toward the door. "Guess I'd better go. Henry didn't want to make the deliveries this morning, and he's supposed to be in the store helping Mom. I need to get back there in case he's not cooperating."

"Okay, I'll see you some evening later this week."

Amy opened the door, but before she could exit the store, Sara's father, Herschel Fisher, stepped in. His towering form was unmistakable. He offered her a warm smile. "It's nice to see you, Amy. How are things going for you and your family?"

"We're getting by."

"I wish I lived closer and didn't have my store to run, or I'd come by and help out with some chores."

"It's okay, Herschel. We're managing." Amy started out the door, calling over her shoulder, "If you think about it, please let your mamm know that we're having a sale at the greenhouse next week."

"I surely will."

Amy waved and hurried to get into her driver's van. She didn't know Herschel all that well but remembered him coming to the greenhouse a few times with his mother. Amy thought he was a nice man, and it was refreshing to see how kind he was to his mother. Even though Herschel was in his early sixties, he seemed attentive to his mom's needs.

Not like Henry, she thought with regret. *He's too caught up in his own little world of grief and anger to care about how Mom feels these days.*

Rolling her shoulders to loosen the tension she felt, Belinda glanced at the battery-operated clock sitting on the counter. Just another hour and it would be time to close the greenhouse for the day; then she could hitch her horse to the buggy and pay a visit to Preacher Thomas Raber and his wife. Thomas was one of the older ministers in their church, and he'd had plenty of experience in the thirty-some years since he'd acquired the position through the drawing of lots. She felt confident that he'd be willing to speak with Henry. She just hoped her son would listen to the minister's words and heed his counsel, because she really didn't want to trouble Ezekiel again. Besides, it hadn't worked last time, so he probably wouldn't succeed with Henry anyhow.

"Oh, I forgot to tell you something." Amy interrupted Belinda's thoughts. "Sara and her husband might come by some evening soon. I asked her to take a look at how things are arranged here in the greenhouse and give me some ideas on how to feature our plants and flowers in a way that will draw the customers' attention."

Belinda tapped a pen against the tablet in front of her. "I suppose it couldn't hurt, but I don't see what's wrong with the way we're displaying things now."

"It couldn't hurt to get Sara's professional opinion."

"I guess you're right."

"She's going to ask her husband to come along, and I suggested that he might want to have a talk with Henry."

Belinda's toes curled inside her shoes. "Why would you do that, Amy? Didn't I tell you that I was planning to speak with one of our ministers about Henry's attitude?"

Amy's cheeks flushed. "Well, jah, but Brad's also a minister so I just thought—"

"You shouldn't have been talking to Sara about our problems."

"Why not?"

"Because they aren't a part of our family."

"Neither is Preacher Raber."

"No, but he is an important part of our Amish church—not to mention that he knows us quite well." Belinda rubbed her chin, mulling things over. "Since there are only a few people here at the moment and it's almost time to close up the greenhouse, I'm going to head over to the Rabers' right now. Will you please lock up after the last customer leaves, and then go help Sylvia get supper started?"

"Of course." Amy touched Belinda's shoulder. "I hope you're not umgerennt because I talked with Sara about Henry. She already suspected he was having a hard time because of how he's acted when he's made deliveries to her flower shop."

"Sorry, I probably overreacted. If Preacher Raber doesn't get through to Henry, then I have no problem with Sara's husband talking to your bruder." Belinda gave a deep sigh. "I just hope that someone will be able to get through to that boy. It's difficult enough to face all the negative things life can dish out. I can't stand the thought of losing Henry because he's chosen to pull away from us all."

As Amy stood in the kitchen next to her sister, each working on a different dish for supper, she couldn't help noticing the dark circles beneath Sylvia's eyes. With Amy's bedroom being across the hall from the room Sylvia shared with her children, she could often hear heart-wrenching sobs. Amy shed tears some nights too, but it was quiet crying, and at least she was able to sleep.

"Did you get a nap today?" Amy's question broke through the silence.

Sylvia shook her head. "I tidied up in the bedroom and bathroom, but afterward I felt drained." She gave the salad a quick toss. "A little later, I lay on the bed with the kinner, but I was unable to sleep—could not turn off the thoughts."

"I'm sorry." *Maybe Preacher Raber should talk to my sister too,* Amy thought. *She may not be grumbling all the time and saying hurtful things, but she hasn't even begun to let go of her grief and could certainly use some spiritual guidance.* When the minister came by to talk to Henry, Amy hoped he would see how badly Sylvia was hurting and spend some time counseling her as well. With the way things were now, it didn't look like Sylvia would ever be able to function as she once had. And if things didn't change, Henry might spend the rest of his life mad at God and taking out his frustrations on the rest of the world.

Chapter 15

The next day, shortly after the greenhouse opened, Preacher Raber and his wife, Rebekah, came by.

"Is your brother around?" the minister asked when Amy greeted them near the door.

Amy shrugged. "I think he's in the barn, but I'm not sure. Knowing Henry, he could be most anywhere." *Trying to get out of work,* she mentally added.

"I'll look there first, while my *fraa* does some shopping for gardening things." The preacher grinned at his wife and gave her a thumbs-up before heading out the door.

Amy smiled. *I hope if I ever get married, my husband is as generous as Thomas Raber.* Her smile faded. *But it doesn't look like I'll ever become a married woman. My responsibility is here helping Mom. That's just how it is.*

She had to admit though, seeing Jared at the biweekly services was a challenge. She would look anywhere but in his direction. She'd made up her mind about not seeing him anymore and wouldn't budge from her resolve. Sylvia had asked about Jared, but she didn't push at all or try to sway Amy's decision. Amy also had to admit, her life had become pretty boring staying home so much and not going to young people's gatherings with Jared. She kept so busy at the greenhouse, there wasn't time to even get together with Lydia anymore.

Maybe it's for the best, Amy told herself. *Lydia might try and talk me into seeing Jared again. She did go to bat for him when he asked for her help.*

While Amy sauntered through the greenhouse, absorbed in thought, her foot caught hold of a watering hose that had been left on the concrete floor. She nearly fell but caught herself in time. Amy looked around and brushed some dirt off the bottom of her dress. Mom's back was turned, so she apparently hadn't noticed Amy's near spill.

Since her mother was busy putting new seed packets on a shelf, Amy took a seat behind the counter. There were no customers other than the preacher's wife at the moment, which gave Amy more time to let her mind wander. *I wonder what Jared is doing today. Has he had many roofing jobs this week?* She leaned forward, resting her elbows on the counter. Amy pictured herself and Jared as a married couple, out running errands together.

She shook those unrealistic thoughts away and chided herself. *I have to stop thinking about him.*

Sitting up tall and looking around the greenhouse, Amy remembered her walk out to the mailbox this morning. She'd been relieved when she found the new box intact. Amy figured the attack on their old mailbox had most likely been done by some rowdy kids looking for something to do that they could brag about to all their friends. She didn't want to believe her brother could have done something like that, for if Henry was the guilty one, then his anger had gotten the best of him and needed to be brought under control.

Amy hoped Preacher Raber had been able to locate her brother and that Henry would listen to and heed everything being said.

Mom finished watering the closest plants and then coiled the hose and hung it on the hooks above the shelf. "I'd better get this up and out of the way before someone trips over it."

Too late, Mom. I already did. Amy snickered at her failure to watch where she stepped. It was a good thing it had happened to her though, and not one of their customers.

"How'd things go with the preacher and Henry?" Amy asked her mother after Thomas and Rebekah Raber left with a few bedding plants. "I assume the minister told you how his conversation went?"

"Jah, he did." Mom bobbed her head. "Apparently, Henry seemed to be listening, but that doesn't mean he will heed the preacher's words and change his attitude."

Amy nodded along as her mother spoke. "I guess we'll have to wait and see how it goes."

Her stomach growled, and she strolled over to the snack bag and took out an orange, which she peeled. "Mom, would you like half of my *aarensch?*"

"An orange sounds good. I could use a little pick-me-up."

They'd finished the treat, when Henry entered the building. His face was red, and a sheen of sweat glistened on his forehead. "Did you *hetze* the preacher on me?" He moved close to their mother.

"I did not sic Thomas Raber on you, Henry. I just told him you were having a hard time dealing with the death of our family members and asked if he would talk to you—offer some words of encouragement."

Henry's features tightened as he crossed his arms. "Sounds like siccing to me." He looked over at Amy and squinted. "You don't need to stand there lookin' so perfect, either. You miss Dad and Abe too, and truth be told, you don't like workin' here anymore than I do. You're just too nicey-nice to say so."

Amy drew a deep breath and held it as she counted to ten. *How could Henry speak that way to Mom? If Dad were here, he'd have something to say about this. Furthermore, I don't appreciate Henry's tone and what he's been saying to me either.* She had half a mind to put her brother in his place once and for all.

Mom stood up straight and looked at Henry. "I'll have you know, young man, that your sister hurts just as much as you do over the loss of your daed and bruder. I'm sure she misses Toby too. But Amy cares enough about this family to work in the greenhouse without complaint, and she doesn't take her frustrations out on others."

Mom's voice had grown louder. It was a good thing there were no customers at the moment. "She sacrificed being courted by Jared in order to give all her time and attention to helping me keep this business running and bringing in the money we need to survive." She pointed at Henry. "What sacrifices have you made, Son?"

"I guess none. At least that's the way you two see it." Henry whirled around and dashed out the door.

Amy lifted her gaze to the ceiling. "That didn't go over so well, did it?"

Mom shook head. "No, I should say not. We need to keep praying for your brother and not let up until we see a change."

"Jah, and the same goes for Sylvia. I think it would help if she kept busy with something other than household chores. And for sure, she needs to be around people and socialize more." *Just like Mom, I'll be praying too. I hope there will be a change for someone in our family soon.*

Sylvia was resting on the couch while the children napped, when she heard the back door open and slam shut. Henry stomped into the room.

"You'd best be ready, Sister, 'cause you'll probably be next."

"Next for what?" she asked, sitting up. "And please lower your voice. Your niece and nephew are asleep."

"Sorry." He sank into their father's favorite chair. "As I was saying. . . You'll probably be next to get chewed out by Mom. Maybe Amy will put in her two cents' worth too."

"Why would they do that?"

" 'Cause they did it to me—at least Mom did. Our sister just stood there listening and bobbing her head." Henry groaned as he leaned back in the chair. "Mom asked Preacher Raber to have a little talk with me, and later she got all over my case. It really irked me when she started comparing me to her sweet little Amy." With a stony face, he stared at Sylvia. "Mom favors Amy over us, ya know."

Sylvia shook her head. "No, she doesn't. I'm sure that's not true."

"Jah, she does. Started singin' Amy's praises because she works hard in the greenhouse without complaint, and she even brought up the fact that Amy broke things off with Jared so she could help Mom all the time."

Sylvia tugged at her sleeve. "Did she say anything negative about me?"

"No, but I'm sure Mom and Amy have talked about you—how you stay cooped up here in the house most of the time." Henry stomped his foot. "If I have to take care of the livestock, tend to those stupid bees, work in the greenhouse, and do a bunch of other chores, then I think you oughta find someone to watch the kinner so you can do some work out there too."

Her brother's harsh words stabbed Sylvia to the core. He didn't understand how exhausted she felt. Just taking care of the children and keeping the house running as smoothly as she could wore her out. Every single thing she did took all her energy and willpower, and as the days went on, it didn't get any better. The agony Sylvia felt over the loss of her husband, father, and brother felt so heavy that at times she almost couldn't breathe. If she even tried to go out to the greenhouse to work, she feared she might collapse. The idea of talking to people and answering questions all day was unfathomable. It was all she could do to face people when they went to church, which was why she sometimes looked for reasons to stay home.

Sylvia didn't mention it to Henry, but the preacher had stopped at the house to speak with her too. She hadn't felt up to talking to him and made the excuse that the children were sleeping, so it wasn't a good time to talk. He'd left, saying he would drop by some other time.

Sylvia lay back down and closed her eyes. *If Mom and Amy have been talking about me behind my back, so be it. The only thing I'm capable of doing right now is taking care of my kinner's needs. Don't know if I'll ever feel up to working in the greenhouse again.* Sylvia's heart clenched. *Could what Henry said about Amy be true? Does Mom care more about her than me and Henry?*

Jared was on his way to the Kings' place to try once more to get Amy to change her mind about seeing him when Dandy began limping.

Jared slowed the horse and found a suitable spot along the shoulder of the road to pull off. "This is not good." He shook his head. "Not good at all. He probably threw a shoe."

He set the brake, climbed down from buggy, and took a look at the horse's hooves. "It's okay, boy," he soothed. "I just need to see your shoes." After patting the horse's neck, Jared lifted the animal's right front leg. Sure enough, the shoe was missing.

Letting go of the gelding's limb, he stepped back. "Well fella, it's back to the barn for you this evening." Hopefully, he'd be able to get a farrier to come out in the morning. Otherwise, he'd have to borrow one of his parents' horses or call a driver.

"Maybe it's for the best," Jared muttered as he took his seat in the buggy again. "Amy would probably tell me the same thing as before, and then I'd be hurt all over again."

Jared thought about the last few Sundays when he'd seen her at church. He had tried to make eye contact with Amy a couple of times, but she never looked his way. After the noon meal, when he tried to seek Amy out, he discovered that she and her family had left for home.

He clenched his jaw. *If only Amy could give me a shred of hope, I'd hang on and wait for her.*

Jared wasn't sure what to do anymore. His heart told him to keep pursuing Amy, but his head told him otherwise. *If she loved me the way I love her, she'd let me help out whenever I could. And she wouldn't shut me out but would accept my love with open arms. Maybe Mom's right. Maybe Amy's not the woman God meant for me.*

Jared felt like a young boy who couldn't make up his mind about what flavor of ice cream to choose. *First vanilla and then chocolate. No, maybe strawberry would be better instead.* One thing Jared was certain of: if he prodded Amy too much, trying to get her to change her mind, he would likely push her farther away. *So maybe it was a good thing Dandy lost his shoe. It probably kept me from making a mistake this evening. If Amy wants a relationship with me, she needs to make the first move. It won't be easy, but I'll try to sit back and wait till she realizes how much she needs me.*

Chapter 16

"Ouch!"

"What happened?" Virginia turned from rinsing out a cup at the sink.

"I touched the cast-iron skillet on the stove, and it was still hot." Earl held up his index finger.

"Come on over here and run your finger under the cool water."

He shook his head. "It'll be okay. I'll just have a seat at the table, since you have our breakfast ready."

She gave a brief shrug and dished up some scrambled eggs on both of their plates.

"What are your plans for the day?" Earl asked.

She offered him some toast and butter. "Nothing yet. I need to take a shower first." Virginia pointed to the cardboard boxes on the other side of the room. "And I still have some things to put away in the kitchen cupboards."

"Yep. You better get busy then."

Virginia's brows furrowed as a fly buzzed her head. "Do you know what happened to our flyswatter? I've looked everywhere for it."

"We had one at the other house, and I thought we packed it." He scratched at his thinning hair. "Guess we may need to buy a new one."

She swatted at the fly hovering near her plate. "I don't remember having so many pesky flies at our place in Chicago."

Earl rubbed the spot on the finger he'd burned. "You have a point, Virginia."

Slapping at the table and missing the insect, she scowled. "I'm sure it's because of all the dirty critters living around us out here in the boonies. It's the perfect breeding ground for filthy flies."

"It might help if we get some fly tape and hung it here in the kitchen. That stuff works pretty good."

Virginia pulled her fingers through the ends of her short hair. "Looks like I oughta drive into town and do some shopping today."

"Good idea."

They ate in silence for a while, until Virginia looked at the open window. The subtle breeze moved the checkered curtains a bit, and she caught sight of something. "The screen in our kitchen window has a couple of holes in it. I bet that's how all the flies are getting in."

He glanced that way. "I can tape up those holes in a jiffy."

"That's just a temporary fix, Earl. We need a new screen."

"I'll tape it for now and will get a new screen as soon as I can."

She smiled. "Sooner, the better."

"What about that?" Earl gestured to the plastic container on the counter. "It's been empty for a couple of days. Don't ya think you should return it to the young neighbor woman who brought those tasty cookies to us?"

"I'll be too busy today. Besides, the little gal knows where it is. If she wants the container, she can come over and get it." Virginia blew on her coffee and drank some.

Earl's eyes narrowed as he stared at her from across the table. "You're kidding, right?"

"Not really. I have no desire to hightail it over there to meet that girl's family." She reached for a piece of toast and slathered it with butter. "Those people are strange. Not only do they dress in plain clothes like the pioneers, but they use those smelly horses that draw flies to pull their old-fashioned gray buggies." Virginia rolled her eyes. "There are no electric wires running to their house, so I can only imagine how they must live in that place."

He dipped his toast in the runny egg yolks. "Did you ever think that their plain ways may be better than ours?"

"Nope. I'd never want to live the way those folks do. I like having our modern conveniences. And what would I do without cable TV?"

"Maybe you'd get more unpacking done if you left the television alone for a while."

"I don't know what you're talking about, Earl. You act like I'm addicted to the thing."

"All I can say is, whenever you're watching some show and I try to ask you a question, you don't even hear me."

"You're exaggerating." She folded her arms. "Now, back to the topic of those Plain People living across the road—there is nothing on this green earth that would make me want to live the way they do."

"As long as we pay our electric bill, you'll never have to." Earl finished his breakfast and pushed away from the table. "And speaking of bills. . .I need to head for work or we won't have money to pay any of the bills that come in."

"I suppose you'd like me to look for a job so I can pay my share?"

Earl shook his head. "With that bum leg of yours, I don't expect you to do anything more than you're capable of." He picked up the container the cookies had come in and handed it to her. "But I do expect you to find some time today to return this. It's the polite thing to do."

"Okay, okay. I'll head over there as soon as I clear the table and put the dishes in the dishwasher."

Earl smiled and kissed her cheek. "Good girl."

It had been two days since Thomas Raber spoke to Henry, but the boy's attitude hadn't changed. In Belinda's opinion, her son had gotten worse. As she headed down the driveway to retrieve the mail, her thoughts took her back to the night before. Henry had been fairly quiet most of that day, until shortly before nine o'clock, when he'd said he wanted to go out for a buggy ride. When Belinda asked where he planned on going at such a late hour, Henry said nowhere in particular; he just wanted to be by himself for a while and enjoy some fresh air. Belinda was tempted to tell Henry he couldn't go anywhere but kept silent. After the discussion they'd had two days ago, she was fully aware of Henry's feelings and thought the buggy ride might do him some good. With a clearer head, he might have a new perspective on things. This morning, however, Henry had been just as sullen as ever.

Last night, Belinda had listened to a message from Sara, saying that she and her husband would be coming over sometime tomorrow evening. *Maybe if Brad talks to Henry, he will be able to get through to him. I can at least hope and pray for that.*

Belinda couldn't give up hope that things would change. She longed to have Henry back and reacting to things the way he used to when his father and brother were alive. "Oh Vernon," she whispered. "I wish you were still here."

That must be our new neighbor. Here's my chance to make her acquaintance. Belinda reached the mailbox about the same time as the red-haired woman across the road left her yard. Holding a plastic container in one hand while walking with a bit of a limp, she came up to Belinda.

"You must be Virginia." Belinda smiled at the woman.

"Yeah." Virginia rolled her blue eyes from side to side, pausing briefly to glance at Belinda. "Came on over here to return this." She held out the container. "The young woman—I guess she's your daughter—brought us some cookies in the container."

"Yes, that was my daughter Amy." Belinda took the container with one hand and reached to shake Virginia's hand with the other. "My name is Belinda King. It's nice to finally meet you, Virginia."

"Umm. . .yeah. Same here." Virginia glanced back toward her place.

"Where are you from?"

"Chicago." She looked toward Belinda's home. "It's taking a bit of getting used to, living around here."

"I see. Well, I've been meaning to come over and welcome you properly, but things have been so busy at the greenhouse, I kept putting it off."

"No problem." Virginia dropped her gaze. "I'm still unpacking boxes and arranging furniture, so I don't have much time for standing around yakking."

"I understand. Moving into a new home can be quite daunting." Belinda smiled, but when Virginia did not reciprocate, she figured it was time to wrap up their conversation. "When you're not so busy, why don't you come over sometime? I'd be happy to show you around the greenhouse, and if we're not too busy, maybe we can sit and visit over a glass of cold meadow-mint tea."

Virginia's nose wrinkled. "Never heard of it, but then I'm not much of a tea drinker. I prefer coffee."

"My other daughter, Sylvia, usually has a pot of coffee on the stove, so if that's what you'd prefer, we can drink coffee instead."

Virginia gave a brief shrug. "Maybe. I'll have to wait and see how it goes." With a mumbled goodbye, she turned and walked back across the road.

Belinda went to the mailbox, unlocked it, and took out the mail. It hadn't taken her long to realize that their new neighbor was certainly not the friendly type. She hoped after Virginia had been here awhile, she'd be a bit friendlier.

Belinda was about to start back up the driveway, when she caught sight of their sign at the left end of the driveway, advertising the greenhouse. Instead of hanging from the heavy wire where it had been attached to a metal frame, the sign now lay off to one side among some tall weeds. Leaning down for a closer look, Belinda realized the wire had been cut. *What is going on here?* Someone had obviously done it on purpose and tossed the sign in the weeds.

Who could have done this and why? Belinda rubbed her forehead. *Oh, I hope it wasn't Henry.*

"You're awfully quiet this morning." Lydia's mother tapped her shoulder. "Didn't you sleep well last night?"

Lydia turned from the stove, where she'd been stirring a kettle of oatmeal. "It wasn't the best sleep. I'm worried about Jared."

"Is he *grank*?"

"He's not physically ill, Mama, but Jared's heartsick because Amy broke up with him."

"Has he actually said that to you?"

"Well, no. It's just the way he's been acting. I can see the pain in his eyes."

"I'm sure he will get past it and move on to someone else who won't break his heart."

Mama lifted Lydia's chin so she was looking directly into her eyes. "Maybe that someone will be you."

Lydia's lips pressed together as she tugged on her apron. "Even if Jared seemed interested in me, I could never come between him and my best friend."

"You can't come between two people who aren't together anymore. Amy obviously doesn't want to be with Jared now, or she wouldn't have ended their courtship."

"She only did it because she has so many responsibilities now. I'm sure Amy still loves Jared. Maybe once things slow down for her, they'll get back together."

Mama got a faraway look in her eyes. "Jared's a nice young man. He'd make a good husband."

"Jah, he would, but not for me. He's in love with Amy."

"But if he took an interest in you, would you be willing to let him court you?"

"No. Amy is my friend, and I'm sure she still has feelings for him." Lydia turned back to the stove and continued stirring the oatmeal. *There is no way Jared will ever be interested in me, so this conversation is just plain silly.*

Sylvia had finished drying the breakfast dishes when Mom entered the kitchen. "Here's the mail." She placed it on the table and handed Sylvia a plastic container she held in her other hand. "Our new neighbor lady across the road returned this to me, but it doesn't look like it's been washed." She shook the container. "See, there are still some cookie crumbs inside."

Sylvia opened the lid and dumped the crumbs into the garbage can under the sink. Then she placed it in the sink and ran warm water and liquid detergent into it. "Wouldn't you think she would have washed the container before bringing it back?"

Mom nodded. "I'll admit that was my first thought, but I'm sure Virginia's been busy what with unpacking and trying to get settled in her new home."

"What's she like? Do you think she'll be a good neighbor?" Sylvia sloshed around the dishrag inside the container.

"I can't say for sure, since we only spoke with each other for a few minutes." Mom paused and cleared her throat. "She did seem a bit standoffish though. Makes me wonder if people from the big cities are different than small-town people."

Maybe she's like me, Sylvia thought. *Could be that she doesn't feel comfortable around people.*

"Well, I just came in to deliver the mail and drop off the container, but now I'd better get out to the greenhouse so Amy's not there by herself when customers begin showing up. Oh, and then I'll need to seek out your brother. Someone cut the wire that holds up our sign at the end of the driveway, so I'll need him to get it hung back up right away. We don't want to lose any customers because they can't find us."

Sylvia whirled around. "You think it was cut down on purpose?"

Mom nodded. "I found it lying in the weeds, and the wire had definitely been cut."

Sylvia's hand went to her mouth. "Oh my. First the mailbox and now this? Who do you think is responsible, Mom?"

"I—I don't know for sure, but I still think it may be your brother. He could have bashed in our mailbox and let the bees in the greenhouse too."

Sylvia's mouth opened slightly. "But I still don't understand why Henry would do something like that."

"He's angry and could be acting out."

"Have you asked him right out if he's the one responsible for knocking down the sign?"

"Not yet. You're the first person I've told about it."

"If he did do any of those things, he needs to be called out."

"Agreed." Mom emitted a noisy huff. "Henry's attitude seems to worsen every day, even though Amy, Ezekiel, Preacher Raber, and I have tried talking to him." She blotted at the tears that had fallen onto her cheeks. "I'm concerned that your bruder may never come to grips with the death of our dear family members."

Sylvia nodded. That much she understood, for she wasn't sure she would ever be free of the agony she'd felt every day since Toby, Dad, and Abe had died.

Chapter 17

"I can't believe someone would deliberately take down our sign," Amy said after listening to her mother explain what she had found. "Do you still think Henry could be behind all these incidents?"

"Yes, although he denied it when I asked him a few minutes ago." Mom kept her voice low as she took her seat on the stool behind the checkout counter in the greenhouse.

"Where is Henry now? Maybe I should go talk to him."

"He's outside rehanging the sign." Mom fiddled with the paperwork lying on the counter. "I don't think it would do a bit of good for you to talk to him, Amy. If Henry is acting out and releasing his emotions by doing destructive things, I doubt anything you or I can say will get through to him."

Amy leaned in closer to her mother. "What are we going to do? There has to be someone who can get through to my little brother."

"I ain't little, and I wish you two would quit talkin' about me behind my back."

Amy whirled around at the sound of her brother's angry voice. She'd been so engrossed in the conversation that she hadn't heard him come in.

"If you'd quit doing bizarre things, we wouldn't need to talk about you." Amy's fingers clenched as she tapped them along the counter. "How do you think Dad would feel if he knew you'd done things to destroy our property?"

He sauntered up to her and stood so close she could smell his minty breath. "I haven't destroyed anything. In fact, I came in here to tell Mom I fixed the sign—it's back in place." He glanced at their mother then back at Amy. "And if I'd bashed in the mailbox, do ya think I woulda gone to town for a new one and then helped put it in?"

"You did it because I asked you to," Mom interjected. "And it's certainly no proof that you're not the person responsible for the pranks."

"Mom, they were more than pranks." Amy flexed her fingers to keep from grabbing hold of her brother and giving him a good shake. "What was done to the mailbox and our sign out front was vandalism."

Henry held firm in his stance. "Jah, well you can believe what you want, but I'm not the person who did those things." He whirled around and stomped out the door.

Mom lowered her head, making little circles with her fingers across her forehead. "I hope and pray that if Henry is the guilty person, he'll realize he's done wrong and won't do anything like that again."

"I hope not either, but I wouldn't hold my breath." She pursed her lips. "I hope neither Dad nor Abe can look down from heaven and see the way Henry's been acting. If they could, they'd be very disappointed."

Mom gave no reply as she continued to rub her forehead.

"We'd better pull ourselves together," Amy announced. "I heard a horse and carriage coming up the driveway, so we need to put smiles on our faces and welcome our first customers of the day."

By late afternoon, Belinda had lost track of how many customers had come to the greenhouse in response to the ad about this week's sale that they'd run in their local paper. In the past, Vernon had been in charge of all the advertising for their business.

Recently, Belinda had gone through some old ads and gotten ideas from her husband's way of doing things. She'd also asked Henry to go into town and hang some flyers on bulletin boards. Belinda wanted to make the public aware of their business with minimal effort and little expense. Having a sale today made her think of how it was when Vernon had still been with them and the anticipation they'd felt getting everything ready for the event. Like she had in the past, Belinda hoped everything would go according to plan.

Pauline, their driver, entered the greenhouse and came over to the counter where Belinda stood. "Amy invited me to come by and have a look around."

"I'm glad she did." Belinda glanced at a large area where several customers mingled. "I believe my daughter is here somewhere."

As if on cue, Amy came up and greeted Pauline. "I'm glad you could come by for the sale. Let me show you around." The two of them headed off and disappeared among the other shoppers.

Belinda smiled. It was good to see more new customers venture into the greenhouse. Having a sale this week had been an excellent idea.

The best part of the day was when an English couple came in a few minutes later and bought over five hundred dollars' worth of plants and shrubs. Soon after they left, an elderly man showed up who was obviously hard of hearing. Amy pointed him out, saying he'd been here before, when Belinda was gone. The gray-haired man asked a lot of questions, and Belinda had to repeat herself several times. Remembering the phone call she'd had not long ago from a man who struggled to hear what she said, Belinda figured he might be the same person she'd spoken to on the phone. The gentleman ended up buying some pots of petunias and a bag of grass seed. He seemed nice enough. It was a shame he couldn't hear well. Belinda wondered why he didn't wear any hearing aids. Perhaps he was either embarrassed or too stubborn to wear them. Or else he wouldn't acknowledge that he was hard of hearing.

I wonder if Henry will be stubborn when he gets old. I love my son, but he certainly can be hardheaded.

Belinda smiled when another customer stepped up to the counter pulling a wagonload of plants and several gardening supplies. She couldn't let her negative thinking get the best of her, or she might appear unfriendly.

"Mom, you look like you could use a break." Amy slipped in behind the counter. "Why don't you let me take over here so you can go up to the house and rest for a bit? Henry's supposed to come into the greenhouse in a few minutes, and I'm sure the two of us can manage on our own for a while."

Belinda pushed some unruly hairs back under her head covering. "I could use a break—but only a short one. If things get busy again, you'll need my help out here."

"No problem. If too many customers show up, I'll send Henry up to the house to get you."

"Okay, you talked me into it." Belinda slid off the stool. "Is there anything I can get you when I come back out?"

"Maybe a glass of meadow-mint tea."

"Consider it done."

Virginia paced the length of her kitchen, gritting her teeth and slamming cupboard doors. She marched into the living room and looked out the window at the cars pulling onto the driveway across the road. She continued to watch as a horse and buggy came down the road and pulled onto the Kings' driveway.

"Just look at the mess that horse left on the pavement." She shook her head. "I wonder who is gonna clean up that nasty debris."

This morning, Virginia had been too tired to get much done, and by the time she'd felt like doing anything, the steady roar of vehicles, mingled with the irritation of the *clippity-clop* of horses' hooves on the road out front nearly drove her batty.

"And it's all the fault of that stupid greenhouse across the way." She paused and kicked one of the lower cupboard drawers but winced and had to sit down when a searing pain shot through her bad leg.

I've told Earl those Amish are strange, and now we're stuck dealing with their conservative lifestyle across the street.

Virginia shifted, trying to find a comfortable position, and reached down to rub her knee. *The pain from that fall I took down the stairs twelve years ago is always here to remind me of how stupid I used to be. Guess I got what I deserved.*

Another influx of customers arrived, and Amy was tempted to send for Mom. But before she could make the effort to call upon Henry, the man who used to court her mother showed up.

"Is Belinda around?" His eyes seemed to glow as he spoke her mother's name.

"She's up at the house, taking a break."

"Oh, okay. Guess I'll go knock on the door."

Amy was prepared to ask him not to bother Mom, when another customer stepped up to the counter, asking a question about the tomato plants that were being sold for 25 percent off. Amy didn't want to lose a sale, so she told Monroe she'd be right back and went off with the woman who'd asked the question to show her which plants were on special.

I hope Sylvia answers the door and tells Monroe that Mom is resting and can't be disturbed. There's something about Mr. Esh that doesn't set well with me. Don't know why, but I get the feeling he's not as nice as he appears to be. Maybe there's a reason Mom broke things off with him when they were courting.

It wasn't fair to judge the man when she didn't really know him, but Amy had always been able to read people well, and she'd rarely been wrong. Of course, there was a first time for everything, so in all fairness, she needed to give Monroe Esh the benefit of the doubt.

She pushed her nagging doubts aside and led the customer over to the vegetable plants. It wouldn't do Amy or anyone else one bit of good if she couldn't keep her focus on work.

When Belinda glanced out the kitchen window and spotted Monroe heading for the house, she quickly set her empty glass in the sink and hurried out the front door to meet him. *I wonder what he wants. Is he here to buy something this time, or is it a friendly visit?*

"When I heard you weren't in the greenhouse and had come over here, I decided to head on over and see how you are doing." Monroe offered Belinda a most charming smile. Back when they were young people, he would often smile at her that way.

"I'm doing as well as can be expected," she replied. "It's nice of you to ask."

He leaned on the porch railing but pointed to the front door, which hung slightly open. "Mind if I come in?"

"Actually, my grandchildren and oldest daughter are sleeping right now, so our voices might disturb them."

"Oh, okay." Monroe inched a bit closer to Belinda then gestured to the wicker chairs on the porch. "Is it all right if I sit down out here?"

"Help yourself." Belinda stepped back, out of his way.

"Aren't you going to take a seat? It'll be easier for us to talk that way."

Oh, bother. Belinda felt trapped. It would be rude to say no, but at the same time, she'd come to the house to spend some quiet time alone and wasn't in the mood for company right now. Reluctantly, she forced a smile and seated herself in the chair beside him.

Monroe took off his hat, and holding it by the brim, he fanned his face. "Sure turned out hot today, jah?"

Glancing toward the greenhouse, she gave a nod. Now that Belinda was outside, her focus returned to how things were going out there.

"Say, I was wondering if there's anything you'd like me to do around here—in the house, barn, or even the greenhouse."

"It's kind of you to offer, but we're managing okay with things."

"Your furrowed brows make me wonder if you're feeling stressed about something. Is everything okay with you, Belinda?"

"I'm fine." No way would Belinda make mention of the things she suspected her son of doing. Henry was her business not Monroe's, and if she brought him into it, things would get worse where Henry was concerned. If her son wouldn't listen to anything family members and close friends had to say, he sure wouldn't appreciate a stranger's two cents' worth.

From where she sat, Belinda saw people coming and going from the greenhouse. It wasn't easy to listen to Monroe talk about the custom-built furniture shop he'd purchased after moving back to Strasburg and how he had several employees and didn't need to be in the shop all the time.

"Just have to be there enough to make sure things are going as they should," he said with a nod.

Truth was, Belinda had other, more important things on her mind. *I hope Amy is managing okay.* She adjusted the pillow behind her back. *I wish Monroe would quit staring at me. It makes me feel uncomfortable.*

They talked for a few minutes more about the struggle to keep cool in the warm weather, and then Belinda stood. "I'm sorry to have to cut this visit short, but I need to get back to the greenhouse. I only came over here for a short break, and from the looks of all the buggies and cars parked outside the building, I'm quite sure my help is needed there right now."

Monroe's shoulders drooped a bit as his lips pressed together. "Are you sure there isn't something I can do out there to help you?"

She shook her head. "Unless you've ever run a greenhouse, I doubt you would know what to do."

"I doubt it can be that hard."

"People ask a lot of questions about gardening."

He rubbed his beardless chin. "Guess I'd be stuck either asking you or makin' something up."

She offered him another forced smile. "Have a good rest of your day, and danki for dropping by."

"You're welcome." Monroe plopped his hat back on his head and headed off toward the hitching rail.

Belinda hurried to the greenhouse, and without a glance in his direction, she stepped inside.

"You didn't take a very long break, Mom." Amy tilted her head to one side. "Monroe Esh was here. Did he come up to the house to talk to you?"

"Jah. We sat out on the porch for a few minutes and talked. Then I said I needed to get back here to help out."

"I see."

"Oh, and I'm sorry, but I forgot to bring you some mead-ow-mint tea."

"No problem, Mom. I still have plenty of *wasser*." Amy lifted her water bottle. "I'm just glad you cut your visit with Monroe short and came back here to help."

Is that a look of relief I see on my daughter's face? Belinda studied Amy for a few minutes. *I have a hunch she doesn't care much for Monroe. Well, that's fine with me, because he's just an old acquaintance and will never be anything more than that.*

Chapter 18

The next day seemed to drag on and on. It wasn't that they weren't busy; there had been plenty of people coming to the greenhouse. Amy was so tired, and she figured her mother was as well. She'd be glad when their workday ended and they could be back in the house where there wouldn't be a group of people posing questions and asking for assistance.

"I'm going to the house to take my lunch break." Mom tapped Amy's shoulder. "Is that okay with you?"

"Sure, Mom. Enjoy your hot meal." Drumming her fingers on the counter, Amy noticed that the bags of hummingbird food had gone down. She wasn't surprised to see the powdered nectar selling so well. She had observed the feeders at their house going empty with the steady flow of hungry hummers and figured many of their customers were also feeding the tiny birds.

Amy rose from the stool and strode toward the storage room. The bags that were ready to be put out sat off to one side. She grabbed all she could and toted them to the display area then put each bag in its place and straightened the rows. Afterward, Amy went to the seed display, where she discovered that certain packets were either low or out of stock.

She went back to the storage room to see if she had replacements to fill the rack that had been depleted. Amy took a notepad and pencil to jot down each item. She would need to get more green bean, radish, and carrot seeds.

"Amy, I'm gonna go eat since we're not busy," Henry hollered.

"Just give me a second with this list, and allow me enough time to get the packets of seeds before you leave."

Frowning, he stepped over to the rack. "What have you written down so far?"

She showed him the list. "I'm about done."

"I'm *hungerich*, Sister. I'll get the items you have listed, but only because I wanna eat." He snatched the piece of paper out of her grasp.

Amy's mouth dropped open. "Don't be so impatient."

Henry took off, and it wasn't long before he emerged with a brown bag full of seed packets. "Here ya go. Now, I'm outta here."

Watching him leave, Amy picked up the sack. She pulled out a few pieces at a time and began her work. When the rack was half done, she realized that the bag was empty. *Why am I not surprised that my brother didn't get all that I needed?*

Amy grabbed the paper sack and went to the back room to get the rest of the needed inventory. She peeked out twice to make sure there were no customers waiting at the checkout. Seeing no one, she went to the seed rack and finished her work.

A short time later, Mom returned with a box full of canned pickles. "I got to thinking about these *bickels* we canned from the garden last year." She gestured toward the storage room. "There's an empty wooden shelf in there that could be brought out and used to display these. We can also sell some extra jars of honey."

"That's a good idea. With all the tourists we get coming in, they don't often buy live plants. But they do seem to be interested in our jellies, jams, and honey, so why not try to sell some bickels too?"

Mom rested a hand on her hip. "The strawberries in the garden are coming along well, and it'll soon be time to make strawberry jam, and we can sell some of that as well. Sylvia agreed to make it, so that's one less thing for us to worry about."

"I like the idea." Amy nodded. "I'm sure the tourists will too."

"We have to come up with some ways that will set us apart from the new greenhouse." Mom slid the box aside. "Right now, however, I need to check on your brother and ask him to move some plants around for me."

"Okay, I'll stay close by." Amy yawned. *Maybe I'm just overly tired from rushing about for the last few days, helping people choose items that are on sale and answering far too many questions.*

She heard the door open and turned to see the homeless lady enter the greenhouse. *If she lives in that old shack quite a ways down the road, guess she's not exactly homeless,* Amy reasoned. *It's certainly not much of a home though. I bet she doesn't have hot and cold running water or indoor plumbing like we are fortunate to have.*

Amy glanced at the poor woman, wishing there was more they could do to help other than offering her free baked goods and garden produce from time to time. She remembered the day Lydia bought a plant for the elderly woman. If Maude had any money, it wasn't much, for she never bought anything from the greenhouse, just came in and looked around. Maude's clothing was worn and faded, and her hair never appeared to be combed. Amy wondered how the woman came to be in this predicament. Could something tragic have occurred that changed things for Maude?

Amy tried not to stare as the elderly woman ambled down one aisle and then another, looking at the various plants and flowers. Every so often, Maude stopped and glanced Amy's way then just as quickly averted her gaze.

When Amy's mother came in with a plate of chocolate chip cookies, which she placed on the counter, Maude ambled up and helped herself to six of the treats. She paused briefly and glanced at Amy then just as quickly looked away. It was almost as though the woman felt guilty about something. Without a word, she slipped out the door with her slender shoulders drawn up and her arms tucked against her sides.

Amy wondered if Maude had stolen some small gift item from the greenhouse and hidden it in the pocket of her baggy dress. *Guess I won't worry about it,* she told herself. *Even if she did take something,*

Mom would probably look at Maude in a kindly manner and say, "It's wrong to take things without asking. Next time you want something from the greenhouse, please come to me and ask."

Amy sighed. Sometimes her mother could be a little too nice.

Toward the end of the day, Herschel Fisher and his mother came into the greenhouse. They were all smiles as they made their way over to greet Belinda. It had been awhile since they'd dropped by, and she was pleased to see them. Vera seemed to be doing well, despite having to use a cane, and it was nice to see Herschel again. He always seemed so pleasant and sincere. The widower was quite attractive for a man his age. Belinda was surprised he'd never gotten married again. *But then,* she reasoned, *Herschel probably still loves his wife, just as I will always love Vernon.*

"Our sale is winding down," she said, after shaking both of their hands, "but there are still several nice plants and other things to choose from." She gestured to the items on sale. "You're welcome to look around, and feel free to ask either me or Amy any questions you may have."

"Danki, we will." Vera hobbled over to the hanging baskets, but Herschel held back. "How are things going for you, Belinda?" he asked.

"With the exception of a few minor mishaps, things are well enough, I suppose." She couldn't help noticing the kindness in his eyes. Although Belinda didn't know Vera's son very well, she'd heard from Sara what a kind, gentle person he was. He'd certainly taken an active interest in his daughter since learning that he was her biological father.

"What kind of mishaps?" Herschel's brows drew together.

Belinda mentioned the situation with the broken pipe in the garden shed, the bees that had found their way into the greenhouse, the vandalized mailbox, and the greenhouse sign that had been cut down and tossed in the weeds.

Deep wrinkles formed across his forehead. "Do you think all those things were done intentionally?"

Belinda shrugged. "The mailbox and our business sign for sure, and maybe even the ieme, but I believe the pipe that broke was ready to go because it was so old and rusty."

"Have you notified the authorities about the vandalism out front by the road?"

She shook her head. "Didn't see any reason to since we have no idea who did those things. I figure they could have been done by rowdy teenagers sowing their wild oats. You know how some of them can be when they're going through *rumschpringe*." She made no mention of Henry as a suspect since she had no proof it was her son who'd done those things. Even if he was the one responsible, it wasn't something she wanted anyone outside the immediate family to know.

Herschel gave a nod. "I can't speak on this firsthand, since I never knew I had a *dochder* until she was in her twenties. But from what other parents have told me, those growing-up days can be difficult to deal with, never knowing what your children might do during that time."

"And always wondering if they will ever settle down and join the Amish church," Belinda put in.

"Exactly."

"My son Henry isn't actually running around, but he's been a problem for me ever since his father and brother were killed." Belinda didn't know why she felt led to share this with a man she barely knew, but it felt good to get it out.

"I'm sorry to hear that. Would it help if I had a talk with Henry?"

"I don't think so. Others have tried, and it's made no difference at all." Belinda shifted her weight, leaning against the front side of the checkout counter. "Henry might resent hearing it from a near stranger even more."

"I understand, so don't worry. I won't bring up the topic should I see him. However, if he brings it up, would it be okay if I said something?"

Belinda nodded. "I think it's rather doubtful though. Henry keeps to himself as much as he can, and he's been bottling up a lot of anger and resentment."

"I know all about that." Herschel's eyes darkened. "I spent a good many years angry at God after my fraa died. Learning about Sara and being able to spend time with her has helped me so much. There's a purpose to my life, and she's given me a reason to live and love again."

"I still have my children and grandchildren, which I'm thankful for." Belinda's eyes misted. "I love them all dearly, and they are my reason to keep on living and doing the best I can."

Since the Fishers were the only customers in the greenhouse and it was almost closing time, Amy left them in Mom's capable hands and went up to the house to see about helping Sylvia with preparations for supper. She assumed she'd find her sister already in the kitchen.

When Amy entered the room, it was quiet and there was no sign of Sylvia. She and Mom had discussed this morning what they would eat for supper. *I suppose it won't be any trouble for me to get the bacon frying for the turkey-bacon club sandwiches.*

She washed her hands at the kitchen sink and got to work heating the pan after getting out the bacon to fry. Once the meat was done and she'd placed the pieces on paper towels to soak up the oil, Amy left the kitchen. She found Sylvia lying on the living-room couch with her eyes closed. *Is she really that tired, or is sleeping the way my sister copes with her sorrow—trying to shut it out?*

Amy glanced across the room, where Rachel sat in her playpen, holding a rattle in her chubby little hands. Allen knelt on the floor nearby, piling up wooden blocks and then knocking them over. It was a wonder the noise didn't wake his mother.

Amy was tempted to wake Sylvia herself but decided to let her sleep. Maybe once she got the rest of their supper going, her sister would smell the food and wake up. Or Allen might become louder and that would do the trick.

Amy returned to the kitchen and took a loaf of bread out, along with some lettuce and tomatoes. Some evenings when she felt extra tired, like now, Amy wished they could all go out for an evening meal. But in addition to going through the trouble of getting everyone ready, there was the cost of a restaurant meal to consider. Another reason the family hadn't gone out to eat was because of Sylvia. She still could hardly stand to be around people.

Amy took a knife from the drawer and grabbed the cutting board. The tomatoes and lettuce came from their garden, which she had picked yesterday. Mom possessed a green thumb for growing produce. Sylvia enjoyed it too, and she'd seemed to be following in their mother's footsteps until the accident happened.

I wonder how long it will take my sister to overcome her depression and realize she can't dwell on the past. For the sake of her children, she must eventually move forward with her life. Sylvia needs to find some joy in life and share it with them.

Amy gave a slow shake of her head. *Who am I to judge my sister for a lack of joy? All I've done since our dear family members' deaths is try to keep things running smoothly in the greenhouse and here at the house. I rarely feel any real joy these days, yet I force myself to smile so I appear cheerful—especially while at the greenhouse.*

Sometimes Amy felt as though she had the weight of the world on her shoulders, even though it was only five family members who shared this home with her.

"It's okay though," she whispered. "I love them all dearly and would make any sacrifice on their behalf."

"Who ya talkin' to in here, Amy?"

She turned at the sound of Henry's voice. "Myself," she admitted.

His brows lifted. "If you're that desperate to talk to someone, why don't ya go outside and visit with Sara and Brad? They just showed up, and wouldn't ya know it—Mom invited them to stay for supper."

Amy was glad they had plenty of sandwich makings to share, and she would also put together a fruit salad and open a bag of chips.

Henry gave an exaggerated roll of his eyes. "I'll bet that preacher husband of Sara's will end up givin' us all a sermon while we eat."

"That wouldn't be such a bad thing, would it?"

"Guess it all depends on what he decides to preach about."

Amy bit back a chuckle. It would do her brother some good to listen to another sermon. For that matter, it might be just what the rest of the family needed too.

Chapter 19

The following day, Amy hurried to the greenhouse, carrying a couple of hanging baskets her sister had made. Once inside, she found some empty hangers to put them on. At least her sister was willing to help, even though it was a nuisance to haul them from the house.

Amy picked up two more baskets from the porch then glanced over at their hitching rail where her buggy and horse waited. She would be going into town soon to grocery shop. That meant Mom and Henry would be working alone in the greenhouse until she returned. Amy hoped Henry would cooperate with their mother while she was gone for a few hours today.

Sylvia came out the door and stepped onto the porch. Allen was with her. "I hope those will sell." She gestured to the hanging baskets. "The plants I used this time were smaller than the last bunch, so the pots aren't quite as full."

"Don't worry. Lots of people have been buying lately, so I'm sure these won't last long."

Allen toddled over and tugged on the edge of Amy's apron. She reached down and tousled the little guy's hair. Her nephew was such a sweet child. Amy wished she could have a little boy like him some-day. But she had to accept the fact that it might never happen. She could be an old maid all her life, helping to keep the greenhouse running.

"Guess I'd better get the rest of these baskets over to the green-house." Amy bent to pick them up when Allen squealed and pointed at a squirrel running through the yard.

Sylvia frowned. "Those rascals are sure pesky. Just what we don't need getting into the bird feeders."

"I know, but most of our feeders have been squirrel-proofed, thanks to Dad."

"Jah, he did a good job taking care of problems around here—big and small."

Amy nodded. Gripping the flower basket handles, she headed toward the greenhouse. "I'll see you both later," she called over her shoulder.

"Are you sure you wouldn't rather go grocery shopping and leave me here to run the greenhouse?" Amy asked her mother when she entered the greenhouse.

Mom shook her head. "Henry will be here with me, and I feel certain we can manage. If I go for groceries, I'll no doubt see people I know and end up talking too long." She smiled at Amy. "You, on the other hand, will hurry through the store, get what we need, and come right back home."

Amy couldn't argue with that. She was less likely to visit with people when she was on a mission to shop for food. "Okay, I'd better get going so I can get back here before noon. I just hope you don't get a swarm of customers while I'm gone."

Mom gave Amy's shoulder a squeeze. "Don't worry. We'll be fine."

Amy set the hanging baskets down, gave her mother a hug, and opened the door, nearly colliding with Henry.

He glared at her. "You oughta watch where you're going."

"I could say the same for you," she countered. Before her brother could think of another comeback, Amy clasped his arm. "I'm going shopping for groceries, so please make sure you stay in the greenhouse with Mom and don't go outside or wander off."

Refusing to look at her, he muttered, "You ain't my boss, so quit tellin' me what to do."

Amy opened her mouth to say something more, but thinking better of it, she hurried across the yard to where her horse and buggy waited. It seemed that no one could get through to her brother, regardless of how hard they tried, so what was the use? Last evening, when Sara and Brad joined them for supper, Brad had tried to engage Henry in conversation several times, but Henry gave little response. While it wasn't a reflection on their mother, Amy could tell how uncomfortable Mom had felt when Henry acted so disinterested in everything Brad or the rest of them said to him.

"Well girl, it's just you and me from here to the store and back again." Amy patted her horse's neck before untying the chestnut mare from the rail. "At least you're more cooperative than that stubborn brother of mine. And you don't talk back either."

Amy had only been gone a short time, when something unexpected occurred in the greenhouse.

"Look—there's a hummingbird in here!" One of their English customers pointed at it.

Ten other shoppers were in the building, and Belinda stood behind the counter, watching as people either ducked or began chasing after the poor bird.

"Be careful!" she hollered above all the noise. "Hummingbirds are delicate, and we don't want to hurt it."

"Here's the reason it got in." Frowning, Henry pointed to the screen door that someone had left open. "Maybe I need to stand guard and make sure it gets closed after every customer comes in."

"That won't work, Henry. Don't forget the back entrance is open during business hours for ventilation. The hummer could have flown in through there also."

Belinda rubbed her forehead. "It doesn't matter how the little bird got into the building. We need to help him find his way out." Looking upward, she observed the hummer trying to get through the top of the roof. It was hard to watch, because there were two exits, but the poor little thing was in such a frenzy, it couldn't find its way out either of the now open doors. The hummingbird soon became the focal point of everyone in the greenhouse. Belinda could only imagine how distraught the poor creature was.

"Well, chasin' after it sure isn't the answer." Henry cupped his hands around his mouth. "Everyone, please stop chasing the hummer and let me handle this situation."

As soon as the commotion died down and all the people stopped running around, Henry looked at Belinda and said, "I'll be right back." He made a hasty exit and came back a few minutes later with a hummingbird feeder in his hand.

"This oughta do the trick." Henry stood by the open front door-way, holding the feeder up high. "Come on, little guy. You're all confused, aren't ya? It's okay. Don't worry. Everything's gonna be all right."

Several minutes passed, and Belinda watched, along with the rest of the people, as the hummingbird made its way over to the feeder. Once it began eating, Henry backed slowly away until he and the tiny bird went out the door along with the feeder.

Everyone cheered as Belinda shut the screen door. It pleased her to see the softer side of her son, even if only for a few minutes. If Henry could show this much concern for one of God's wee creatures, she couldn't help but hope that the kind, gentle young man she and Vernon had raised would eventually resurface. It might take time and lots of love and encouragement, but she would never give up believing in any of her children.

Jared had come out of the bank, where he'd gone to make a deposit, when he saw Amy's friend Lydia walking down the sidewalk in his direction. She smiled and waved, so he waited for her to catch up.

"It's nice to see you." Lydia smiled when she joined him in front of the bank. "How are things going, Jared?"

I'd like to say I'm miserable, but I won't. "Everything's okay as far as work goes, at least."

"Have you been by to see Amy lately?"

He shook his head. "I want to, but I'm afraid she'll reject me again, and then I'd feel worse than I already do."

Lydia placed her hand on his arm. "I'm sorry, Jared. Amy's making a huge mistake, but she's so caught up in her work and trying to help her family get through their grief, it seems to be all she can think about or deal with right now."

"I get that, but she could deal with it better if she'd let me help."

"I agree." Lydia glanced at the restaurant across the street. "I came to town to buy some things for my mamm, and since it's almost noon, I'm going to have some lunch. Would you care to join me?"

Jared hesitated at first, but he hadn't eaten much for breakfast, and after finishing up a roofing job a short time ago, the thought of a good meal appealed. "Jah, okay, some pizza or a sub sandwich sounds real good."

"The pizza is sure *gut* here." Lydia smiled at Jared from across the table.

He nodded and swiped a napkin across his lips. "Messy but good."

"How's your summer going? Are you keeping busy with the quilts you and your mamm make?" Jared asked. It was an unexpected question; he hadn't said much since they'd ordered their lunch.

"Jah," she responded. "We keep plenty busy quilting and also working in the garden. Whenever I have some free time, I like to read."

"Do you enjoy quilting?"

"I do, but someday I hope to get married and start a family, so my life would then be going in another direction."

Jared picked up his glass of lemonade and took a drink. "If things would have worked out between me and Amy, we'd be planning our wedding right now."

"It's too bad I couldn't get through to her." Lydia studied Jared's handsome face. In addition to being so good-looking, he was such a nice man. She couldn't imagine Amy being foolish enough to let him go no matter what the circumstances.

After Amy left the grocery store, she stopped at Sara's flower shop to say a quick hello only to discover that Sara wasn't there.

"She had a doctor's appointment," Misty said. "I'm not sure what time she'll be back, but you're welcome to wait if you want."

"I'd better not. I have groceries in the buggy that need to be refrigerated, so I need to get them home." Amy smiled. "Please tell Sara I said hello and that we enjoyed our visit with her and Brad last evening."

"I'll give her the message." Misty came around from behind the counter and gave Amy a hug. "I haven't had a chance to tell you this, but I was sorry to hear about the horrible accident that took three of your family members."

Amy's chin trembled at the mention of their loss. It was easier not to think about it if people didn't bring up the topic. "Thank you," she murmured. Keeping her gaze fixed on a bouquet of pink carnations inside the standup cooler on the other side of the room, she said, "I'd better get going. It was nice seeing you, Misty."

"Same here. Take care."

When Amy exited the shop, she paused for a few minutes to gain control of her emotions. No matter how much time passed or how busy they kept, she was certain there would always be a huge void in her family's lives.

Amy heard laughter, and for a split second she felt as if her breathing had been suspended. There stood Jared in front of the pizza place. Lydia stood beside him with her hand on his arm.

Amy ducked under the canopy above the flower shop door and angled her body so that her face could not be seen. *Is my good friend being courted by Jared now? Could he have forgotten about me so quickly and moved on?* A surge of jealousy coursed through her body.

Amy glanced over her shoulder and watched as Jared and Lydia headed down the sidewalk together. When they were far enough away, she hurried to the area where her horse and buggy waited. She'd told Jared he should move on, but did it have to be with someone she knew—her best friend, of all people?

Chapter 20

"Would you mind watching the kinner for me?" Sylvia asked her mother after the supper dishes had been done one Friday evening. "I need to take a walk outside and get some fresh air."

"I don't mind at all." Mom smiled as she wrung out the wet sponge. "It's not good to be cooped up in the stuffy house with the little ones all day. I'm sure you could use a break, and the blueberry cobbler I made can wait. We'll enjoy the dessert with vanilla ice cream when we're all ready for it."

If only a walk would help me feel better or the fruit crisp, for that matter. Sylvia's jaw and facial muscles tightened. She hoped she wouldn't be subjected to another of Mom's lectures on the importance of getting back into life and a normal routine. Sylvia's routine had been derailed the minute her husband, father, and brother had been killed. While it may have been true that the glare of the sun had been in the driver's eyes, he should have been going slower.

Instead of responding to her mother's comment, Sylvia merely smiled and said, "Danki, Mom. I won't be outside very long."

"Take all the time you need," Mom was quick to say. "Amy will be upstairs from the basement soon, so if I need any help with the children, I'll call on her for assistance."

"Okay." Sylvia removed her work apron and was about to head out the back door, when she paused. "Can I ask you a question, Mom?"

"Of course."

"Is Amy your favorite over me and Henry?"

Mom blinked a couple of times. "Of course not, Sylvia. Why would you even ask such a question?"

"Because she willingly helps out in the greenhouse, and you can count on her for support."

Mom slipped her arm around Sylvia's waist. "Amy has been a big help to me in the greenhouse, but each one of my kinner is special to me, and I love you all the same."

"I'm happy to hear that, because sometimes I feel like I'm letting you down by staying here with my little ones and—"

Mom held up one hand. "You're where you need to be right now, and I'm grateful for all the chores you do in the house, not to mention so many meals you have prepared for us at the end of a long day. Danki for that."

"You're welcome." Feeling a little better about things, Sylvia stepped out the back door.

From where she stood by the railing, Sylvia saw their new neighbor man out by the road, closest to his side. He held a shovel and appeared to be scooping up something.

I wonder if he's getting some of the horse droppings left behind from all the buggies that travel this road. Sure hope he's not planning to spread the fresh manure on any of his plants in the flowerbeds, or worse yet, in a vegetable garden. Sylvia had a lot of knowledge when it came to what could or couldn't be mixed into the soil. She was fully aware that fresh horse manure could damage young plants. It also attracted flies and had a strong odor. Hopefully, the man across the road knew this too and would add the manure to a compost pile. It would take four to six weeks to turn from stable waste to being ready to put around the plants or in a garden. Sylvia wondered if either the man or his wife knew anything about composting.

After some time, the neighbor man went up the driveway and into his yard with the shovel. Sylvia thought it was a bit odd that he would be so eager to go out and collect horse droppings from the road. She had seen the wife a time or two, when she came out to her front porch. The new neighbors kept pretty much to themselves—nothing like Mom and Dad's previous, friendly neighbors.

Those nice people are surely missed. Sylvia wiped the perspiration from her forehead. "Typical weather for the second week of July," she muttered, stepping off the porch. The grass felt soft and cool under her bare feet. Sylvia paused to admire the newest flowerbed Mom had created. It was filled with summer colors.

Sylvia's first inclination was to lie in the free-standing hammock awhile, but that would only remind her of Abe. When they were teenagers, on hot summer nights he often slept out here under the stars. Whenever Sylvia and Amy slept outdoors, Dad set up cots for them on the porch. Ezekiel had never cared much for sleeping outside, but occasionally Sylvia and the rest of his siblings would convince him to join them. Even though Henry was several years younger than the rest of them, Mom and Dad sometimes agreed to let him take part in the sleep-outs.

Tightening the black scarf wrapped around her head, Sylvia remembered one time when Ezekiel and Henry lay on the grass in sleeping bags with a canvas tarp beneath them. Abe, like most big brothers, decided it would be fun to tease Henry by telling him made-up scary stories. One story in particular had made Henry cry and run for the house. It was about a wild animal that would sneak into the yard under a full moon and steal small children.

A few minutes after Henry ran screaming into the house, Mom came out, shook her finger at Abe, and said, "If you keep tormenting your little brother, you'll be sleeping in the barn by yourself, and Henry can have the comfortable hammock."

Sylvia's eyes filled with tears as she recalled more childhood memories. *I would give almost anything to have those carefree days back again.*

She smoothed the black fabric of her dress. Amy, Mom, and Sylvia all wore the drab color every day in remembrance of their loss. Wearing black during the mourning process was part of their Amish way. After a year of grieving, they would put away the dresses and wear regular colored frocks again. In the meantime, they all said that they hoped it would be a very long while before any of them would have to wear mourning garb again.

Sylvia's thoughts went to Toby's parents and siblings, who lived in Mifflin County. She'd received a letter from Toby's mother, Selma, the other day, asking how Sylvia and the kinner were getting along and stating that she and the rest of the family were still missing Toby and spoke of him often.

Feeling restless and struggling to keep her raging emotions under control, Sylvia made her way down the driveway until she came to the phone shed. Stepping inside, she took a seat, leaving the door hanging open. Despite the sting of losing loved ones, life continued to move on. It hadn't stopped or changed because of what had happened to Toby, Dad, and Abe.

The message light blinked, so she clicked the button then picked up the pen to write down any information they would need. The first one was from a man wanting to sell them something she was sure they didn't need. Sylvia deleted the message and listened to the next. This was from Ezekiel, letting them know that Michelle had delivered a nine-pound, twenty-one-inch baby boy at two o'clock this afternoon. They'd decided to call him Vernon Lee.

Sylvia felt a tightness in her chest that would not loosen. *Oh Dad, I wish there was a way you could know that you have a namesake. If only you could be here to hold the new boppli.*

She wrote down the details of the baby's birth, tore off the paper from the tablet, and stepped out of the phone shed. Sylvia couldn't help the envy circulating within her. *Michelle has a husband to share in the joy of raising their children. I, on the other hand, am without my mate and need extra support from my mamm and sister.* Sylvia hoped that in time things would get better—not just for her but for the others in her family, who'd also suffered a great loss.

As she started back toward the house, a crow flew over her head, screeching out its shrill call. It landed on a nearby treetop and let out several more aggravating calls. *I hope that silly thing doesn't have a nest somewhere in our yard.*

Ignoring the black bird, Sylvia hurried up the back steps and into the house. "Mom, there was a message from Ezekiel on our answering machine!" She rushed into the living room, where her mother and sister sat on the sofa. Mom held Rachel, and Allen sat on Amy's knee.

"What did your brother have to say?" Mom patted the baby's back.

"Michelle had her boppli this afternoon, and they named him Vernon."

Mom squealed so loud, Rachel began to howl. "Oh, sorry, sweet baby." She continued to pat the little girl's back as she looked over at Sylvia. "That is such good news. Are Michelle and the boppli doing okay?"

"They're both fine." Sylvia gave them all the details then leaned down and scooped her baby daughter into her arms.

"Dad would be so pleased to know they named their son after him." Tears welled in Amy's eyes as she looked at their mother. "Michelle's going to have her hands full now, with two little ones to look after."

Tearfully, Mom bobbed her head.

"She's no doubt going to need some help." Amy reached over and touched Mom's hand. "You should go there for at least two weeks to lend a hand." She looked at Sylvia. "Don't you agree, Sister?"

Sylvia shrugged. "I suppose so, but it would be a lot for you to handle the greenhouse by yourself. Every time I've looked out the window the past few weeks, there have been a good many cars and horse and buggies in the parking area. Busy is good, but not when you are working in the greenhouse pretty much by yourself."

"I'll have Henry's help."

"Jah, when he feels like helping," Mom put in. "Sylvia's right, Amy. I can't leave you here to run the place by yourself."

Amy set Allen on the floor, jumped up, and faced Sylvia. Planting her feet in a wide stance, she spoke with assurance. "We'll get someone to come here to watch the kinner, and then you can help me in the greenhouse."

Sylvia's forehead wrinkled as she gave a determined shake of her head. "No, Amy. . .I can't."

"Can't or won't?" Amy pointed at Sylvia with her index finger. "If you care about Ezekiel and Michelle, you'll step out of your comfort zone to help out so Mom can go there to help."

Sylvia took a deep, pained breath and closed her eyes. She disliked being made to feel guilty. Didn't her sister realize how hard it would be for her to leave the children with someone else and spend a good portion of her days in the greenhouse? *I can't do it,* she told herself. *It would be too difficult to deal with people asking me questions all day and giving me looks of pity. Hiring someone to help out in the greenhouse would be better.*

Sylvia bit down on her lower lip. *But honestly, it would take some time to train a new person, and I already know what to do.*

"Don't feel like you have to say yes, Daughter." Mom looked at Sylvia with a tender expression. "But it would be ever so nice if I could go to Clymer to see my newest grandchild and stay a few weeks to help out."

No pressure. I really do need to deal with my stress and anxiety, so I'll force myself to do it. Either I'll be able to work through the two weeks Mom's gone, or I'll be very desperate for her return.

Sylvia stroked the sides of her little girl's silky head while clearing her throat a couple of times. "All right, I'll do it. I will help in the greenhouse, but only till Mom gets back. After that, I'll be right here with my precious kinner again."

"You've been actin' like a bumble grumble all evening. What's the problem?" Earl moved closer to Virginia on the couch and bumped her shoulder.

"You'd be a bumble grumble too if you had to be stuck in this house all day listening to all the traffic coming down the road in front of our place." Virginia wrinkled her nose. "I tried sitting on the front porch for a while, but the nasty stench from all those horses was unbearable."

"That's good ole' country air." He nudged her again. "You'll get used to it in time."

She folded her arms. "I doubt that. Also, Earl, I'll have you know that my car has horse stuff on most of its wheels. That sort of thing would never have happened in good old Chicago."

"Well, dear, you'll just have to try harder to dodge all the road apples when you're out driving." Earl chuckled. "Actually, I went out earlier and collected some of that stuff. A guy from work told me that it's good for fertilizing around the shrubs in the flowerbeds."

Virginia merely glanced at him and gave a look of disapproval.

"Did you get started on the garden yet?"

"Nope."

"How come? I got the plot all ready for you."

"I'm still unpacking boxes. Besides, I don't have any vegetable seeds."

Earl gave a disgusting snort. "Really, Virginia, there's a green-house right across the street. I bet ya anything they sell packets of seeds. Probably have some vegetable plants already started too, which would be your best bet since it's already the middle of summer." He pointed toward the front window. "You oughta go over there tomorrow morning and check it out."

She groaned. "Do I have to? Can't we buy the seeds at a hardware store or anyplace else that might sell them?"

Earl shook his head. "Don't be ridiculous. There's a place right across the road, so why make a special trip into town to get what you need?"

With my luck, that Mrs. King will try to arrange a tea party with me. I feel stuck in the middle with Earl making me go over there and me trying to avoid any contact with those Amish people.

Virginia sighed. "Okay, okay. Sometime tomorrow I'll head over there and see what they have." *Maybe I'll tell 'em what I think of the stench their place causes too.*

Amy stood in front of her bedroom window, staring out at the night sky. Only a sliver of the moon shown tonight, and a light wind blew in through the partially open window. Tomorrow morning Mom's driver would be by early to pick her up for the roughly six-hour journey to Clymer.

Amy figured her mother must be pretty excited about seeing Ezekiel and Michelle's new baby. It would be good for her to get away for a few weeks to help out and enjoy two of her grandchildren.

Amy moved away from the window and picked up her hairbrush. As she pulled the bristles through her long hair, she thought about Sylvia agreeing to help in the greenhouse. *It will be nice to have my sister working in there with me again.*

Amy clicked her tongue. She hoped Sylvia's little ones would adjust to having an unfamiliar person taking care of them. Mom had been in touch with Mary Ruth, and she'd agreed to come over each workday to watch Sylvia's children while Mom was away.

Amy wished she could go with their mother to see Michelle and Ezekiel's new baby. How exciting it must be to have a new addition to their growing family. Once more, Amy thought about how her plans for marriage and children had been changed.

She continued to run the brush through her smooth waves. *I hope it all goes well tomorrow and that it's not too much for Sylvia to work with me in the greenhouse.*

Amy's thoughts turn to Jared and the jealousy she'd felt seeing him with Lydia. *But can I really blame him? I did tell Jared he was free to court someone else. And who better than my dear sweet friend?*

She set the hairbrush down and sank to the edge of her bed. *If Jared decides to marry Lydia or someone else, I'll have to accept it and try to be happy for them. In the meantime, I need to keep my focus on running the greenhouse and helping everyone in the family overcome their depression.*

Chapter 21

Sylvia swallowed multiple times as she hugged her mother and told her goodbye the following morning. Mom would be gone for at least two weeks, and during that time Sylvia was expected to help in the greenhouse. She could hardly believe she had agreed to do it.

Sylvia gripped her hands together behind her back as she watched Henry put Mom's suitcase in her driver's van. Sylvia's apprehension increased when Henry and Amy hugged their mother and then Mom got into the van.

How am I going to be able to cope? Sylvia asked herself. *What if I can't carry through with my promise?* Mary Ruth would be here soon to look after the children, so that problem had been taken care of. Sylvia felt sure Allen and Rachel would be in good hands, but that didn't make her job of waiting on customers and being available to answer questions at the greenhouse any easier. There was no turning back now. The vehicle had pulled out of the yard and turned onto the road.

As if she were able to read Sylvia's thoughts, Amy joined her on the porch and slipped her arm around Sylvia's waist. "I have every confidence that you'll be able to do this, dear sister." She glanced toward the greenhouse, where Henry had already gone. "It will be time to open soon, so I'm going to head out there now. You can join us as soon as Mary Ruth shows up."

"Okay." Sylvia's single word came out in a squeak. It was selfish to think such thoughts, but she wished Mom hadn't agreed to help at Michelle and Ezekiel's. *But she came over to my house to help when both of my bopplin were born,* Sylvia reminded herself. *It's only fair that she would do the same for my brother and his wife.*

"I'll be there as soon as I can," Sylvia said, turning toward the front door of the house. She glanced over her shoulder and saw Amy sprinting across the yard toward the greenhouse.

For the umpteenth time, Sylvia wished she could turn back the hands of time and be living at her own home again with Toby and the children.

Clymer

Ezekiel sat beside Michelle on the couch while she fed their precious son. He held Angela Mary on his lap, stroking her soft cheek.

"Your little brother is Vernon Lee and is named after your grandfather," he said in Pennsylvania Dutch.

"Bruder?" The little girl tipped her head back and looked up at him with wide eyes.

Ezekiel nodded. "Jah. Someday when he's a little bigger, the two of you can play together."

Angela Mary reached over and touched Vernon's arm. "*Mei boppli.*"

"He is your baby, but he's also your mama's and my baby."

Angela Mary nodded as though she understood and then leaned her head against Ezekiel's chest and closed her eyes. It was a special moment, the four of them here in the living room, waiting for Ezekiel's mother to arrive. "It'll sure be good to see Mom again and introduce her to Dad's namesake."

"Yes, it will be very nice."

When Michelle finished nursing the baby, she put him over her shoulder and patted his back. It wasn't long before a good burp came forth.

Angela Mary sat up straight and pointed at her brother. "*Der boppli waar am uffschtoose.*"

Michelle chuckled, and so did Ezekiel. "Jah." With a gentle touch, he rubbed his daughter's back. "The baby was belching." He looked over at Michelle and grinned. "Our daughter is pretty *schmaert*."

"Jah, she's a very smart little girl."

Ezekiel's head turned toward the door when he heard a vehicle pull into the yard. "I bet that's my mamm and her driver right now."

Belinda had no more than stepped out of the van, when she saw Ezekiel come out of the house and sprint toward the vehicle. She greeted him with open arms. "*Ach*, it's so good to see you again."

"Likewise, Mom." Ezekiel hugged her tightly. "Michelle's in the house with Angela Mary and the boppli. They'll be excited to see you too."

While Ezekiel opened the back door to retrieve Belinda's suitcase and tote bag, she paid the driver and reminded her of what day and time she would need to be picked up for the return trip to Strasburg. With Ezekiel carrying the suitcase and Belinda the tote, they hurried toward the house.

Excitement welled in Belinda's chest when they entered the house.

"Go on into the living room," Ezekiel said. "I'll put your things in the guest room while you visit with Michelle and the kinner."

"Okay."

Belinda found Michelle sitting on the couch holding the baby, and Angela Mary sat beside her.

Seeing her granddaughter's eyes light up when she saw her, Belinda bent down, swooped the little girl into her arms, and gave her a kiss.

Angela Mary giggled and touched Belinda's cheeks. She turned her head and pointed at her baby brother, snuggled in his mama's arms. "Mei bruder."

Belinda placed the child on the couch and took a seat between her and Michelle. "Jah, sweet Angela Mary, you have a little brother now." A lump formed in Belinda's throat as she gazed for the first time on her newest grandchild. *"Er hot en lieblich boppli."*

"We think he's an adorable baby too." Michelle reached around Belinda's shoulders and hugged her. "Danki for coming. It's so nice to see you again."

"I am glad Sylvia agreed to help out in the greenhouse, or it would have been hard for me to get away." Belinda stroked the baby's soft cheek.

"Would you like to hold little Vernon?"

"I surely would."

When Michelle placed the baby in her arms, Belinda choked up. "If only his grandpa could be here to see him right now. He would feel honored that you named the boppli after him."

Ezekiel stepped into the room. "It was my fraa's idea, Mom, but I was in total agreement."

Belinda smiled and touched her daughter-in-law's arm. "It was a sweet thing to do."

"If our little Vernon turns out to be even half as kind and loving as your husband was, Ezekiel and I will be happy parents."

"Those are my thoughts too." Ezekiel took a seat on the other side of Belinda and pulled Angela Mary onto his lap.

"How are you and the rest of the family doing?" he asked, reaching over to stroke his son's forehead.

If only I could be forthright, but... "We're getting along okay." No way would Belinda say anything to the contrary. The last thing she wanted was for Ezekiel to worry about them or believe things were not going well in the greenhouse or even within their home.

"How's Henry's attitude? Has his temperament improved any since I last talked to him?"

"Some. One of our ministers spoke to him, and so did Sara's husband, Brad."

"That's good. The more people who take an interest in him, the better it will be."

"Jah." Belinda changed the subject by asking how Michelle was feeling since the birth of her second child.

"I'm doing okay physically but not well enough to be on my own yet, so I'm ever so thankful you'll be here for a couple of weeks." Michelle's eyes glistened with tears. "I have no mother to help out, but I feel blessed to have you."

Belinda teared up too. Although Michelle wasn't the woman she would have originally chosen for her son, she'd come to care deeply for her. Michelle had proven her loyalty and love many times since she joined the Amish church and married Ezekiel. Belinda felt bad for the cool way she'd treated her daughter-in-law in the past but was thankful for the opportunity to make it up to her now.

Strasburg

Amy felt concern when she saw her sister's rigid posture as she clutched a pot of petunias close to her chest as though it were a shield. Sylvia was undeniably filled with unease. She'd made it through the morning but avoided speaking to anyone unless they spoke to her first. When Sylvia had come back to the greenhouse after taking her lunch break, Amy noticed her sister's glassy stare and trembling hands.

Less than an hour later, Sylvia announced that she wanted to go check on the children. Amy didn't argue. They didn't have any customers at the moment.

After Sylvia left, Amy stepped outside in search of Henry. If they did end up with any customers while Sylvia was in the house, she would need her brother's help.

"Henry! Where are you, Henry?" Amy called.

"I'm right here."

She glanced toward the barn and spotted him sitting in the wide opening of the hayloft, crossed-legged and looking out as if he didn't have a care in the world.

"What are you doing up there? Don't you know there's work to be done?"

"I like to be up high so I can watch the birds," he hollered. "I've seen a cardinal, a few robins, and look. . .there's a big black crow over there."

Amy turned to look at the roof of the greenhouse where Henry pointed. *Caw! Caw! Caw!* The bird flapped its wings and swooped to the ground, continuing to make a racket. Amy shuddered. It seemed like every time that annoying bird came around, something bad happened.

Amy's slender covering ties swished across her face as she shook her head. *I need to stop such superstitious thoughts.*

She looked up at Henry, sitting in the same spot, and pointed her finger. "You'd better come down here right now, because I need your help in the greenhouse."

Henry cupped his hands around his mouth. "I thought Sylvia was helpin' you today."

"She went in the house a few minutes ago to check on the kinner."

"Well, you'd better get back to the greenhouse then 'cause I see that new English neighbor lady from across the road walking up our driveway. I forgot her name, but I bet she's needin' some kind of plants or gardening supplies."

"Her name is Virginia."

It wouldn't be good to have customers walking around the greenhouse without anyone to wait on them, so Amy turned and ran back inside.

I wonder how this is going to play out while Mom's away. Since she left us, Sylvia's apprehensive about helping me, and Henry thinks he can sit in the barn during business hours and bird-watch. Amy moaned in despair. *I hope these two don't leave me on my own out here to manage things, because if they do, I'm going to be real upset and disappointed. Why don't they understand that I am struggling to function too?*

A few minutes later, Virginia came in, dressed in a floral print, citron shirt and tight-fitting lime green pants that matched the color of her sandals. The woman's flashy attire caught Amy off guard, and it was hard not to stare.

Without saying a word, the neighbor headed over to the racks where the seed packets were located. She picked out a few before meandering down the row of vegetable plants.

Thinking she might need some assistance, Amy hurried over to her. Virginia's bangle bracelets rattled together on her wrist as she withdrew a small vegetable plant and looked it over. Amy greeted the woman and asked if she needed help with anything.

Virginia placed the tomato plant down. "Wouldn't be here if I didn't need somethin'." A sheen of sweat covered the woman's cheeks, nose, and forehead. She took out a handkerchief from her bright yellow cross-body bag and dabbed at the sweat. "Sure is warm in here. If you had electricity, you could cool the place down."

Amy smiled. "What are you in need of?"

"I'm lookin' to buy some tomato plants that already have fruit on them and will ripen soon." Virginia avoided eye contact with Amy. "What other varieties do you have?" She gestured to the smaller tomato plant. "I put that one back since it only has flowers on it."

"Since it's the middle of July, most of our vegetable plants are pretty picked over, but I'm sure I can find you a few good ones." Amy stepped over to another spot and picked up a cherry tomato plant. She also grabbed one of the larger types of tomatoes that would make good slicers. "Will these do?"

"Yeah, sure." Virginia's eyelids twitched. "I read in the paper that there will be another greenhouse going in not far from here. Sounds like it'll be a pretty good size."

"Yes, I've heard about it."

"Aren't you worried that it'll take a lot of your customers away?"

"I'm not bothered." Amy spoke with assurance, although she did have some concerns. But as a Christian, she needed to have the faith to believe that things would work out according to the Lord's plan, and she reminded herself that worrying over things wouldn't help. She figured Virginia wouldn't be interested in her way of dealing with the knowledge that they would soon have competition.

Amy placed the plants in a wagon. "Is there anything else you would like?"

"Well, I'm not sure. Let me think about it for a sec." With her backside to the shelf where the vegetable plants sat, Virginia folded her arms and leaned back. She stood that way several seconds, and then, slapping her hands against her reddened cheeks, she jumped away from the shelf as if she'd been stung by a bee. "For goodness' sakes!"

"What's wrong?" Amy felt concern, seeing Virginia's curling lip and wrinkled nose. "The back of my pants is all wet. Someone in here obviously doesn't know what they're doing with a hose."

Before Amy could respond, Sylvia, who only moments ago had returned to the greenhouse, stepped up to Virginia and apologized. "I'm so sorry. I–I must have watered a little too much this morning."

"Yeah, well, it's just a good thing it's only water I backed into and not somethin' I can't get out of my pants." With a huff, Virginia grabbed the wagon's handle and pulled it up to the front counter.

Amy followed.

After the woman paid for her purchases, Amy put them in a cardboard box. "Would you like me to ask my brother to carry the tomato plants over to your house so you can walk with your hands free?"

Virginia shook her head. "No thanks. I'll haul it over there myself." She paid for her items, and carrying the box, she limped out the door.

"I wish she would have let me ask Henry to help her," Amy said when Sylvia joined her a few minutes later.

Sylvia looked down at the floor. "I can't deal with this right now, Amy. I wish I'd never agreed to help you in the greenhouse while Mom is gone." Without waiting for a response, Sylvia flung the door open and dashed out.

Amy sank onto the stool behind the counter with a groan. *What if Sylvia won't come back to help tomorrow? How am I going to manage things for the next two weeks with only a little help from Henry?*

Chapter 22

Clymer

A multitude of thoughts swirled in Belinda's head while she stood at the kitchen window and watched her son head to the barn to do his chores. Ezekiel's mannerisms and the way he carried himself reminded her of Vernon. After not seeing Ezekiel for a while, it caught Belinda off guard when she witnessed her son's comforting traits.

Through the open window, she heard him whistling a cheery tune; again, something her husband had done now and then. Belinda also noticed the way Ezekiel's arms swung as he strolled across the grass.

Aside from her own pain of missing Vernon and seeing him in a way through her eldest son, she ached to be close to all four of her children. *I won't be selfish. The Lord has given Ezekiel a new path to follow. I can't stand in the way and cause him to deviate from it.*

Belinda lowered her head. Staring at the floor, she pondered the happenings of the day before. *He's happy here,* she noted. She'd heard it in his voice and seen the sparkle in his eyes last evening during supper when he talked about his role as a minister. Ezekiel read his Bible in the evenings and said he wanted to walk close to the Lord. He'd also mentioned the satisfaction of owning his own business, saying he was glad he had the chance to do something for a living that he truly enjoyed. He downplayed his disinterest in the work he used to do back home but said if the need arose, he would go back to it. Although it was kind of Ezekiel to offer, Belinda wouldn't hear of her son leaving his new life here in Clymer.

She filled the coffeepot with water and put the right amount of coffee in the filter then set it on the stove and turned on the gas burner. Her thoughts went back home for a spell. *I wish Henry took some pleasure in helping us in the greenhouse and taking care of the bees.*

Belinda watched the bluish flame heating the pot. *My youngest son needs support, and I pray he'll wake up and feel the love and encouragement from his family as well as those in our church district.*

Belinda was well aware of Henry's frustration and dissatisfaction with his new tasks, but she saw no alternative to his situation—at least not until he was a few years older and she felt sure they could run the greenhouse without him.

I wonder what kind of work Henry would like to do. He's never really said. It might be good for me to ask and let him know that eventually he will be able to branch out on his own if he still wants to by then. Belinda moved away from the stove and opened the refrigerator to take out a carton of eggs. *At least it would give Henry a ray of hope, which might help to improve his negative attitude.*

Their lives had changed so much after the accident. The light at the end of the tunnel wasn't there yet. They all seemed caught in a perpetual unrest, trying to balance their everyday tasks around home and keeping the business running.

Belinda realized that most of Henry's problem was due to the anguish of missing his father and brother. She wished there was some way to help him rise above it and see that his life must go on. *Maybe if Henry found some things to do that he enjoyed, it would give him something positive to focus on. Perhaps a new hobby or time spent with his friends would be helpful. I dare say he could probably use a good role model in his life. But it won't be with a stepfather.* Belinda shuddered. *I can't see anyone in the future for me. Oh Lord, I miss my Vernon so very much.*

She drew in her bottom lip. *I might be expecting too much of Henry. He's not a man yet—still a teenage boy. It could help if I give him a bit more freedom to do some things on his own—things that don't involve working all the time.*

Belinda resolved that when she returned home, she would have a talk with Henry and express some of the things she'd been mulling over this morning. *Perhaps this time away from me telling him what to do will help too,* she reasoned.

Belinda glanced at the battery-operated clock above the refrigerator and noted the time. It was 6:30 a.m. No doubt her daughters would be up by now, preparing breakfast, and would soon be getting ready for another day in the greenhouse. *Should I call and leave a message for them today? I really need to check and see how things are going. I hope everything is fine and that Sylvia doesn't feel too overwhelmed working in the greenhouse while I'm gone.*

Belinda sniffed the air. The brewing coffee filled the kitchen with a wonderful rich aroma. Thoughts of home still drifted into her mind though, and it was difficult not to rethink things. Belinda needed to know she'd made the right choice in coming here and wasn't being selfish somehow. *Sylvia might have only been trying to please me by agreeing to help while I'm gone even if she didn't feel ready. I certainly hope that's not the case.*

Belinda's eldest daughter had begun working in the greenhouse as soon as she graduated from the eighth grade, so she knew what needed to be done. Hopefully, her nerves had calmed down and her reluctance to talk to customers was a thing of the past.

A shrill baby's cry halted Belinda's thoughts. She needed to get breakfast made so that all Michelle had to do was take care of little Vernon. Belinda couldn't wait to see the grandkids this morning. Their pure hearts and sweet faces were a joyful tonic. She'd brought along her journal to write down all the things that were taking place. Belinda wanted to remember as much as she could about this special visit. It would be fun someday to read to her grandchildren what she'd written about them. She could also share the notes with her family back home. Every person in Belinda's family was special, and she felt blessed to have each of them in her life.

Belinda heard the patter of little feet and looked toward the doorway of the kitchen. She smiled when she saw Angela Mary enter the room holding the baby doll Belinda had given her yesterday. The child padded up to her wearing a tender smile.

"Are you hungry, sweet girl?" Belinda asked in Pennsylvania Dutch.

Angela Mary nodded and rubbed her tummy.

"What would you like for breakfast?"

"*Pannekuche.*"

Belinda grinned. "Are you sure?"

"Jah, *Grossmudder.*" Angela Mary gave a little hop.

Belinda hadn't planned on making pancakes today, but she didn't want to disappoint her granddaughter. "All right, Angela Mary—pannekuche it is." She set the eggs on the counter, picked the little girl up, and gave her a kiss. Spending time with her grandchildren and doing things to make them smile—that's what would keep Belinda going and looking to the future with hope.

Strasburg

The sunlight pouring into his room caused Jared to wake up with a start. When he checked his alarm clock, he realized it had never gone off.

"Maybe I forgot to set it last night." He picked it up. Sure enough, the button on top had not been pulled out. He'd been forgetting a lot of things lately—phone calls he hadn't returned; notes he'd made about jobs; and errands he should have run. Jared's only excuse was that his mind seemed to be elsewhere most of the time. No matter how hard he tried, Jared couldn't get Amy out of his thoughts. Common sense told him to move on with his life and find someone else, because it didn't look like she would change her mind. When he'd talked to Lydia the other day, she had commented that Amy kept really busy with her responsibilities at home and in the greenhouse. Lydia also stated that her friend didn't have time anymore to go out to lunch or take a few minutes to talk.

Jared grunted as he rolled out of bed. He wanted so badly to drop by the greenhouse to check on her but figured Amy would be too busy. More than likely she'd think he only came over to pressure her into letting him court her again. He saw Amy every other Sunday, but her body language remained the same. Amy kept her distance, but at least he could see that she was okay. The only news Jared had about Amy and her family these days was through the Amish grapevine. His mom had talked to someone who'd stopped at the greenhouse for something the other day, and whoever it was (Mom wouldn't say) had informed her that Amy's demeanor was always so serious, and the dark circles beneath her eyes revealed extreme fatigue.

Jared pinched the skin at his throat. *Even though she doesn't want to see me, I think I'll come up with an excuse to visit the greenhouse sometime this week.*

When Amy approached the greenhouse early the following morning, she was surprised to see the front door standing open; although the screen door was shut. She poked her tongue against the inside of her cheek and inhaled a long breath. *Henry King, didn't you close and lock the door like I told you to yesterday evening?*

After she'd closed the greenhouse for the day, Amy remembered later that she'd left some money in the till and had asked Henry to fetch it. He'd returned to the house with the cash, so she assumed he would have locked both the front and back doors, since that was the standing rule.

Cautiously, she stepped inside. All was quiet, and there was no sign of anyone, but when Amy walked down one of the aisles, she was stunned to see several of the potted plants had been dumped onto the floor. *Oh, no—the flowers!* She looked around again in desperation.

"How in the world did this happen?" Amy drew a shaky breath, walking backward toward the entrance to the building. Whoever had done this might still be inside, hiding somewhere. She wasn't about to turn her back on them.

"How did what happen?"

Amy gasped and whirled around. "Henry, you about scared me to death. I thought you were still in the barn feeding the livestock."

"I'm done with that." He tipped his head to one side. "You never answered my question? What happened in here?"

She explained about the plants and led the way so he could see the evidence.

"Oh, great." He thumped the side of his head.

"When you came out to get the money last night, did you make sure to shut and lock both doors?"

He shifted his weight from one foot to the other. "I remember shutting them, all right, and I—I think I locked the doors too."

"Do you actually remember doing it, Henry?"

"Umm. . .let me think." Henry rubbed the bridge of his nose.

"Well, did you or not?"

"I don't actually remember doing it, but I'm pretty sure I did." He glanced at the ruined plants then back at Amy. "Are you gonna let Mom know about this?"

"No, I am not." She placed her hand on his shoulder. "And I don't want you to mention it either."

"How come? Don't ya think she has a right to know about the vandalism that's struck us again?"

Amy was on the verge of offering a response when Henry spoke once more.

"And don't try to put the blame on me for what happened either." Henry's eyes narrowed as he pointed at the plants. "What reason would I have for ruining all these?"

"Well, umm. . ."

He held up his hand. "You think I did it, don't ya?"

Amy shrugged her shoulders. "Truthfully, the thought had crossed my mind."

"Why?"

"You've made it more than clear that you don't like working here. And last night, when you didn't know I was within earshot, I heard you mumble that you were sick and tired of the greenhouse as well as caring for the bees."

"Jah, well, I don't like either of those jobs, but I wouldn't be dumb enough to wreck plants or do anything else destructive in the greenhouse. After all, the money we earn here is what pays the bills and keeps food in our bellies." Henry thumped his stomach.

"Okay, okay, calm down, little brother."

He raised his eyebrows and gave Amy a glassy stare. "I ain't little, so quit callin' me that."

"Sorry, it was just a figure of speech. Don't forget, you are my youngest bruder, Henry."

"Yeah, with Ezekiel living far from us now and God taking Abe away, I feel like I've become your *only* brother."

The look of hurt Amy saw in Henry's eyes let her know that she'd said enough. She moved closer and hugged his shoulders. Relieved that he didn't pull away, she said, "Let's try to work together from now on, okay?"

Henry gave a slow nod. "Sure. Whatever you say." He moved away and set to work cleaning up the mess that had been made. "I have to wonder if some animal got into the greenhouse and pawed through these plants, which knocked 'em to the floor."

She shook her head. "It looks more intentional to me, but I could be wrong."

"This is a waste, though it won't take long to clean up." Henry picked up all the ruined plants and hauled them away.

Amy watched as her brother grabbed a broom and swept up the remaining soil. Nearby sat a bucket he dumped all the dirt into. Then Henry carried off the emptied containers toward the storage room.

Amy sighed. She'd helped Mom months ago get those plants started from seeds. *I agree with Henry—it is a waste.*

She groaned inwardly. Their mother had only been gone two days, and already unpleasant things had happened. She hated to think of what else might occur during Mom's two-week absence.

Try not to borrow trouble, she told herself as the distinctive sound of the crow's call filtered in through the open door. *Caw...Caw...Caw...*

Chapter 23

"I hear a steady *clip-clop* of horses' hooves this morning. I bet that greenhouse across the road is getting business already this morning." Virginia's fingers tightened as she handed her husband a piece of toast.

"Yep. You're probably right." Earl kept his focus on the sports section of the newspaper lying next to his plate.

"I am still a bit irritated about getting my lime green pants wet when I went to the greenhouse yesterday."

He chuckled. "You should be more careful where you're leaning your backside."

She lifted her gaze to the ceiling. "You would say something like that."

"I have to say, that greenhouse of theirs was plenty warm inside. It made me sweat like a pig. If they had electricity at their place, they could have several fans running to circulate the air."

"Well, dear, they are Amish, and who knows what else they don't do." Earl pushed the paper aside and drank some coffee. "Did you get the tomato plants you bought put in the ground?"

Virginia shook her head and buttered the toast on her plate. "Not yet." She took a bite of it and tried to relax.

"When ya do, don't forget to add some of that horse manure into the soil."

"Earl, I'm eating. Can't you see that?" She wrinkled her nose. "I'm not about to touch any of that yucky stuff, and I sure don't wanna talk about it at the breakfast table."

Earl set his coffee mug down and gave an impatient huff. "I'm not suggesting you handle the manure with your bare hands, Virginia. Dig a hole in the area where you want the tomato plants to go, and then shovel some of the manure in and spread it around. After that, put the plants in the hole and cover the rest of it with dirt. The last step will be to give the tomato plants plenty of water."

She flapped her hand. "That sounds like a lot of hard work. Anyway, is that how you think those Amish folks do their gardening—by mixing all their horse droppings into the soil?"

"I suppose." He finished his toast. "Why don't you ask 'em?"

"No way!"

"I did notice at the Kings' place that their plot of vegetables looked healthy, and all the flowers they grow to sell are gorgeous."

"What else would they use, Virginia? They've got an endless supply of horse manure."

"All I know is they run around barefoot a lot over there. Don't they worry about stepping in some of it?"

Earl laughed. "Good question. Why don't you run on over there and ask that question too?"

"Very cute, Earl. I was just pointing out what I've noticed is all."

"Have you been using my binoculars to spy on them?"

"No, of course not. But I have good vision and can see details that are pretty far away."

Virginia drank the rest of her apple juice, pushed her chair aside, and stood. "As soon as I put our dishes in the dishwasher, I'll get started on the garden plot. I can't wait to see how well our plants grow."

"Sounds good." He stood and kissed her cheek. "I'd better get to work. I hope you have a nice day."

"You too, dear."

After her husband went out the door, Virginia watched out the front window as he got into his truck. Since their place had only a one-car garage, Earl let Virginia park her car inside, and he left the truck in the driveway.

She walked out onto the porch and waved to Earl as he backed his rig out of the driveway and headed down the road in the direction of Lancaster. When he was out of sight, she glanced across the road and noticed a lot of cars in the greenhouse parking lot. *They're sure busy over there again. No doubt there'll be more noise for me to put up with today.*

Virginia moved away from the porch railing and went back inside the house. *One good thing. . . . At least Earl and I will have a nice crop of tomatoes to enjoy in the days ahead. Maybe country living won't be so bad after all—at least in that regard.*

When Virginia returned to the kitchen, she cleared the table. After placing the dishes in the dishwasher, she found her gardening gloves and went out the back door. *Even though it was my idea to grow some fresh produce, I hope this project isn't more than I can handle.*

Jared had quit working a little early today so he could go home and take a shower before heading to the greenhouse. He didn't want to show up at the Kings' smelling like a hog or with clothes covered in dirt and sweat.

Jared snapped the reins to get Dandy moving along. "If Amy saw me like that, she might never change her mind about us."

The gelding's ears twitched, and he bobbed his head. It seemed as if Dandy agreed with Jared. He couldn't control the nervousness he felt as he drew closer to the Kings' place. But, oh, how he looked forward to seeing Amy, even if the reception awaiting him would be less friendly than he'd like.

When Jared guided Reckless up the Kings' driveway, he was pleased to see four cars in the graveled parking lot as well as two horse and buggies at the hitching rail. *Their business must be doing well, and that's a good thing. I wonder how Amy and her family are doing emotionally though.*

Jared directed Dandy to the rail and set the brake. Then he

climbed down and secured the horse. Jared paused to brush away a few smudges on his trousers from the carriage wheel he'd come in contact with, although he was sure his efforts in looking nice wouldn't do anything to help him win Amy at this point. Jared still loved her, and his heartbeat quickened, thinking about being close to her.

As he walked toward the entrance of the building, an English man he'd done business with came out carrying a hanging basket in one hand. He smiled at Jared as he approached. "It's nice to see you."

"Nice to see you too, Mr. Chandler."

"You and your crew sure did a good job on my roof. In fact, I've handed out several of your business cards to others who have complimented the job you did." The man shook Jared's hand. "Would you have any more of those cards on you? I'll give some of them out to the fellows I work with in case they might be thinking of having a new roof put on their home, shop, or garage."

"Sure. That'd be great." Jared pulled his wallet from the pocket in his trousers and withdrew ten of his cards. "Is that enough?"

"I believe so. At least for now." Mr. Chandler clasped Jared's shoulder. "I've had other work done by Amish men and have always been satisfied, so keep up the good work."

"Thanks, I will. And I appreciate you spreading the word about my business."

"Not a problem. When I know a good thing, I always like to tell others." He tapped Jared's arm. "Have a good evening."

"Same to you, sir."

When Jared entered the greenhouse, he saw Amy standing behind the checkout counter with three people lined up on the other side, waiting to check out.

Jared didn't want to interrupt, so he headed down one of the aisles in search of the right birthday gift for his mother. About halfway down, he spotted Henry moving some plants from one wooden shelf to another. "How's it going?" Jared asked when he approached the boy.

With tight lips, Henry merely gave a shrug.

"It looks like you're keeping busy."

"Yeah, too busy," the boy mumbled. "Amy's always tellin' me what to do, especially now that Mom's not here."

Jared glanced over his shoulder and saw Amy still waiting on customers, then he turned back to face her brother. "How long till your mamm returns?"

"She'll be gone at least two weeks. I'm guessin' maybe longer if they need more help."

Jared didn't want to appear nosey, but he was curious as to where Belinda had gone and who needed her help. Under the circumstances, it seemed unlikely that she'd leave her home, greenhouse, and family that long. "If you don't mind my asking. . .where'd your mother go?"

"Up to Clymer, New York, where Michelle and Ezekiel live. Michelle had a baby boy recently, and Mom went there to help out."

"I see. Makes sense that she'd want to be there."

When Henry gave no response, Jared posed another question. "So, is it just you and Amy working in the greenhouse while your mamm is gone?"

Henry shook his head. "Sylvia's helpin' out too, and Mary Ruth is taking care of her kinner while she's out here." He pulled his suspenders out with his thumbs and gave them a snap. "I don't like working here and having someone always tellin' me what to do. You're lucky to be your own boss."

"Running my own business has its good points, but there are some negative things about it too."

Henry folded his arms. "Like what?"

"Well, being my own boss means I have to be responsible for hiring a good crew of roofers. There is also lots paperwork to do when you run a business."

"I'm well aware. Amy does that kind of stuff for the greenhouse. She's always busy with something or other, even when the greenhouse is closed." Henry's brows furrowed. "Whenever she's not workin', she's reminding me about chores and saying something I've done is wrong."

"Anything specific?" Jared asked.

Henry's voice lowered. "Well, someone got into the greenhouse last night and dumped over some of our potted plants. Amy accused me of not locking the doors." His face colored as he reached up to rub the back of his neck. "I'm sure she thinks I'm responsible for all the vandalism that's happened here since my daed, brother, and brother-in-law died."

Jared's eyes widened. "What are you talking about, Henry? What kind of vandalism?"

He listened with concern as Henry told him about the mailbox, greenhouse sign, and a few other things that could have been done on purpose. "Does Amy believe those things were done intentionally?"

"Jah, and as I said before, she thinks they were done by me."

"Did you do any of them, Henry?" Jared felt led to ask.

He shook his head vigorously. "Wanna know what I think?"

"Of course."

"I think some of my friends might have done all those things."

Jared tipped his head. "Why would they do that?"

"Cause they're mad about me not bein' able to do anything fun with them this summer, thanks to all the work I have to do here." Henry groaned. "Me and my buddies had planned all sorts of fun things to do after we got out of school. Now I can't do nothin' because of all the work that's been forced on me." There was a hard edge to the young man's words, and Jared saw a look of bitterness on Henry's face.

Jared searched for the right words to offer comfort or advice, but before he could form another sentence, Henry turned away and tromped off.

Jared rubbed his jaw in contemplation. *I believe that young fellow needs someone to talk to. I may not be the one he'll open up to, but I can sure be praying for his situation.*

Jared picked up a hanging basket filled with pink and white petunias and started down the aisle toward the checkout counter. As he approached, he couldn't help but notice the look of exhaustion on

Amy's face. There was no doubt about it—she'd been working too hard. "Hi, Amy. It's nice to see you."

"Hello, Jared." Amy drew in some air, trying to slow her breathing. Even though they couldn't be together, her feelings for him hadn't changed. "That's a lovely basket you've chosen." *I wonder if it's for Lydia. I'm sure they must be courting.*

He gave a nod. "It's for my mamm. Today's her birthday."

"Oh. I'm sure she will like it. Please tell her I said happy birthday."

"I will." Jared's eyes darkened. "How have you been, Amy?"

"Okay." She kept her gaze fixed on the basket.

"You look mied."

"I am tired, but it's nothing I can't handle."

"Are you sure about that?" He sounded concerned.

Her head came up. "Of course, I'm sure."

"I was talking to Henry earlier, and he mentioned that your mamm's in New York, helping out since your sister-in-law had her baby."

"That's correct."

"Henry also said he and Sylvia are helping you here."

"Jah."

"I'm glad your sister is able to work again."

"I am too." Amy didn't mention how hard it was for Sylvia to be around people or that she went into the house several times a day to check on the children, as she had done a while ago. Since they weren't a courting couple anymore, she saw no need to fill him in on any of their personal business.

"Henry also said you've had some problems with vandalism."

Amy shifted as she gave her apron a tug. "It's nothing serious, and we're all okay, so please don't mention it to anyone."

"Why not? If somebody has singled you out for some reason then—"

Amy shook her head. "Jared, I'd rather not discuss this right now."

"Okay, but please be careful, and if any more damage to your property occurs, you should call the sheriff's office right away."

"We'll deal with it in whatever way we feel is best." Amy made sure to keep her voice down during this conversation. "Did you need anything else?"

He shook his head. "No, but I was wondering if you've talked to Lydia lately." He leaned against his side of the counter.

"I just spoke a few words to her at the last church meeting." Amy gave a sidelong glance when another customer came into the store. Truth was, she'd been avoiding her friend. It would be too painful for Amy if Lydia were to admit that she'd been seeing Jared socially.

Amy rang up Jared's purchase, and he gave her the money. "I hope your mother likes what you got her."

"I'm sure she will." Jared picked up the hanging basket. "Tell your family I said hello." He started toward the door but turned around. "If you need anything while your mom is gone, please let me know."

All Amy could manage was a slow nod. Her throat felt so thick, she couldn't utter another word. She watched Jared as he walked out of the building. It had been difficult to chat with him and maintain an indifferent attitude.

After Jared left the greenhouse, she turned her attention toward the young English woman who had come in. "May I help you with anything?"

At that moment, Sylvia arrived with two bottles of water, which she placed under the counter before stepping behind it while Amy dealt with the customer.

The English woman moved closer to her. "My grandmother is in the hospital, and I'm looking for a pretty plant to give her."

"Right this way. I'll show you what we have available." As Amy headed down the aisle where the houseplants were displayed, one more thought about Jared popped into her head. *If we were still a couple, I would have talked more with him about the troubles we've had here lately. But I'm sure I did right by not discussing it further. But really, what would be the point? There's nothing Jared can do for us.*

Chapter 24

Virginia moaned and rolled over in bed. Her throat hurt something awful. She'd coughed and sneezed so much last night that Earl had slept in their guest room. Virginia hadn't been out of the house for two days and had spent most of her time in bed or on the couch. She eyed the throat discs lying on her nightstand, grabbed one, and popped it into her mouth. They helped a little with her pain when she needed to swallow.

"I see you're awake." Earl stepped into the room and handed her a glass of water. "Maybe you ought to see a doctor."

Virginia grabbed a tissue from the nightstand and blew her nose. "I might do that if we had a doctor. Since we're new to the area, I wouldn't have any idea who to call. Besides, it's rare when a person can get in to see a doctor the same day they call."

"You have a point. Might be best for you to go to the hospital emergency room."

She shook her head. "Think I'll go to the pharmacy in town and see what they have to offer."

"Suit yourself." Earl stepped away from the bed. "I've gotta go. I'll see you this evening when I get home from work. Hopefully, by then you'll feel somewhat better."

After Earl left the room, Virginia lay in bed for a while. Finally, mustering up her strength, she pulled herself out of bed. "If Earl cared anything about me, he would have taken time off work to look after me," she grumbled.

Virginia threw on a pair of jeans and a button-down blouse before stumbling into the kitchen. With a diminished appetite, nothing appealed to her, so she fixed herself a cup of tea. Even though she didn't care much for the taste, the warm liquid felt good on her scratchy throat. When the cup was empty, she placed it in the sink, which was devoid of any breakfast dishes. Apparently, Earl had put his dishes in the dishwasher. She felt thankful for his consideration in doing that much at least.

Guess I can't blame him for not taking the day off to be with me. He's a new employee at the car dealership, and it probably wouldn't go over well with his boss. Besides, we're not rich, and we need a steady income to stay up with the bills coming in, not to mention food, clothes, and other essential items.

Virginia grabbed the car keys and her handbag then opened the back door. She wanted to check on the tomato plants she'd put in the ground two days ago, before getting her vehicle out of the garage.

Walking toward her small garden patch, she was shocked to see that her tomato plants had both died. They looked like someone had struck a match and lit them on fire. It made no sense. The last two evenings it had rained, so the plants had to have gotten enough water.

"I don't understand this. All my plants seemed healthy the day I brought them home. I bet that young Amish woman sold me some diseased plants." She broke off a piece from one of the plants. "I don't think those people across the road can be trusted." Virginia continued to bluster out loud as she tossed the plant debris away. "My poor garden looks terrible. Maybe if I go back there and complain, she'll give me all new plants." She paused from her ranting and rubbed her sore throat. *I need to quit talking to myself.*

Virginia kicked at a clump of dirt with the toe of her sneaker. *I wonder what went wrong with those tomato plants.*

Sylvia yawned as she sat at the kitchen table, trying to eat her breakfast while feeding Allen from his highchair. The baby had been fed and gone back to sleep, so she only had one child to worry about before Mary Ruth showed up.

"Would you like me to take over helping Allen eat his breakfast?" Amy asked. "That way you can eat yours in peace."

Peace? Sylvia's jaw clenched. She hadn't felt a moment of peace since her husband, father, and brother had died. Now with their mother away in New York and Amy counting on Sylvia to work in the greenhouse, she felt more stressed than ever.

"Sister, did you hear what I said?" Amy reached over and touched Sylvia's arm.

"Jah, I heard. If you're willing to oversee Allen trying to feed himself, that's fine with me."

"Course I'm willing."

"And are you also willing to clean up the mess he makes?"

Amy nodded. "If it takes too long, our brother can open the greenhouse today."

From his seat across the table, Henry gave no response.

When Amy took over with Allen, Sylvia picked up the newspaper lying on the corner of the table. "There's an article in here about the new greenhouse. Seems they're having a big grand opening sale this weekend—including Sunday." She looked over at Amy. "With them being English, they're bound to be open on days we are closed."

"We can't worry about it." Amy spoke softly, although wrinkles had formed across her forehead. "We just need to be confident that God will take care of our needs."

Sylvia pursed her lips. "If He was really taking care of our needs, Toby, Dad, and Abe would still be here. A lot of good it's done us to try and live a good Christian life." Her feelings were out, and Sylvia was glad she'd voiced her thoughts. As far as she was concerned, God had abandoned them, and they now had to fend for themselves.

"Remember, Matthew 5:45 says that the rain falls on the just as well as the unjust," Amy said.

"You sure know how to quote scriptures." It was the first thing

Henry had said since they'd sat down to eat breakfast.

"I've learned by reading the Bible every day and also from listening to our ministers' sermons during worship services." Amy looked over at Sylvia. "You know God's Word as well as I do. Your faith should be as strong as mine."

"Well it's not." Sylvia leaped out of her chair, nearly knocking it over. "I'm going to check on Rachel before the babysitter arrives."

As she fled the room, a strangled cry of frustration burst from her throat. *Will I ever feel whole again?*

Amy's gaze settled on her nephew as she took a couple of deep breaths. "Your mamma feels cheated from the loss of our family members. But as a Christian, she needs to let go of her anger and bitterness because it's not doing any good."

Allen looked up at Amy with a curious expression. She realized the little guy had no idea what she was talking about.

After Allen finished eating and she cleaned him up, Amy took her nephew to the living room to play. Then she returned to the kitchen, where Henry still sat at the table, looking at his pocketknife.

Amy picked up the small container of raspberries sitting on the counter, poured them into a colander, and turned on the water to wash them. "I was surprised to see these had already turned red, so I collected all that there was."

Henry only grunted.

"Would you please go out and open the greenhouse now?"

He squinted at Amy from across the table. "Why don't you do it, like you usually do?"

"I still have a few chores to do here, but I should be out there before any customers show up. Sylvia will come out with me as soon as Mary Ruth arrives."

"Okay, but can I borrow your *schlissel?*"

Her brows furrowed. "Why do you need my key when you have your own?"

"I—I can't find it. Must have lost it somewhere," he stammered.

"When was the last time you saw the schlissel?"

With palms up, Henry shrugged his shoulders. "Guess it's been a few weeks—maybe longer, since I wasn't asked to unlock the doors for some time."

"Did you have your key when you were asked to lock the doors at the end of the workday?"

"Don't know, but I never locked 'em with a key anyways. Always just turned the lock on the door knob before pulling it shut."

Amy stiffened. "Maybe the person who knocked over the potted plants found your key and picked it up. That could be how they got into the greenhouse."

"Yeah, maybe, but I'm gonna start lookin' for the key." Henry jumped up from his seat and made a mad dash for the back door.

Amy leaned forward with her hands resting on her forehead. *Heavenly Father, if Henry's key is still around, please, help us find it.*

Clymer

Warm water churned the soap into frothy suds as Belinda filled the kitchen sink and added liquid detergent. With breakfast over and the dishes soaking, she was ready to take care of another task she had wanted to do this morning. "Before I start washing the breakfast dishes, I'd like to walk out to the phone shed and make a call to the family at home. I want to let them know how things are going here and see how they're all doing," Belinda announced.

"That's a good idea, Mom." Ezekiel poured himself a second cup of coffee and added a spoonful of sugar. "Feel free to check the answering machine. There could be a message from Amy, Sylvia, or even Henry."

"I will. If there are other messages, I'll make sure they don't get erased, and you can check them when you have time."

"Sounds good." He smiled, dropping his spoon into the sink. "It sure is nice having you here—and not just to help out. We enjoy your company."

Belinda returned his smile. "And I enjoy yours." She looked at Angela Mary, sitting on a wooden booster seat Ezekiel had made to heighten the chair the little girl occupied. Although it saddened Belinda to miss out on so much that would go on in her son and his wife's family here, she wouldn't say a word about it. She wanted Ezekiel to feel good about remaining in Clymer.

Michelle entered the kitchen and took a seat at the table. "I finally got little Vernon settled. He did a lot of fussing throughout the night and even when he woke up this morning." She shook her head. "Angela Mary wasn't like that at all when she was a boppli. In fact, the only time she cried was when she was hungerich or her windel needed to be changed."

"All babies are different. I'm sure once you've established a routine, things will improve."

Michelle massaged her forehead. "I sure hope so, and I hope it happens before you have to return to Strasburg. I don't know what I'd do without you right now."

"Well, not to worry; I'll stay as long as you need me." Belinda hoped it wouldn't be more than two or three weeks at the most. As much as she enjoyed being here, she had responsibilities at home.

"I'm going to head out to the phone shed now." Belinda tightened the dark scarf on her head and went out the back door.

When she got to the phone shed, she stepped inside and took a seat. The green button on the answering machine blinked, so there were definitely some messages.

She clicked the button and listened to each one. Most were from customers interested in purchasing supplies for their bee business, but the last one was from her youngest daughter.

"Hi, it's me, Amy. I'm calling to see how things are going there and to tell Mom not to worry about us or the business. We're getting along fine here and keeping plenty busy."

Belinda decided to return the call right away and respond to

Amy's message. She dialed the number and was surprised when Henry picked it up after the second ring.

"Hello. If you're calling about the greenhouse, we're not open yet. If you have a message for someone in the family, I'll be glad to take it."

"Henry, it's your mamm."

"Oh, hey. How are ya, Mom?"

"I'm fine. We're all fine here. How are things going there?" When Henry gave no response, she phrased the question again.

"Umm. . .well. . ."

"Is there a problem, Henry?"

"I lost my key to the greenhouse. I've been lookin' everywhere I can think of, but it hasn't turned up."

"It's nothing to worry about, Son. Amy and Sylvia both have a key."

"I know, but. . ." Henry's voice trailed off.

"But what? Is there something going on I should know about?"

"Jah, but Amy told me not to say anything to you about it."

"About what?" Belinda pressed her trembling fingers against her chin. "I need to know what's going on, Henry."

"Okay, I'll tell ya. A couple days ago, someone got into the greenhouse during the night—or maybe it happened in the wee hours of the morning."

"Who was it? Did they take anything?"

"We don't know who it was, and nothing seemed to be missing. Amy told me that as soon as she has the time, she'll go to the hardware store and get another lock and all new keys made just in case we don't find mine. We'll ask Jesse Smucker if he has time to put it on." There was a slight pause before Henry continued. "We found a bunch of potted plants dumped over onto the floor."

"Maybe your *hund* or one of the *katze* got in and knocked over the plants."

"I don't think so, Mom. Blackie slept in my room that night, and I don't think any of our cats would be strong enough to knock over the pots. They were some of the heavier ones. Besides, how would a dog or one of the cats get the door to the greenhouse open?"

Belinda blinked rapidly as she clutched the folds in her dress. "I don't like the sound of this, Henry. I'm needed here, but I might be needed there more."

"It's okay, Mom. We're all fine, and there's no need for you to come home right now. If it'll make ya feel any better, I'll ask one of the men in our community to come over and take a look around."

"Jah, that would put my mind at ease. Oh, and Henry. . . I want you to let me know right away if anything else out of the ordinary happens at our place. Understood?"

"Jah, Mom."

"All right, Son. Give your sisters my love, and let them know that I'm praying for all of you."

"Okay. Bye, Mom."

"Goodbye, Henry."

When Belinda hung up the phone, she remained in the shed for several minutes, mulling things over. She felt sure that the vandalism that had been done to their mailbox, the sign out front, and now this happened for a reason. Someone either didn't like them or wanted their business to fail. The question was who and why?

Chapter 25

Virginia lay on the couch, reading a magazine she'd picked up at the pharmacy. She had slipped back into her comfy pajamas as soon as she got home. Swallowing still hurt, and the cherry-flavored lozenges weren't helping anymore. Virginia wanted so badly to feel better.

Thinking a cup of herbal tea might help, she pulled herself up and plodded into the kitchen. After filling a cup with water and putting it in the microwave, Virginia took a seat at the table. Once it was hot enough, she added a teabag along with a heaping spoonful of honey.

Once the tea had steeped, Virginia took the cup and went back to the living room. Sitting on the couch, she sipped the warm brew gratefully. Even though she wasn't much of a tea drinker, the soothing lemon herb tea went down easy, and it tasted pretty good with the addition of the honey.

Virginia hadn't started anything for supper and didn't plan to. Earl would have to either get them takeout or barbecue something on the grill. Of course, there wasn't much Virginia was in the mood to eat. She'd picked up a few things to help her cold and sore throat, but so far, it hadn't helped much. She'd gargled with salt water and nearly gagged. *There oughta be something that'll make me feel better. Maybe I should have gone to the ER.*

Virginia reclined on the couch again and had rolled onto her side when Earl came in through the front door. "How'd your day go?" he asked. "Do you feel any better?"

"Not really. I got some things at the pharmacy, but I still feel lousy." She pulled herself to a sitting position. "By the way. . .those tomato plants I got from the greenhouse across the street are dead. I think that young Amish woman sold me some defective plants."

He took a seat at the end of the couch, picked up her feet, and put them in his lap. "Oh, oh. I'm afraid it might be my fault they died."

Virginia coughed and massaged her throat. "How was it your fault?"

"The fellow at work who told me about putting horse manure on plants brought up the topic again today." Earl cleared his throat a couple of times, and spots of color erupted on his cheeks. "Said he forgot to mention that fresh manure was too strong to put on the plants. It needs to age, and mixing it with compost then letting it set a few months would be the best way."

"Oh boy. No wonder those plants keeled over."

"I'll go over to the greenhouse and get you two new plants, and then we can start over."

"I wanted to have a small garden, but with me not feeling well, I've lost my desire. So, don't worry about getting any new plants. I'll forget about gardening this year and buy our tomatoes at the grocery store or one of the local farmers' markets."

"Suit yourself, but I wouldn't mind going to the greenhouse and buying some new plants."

Virginia shook her head forcibly. "I don't want anything more to do with those people. The way they live is strange to me—sort of like the Quakers and pioneers did many years ago." She waited to see if Earl would comment, but when he remained silent, she added something else. "While I was at the pharmacy today, I saw a couple of Amish women there. They were speaking to each other in a strange, foreign-sounding language."

"It's Dutch, Virginia—or more to the point, Pennsylvania Dutch."

"Well, whatever it's called, it seems odd-sounding to me." She pulled her fingers through the ends of her tangled hair. "Anyway, back to my dilemma. They should have given me instructions on how to plant the items I bought. I hope that new greenhouse runs the King family right out of business."

Earl's eyes widened as his mouth fell open. "That's a hateful thing to say, Virginia. What have you got against those people?"

"I keep telling ya, but you're not listening—they're strange, and all the traffic on this road, mostly brought on by their business, gets on my nerves. I thought by moving to the country everything would be quiet and peaceful."

"I do listen to you, by the way, but I don't know what you think can be done about our neighbors. It's a new place, and we haven't even finished unpacking." He gave her feet a little squeeze. "Trust me, Virginia, you'll get used to it in time."

"No, I won't. I don't like livin' here, and I never will."

By the time Jared finished bidding a new job, it was almost noon, so he decided to stop at Isaac's Famous Grilled Sandwiches for lunch. He'd always enjoyed coming here to eat, since it was near the Choo Choo Barn model train layout and the Strasburg Train Shop.

Jared's fascination with trains began when he was a boy and he and his folks had traveled by train to see relatives in South Bend, Indiana. Someday he hoped to make a trip by train all the way out to the West Coast. He'd heard others who had gone there talk about the Rocky and Cascade Mountains, as well as the Pacific Ocean. One of Jared's friends who'd made such a trip came back with all kinds of interesting stories.

Jared had thought if he and Amy ever got married, he would take her on a trip to see some of the western states. Maybe they would be able to see the Grand Canyon or Yellowstone National Park.

But if I can't convince Amy to let me court her again, there will be no marriage or train ride out West. Jared gripped the reins as he guided Dandy to the hitching rail. *It wouldn't be any fun to take a trip like that by myself.*

When Jared entered the restaurant a short time later, he spotted

Lydia sitting at a table by herself. He placed his order then walked over to her table. "Mind if I join you?" he asked.

A deep dimple formed in her right cheek as she smiled up at him. "You're more than welcome to eat here at my table."

Jared pulled out a chair and sat down. "What's new with you these days, Lydia?"

"Nothing exciting. I'm still helping my mamm make quilted items. In fact, before I came here, I was out delivering some finished quilts to a couple of shops in the area that sell on consignment."

"Sounds like you're keeping busy then."

"Jah. How about you? Have you been doing a lot of roofing jobs this summer?"

"Sure have. I'm keeping my crew plenty busy, and I always make sure to have plenty of water on hand for my guys so they don't get overheated up there on the rooftops."

"I'm sure they appreciate it."

They visited more about the warm weather, and then Lydia posed another question. "Have you seen Amy lately?"

He gave a brief nod. "I stopped by the greenhouse the other day and bought a plant to give my mamm for her birthday."

"How's she doing?"

"You mean my mother?"

"No, I meant Amy."

"Oh. Well, it was great to see her and talk a short while. But I must tell you, I do have concerns about her."

"Anything specific?"

"She looked awful tired, and when we spoke, her voice sounded strained." Jared wasn't sure if he should tell Lydia what Henry had told him, but he decided to bring up the topic and see if she already knew about the vandalism that had taken place. "Did you know that there's been some damage done to the Kings' property?"

Her eyebrows rose as she gave a little gasp. "I had no idea anything like that was going on. Did Amy give you any details?"

"Not much, but Henry's actually the one who told me about the things that have been done." Jared spoke in Pennsylvania Dutch so none of the English people who might be nearby would understand what he said.

"What exactly was done?"

After Jared told Lydia all that he'd learned, he thought about Amy and hoped she wouldn't mind that he'd discussed this with Lydia. She had asked him not to say anything, and he didn't want to do anything that might push away any hopes of them getting back together. Even so, Lydia and Amy had always been close. Surely she wouldn't care if her best friend knew about the vandalism.

"Oh, my! Do you think somebody is out to destroy their business, or could someone in the King family have an enemy they don't know about?"

Jared shrugged. "It could be either one, I suppose, or maybe it's just some teenage kids sowing their wild oats. Henry mentioned that his friends might be upset because all of his chores have kept him from spending time with them."

"Have they called the sheriff or told anyone else about it?"

"Amy said they haven't notified the sheriff, but I don't know about friends. I doubt it though, since she asked me not to say anything." Jared paused for a quick breath. "I wish there was an adult male present on the property. I mean, Amy's brother is fine and all, but I really think if whoever is doing this had to deal with a man living there, it could deter the problem."

"I agree." Lydia picked up her glass and drank some water. "I'll have to stop by the greenhouse soon and talk to Amy."

"That's fine, but it would probably be best if you didn't tell her that I told you."

"Okay, I'll just drop by to see how things are going. Hopefully, since we've been friends a long time, Amy will open up to me."

Jared hoped that would be the case, but he had his doubts. He and Amy had been friends for some time too, but she hadn't opened up to him. If not for Henry blabbing, Jared wouldn't know a thing.

'I'm going up to the house to get my sack lunch and check on our sister," Amy called to Henry from her place behind the counter. Since there were no customers at the moment, she figured it would be okay to leave him alone in the greenhouse for the short time she'd be gone.

"Yeah, okay," Henry hollered from the other end of the building. "Would ya bring my lunch out too?"

"Of course, but you'd better come up here and keep an eye on things while I'm gone. If someone shows up, it wouldn't be good to leave the cash register unattended."

"No problem. I'm coming."

Amy left the greenhouse and hurried toward the house. Sylvia had developed a bad headache and gone up an hour ago to take something for the pain.

When Amy entered the house, she found Mary Ruth in the kitchen fixing lunch for the little ones.

"Where's Sylvia?" Amy asked.

"She's in there." Mary Ruth nodded with her head in the direction of the living room.

"I'd better check on her." Amy made her way to the living room, where she found her sister lying on the couch with a washcloth over her forehead.

"Has your *koppweh* gotten worse?" Amy rushed across the room.

Sylvia moaned. "Jah. I feel like a stampede of horses is inside my head. Sorry, Amy, but I don't think I can work in the greenhouse anymore today."

"Well, as long as we don't get too busy, I guess Henry and I will be fine on our own."

Amy leaned down and patted her sister's hand. "Is there anything I can get for you before I head back outside?"

"No, but would you please let Mary Ruth know I'll be staying inside? I hope she's willing to stay and watch the kinner until you close the greenhouse and come in for the day. With the way my head is pounding, I don't think I could manage to take care of

Allen and Rachel right now."

"I'll let her know. And don't worry about anything, Sylvia. Just get some rest."

"Danki." Sylvia's voice, filled with emotion, told Amy that her sister was close to tears.

Amy returned to the kitchen and took her lunch sack as well as Henry's from the refrigerator. Then she grabbed two bottles of water. "Sylvia's not feeling well enough to return to the greenhouse today, so she's going to stay here and rest." She looked at Mary Ruth. "Are you willing to stay until I close the greenhouse late this afternoon?"

"Most certainly." Mary Ruth smiled. "I'll try to keep the kinner quiet so your sister can sleep."

"You might suggest that she go to her room. If she remains in the living room, she'll never get any rest."

"I will." Mary Ruth moved closer to Amy. "Do you think you and your brother can manage things in the greenhouse without your sister's help?"

"We don't have much choice, but I believe we should be okay. Business has been kind of slow—probably because of the extreme heat, so I doubt we'll have too many customers this afternoon." Amy said goodbye and scooted out the door.

As she approached the greenhouse, she saw a horse and buggy at the rail. She hurried into the greenhouse and placed the water and lunch sacks on the counter.

Mom's old boyfriend stood nearby. "Good afternoon, Amy. I came to talk to your mother. Is she here?" Monroe asked.

"No, she's at my brother's place in New York, helping out with their new boppli."

"How long will she be gone?" He looked at Amy intently as though he didn't quite believe her.

"She should be back the week after next. Would you like to leave her a message?"

He moved his head from side to side but then changed it to a nod.

"Just tell her I came by to see her and that I'll come back when she gets home."

"Okay, I'll let her know." Amy was glad she could tell Monroe that her mother wasn't there. She still couldn't put her finger on it, but there was something about the man that made her nervous.

Monroe looked around as though he was inspecting the building. "So, there's no man here to protect you?"

Amy stood tall with her head erect. "My brother's here and we're getting along fine."

Monroe snorted as he looked at Henry, who stood a few feet from them sweeping some dirt off the floor. "That brother?"

"Jah."

"Why, he's hardly a man. He's not much more than a boy."

Amy's fingers curled into her palms. "Henry is old enough to do most chores a fully grown man can do."

"If you say so. Maybe I misjudged him."

Maybe you did. Amy bit back the words on her tongue. "Is there anything else I can help you with, Mr. Esh?"

He shook his head. "Nope. Just remember to tell your mamm I was here." He turned and went out the door.

Amy looked at Henry to see if he would comment, but he merely kept sweeping the floor.

She picked up one of the water bottles and took a drink, allowing the liquid to cool her mouth. *I hope that man doesn't keep coming around, and I especially hope he has no designs on our mother.*

Chapter 26

The following Monday as Amy finished watering the two hanging baskets on their front porch, she thought about her mother and how much she missed her.

I am glad Mom will be home soon. Even though they'd been managing the greenhouse okay, Amy felt as though she carried most of the burden. She'd handled all the customer relations so far, and Henry usually needed prompting to get things done each day.

Amy turned off the spigot and put away the hose then headed for the greenhouse to get things in order for the day.

The first thing she did after entering the building was to put the Open sign in the front window. Following that, Amy went to open the back door and check the plants, making sure everything looked in order. Ever since the incident with the potted plants, Amy couldn't help being a bit skittish when first coming in to open things up. She liked it better when she and Henry went in together. But not every day played out the way she wanted. This morning, Henry had been delayed for a bit while helping Sylvia take down some clocks to change the batteries.

After Amy gave a thorough look around and felt satisfied with things, she headed up front to check the shelves that displayed her mother's jellies, jams, and honey. She tidied up the pieces and moved back to the register. They'd been selling a lot of her mother's canned goods, which Amy knew would make Mom happy to hear when she returned.

A few minutes later, the front door opened. Amy was surprised when Lydia came in. It had been awhile since she'd been by, and the only time Amy had seen her friend recently was at church yesterday.

"How are you?" Lydia stepped up to the counter.

"Doing okay." Amy hoped her tone sounded sincere. "How are you?"

"I'm keeping busy helping my mamm but otherwise good." Lydia's voice lowered, although Amy didn't know why. She was the only customer in the building at the moment. "Is anything wrong, Amy? You would tell me if there was, wouldn't you?"

"Everything's fine. Why do you ask?"

"Because you're picking at your cuticles like you've always done whenever you're stressed about something."

Amy glanced down and pulled her hands apart. "It's just a bad *aagewehnet.*"

"Jah, a habit you've had since we were girls, but you only did it when you were stressed or worried about something." Lydia tapped her fingers against the countertop as if to drive the point home.

"Guess I am a little bit stressed," Amy conceded.

"About what?"

"My mamm's in New York right now, helping Michelle with her new baby."

"I didn't realize she'd given birth. What did she have?"

"A little boy. They named him after my daed."

Lydia smiled. "How nice. I bet that made your mom happy."

"It did."

"So, who's helping you run the greenhouse while she's gone?"

"Sylvia and Henry, although they're still at the house right now." Amy touched her temples while closing her eyes briefly. "Things have been really busy here, and there are times when it's hard to keep up even with my siblings' help."

"That would explain why you're tired, but what I see in your expression and tense posture is more than fatigue."

Amy sighed. "Well, we have had a few things go wrong since Mom's been gone."

"Such as?" Lydia leaned forward.

"Just a little episode with some pots of plants getting tipped over."

"Who tipped them over?"

"We don't know." Amy felt relieved when another customer came in. She didn't want to talk about their problems. And why bother? It wouldn't change a thing or keep more vandalism from happening.

"Did you come here to purchase anything?" she asked.

Lydia shook her head. "I just wanted to see you and find out how things are going because that's what best friends do."

"Danki for thinking of us." Amy stepped out from behind the counter and gave Lydia a hug. "Wish I could talk with you longer, but I have to see what the woman who just came in needs."

"I understand. I'll see you at church for our next gathering. In the meantime, if you need anything, please don't hesitate to ask."

"Thank you." Amy glanced toward the door and was glad to see her brother step in as Lydia left. "Will you please stay at the checkout counter until Sylvia comes out?" Amy asked when Henry approached.

"Okay, since you asked so nice." Henry moved away before Amy could comment. She didn't appreciate his sarcastic tone, but at least he hadn't refused to do as she asked.

Sylvia had spent more time in the house than she planned to, but after she and Henry had hung up the clocks, the baby needed to be fed. Afterward, even though Allen had been playing happily with his toys, he started crying and clinging to Sylvia. Mary Ruth had quite a time getting him calmed down so Sylvia could slip out the door. It tore at Sylvia's heartstrings to leave her children so she could work in the greenhouse, but until Mom returned, she had no other choice. She hoped at the end of Mom's two-week stay at Ezekiel's that she wouldn't decide to extend her trip. Sylvia was anxious to resume caring for her children full-time and letting Mom and Amy run the greenhouse with whatever help they could get from Henry. Each day of helping in the greenhouse became a little harder for Sylvia. Some days she wasn't sure she could force herself to go there at all.

As she stepped into the yard and headed for the building, a tour bus pulled in. The next thing Sylvia knew, about forty people got out, all talking at once as they headed for the greenhouse.

Sylvia drew in several quick, shallow breaths. She saw spots in front of her eyes and feared she might faint. No way could she handle being around so many strangers crowded into the greenhouse. She wanted to turn around and run back to the house, but that would leave her sister and brother to deal with the people on their own.

Sylvia rushed in ahead of the tourists. She found Henry sitting behind the counter doodling on a piece of paper. "What are you doing? Where's Amy?"

"I'm doing what she told me while she waits on a customer." Henry pointed to the nearest aisle. "But since you're here now, you can take my place. I've got some things I need to do outside of the greenhouse."

"No, please don't leave me." Sylvia looked toward the open door as people from the bus began filing in. "With all these folks here, I might need you."

Henry stepped off the stool. "You'll be fine. As I said, there's something I need to do." Before Sylvia could protest, he made a dash for the door.

"Oh, this is so exciting." One of the tourists smiled at Sylvia. "It's my first time in Amish country, and I'm having so much fun."

Sylvia forced her lips to form a smile. *Amy. Hurry up, Amy. You're better at talking to people than I am.*

Wiping her damp hands along the front of her black apron, Sylvia went behind the counter and took a seat. Her rigid form relaxed a bit when the noisy group of people dispersed down all five aisles.

"You look a bit overwhelmed," the man who had been driving the bus said. "I take it you're not used to having a bunch of eager tourists roaming around your greenhouse."

"There have been a few tour groups stop by but not since I've been working here." Sylvia took in a few more deep breaths.

"Well, this could be your lucky day." The man grinned at Sylvia. "This group of people has been buying stuff from every store we've stopped at so far. You may make a nice profit today."

Sylvia wasn't sure how best to respond, so she forced herself to offer the man another smile.

"From here we'll be stopping at the Strasburg Railroad so that those who want to can take the short train ride." He reached into his pocket and pulled out a package of gum. "Then our last stop of the day will be at an Amish farmhouse in Paradise for a homemade sit-down supper. I'm sure everyone on the bus will enjoy that."

She nodded. *I wish this man would stop talking to me. I need some time by myself before anyone comes up to the counter with a purchase.*

Sylvia craned her neck to see where Amy had gone. *Sister, why aren't you coming to rescue me?* She glanced toward the door. *Henry, where did you run off to? Mom wouldn't like it if she knew you weren't here helping like you're supposed to be.*

The more Sylvia thought about her situation, the more panicked she became. Sweat beaded on her forehead and trickled down her cheeks. Was it the heat and humidity inside the building or just her nerves?

Sylvia heaved a sigh of relief when she saw Amy heading down aisle 2 with four women following her. Each carried some item—a plant stake, a jar of honey, a candle made of beeswax, and a brass wind chime. Hopefully, once they paid for their purchases, they'd leave the greenhouse and get back on the bus.

As if she sensed Sylvia's distress, Amy joined her behind the counter. "I'll do the talking, and you can take the money and make change if needed," Amy whispered as she bent close to Sylvia's ear.

"Okay." Sylvia pressed a palm to her chest. Now that her sister was here, she felt a little better.

"Where's Henry?" Amy asked after all the customers had left.

Sylvia shrugged. "I don't know. He said he had something to do outside."

Amy frowned. "Well, he'd better get back in here soon. One of those tourists opened a bag of potting soil, and then someone else came along and knocked it over." She puffed out her cheeks. "So now there's a mess to clean up and no Henry."

"Should I go outside and look for him?" Sylvia offered.

"Jah, if you don't mind."

"Don't mind at all. In fact, I could use a bit of fresh air."

When Sylvia left the greenhouse, she headed to the barn, figuring her brother may have gone in there. Although she saw no sign of him, Sylvia detected the unmistakable odor of cigarette smoke. *Now who would have been in here smoking? Could one of those tourists have wandered into the barn to look around and lit a cigarette?*

She cupped her hands around her mouth. "Henry! Are you in here, Brother?"

Except for the gentle nicker of one of their horses, all was quiet within the wooden structure.

"Henry," she called again. Still no response.

Sylvia left the barn and was about to go up to the house to see if Henry had gone there, when he stepped into the yard.

"Where have you been all this time?" Sylvia slapped both hands against her hips. "Amy needs you, and. . ."

"Oh, she always needs me for somethin'. What's she want this time?"

"Someone spilled a bag of potting soil, so. . ."

"And I'm supposed to clean it up?"

"Jah."

Henry's eyes narrowed as he clenched his jaw. "I always have to do the dirty work, and I never get to have any fun." His voice rose. "I'm gettin' sick and tired of it."

"Henry, you're just as much a part of this family as the rest of us, and we all need to pull together."

"Well, I didn't see you doin' much to help out till Mom left, but then you didn't have much choice."

Sylvia recoiled. Her brother's sharp words stung like fire. "You have no right to speak to me like that," she shot back. "You don't know what it's like for me to be faced with two kinner to raise and no husband."

Henry glared at her. "Well, you don't know what it's like to have your dad and older brother killed and be stuck with all the chores they used to do. And besides that, I miss the fun stuff Dad, Abe, and I used to do."

Before Sylvia could think of a response, Henry tromped off to the greenhouse.

Tears sprang to her eyes. *None of us has been the same since the accident that took three precious lives, and I'm not sure we'll ever be again.*

That evening while Amy and Sylvia prepared supper, they talked about the events of the day.

Amy went to the refrigerator and took out a package of ground beef. "Thanks to all those tourists who came in, we sold more today than I expected."

Sylvia bobbed her head. "I would have been even more nervous than I was if you hadn't been up at the counter with me."

Amy joined her sister by the cupboard, where she was busy slicing fresh tomatoes to go on the burgers they'd soon be grilling. "You haven't always been uncomfortable around people. Is there any specific reason they bother you so now?"

Sylvia's features tensed up. "My nerves have been on edge ever since Toby, Dad, and Abe died. And now, with the vandalism that has occurred here, I wake up every morning wondering if something else unpleasant has happened."

"We can't live in fear, and worrying doesn't add even one more minute to our lives." Amy set the ground beef on the counter and placed her hand on Sylvia's shoulder. "Besides, the vandalism that's been done is minor. No one's been hurt or even threatened."

Sylvia lowered her head. "But they could be, and I can't help but be afraid. The fact that some stranger is trespassing on our property, doing damage to things, is creeping me out."

"It's best not to worry—especially about things that are beyond our control. We need to pray every day and put our faith in God. And it wouldn't hurt to ask Him to put a hedge of protection around us."

When Sylvia gave no response, Amy added, "I'm praying for you too, dear sister."

Sylvia's chin lowered, almost to her chest. "You can pray all you want, but I doubt it'll do any good."

Amy felt helpless at that moment. All she could do was lean on her heavenly Father. She closed her eyes. *Lord, we need Your strength to get through this time of trial. Please help me to be a reflection of You to my family.*

Amy wouldn't say anything more to Sylvia right now. If her sister's faith was going to be restored, it would come through loving words and lots of prayer.

Chapter 27

"I can't believe Mom will finally be coming home tomorrow." Sylvia wiped her hands on a paper towel after she finished clearing their messy supper dishes. They'd had baked spareribs with barbecue sauce, and as good as the meal had been, their plates showed the telltale sign of sticky sauce.

Amy smiled as she took out the dishtowel in readiness to dry the dishes her sister would soon wash. "I wonder if she's as excited to see us as we are to see her."

"No doubt she is, but it will be hard for her to leave Ezekiel and his family. I'm sure Mom enjoyed getting to know her new grandson and spending time with sweet little Angela Mary." Sylvia rinsed off their dishes and put them in the warm, soapy water that awaited them.

"Jah, but she'll be equally happy to be here with us and your adorable kinner."

"You're right, I'm sure." Sylvia sloshed the sudsy dishrag over a plate, rinsed it well, and placed it in the dish drainer. "If Ezekiel and his family moved back here, it wouldn't be a problem for Mom at all. We'd all be together in the same town and could be there for each other when there was a need."

Amy nodded. "I agree, but Mom's dead set against them leaving Clymer. They're settled there, and our brother's happy with his business and new role as minister. Mom thinks it wouldn't be fair to ask him to give that all up."

"Nothing's fair. Not in this life anyway." Sylvia slapped the dish-rag against the next plate so hard, some water splashed up, almost hitting her in the face.

Amy didn't respond. It was difficult to see her sister in this state. Although Sylvia needed to come to terms with her bitterness and anger toward God in her own way and time, Amy hung to the hope that things would eventually get better.

She heard a knock on the front door and voices in the living room. It sounded like Henry was talking to someone. Amy tried to listen while drying another dish, hoping to hear who the other person might be. *I hope it's not Monroe. He's been wanting to see our mamm. Is he interested in her the way he was when they were young adults?* Something about the man still didn't set well with Amy.

A few minutes later, Henry entered the room. "My friend Seth is here. He wants me to sleep over at his place tonight and then go fishin' with him tomorrow morning."

Amy felt relieved that at least it wasn't Monroe. "Tomorrow's Saturday, Henry, and as you know, that's always a big day at the greenhouse. Sorry, but you'll need to be here to help out."

"Not only that," Sylvia spoke up, "but Mom's coming home tomorrow, and she'd be disappointed if you weren't here."

"Great! You're both ganging up on me now." Henry's brows drew together. "If Mom leaves there in the morning, she won't be here till late afternoon. I'll be home by then."

"Sorry, Brother, but the answer is no." Amy spoke with authority.

Henry looked back toward the other room, where Seth obviously waited. "I think I've been more than helpful since Mom left for Clymer. I've put up with bein' told what to do the whole time, and I'm sick and tired of it. You two ain't my mamm," Henry mumbled as he tromped out of the room.

A moment later, Amy heard the front door open and slam shut.

Sylvia looked at Amy. "That didn't go too well, did it?"

"It never does unless Henry gets his way. One minute he promises to cooperate, and the next minute he gets belligerent and shows us his temper." Amy sighed. "I'll be glad when Mom is here so she can deal with our brother, and I won't have to be the voice of authority."

Once the dishes were done, and the little ones had been put to bed, Amy and Sylvia retired to the living room to do some mending and enjoy a glass of cold root beer Mary Ruth had brought them this morning. She said Lenore's husband had made it with a recipe that had been handed down in his family.

"This root beer is sure good, isn't it?" Amy licked off some of the cool liquid that had stuck to her upper lip.

Sylvia nodded. "Are you sure you don't want some, Henry?"

Henry looked up from the newspaper he'd been reading. "No thanks. In fact, I'm headin' upstairs to bed."

"So early?" Amy glanced at the clock on the far wall that played music on the hour. "It's not like you to be tired at eight o'clock in the evening."

"Who says I'm tired? I just wanna be alone." Henry tossed the paper on the coffee table and stood. Without telling them good night, he ambled out of the room and clomped up the stairs.

"Maybe he's punishing himself for his harsh words earlier by not having any root beer and going to bed before he normally would," Sylvia commented.

Amy set her empty glass on the side table by her chair. "I think it's just his way of trying to show us that he can make some decisions for himself."

"Well, whatever the case, I'm kind of glad Henry went to bed early. He's beginning to get on my nerves." Sylvia leaned back in her chair. "Truth be told, nearly everything bothers me these days, and I'll be glad when I don't have to work in the greenhouse anymore."

Amy's chin tilted down as she frowned. "I was rather hoping you'd continue to work there with me and Mom. It would be like old times, before you got married."

Sylvia's mouth twisted grimly. "Being around so many people is too stressful for me, Amy. My place is with the kinner. They need their mamm not a babysitter who isn't part of our family."

"Hasn't Mary Ruth done a good job taking care of Rachel and Allen?"

Sylvia nodded. "But she's not family, and even if she was, I don't want to work in the greenhouse once Mom returns home. It's just that simple." Sylvia rose from her chair. "I am going to check on the kinner, and then I think I'll also go to bed."

"Oh, okay. I'm going to stay up for a while and do a bit more mending."

"All right then. Good night, Amy."

"Night. I hope you sleep well."

Sylvia mumbled something Amy couldn't quite understand and quickly left the room.

Amy set her mending aside and picked up her Bible to read a few verses from Psalms. She couldn't let her discouragement tear down her faith. The best remedy was reading God's Holy Word.

"Giddyap, Dandy. Don't be such a slowpoke." Jared snapped the reins. He'd left Lydia's house a short time ago and was eager to get home. He'd gone there to give them a bid on a new roof for their house, and Lydia's mother had invited him to stay for supper. Jared didn't want to be impolite, so he had accepted the invitation. He'd hoped it would give him a chance to talk more to Lydia about Amy, but that never happened. Lydia's mother had monopolized the conversation. Jared wondered if she'd been trying to impress him. Darlene kept trying to get Jared to eat more and then almost insisted that he have seconds on dessert. When it was time for him to leave, she seemed intent on keeping him there by bringing up even more topics. Lydia's poor dad barely got a word in during supper because his wife monopolized the conversation.

Maybe it's just as well that I left when I did, Jared thought. *Lydia's mamm is a bit of a gossip, and I wouldn't want her listening to or commenting on anything either Lydia or I might have said concerning my broken relationship with Amy.*

As Jared's horse and buggy approached the Kings' place that evening, he saw a car pull up along the road about six feet from the Kings' driveway. A few seconds later, Amy's teenage brother ran out from behind some bushes and got in the passenger's side of the vehicle. It was well after nine o'clock and almost dark. *I wonder where Henry could be going at this hour. I doubt that Amy or Sylvia would allow him to go anyplace at this time of the night.*

Jared was tempted to stop at the house and say something to Amy or her sister but swiftly concluded that it was none of his concern. *If they knew Henry was out and about, they might not appreciate me butting into their business.*

Clymer

The following morning, Belinda said a tearful goodbye to Ezekiel, Michelle, and the little ones. It had been a joy to spend the last two weeks with them, but Michelle insisted she was doing well enough to be on her own now, and it was time for Belinda to go home.

"We promise to come for a visit as soon as the baby is a little older and Michelle gets all of her strength back." Ezekiel gave Belinda another hug.

She sniffed. "That would nice. We'll look forward to it."

"Danki for all you did to help out." Michelle, holding the baby, hugged Belinda with her other arm. "I couldn't have managed without you."

Belinda leaned down and kissed Angela Mary's soft cheek. She tried to capture in her mind the softness she'd felt. "Be good for your mamm and help her out when you can, okay my sweet girl?" As usual, Belinda spoke to her granddaughter in Pennsylvania Dutch since the child spoke no English yet.

The little girl nodded soberly, then her face broke into a wide smile.

It melted Belinda's heart, seeing the special look on her grand-daughter's face. *Oh, how selfish I feel right now. If only it were possible, I'd bring all of them home with me to Strasburg.*

Belinda kissed baby Vernon's forehead. "I hope he doesn't grow too much before I see him again."

"Maybe by the first week of September we can come for a visit." Ezekiel put Belinda's bags in her driver's vehicle. "Tell everyone hello and please give them our love. We pray for each of you every day."

"Prayers are always appreciated, and we'll pray for you too."

Belinda gave them all one last hug before climbing into the passenger's seat. With a lump in her throat, she waved goodbye as the van backed out of the driveway. Even though Belinda felt sad about leaving her family here, she had something to look forward to at home. Later today, Belinda would be hugging Sylvia, Amy, Henry, and her other two grandchildren. She could hardly wait to see everyone and find out how each of them was doing.

Strasburg

For a second time, Amy stood by the kitchen doorway and called Henry to come eat breakfast. "He should have been down here an hour ago to do his outside chores," she told Sylvia.

Her sister nodded. "Maybe he forgot to set his alarm clock."

After a few more times of calling him, Amy went upstairs. She knocked on his door, and when there was no answer, she opened it. Henry was not in his room, but the bed had been made. She lifted her gaze to the ceiling. *If Henry made his bed without a reminder, that's a first. I wonder what came over that boy.*

Amy went back to the kitchen and let Sylvia know that their brother was not in his room. "But the strange thing is, his bed was made, and neatly at that," she added.

"Since he knows Mom's coming home later today, maybe he wants to make a good impression," her sister replied as she set the table.

"Or maybe," Amy said, "our brother was trying to impress us by making his bed so we won't mention anything to Mom about him being uncooperative most of the time while she was gone." Amy moved toward the back door. "Guess I'll go outside and tell him breakfast is ready. He probably got up earlier than usual and is still out in the barn taking care of the livestock."

"When you see Henry, tell him to hurry because the quiche is getting cold."

"Will do." Amy stepped into the yard but saw no sign of Henry. All seemed quiet as though her sibling was nowhere around. She went to the barn but didn't see or hear any sign of her brother there, even though she called his name several times.

Amy was about to leave the barn when she spotted an empty cigarette pack on the floor. *I wonder where that came from.* She picked it up and tossed it into the trash can near the barn entrance.

Back outside, Amy checked inside the greenhouse, pump house, potting shed, and even in the phone shack, but her brother wasn't in any of those places.

She tapped her chin. *This is so odd. What's going on here this morning? I'll look one more place before I begin to panic.*

In desperation, she walked down the driveway to see if he might have gone to the mailbox to mail a letter or get the mail. She and Sylvia had been so busy yesterday that neither of them had taken time to get the mail.

Amy went to the box and put the key in the lock. Sure enough, there was mail inside. *At least I know my brother didn't take care of this.* Holding onto the stack of letters, she looked up and down the road. No sign of Henry, but Amy noticed the neighbor man leaving for work and his wife waving to him from their front porch. Amy gave a wave too before heading back to the house.

"Did you find Henry?" Sylvia asked when Amy entered the kitchen.

She placed the envelopes on the counter near the door. Full of frustration, Amy shook her head. "The only thing I found was this morning's mail. There was no sign of our brother in the yard or any of our buildings. She made no mention of the cigarette pack she'd seen in the barn. No point in upsetting Sylvia further. "I'm worried. I think I should hitch my horse to the buggy and go looking for him."

"That's a good idea." Sylvia's gaze flitted around the room, never settling on any one thing. When she looked at Amy again, tears welled in her eyes. "If we haven't found Henry by the time Mom gets home, I don't know what we're going to tell her."

Chapter 28

"I bet our bruder never slept in his bed at all. I believe he may have snuck out of the house after you and I were in bed and gone over to Seth's." Amy looked at Sylvia with a firm resolve. "I can't believe it. Neither of us ever did anything like that during our *yuchend*. Yet our kid brother did even though he knew it was wrong." She drummed her fingers on the counter. "Henry's not going to get away with it, and he can't use the excuse of being young, either. If he's not here by the time Mom arrives, she's going to be very umgerennt."

"It sounds to me like you're a little upset yourself." Sylvia gestured to the kitchen table. "Why don't we take a seat? We can talk about the situation while we eat our sausage and vegetable quiche. It'll give us a chance to decide what we should say when Henry's confronted."

"Okay." Amy moved over to her chair but didn't sit down. In addition to the egg dish, there was fresh fruit and moist banana bread. It was a shame to have all this nice food and their brother wasn't here to eat it with them.

Normally, Amy's mouth would water in anticipation but not today. The concern she felt about Henry had diminished her appetite.

"We'll have plenty of leftovers for Mom to have tomorrow morning." Sylvia poured herself a glass of orange juice and gave one to Amy. "When we're finished eating breakfast, you can go over to Seth's place and see if Henry's there."

"I suppose it could wait till after we eat, but while I'm over there, you'll be stuck opening the greenhouse and working by yourself until I get back."

Sylvia stood next to the table with one hand clasping the other at the elbow. "I—I hadn't thought about that. I'm not sure I can handle being by myself in the greenhouse with customers." Perspiration beaded on her forehead.

Amy had hoped by the end of these two weeks, her sister's apprehension would have lessened some and she'd be more at ease around other people. Amy certainly felt her sister's stress. *I think it's necessary to give Sylvia some relief right now. If I were my sister, what would I need to hear?*

She slipped her arm around Sylvia's waist. "Maybe you'd rather go after Henry once Mary Ruth gets here."

Sylvia shook her head. "I can't drive the horse and buggy yet. It would make me too nervous."

"Then I'll go—either now or after we eat our breakfast."

Sylvia pulled out a chair and sat down. "I am really not that hungry, but let's eat now. Once Mary Ruth shows up, you can go over to Seth's place and I'll open the greenhouse."

"Danki, Sister." Amy sat too.

"After we've finished eating, I'll check on the kinner and see if either of them is awake. They were both sleeping soundly when I left the room, so I decided it would be best not to disturb them."

"I agree. Now shall we bow for prayer?"

Sylvia bowed her head, though Amy suspected her sister wasn't praying.

Heavenly Father, Amy silently prayed, *if I don't get to Seth's house before Henry leaves there, please bring him home safe.*

When Amy's prayer ended, she opened her eyes. About to reach for the salt and pepper, she lowered her hand when she heard the back door open and shut. A few seconds later, Henry stepped into the kitchen. His hair looked disheveled, and his clothes were a rumpled mess like he'd slept in them. *Thank You, Lord, for bringing my brother home safe and sound.*

Amy left her chair and marched up to her brother. "Where have you been, young man?" She stood with both hands firmly against her hips. "You were gone all night, weren't you?"

He gave a slow nod.

"That wasn't a schmaert thing to do, sneaking out at night and without our permission."

"Where did you go? Were you at Seth's?" This question came from Sylvia, who had also left her seat and turned to face their brother.

Silence filled the room as they stood waiting for Henry's response.

"Jah, I went over to Seth's, and I spent the night." Henry lowered his head. "Figured I'd be back early this morning before you missed me, but we overslept."

Amy was so angry, her hands shook. She was about to give Henry a piece of her mind, but Sylvia spoke again. "You'd better get cleaned up, Brother, and then eat some breakfast. You have chores yet to do, and we expect you to be in the greenhouse on time for opening."

Henry stared at his feet and then shuffled out of the room.

Amy looked at Sylvia and heaved a sigh. "Wait till Mom hears about this."

"Maybe we shouldn't say anything to her," Sylvia responded.

"How come?"

"It might take the joy out of her trip and make her wish she hadn't gone at all. Besides, our brother seemed quite desperate to have some sort of fun yesterday."

"Yes," Amy said, "and then he went ahead and got his way without our consent."

Sylvia frowned deeply. "He sure did, but honestly, did he look happy this morning?"

"It didn't appear so to me."

"So how about if we keep quiet about Henry's escapade?" Sylvia suggested again. "We don't want to stir things up when our mamm gets home."

"I see your point. And with Mom here to take control of things, it's not likely that Henry will pull another stunt like that."

Soon, the soft patter of little feet came into the kitchen. Amy bent down and scooped her nephew into her arms. "Guder mariye, sweet boy."

Allen grinned at her.

Sylvia stepped over and tickled her son's chin. "Are you hungerich?"

He bobbed his head.

"I'll take Allen back and get him dressed while you fix his cereal. We won't be long." Amy left with the giggling boy in her arms.

"Where'd you go last night?" Jared's mother asked as he sat at the table with his folks, eating breakfast. "I heard you come in, but your daed and I had already gone up to our room and were in bed."

"Figured as much." Jared drank the rest of his apple juice. "I had supper at Lydia's house."

"Is that so?" Mom leaned slightly forward. "Does that mean the two of you are courting?"

Jared shook his head. "I went over to her folks' to give them a bid on a new roof, and Lydia's mamm asked me to stay for supper. I didn't want to be rude, so I accepted."

In order to take the pressure off himself, Jared turned the conversation in a different direction. "On the way home, I saw something that has me kind of worried."

Jared's dad tipped his head. "What was that, Son?"

"As I was going past the Kings' place, I saw Henry run out of the bushes and jump in a car that had stopped along the side of the road." Jared squeezed the bridge of his nose. "It was after nine o'clock, which seemed a bit too late for Amy's brother to be out with a friend."

"How do you know it was a friend?" Mom asked.

He shrugged. "I don't for sure, but I suspect it was. I almost stopped to talk to Amy about it but decided it was none of my business, so I kept going in the direction of home."

"You did the right thing, Son." Dad thumped Jared's arm. "A person who goes around stickin' their nose in other people's business is likely to get it chopped off."

Mom squinted her eyes at Dad. "That's an awful thing to say, Emmanuel. Besides, I wouldn't be one bit surprised if Amy's brother was up to no good. He has a sneaky look about him."

Dad shook his head. "Now how in the world can you tell if someone's sneaky by lookin' at them?"

"I just can. In my younger days, I was a schoolteacher, don't ya know?" Mom added a spoonful of sugar to her coffee cup and stirred it around. "None of the scholars in my school could pull the wool over my eyes because I could tell by their expressions whether they were telling the truth or trying to pull a fast one."

"Well, Ava dear, even if you're right about Belinda King's boy, it's none of our business." Dad gave Jared's arm another thump. "Right, Son?"

Jared managed a smile, but he couldn't help feeling concerned about Henry. He hoped the boy wasn't hanging around with a rough crowd, which could eventually get him into trouble.

Virginia woke up in a stupor and crawled out of bed. *I need to get some coffee into me to clear my head.*

As she stood at the window, after opening the shade, Virginia thought about how yesterday she'd seen a beautiful cardinal in their yard. *Maybe I could ask Earl to get me a nice birdfeeder to hang in that tree where the cardinal sat. It would be nice to see birds in the yard more regularly.*

Virginia yawned. She didn't feel like she'd gotten a good night's sleep and could barely keep her eyes open, yet she didn't want to go back to bed. She'd probably feel worse when she woke up again. At least she'd finally gotten over her cold and sore throat. That was something positive to think about.

When she reached the kitchen and saw the clock, Virginia realized that her husband had already left for work. *It was nice of Earl to let me sleep in. I sure must have needed it, because I slept right through him getting ready for work.*

The coffeemaker was turned off, but if Earl had used it this morning, the coffee might still be warm. Curious, she touched the carafe, but it felt cold. Virginia poured some into a mug and heated it in the microwave.

Think I'll go out on the front porch and see what's happening across the road. She stepped out the door and took a seat on one of the chairs.

Last evening, Virginia had seen the neighbors' teenage boy getting into a car that had pulled onto the shoulder of the road. She could only imagine what a teenager would be doing out at that time of the night with his friends. Why hadn't the vehicle pulled into the Kings' driveway by the house to pick him up? In Virginia's suspicious mind, it didn't add up.

She squinted against the glare of the sun and spotted Amy outside on the lawn with a toddler. They seemed to be looking at something in the grass, but Virginia had no idea what it was. It was endearing to see them together. Virginia wished her kids were still little and she could be with them right now. She'd sure do things different if she could raise her children again.

When Amy was about to bring Allen inside, she spotted Henry standing by the fence dropping birdseed on the ground.

"What are you doing?" she asked.

"I'm feeding the pretty crow that likes to hang around here all the time. I've discovered, in addition to eatin' lots of bugs, he likes birdseed."

Amy frowned as she gazed at the black bird. It did have a blue tinge to its tail feathers, although it was not what she would call *pretty*.

"That noisy crow is nothing but a nuisance, and if you feed it, it'll just keep hanging around."

"I thought you liked birds."

"Not *grappe*."

"What have you got against crows?"

"This one in particular makes too much of a racket." Amy didn't mention that the crow always seemed to make an appearance right before or after something bad happened. Henry would probably laugh and say she was superstitious.

"Just don't keep feeding it," she warned. "There are enough birds around here already."

Henry said nothing, but the crow responded. *Caw. . .Caw. . . Caw. . .*

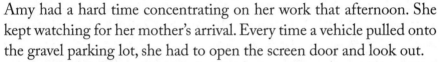

Amy had a hard time concentrating on her work that afternoon. She kept watching for her mother's arrival. Every time a vehicle pulled onto the gravel parking lot, she had to open the screen door and look out.

At four o'clock, when there were no customers in the building, Amy heard another vehicle pull in. She hurried to open the door and was pleased to see their driver's van pulling in.

"Mom's here," Amy hollered to Sylvia and Henry. They joined her as she stepped outside.

"It's so good to see all of you!" Mom stepped down from the van and rushed forward.

"It's good to see you too. Welcome home!" Sylvia hugged Mom first, followed by Amy and Henry.

They all tried to talk at once, and after Mom got her luggage and paid the driver, she suggested they go into the greenhouse.

"Everything looks good." She smiled. "I appreciate how you all handled things so well while I was gone."

Amy wanted to tell Mom that things hadn't gone well all the time, but she kept quiet, not wanting to ruin their mother's happy homecoming.

"Tell us all about the new boppli," Sylvia said after they'd entered the building.

"He's a sweet baby." Mom gave them an update on Ezekiel and his family. "He said they would try to come see us in early September."

"Oh, that'd be so nice." Amy smiled and gave Mom another hug.

"Now I'd like to go to the house and see my other two precious grandchildren." Mom looked at Sylvia. "Since there's no activity in the greenhouse right now, why don't you go with me?"

"That's a fine idea."

Mom and Sylvia locked arms and headed out the door. "Amy, as soon as you close the greenhouse for the day, please come right up to the house so we can visit more while we fix our evening meal," Mom called over her shoulder.

"Okay, Mom. Henry and I will both be there."

When the door shut behind Mom and Sylvia, Amy turned to face her brother. "Please make sure that all the plants are watered well. We can't afford to have any of them die from lack of water on these hot days like we've been having."

"Jah, okay." He scuffed the toe of his boot on the concrete floor. "Will ya do me a favor, Amy, and not say anything to Mom about me bein' gone last night?"

"I won't say anything this time, but if you ever pull another stunt like that, Mom will be the first to know." She shook her finger in Henry's face. "And I guarantee you, she won't like it one bit."

Chapter 29

"Guder mariye," Amy said when she entered the kitchen Sunday morning and found her mother at the table going through a stack of mail Amy had set aside for her.

Mom looked up and smiled. "Good morning."

"Did you sleep well?"

"Jah. It felt good to be back in my own bed." Mom gestured to the mail. "I surely appreciate all that you, Sylvia, and Henry did while I was gone. Just keeping up with sorting the mail and paying bills must have kept you busy, not to mention running the greenhouse, plus cooking and cleaning here in our home."

"We were glad to do it so you could be a help to Ezekiel's family." Amy poured them each a cup of coffee and took a seat at the table.

"It was my privilege to help, and I enjoyed my time with Ezekiel, Michelle, and the little ones. But I have to admit, it's real nice to be home. I thought about all of you a lot and always wondered how things were going."

"We managed okay, Mom."

"How did Henry do while I was gone?"

"We had a few problems but nothing I couldn't handle."

"What kind of problems?" Mom tipped her head.

"He complained about some of the chores I asked him to do." Amy drank some of her coffee before she proceeded. "Henry was also a bit careless. Somehow he managed to lose his key to the greenhouse doors, but Lenore's husband came over and put new locks on both doors, so now we have new keys for everyone but Henry. I don't trust him with it. He's so careless, he might lose a new key too."

Mom rubbed her forehead. "So, he never found the old one?"

Amy shook her head. "Henry looked everywhere for it, and so did I."

"That's not good. What if someone else found it and. . ." Mom's voice trailed off as she looked at Amy with a serious expression. "Henry told me about plants that had been dumped over. Why didn't you call Ezekiel's and tell me what happened? Didn't you think I had the right to know?"

"I didn't want you to worry about something that was out of your control." Amy patted her mother's arm. "And you needn't look so concerned now, because not all the plants in the greenhouse were ruined, and none of us were harmed."

Mom sat staring at the table. Amy could almost read her thoughts. Between hearing about the missing key and the overturned pots, her dear mother was undoubtedly worried.

And with good reason. Amy chose not to mention that Henry had snuck out of the house last night, since she'd promised she wouldn't say anything unless he did something like that again. *So, I'll keep quiet for now, but if he messes up again, I won't hesitate to tell Mom.*

Monday morning, Sylvia sat beside Allen on the couch, tying his shoe. In a few years, her precious boy would be old enough to tie it himself.

He looked up at Sylvia with such a tender expression it brought tears to her eyes. Allen reminded her so much of his father—not just his curly black hair. It was mostly the determined set of his jaw when he wanted something. Sylvia could still see Toby's unwavering expression the day he proposed marriage. He'd proclaimed his love to her and said he'd do everything in his power to be a good husband and provider. And he had been, right up until his untimely death.

Sylvia forced her musings aside and finished tying her son's shoes.

Then she lifted him onto her lap and stroked his cheek. "You're such a *gut bu.*"

"Good boy," he repeated in Pennsylvania Dutch.

"Jah, a very good boy."

When Allen began to squirm, she allowed him to get down from the couch. He turned, grinned at her, and then darted across the room for his toy box.

Sylvia leaned against the cushion behind her back and sighed. It was a relief not to work in the greenhouse today. She hoped Mom and Amy wouldn't expect her to work there anymore, because being here with her children was where she belonged, not dealing with anxious or curious customers.

Hearing Rachel's cry from the bedroom, where she'd been sleeping, Sylvia rose from the couch. Today would be a better day for her than the last two weeks.

The greenhouse had been open only a few minutes when Monroe showed up. He seemed to be dressed in nicer clothes today and smelled of some kind of men's cologne—or maybe it was his aftershave. Belinda thought it looked strange to see an Amish man Monroe's age clean-shaven, but since he'd never married, it made sense. *I hope he didn't get all fancied up on my account. Maybe Monroe has some appointment to go to later.*

She smiled and tried to be polite, but the strange way he looked at her made Belinda apprehensive.

"You look real nice today, Belinda." Monroe moved close to the counter where she sat. "It's good to see that you're back home where you belong." His brows wrinkled as the aroma of his cologne grew stronger. "You know, it's not safe for you and your kinner to be alone without a man in the house."

"My children are all grown, and they did fine while I was gone. In fact, we're all getting along well on our own."

"Are you sure about that?" He leaned on the counter so close that

Belinda could feel and smell his minty breath.

Fussing with her apron ties, she moved slightly away. "I am quite sure. Now if you don't mind, Monroe, I have work to do here."

He glanced around. "Doesn't look like you're all that busy. In fact, at the moment, I'm the only customer in the building."

"If you're a customer then I assume you came to buy something?"

"Well, I . . ."

"If so, either my daughter or son can help you." She gestured toward the other end of the greenhouse and the row in front of the checkout counter.

"I really don't need anything right now, but I'll wander around a bit and see what all you have." He grinned at her and headed down the aisle she had gestured to. As Monroe meandered, he seemed to be inspecting things as he went along.

About the time several customers showed up, Monroe came back up the aisle and said goodbye to Belinda. "I'll be back soon to see how you are doing."

When he went out the door, Belinda felt her rigid body begin to relax. Although at one point in her young adult life she'd thought she might care for Monroe, she had no romantic feelings for him now. Belinda was still in love with Vernon and figured she always would be.

When she felt sure Mom could handle things in the greenhouse with only Henry's help, Amy slipped out to get the mail. She took a quick side tour and looked at the garden to see if anything would need picking later. The tomatoes looked like they were doing well, and so did the radishes. *Sometime later I'll come out with a container and collect what is ready.* Amy turned and headed down the driveway.

When she reached their box, she met Virginia, who was also getting her mail.

Amy said hello and tried to make conversation, but Virginia wasn't sociable.

"How are those tomato plants I sold you?"

Virginia wrinkled her nose. "They both died a few days after I put 'em in the ground."

"I'm so sorry. You should have come over right away and told us about it. If you'd like to bring them back, we'll gladly refund your money or give you some new plants."

Virginia shook her head. "The plants weren't bad. It was the fresh horse manure I put in the dirt when I planted them. It wasn't my idea, you understand. I was only doin' what my husband told me to do. He said horse manure would make the plants grow." Deep wrinkles formed across her forehead. "We found out, a little too late, I might add, that it's best to use manure that's been aged awhile."

"That's correct. I should have given you planting instructions when you bought the plants that day."

Virginia shrugged. "What's done is done. I just won't have a garden this year."

"We always grow a big garden, so I'm sure we'll have more than enough produce to share some with you."

Virginia lifted her hand and waved it about. "No need for that. Me and Earl will get by just fine."

"Oh, but we'd like to help out."

"We ain't rich, but we're not poor neither. We'll buy whatever produce we need at the grocery store or one of the farmers' markets in the area."

Amy didn't want to press the issue, so she smiled and said, "Whatever you wish, but please let us know if you change your mind."

"It's doubtful." Virginia grabbed her mail from the box and limped back across the street.

Amy watched until she got safely to the other side. *I wonder if that poor woman has a bad knee and is in need of a knee replacement. She seems able-bodied enough except for that terrible limp. I suppose it would be impolite to ask her about it.*

When Amy turned and headed back up the driveway, she was greeted with the raucous cry of the pesky crow that kept hanging around. *I hope Henry's not feeding the bird again. It's ridiculous that my brother thinks he can make a pet out of the crow. If I had my say, we would figure out some way to get rid of that irritating bird. For me, it's nothing but a reminder of everything that's gone wrong around here since our dear family members perished.*

Virginia came to the front door with her mail and turned the knob. It wouldn't open. "What on earth? Did I lock myself out of the house?" Gritting her teeth with determination, she gave another try. The knob still didn't budge.

Virginia felt in her pockets. *I don't believe this! My key's in the house, and I can't even call for help because my phone's in there too.*

Virginia set the mail on the wicker table that had been placed between two matching chairs and clenched her teeth. If she had her phone, she could call Earl and ask him to come home and let her in. *Of course, he might not take too kindly to me interrupting his workday.*

She eyed the phone shed across the road. *Should I go over there and ask one of those Amish people if I can use their phone?* Virginia shook her head. *That's not a good idea. They don't need to know I was stupid enough to lock the door and go outside without my key or cell phone. I'll deal with this issue on my own. After all, I've been through worse situations and come through them okay.*

Virginia stepped off the porch and limped around back. She tried that door but found it was also locked. Next, she checked every window and discovered that only the kitchen window had been left partway open. "Oh, good. Sure hope I can wiggle my way through the opening, because I'm not sixteen anymore."

Virginia stepped over to it and surveyed the size. She put her hands to her hips, and, keeping the same measurement, put her hands in front of the window. *I think I can fit through there, but I'll need to take the screen off first.*

She noticed how it was fastened and gave it a pull. The screen snapped off, but it had broken apart. "Oops! Earl sure won't like what I did there," she mumbled. "Of course, that screen does have some holes in it that he still hasn't fixed. It's way past time for a new one anyway."

Virginia set the unusable piece aside. She was glad their kitchen window faced the backyard, because she wouldn't want anyone to see her trying to crawl through it. She eased the bottom frame upward, but it stopped and wouldn't go all the way.

Desperate to get inside, Virginia hoped she could squeeze through. She started going feet first, but found out quickly that her bum leg didn't like that one bit. Then she changed her idea to lying on her stomach and wiggling in that way.

Virginia stuck her head through and slowly worked her way in but got hung up. She saw her phone where she'd left it and tried to reach over, but the device wasn't close enough. The sink was right under her, and she could now use the faucet to tug on in order to get herself farther in. Virginia pulled on it hard and screamed when the faucet broke, spraying water everywhere.

"Oh, no!" She worked to get back out of the open window. It took some time, but she finally made it. Now, drenched from the waist up, there was a fountain of water running in her kitchen that she had no idea how to deal with.

Virginia moved from the window to the back door, which had a small window in the upper part of it. As far as she could tell, there was only one recourse. *I'll need to break in; that's all there is to it. I have to shut off the water before the whole kitchen is flooded.*

She looked around for something to use. "Hey, that might work." Virginia grabbed a hand shovel that she'd left in one of the flower-beds and used it to break the window glass. Then she carefully eased her hand inside and released the lock.

Whew! That's a relief.

Once in the kitchen, she waded through the water and opened the cupboard door under the sink. Virginia reached the shutoff valve and somehow managed to close it tight. She stood up and looked at her kitchen in dismay. "Oh, boy. . . I've got some work to do here."

Her first chore was getting the water soaked up, and the second was to clean up the broken glass on the floor by the back door.

Virginia grabbed a mop and began using it but decided old towels might be easier and faster. She got some from the utility room closet and tossed them on the water. Then she wrung out the waterlogged towels in the sink. It took a while to get the floor dried, but the chore was finally done. She then moved on to sweep up the shards of glass. This day had turned into quite a workout.

Virginia would still have to explain to Earl and show him what she'd done to the kitchen faucet. *I'll just call him at work when I'm done and tell him what happened to me. That way it will soften the blow and he'll have a chance to cool off before he gets home.*

She picked up her phone and pressed his number. When her husband answered and asked what was up, she began telling him the story until he interrupted. "Virginia, need I remind you that I'm at work? Can't you wait to tell me what happened after I get home later today?"

"No, it can't wait. I broke the screen on the kitchen window trying to go through in order to get into the house."

"Why didn't you just open the door and walk in?" he asked.

"Because the door was locked, and I didn't think I could get in any other way."

"How come you didn't call me?"

"I couldn't; my phone was in the house."

"You could have asked the neighbors across the road to use their phone."

"I didn't want to go over there. Those people are strange."

"If all you ruined was the screen, that's not so bad. I can replace it with a new one. I'll stop at the hardware store on the way home."

"No, Earl, you don't understand. There's more."

"More what?"

"More that went wrong." She drew a quick breath. "I also ruined the kitchen faucet."

"What?" Earl's voice grew louder. "How'd you do that, Virginia?"

"I used the faucet to pull myself through the window, but I couldn't fit and it broke from all the tugging. I think it must have already been loose and ready to go."

To Virginia's surprise, her husband chuckled. "Your backside got you hung up, did it?"

"It figures you'd say something like that. And quit laughing. It wasn't funny."

"Wish I'd been there to see it. Course, if I had been, it wouldn't have happened because I had my house key with me."

Virginia said nothing in response.

"So, is that it then? You finally got in through the window?"

She groaned. "Not exactly."

"What's that mean? Did you get in or not?"

"I was able to back out of the window and eventually got in through the kitchen door."

"But you said you got locked out, right?"

"Yes."

"So how did you get in?"

"I used the shovel and broke the glass out."

"Are you kidding?"

"Wish I was, but I needed to get in and turn off the water. It was shooting up like a geyser."

He groaned. "Are you okay otherwise?"

"My knee hurts, but other than that I'm fine—just pretty wet, and I'm tired from cleaning up the mess."

"Sorry you had to go through all of that. I'll take care of putting in a new faucet and screen when I get home, but I need to get back to work now. I'll see you later, Virginia."

"Okay, bye, Earl." Virginia pressed the END button. *Whew! I'm glad that's over. Sure hope he doesn't think it over and come home angry at me.* She leaned down and rubbed her throbbing knee. *Who knows what could happen?*

Chapter 30

Belinda couldn't believe she'd been home two weeks already. It seemed like just yesterday that she'd been holding baby Vernon and reading stories to Angela Mary.

Where has the time gone? Belinda wondered as she went outside to see if Henry had gotten her horse out for a trip to the store. *And now here we are, halfway into August.*

Seeing him standing beside her horse at the hitching rail, Belinda realized they had been so busy in the greenhouse lately, she'd forgotten about the talk she wanted to have with her son.

Smiling, she stepped up to him. "There's something I've been meaning to ask you, Henry."

He tipped his head. "Something I need to do in the greenhouse while you're in town?"

"No, it's about your future."

Crossing his arms, he stared at her. "I suppose you want me to take over the greenhouse someday when I'm older."

She placed her hand on his shoulder and gave it a gentle pat. "I would never expect you to take full control of the business unless it was something you wanted to do."

Henry shook his head. "I'd rather do somethin' else, Mom."

"Like what?"

"I'm not sure. Just know it's not in a humid greenhouse with a bunch of flowers, trees, and plants."

"I understand. Ezekiel didn't care for that kind of work either."

Henry dug the toe of his boot in the dirt. "I might wanna learn the woodworking trade or become a roofer like Jared."

"Whatever job you choose will be your decision. However, for the next few years, I'm going to need your help here, just as I need Amy and Sylvia's."

"Jah, right. Sylvia hasn't done anything in the greenhouse since you got home from Ezekiel's. All she does is stay in the house and take care of her kinner."

There was a hard edge to Henry's voice, and the tightness around his eyes reminded Belinda once again that her son still harbored bitterness in his heart. Although she too hurt deeply from the death of their loved ones, Belinda realized she must press on and try to find some joy in life. Spending time with her children and grandchildren had given her a sense of purpose and something to smile about.

"Son, you need to understand that your sister's children are small, and they need their mother's full attention."

"They did all right with Mary Ruth takin' care of them."

"That may be, but friends can't give a child what their mother can. The fact that Sylvia is taking care of her kinner the way she feels best is a good thing." Belinda paused to choose her next words. "Also, Sylvia's still struggling with her loss and doesn't do well in situations where she must converse with a lot of people—most of whom she doesn't know."

"Puh!" Henry pulled off his straw hat and fanned his face with it. "I don't like talkin' to strangers neither, but I put up with it."

Since Belinda was having no success getting Henry to understand his eldest sister's situation, she gave her horse a pat then climbed into the driver's seat. "I won't be gone long, and since it's near the end of our workday, there shouldn't be too many customers. Is there anything you would like me to get you while I'm in town?"

Henry shook his head, but then, as she backed the horse and buggy slowly away, he hollered, "Wait! I'd like some chocolate milk. And Mom, could you stop at the hardware store to get some suet for my pet crow? I think he'd like that better than seeds."

Belinda didn't mind picking up a few things for her son. "You got it, Son!" she shouted.

After putting the cleaning items away, Amy glanced at the Amish couple again, observing their happy expressions. Caleb and Susan were newlyweds from their church district. Their wedding had taken place two weeks ago, while Mom was gone. Amy had been invited to the event, but with so much to do at the greenhouse, she'd decided not to go. She felt it was more important to keep their business open and money coming in than to attend the ceremony for a couple she didn't know that well. Susan and Caleb seemed happy as they walked down the first aisle, talking about all the plans they had for their new home and yard. Susan mentioned planting flowers this fall that would bloom in the spring, and Caleb said he'd like to have a few fruit trees.

Amy had decided to wear her new sandals to work today. They felt comfortable as she sat on the stool behind the cash register, watching a young Amish couple who'd come into the greenhouse a short time ago.

Amy reached for her can of tropical punch, but in so doing, she lost her grip. The sticky liquid spilled onto the front of her apron and dripped all the way down to the floor, just missing her sandals. She hopped off the stool and snatched a roll of paper towels and cleaning spray from under the counter. Amy worked quickly to clean the mess off the floor, and then she moved on to her apron. She did her best to clean it off, but it was too wet to wear any longer, so she took off the apron and hung it from a peg on the wall behind her. She would put it in the laundry room when she went up to the house.

Amy thought about Jared and how well their relationship had been going before the horrible accident. *I can't help thinking about what we'd be doing these days if things would have remained unchanged.* Amy was almost certain that he'd been about to ask her to marry him, and she'd felt ready to accept his proposal.

She struggled to hold back tears. *I have to keep reminding myself not to give in to self-pity. My first obligation is to Mom and keeping the greenhouse running. Maybe someday, when Henry is old enough to take over the greenhouse, I'll be free to begin a relationship again. Only it won't be with Jared because I can't expect him to wait for me that long. Maybe I'll be so old by the time I'm free to marry that no man will want me.*

Amy's self-pity was getting her nowhere, so she shook herself mentally and walked down a row of indoor plants to make sure they'd been getting enough water. They appeared to be fine, so at least it was one less thing to worry about. Now on to the next row.

Virginia had finished her breakfast when the cell phone rang. She left the table and limped over to pick it up. "Hello."

"Virginia, is that you?"

"Yep. Who's calling?"

"It's Stella. I haven't heard from you since that first call you made right after your move to Pennsylvania, and I've been wondering how things are going."

"Not the best. Livin' here with all the country odors has been hard for me to adjust to." Virginia took the phone over to the table and sat in her chair. It had been awhile since she'd talked to her friend from Chicago, and it might take some time to get caught up, so she may as well be comfortable.

"Have you made any new friends in the area?" Stella asked.

"No, not really. Earl's made a few at work, but because of my bum knee flarin' up so often, I hang around the house most of the time."

"That's too bad. You should get out more and maybe attend some community functions. Those kinds of events are good places to seek out new friends."

"Didn't ya hear what I said, Stella? My knee hurts—especially when I walk a lot."

"I assume you're still too stubborn to use a cane?"

"No, I don't use a walking stick. I'm only forty-six years old, and using a support would make me look and feel old." Virginia drank the last bit of water in her glass. Truthfully, she wasn't interested in making new friends, but there was no point in telling Stella that.

"Are you completely unpacked?"

"Pretty much. There are still some boxes in the garage, but I've put all my dishes and other kitchen items away. It's looking pretty good in here." Virginia glanced at her new faucet above the sink, remembering how calm Earl had been over her damaging the old one when she'd tried crawling through the kitchen window. He'd replaced the window in the back door without a complaint too. She had half-expected him to blow up when he saw the mess she'd created.

"Are you still there, Virginia?"

"Yeah."

"I was wondering if you heard my last question."

"Sorry, Stella. What was it you said?"

"I asked if you planted a garden this summer. As I recall, you mentioned wanting to do that when you moved to the country."

"I tried to but didn't have much luck." Virginia went into detail about the tomato plants that had died.

"That's a shame. Guess we have to learn some lessons the hard way."

"You got that right. I've learned a good many lessons over the years." Virginia released a lingering sigh. *Too bad I can't undo the past and start fresh again.*

"Do you think you might try a garden again next year?" Stella asked.

"Maybe." Virginia fingered the edge of her empty plate. "There's a greenhouse across the road where I can buy seeds and plants, but I'd rather not go there again."

"How come?"

"The people who own it are Amish."

"Is that a problem?"

"It is to me. They're so old-fashioned."

"But if they have the items you need for gardening, why worry about the way they live?"

Virginia's toes curled inside her sneakers. "I'm not worried about it. I just don't care to be around them that much."

"Each to his—or in this case *her*—own, I guess."

Virginia determined it was time to hang up before her friend asked a bunch more questions she'd rather not answer. "I should go, Stella. I just finished eating and still have dishes to do."

"All right, but let's keep in better touch."

"Okay. Talk to you later then."

When Virginia ended the phone call, she leaned back in her chair and let out a puff of air. *Stella has no idea how hard it is for me to live here in the middle of nothing but horse sounds and smelly manure.*

Jared felt pleased with how well things were going as he and his crew worked on the roof at the home of Lydia's parents. Even though the place had been added onto through the years and there were different pitches to work with, the challenge was kind of fun. This type of encounter was usually common on Amish farmhouses due to the addition of more children and the attached *daadihaus* for grandparents who either needed or chose to live with their adult children.

It was a hot and sultry day, but Lydia's mother kept them well supplied in snacks and cold drinks. Sometimes Lydia brought the refreshments out. Other times her mother delivered them to the men, like now.

"Our new roof is certainly going to look nice." Darlene directed her comment to Jared. "We should have done this long ago, but I couldn't talk Lydia's daed into putting out the money until now."

Jared smiled and drank a glass of the lemonade she'd brought out. "I'm glad we were able to fit you in, because your old shingles were pretty worn and many were missing. Probably wouldn't have been long before you had a leak in the roof during a bad storm."

"My thoughts exactly." Darlene glanced at the wicker lounge chair on the lawn, where Lydia sat reading a book. "My daughter's birthday is coming up in a week, and we're going to have a little gathering for her. Would you like to come, Jared? I'm sure Lydia would enjoy having you there."

Jared couldn't control the apprehension he felt from his head down to his toes. *Should I do this? What would Amy think if she heard about it?* He reached for one of the peanut-butter cookies Darlene held out to him. *Maybe I'll see Amy at the party.* "What night will it be?" Jared asked.

"Saturday. Will you be free to join us?"

Jared figured that Amy, being Lydia's best friend, would also be invited. So, if he came, it would give him a chance to talk with her for a bit. At the very least, he could find out how she was doing and ask if things were going okay at their place. He swallowed the last bite of his cookie. *I sure do miss my aldi. If only there was a way to win my girlfriend back.*

Jared looked at Lydia's mother and nodded. "Sure, I'll be there. What time will the party start?"

"Six o'clock. We're planning to have a barbecue supper and then play a few games. Of course, there will also be ice cream and chocolate cake for dessert, since those are Lydia's favorites."

"Mine too." Jared finished his lemonade and gave the glass to Darlene. "Danki for the refreshments, and if I don't talk to you before, I'll see you Saturday night."

"Jah, we'll see you then, Jared." Darlene spoke in a bubbly tone. "I have a few things to do inside now, so if you need anything, just let Lydia know." She walked away humming a cheerful melody.

After Darlene returned to the house, Jared glanced into the yard at Lydia. *I wonder if her mother is hoping Lydia and I will start courting. Could that be the reason she invited me to the birthday gathering?*

Belinda's first stop in town was the hardware store, where she purchased two packages of suet. She still couldn't get over her son's attention to the silly crow hanging around their place and his wanting to feed it. Belinda understood that Henry needed a few distractions these days, which might make him happier. But a crow?

After Belinda left the hardware store, she went to Sara's flower shop to see if she might need any more summer flowers.

When Belinda entered the shop, she spotted Jared's mother talking with Sara. She held back until they concluded their business, looking casually at the various things Sara had for sale in her store in addition to floral arrangements.

Maybe we should try selling more things in the greenhouse that might attract people's attention. Although some local people, as well as tourists, bought the jams, jellies, and honey she sold, there might be other items of interest that could bring people into the greenhouse. This was something Belinda would ponder and talk to Amy and Sylvia about.

"Well, hello there." Eva Riehl smiled as she approached Belinda. "I didn't realize you were back from your visit to New York."

"I've actually been home two weeks and was at church last Sunday. I'm surprised you didn't see me there."

Eva rubbed her chin. "Now that you mention it, I do recall you sitting on a bench by your daughters. How have you been, Belinda?"

"Doing fine. And you?"

"Things are going well at our place too." Eva's voice lowered to a whisper. "My son told me what happened with Henry." She clicked her tongue. "It's such a shame when young people think they have to ride around with their friends in cars, especially when they go sneaking around in order to do it."

Belinda's brows furrowed. "I'm not sure what you're talking about."

"One night while you were gone, Henry was seen coming out of the bushes and getting in a car that sped off. Jared was going by at the time and saw it. The next day, he mentioned it to me."

Belinda's facial muscles went slack. She glanced around to see if Sara might be listening, but she'd slipped out from behind the counter and had gone to her desk for something.

"This is the first I've heard of this incident. I'll have to ask Henry about it."

"I hope I didn't speak out of turn. Jared didn't say I shouldn't mention it."

"It's all right. Don't worry about it." Belinda's fingers trembled as she touched Eva's arm. "It was nice seeing you."

"Jah, you too." Jared's mother blinked rapidly. "Since my son and your daughter are no longer courting, we don't get to see Amy or any of your family that much anymore."

Belinda gave a slow nod. "I'm sorry about their breakup. I tried to tell Amy that it wasn't necessary for her to make such a sacrifice, but she wouldn't listen." She sighed. "I wish there was something I could do to get those two back together."

"It might have been for the best. Did you ever think maybe they weren't meant to be together?"

Belinda's thoughts swirled so quickly, it was hard to follow them. Surely Ava didn't mean what she'd said.

"Well, I'd better go. I still have several errands to run." Ava said goodbye and hurried out the door.

Belinda remained in place, trying to let everything Jared's mother had said sink in. *I don't want my son to become the topic of other people's conversations. I hope Ava doesn't mention it to anyone else.*

"It's nice to see you, Belinda. Did you come in to see about my next order from your greenhouse?" Sara stepped up to Belinda, scattering her contemplations.

She cleared her throat and tried to collect herself. "Umm. . .yes, that is why I came by."

"I have a list on my desk of things I need to order. Funny thing, I called and left a message on your answering machine a short time ago." Sara smiled. "If I'd known you'd be dropping by, I would have waited to let you know in person about the flowers I need."

"I came to town to do some shopping," Belinda explained. "So, I figured while I was here, I'd stop in and see if you needed anything from the greenhouse."

"Well, it was perfect timing. Let's go over to my desk and I'll give you the list."

If not for Sara's request, Belinda would have already left the store. She was anxious to get home and speak to Henry.

Chapter 31

"I wonder how things are going for Mom as she runs her errands," Amy commented to Henry while he restocked the shelf full of honey jars.

He shrugged. "Beats me. I hope she gets back soon though. I'm eager to hang out the *fett* she promised to buy for me."

"I'm sure all the birds that come into our yard will appreciate having suet to eat in addition to the seeds we put in their feeders."

"The fett is for my pet crow not all the other birds that hang around."

Amy looked upward and shook her head. "I've told you before—the crow is not a pet. Furthermore, if you hang out the suet, you can't keep other birds from eating it." *I don't even like crows, and this one in particular whenever it caws. I'd be happy if that pesky fowl doesn't get any of the suet and the other yard birds hog it all. Maybe he'd find someplace else to make a home.*

Amy's paranoia over the crow hadn't lessened, but she wished it would. Allowing superstitious thoughts to overshadow her faith was not a good thing. She needed to pray harder and put her trust in the Lord.

Henry set the last jar of honey on the shelf and picked up the empty cardboard box. "I'm gonna put this away in the barn, okay?"

Amy handled the jars on the shelf with care, turning each of them with the label-side forward. "Sure, go ahead. But don't take too long because when more customers show up, I'll probably need your help."

Henry just ambled out the door with the box.

Amy pinched her lips together as she continued the task. *He'd better not fool around. He needs to get back here to help. Mom won't appreciate it if I tell her Henry's not working like she asked.*

Amy thought about the night her brother had snuck out to be with Seth. It was burdensome to be holding the goods on Henry and keeping his misdeed from their mother. How long would it be before Henry did something else wrong? If and when he did, Amy wouldn't hesitate to tell Mom.

Amy finished with the display shelf and moved away. It was quiet in the greenhouse for the moment, which gave her time to ponder. She visualized Jared's face for a few seconds, remembering when he'd been in here last. *He's a handsome guy, and I'm sure in a matter of time he'll be courting someone new—probably Lydia, if my suspicions are correct.* Thinking about this bothered Amy. *I've got to get Jared out of my thoughts. If only there was a better distraction.*

Since there were no customers at the moment, Amy made a trip up and down all four aisles. Everything looked good, so she paused to observe a pretty yellow butterfly flitting from flower to flower. She pursed her lips. *Here I work in the greenhouse nearly every day, yet I rarely take time to enjoy the beauty found in this building.* She drew in a breath, inhaling the lovely fragrance of all the colorful flowers that adorned this row. *Only God could have created such beauty.*

Amy lingered a few more moments before returning to the checkout counter and taking a seat. While sitting there, she reflected on the message from Lydia that had been waiting for her on their answering machine this morning. Amy's good friend would be having a birthday supper this Saturday, and she wanted Amy to come.

Of course I'll go. Amy smiled. *Lydia's been my best friend for a good many years, so I wouldn't miss helping her celebrate a special birthday. It'll be fun for the two of us to spend some quality time together. We haven't done that in a long while.*

A short time later, Maude entered the greenhouse. She hadn't been in for some time, and Amy had begun to wonder if the elderly woman had left the area and moved on.

Amy watched in shock as Maude shuffled down aisle 1, pinching one or two leaves from every plant on the wooden shelves. *Oh dear, she's going to ruin them all if I don't stop her.*

Amy rushed after Maude, calling, "Please don't do that to the plants."

The old woman stopped and turned to look at Amy. With her head tilted to one side, she asked, "Is something wrong?"

"Yes. I—I mean, why are you pulling leaves off the plants and throwing them on the floor?"

"I'm pruning 'em. All plants need to be pruned." The wrinkles in Maude's forehead deepened. "Since you work here, ya oughta know that."

Exasperated, Amy stepped between the woman and the next plant in line. "I do know when a plant or bush needs to be pruned, but the ones you plucked leaves off of are just fine and don't need any kind of pruning at all right now."

"Humph!" Maude folded her arms and stamped one foot. "Shows ya what you know. If this place was mine, I'd sure do things different."

I can only imagine. Amy clenched her teeth. She didn't want to appear rude, but she wished there was a nice way of asking the elderly lady to leave. Then an idea popped into her head. Remembering the apples and grapes she'd brought out for a snack this morning, Amy offered them to Maude.

The old woman's eyes held a hint of a sparkle. "Yeah, sure, I'd be happy to take 'em."

Amy led the way up to the counter, reached underneath, and withdrew a plastic container. "Here you go. Feel free to take the fruit home in the container. You can bring it back the next time you come here."

Maude gave a toothless grin, took the offered gift, and ambled out of the building. Amy heard her mumble something, but it didn't make much sense. The container was an old one, so even if Maude never came back with it, there wouldn't be a problem.

Amy called Henry to sweep up the scattered leaves then returned to the checkout counter. She was about to take a seat on the wooden stool, when a tall English man came in. "Hello. My name is Clarence Perdue. Are you the owner of this greenhouse?" he asked.

She shook her head. "My mother is, but she's not here at the moment."

"I see. Well, I just came in to look around. Wanted to check out the competition."

"Competition?" Amy repeated, pulling back slightly so as not to inhale the lingering cigarette smoke on his clothes.

"Yes. My wife, Patricia, and I own the new greenhouse on the other side of town, and we've been curious about your place and what all is being sold here." He gave her a pointed stare. "Mind if I have a look around?"

Amy wasn't sure how to respond. She wanted to tell the man no, but that would be impolite. "I guess it would be okay." Her voice cracked. Not once since the new greenhouse opened had she thought to visit there in order to see what they sold. *But maybe I should have.*

Amy watched helplessly as Mr. Perdue headed off down aisle 1, where Henry was busy cleaning up the mess Maude had left. *I bet the man thinks our place of business is pathetic compared to his. After a trip through the building, he will probably realize we are no competition to him at all.*

"Where's Henry?" Belinda asked when she entered the greenhouse a little after noon. She was glad no customers were at the front counter, because what she had to say to Amy was not for other people's ears.

"He was supposed to have gone up to the house to get the lunch sacks Sylvia said she would prepare for us," Amy responded. "Oh, and Mom, there's something you might want to know."

"I already know more than I want to." Belinda bent close to her daughter's ear. "Why didn't you tell me your bruder snuck out one night while I was gone?"

Amy blinked rapidly. "I—I promised him I wouldn't say anything unless he messed up again. I didn't want to worry you about something I hoped was a one-time occurrence." She glanced to her right. "Can we talk about this later, Mom? Someone's coming up with their purchases."

"No problem. It's Henry I need to talk to right now." Belinda turned and rushed out the door.

When she entered the house, she found Sylvia in the kitchen feeding Allen his lunch.

"Hi, Mom, I'm glad you're back." Sylvia smiled. "There's a tossed green salad in the refrigerator. Would you like some for lunch?"

"Not right now. I'm looking for Henry. Is he here in the house?"

Sylvia shook her head. "I haven't seen him since this morning."

"Oh, really? Amy said he was supposed to come here to get their sack lunches." With forced restraint, Belinda spoke through her clenched teeth.

"Their sandwiches are still in the refrigerator. Maybe he's out in the greenhouse."

"No, I just came from there, and Amy said. . ." Belinda ended her sentence and tousled Allen's hair when he stopped eating and looked up at her with innocent eyes. *I must not let this little fellow see my irritation.*

She moved across the room and motioned for Sylvia to join her. "I found out from Jared's mamm this morning that Henry was seen getting into a car one evening while I was gone." She was careful to keep her voice down and spoke in English so Allen wouldn't understand any of their conversation. "Amy admitted that she knew about it, so I assume you were also aware."

"Jah. He said he wouldn't do it again, and we wanted to give him the benefit of the doubt. What I don't understand though is how Jared's mother knew about the incident."

"Ava said Jared was going past our place the evening it happened, and he saw Henry come out of the bushes and get in a car." Belinda looked directly at Sylvia. "Do you know where he went?"

"He spent the night at Seth's even though earlier, Amy told him he couldn't go."

"So, he decided he could do whatever he pleased?"

"I guess so."

Belinda's face heated as her muscles tensed. "I'd better go find him and deal with this matter."

She stepped out the back door and stood on the porch, scanning the yard. Then after several seconds, she stepped down into the yard. *Where is that boy of mine?*

She heard a whistle and looked up, surprised to see Henry sitting inside the opening at the top of the barn with his legs crossed.

Belinda cupped her hands around her mouth. "What in the world are you doing up there?"

"I'm talkin' to the birds!"

"Well, come down here right now. I want to talk to *you*."

Henry disappeared, and a few minutes later, he came out of the barn. "What's up, Mom? Did ya get the fett for my crow?"

Belinda took hold of her son's arm and led him back to the barn so they could talk without being heard by any potential greenhouse customers. "I did get the suet but not the chocolate milk you asked for. However, that's not what I want to talk to you about."

"If it's about me not bein' in the greenhouse, Amy sent me in to get our lunches."

"So I heard, but you obviously did not do as you were told."

"I was planning to, but then I spotted the crow." Henry grinned. "I'm gonna make a pet out of him, Mom."

She shook her head. "It's my understanding that you cannot tame a crow. They aren't trainable like a parrot or some other indoor bird."

"Maybe not, but there's always an exception, so I was thinking—"

Belinda held up her hand. "Enough about the crow, Henry. We came in here to talk about you and why you snuck out of the house and spent the night with Seth while I was at Ezekiel's place."

Henry let out a forceful breath and stomped his foot. "I can't believe Amy blabbed—or was it Sylvia who told ya?"

"It was neither of your sisters who did the telling. I heard it from someone I saw at Sara's flower shop this morning."

Henry gave his earlobe a tug. "How'd Sara know about me spending the night with Seth?"

"It wasn't Sara who mentioned it."

"Who then?"

"That doesn't really matter, Son. The point is, you did something you should not have done and then kept the truth from me." Belinda gave a frustrated shake of her head. "I'm disappointed in you, Henry. I thought I could trust you to do what's right while I was away."

He dropped his gaze to the floor and shuffled his boots in the straw beneath them. "Sorry, Mom. I promise, it'll never happen again."

"I should hope not. If your daed was here, he would also be very disappointed."

"I know." Henry looked up. "Guess you're not gonna give me any suet for the crow now, huh?"

"I will give it to you, Henry. There's no reason the bird should suffer because you snuck out of the house and worried your sisters."

"Danki, Mamm."

"But that doesn't mean you shouldn't be punished for your misdeed."

"I figured as much. What's my punishment besides no chocolate milk?"

"You'll have extra chores to do for the next two weeks, and you're not to go anywhere with your friends, or even by yourself, until I say so. Is that understood?"

"Jah."

"All right then, please go into the house and get yours and Amy's lunches like you were supposed to do."

"Okay, I'm on it."

They left the barn, and while Henry sprinted for the house, Belinda made her way to the greenhouse.

Clymer

Ezekiel sat across from Michelle at their kitchen table, eating lunch. "You look tired. Have you been doing too much?"

Michelle shrugged. "Maybe a little. I'm managing on my own, but I sure miss your mamm. She was such a big help to me."

"Jah, she was. I miss her too and so does Angela Mary." He reached over to where their daughter sat in her booster seat and tweaked her petite nose. "I think even the boppli misses his grandma because she held him so much."

"Do you still think it's possible for us to visit there in September?"

"I believe so." Ezekiel took a drink of iced tea. "It'll be good to see everyone."

She smiled and handed him another egg salad sandwich. "Have I told you lately how much I love you?"

He grinned back at her. "Every day, and I tell you the same."

"That's true." Michelle sighed. "The best thing I ever did was to join the Amish church and marry you."

"So I've heard." Ezekiel winked at her. "But I never get tired of hearing it."

"Sometimes, like when I'm in church surrounded by all the others in our district and listening to you preach, I have to pinch myself to make sure I'm not dreaming."

Ezekiel leaned forward in his chair. "How do you think I'm doing with that, Michelle? Do I stumble too much over my words?"

"Certainly not. It's plain to see that God has called you to be a preacher. Your messages are uplifting and encouraging. My only advice is to keep doing what you're doing and stay as humble as you are now."

"No worries about that." Ezekiel thumped his chest. "I have asked God to give me a kick in the pants if I ever become full of *hochmut*. All I want to do is be a good husband, father, and preacher and allow God to work through me so I can minister to those who are in need."

Michelle placed her hand on his arm. "You've always been there to minister to me—even before I invited Christ into my life."

"Well, I wasn't perfect by any means, and I knew in my heart that you and I had a lot to learn during our courting days, and even before when we were full of rebellion. It just goes to show that God can use any person who is willing to repent and turn their life around."

Chapter 32

Strasburg

Saturday evening, as Amy's horse and buggy approached her friend's house, she had mixed feelings. As much as she looked forward to spending the evening with Lydia and helping her celebrate a birthday, Amy worried that Jared might be there. With rumors going around and the fact that she'd seen them together a few times, Amy felt sure they must be courting.

"Well, it's too late now to change my mind," she murmured as her horse picked up speed and turned, of his own accord, into the driveway. Buster had been here numerous times and was probably eager to visit with the Petersheims' horses.

"I'm so glad you could be here." Lydia greeted Amy at the hitching rail. "Tonight wouldn't be the same without you."

Amy smiled, and when she stepped down from the buggy, she gave Lydia a hug. "Happy birthday."

"Thank you. Let's get your *gaul* put in the corral, and we can join the others who have come this evening."

"Okay. Oh, and by the way. . .you smell nice. Are you wearing perfume?"

"No, it's the new hand-and-body lotion my mamm got for my birthday." Lydia walked over, opened the paddock, and waited for Amy's gelding to enter.

Amy unhitched her horse and led him to the corral. His ears perked up, and he whinnied when she put him inside.

Lydia laughed while she closed the gate. "Looks like Buster's happy to be here."

"Jah, I believe he is." Amy stepped along with Lydia and could smell the odor of wood smoke. It smelled good floating through the air, but Amy wasn't very hungry, so she probably wouldn't eat much. Truth was, since breakfast, she'd felt a sense of apprehension about the possibility of seeing Jared this evening.

As they drew closer to the bonfire, Amy heard the voices of her friend's guests. She wondered how this evening would play out with Lydia and Jared.

"Let's head over to the tables my folks have set up in our yard. Several of our friends are here, and I'm sure they'll be glad to see you."

As Lydia led the way, Amy reached up and checked her hair to make sure none of it had come out from under her kapp. The colorful paper plates and napkins looked festive. Amy figured Lydia's mother wanted to make everything just right for her daughter's special gathering.

As they approached the tables that had been set up on the lawn, Amy's heart pounded when she saw Jared sitting on a bench. She wished she could turn around and run back to get her horse and buggy, but Lydia would be disappointed if Amy left now.

Plastering a smile on her face, Amy made the rounds greeting everyone present including Jared.

"It's nice to see you, Amy." Jared smiled. "How have you been?"

"I'm fine. How are you?"

Before he could respond, Lydia's mother came out of the house with a tray full of hot dogs and buns. "Come on, everyone—grab a hot dog and a roasting stick. Lydia's daed has the fire going, so anyone who wants to can roast theirs as soon as we have prayed. He also has some ground beef patties cooking on the grill."

All heads bowed for silent prayer. When it ended, Jared stood and asked Amy if she would like him to roast her a hot dog.

"No, that's okay," she said with a shake of her head. "I can do my own when I'm ready. I may start with a burger."

"Okay." Was that a look of disappointment she saw on his face? Or maybe it was a look of relief. No doubt he'd been trying to be polite.

"You can roast a hot dog for Lydia," Darlene spoke up. "Since she's the birthday girl, she deserves to sit and be waited on this evening."

Lydia's cheeks turned crimson. "Mama, I'm not an invalid or a young child. I can most certainly wait on myself." She grabbed a hot dog and followed the others to the bonfire.

It was indeed awkward for Amy being here this evening. Not to mention having many of hers and Amy's peers who had been invited. She could only imagine what some of them must be thinking about her. *I'm sure they'd like to ask why I broke things off with Jared, but I hope no one does.* Having to respond to a question like that would only make Amy feel worse.

For the rest of the evening, Amy tried to avoid Jared as much as possible and kept her responses short whenever he spoke to her. She visited with some of the other guests during the party, but her heart wasn't in any of it. Fortunately, no one asked about her and Jared's breakup.

Amy couldn't help noticing the care Lydia's mother gave to Jared. It seemed as if Darlene might be paving the way for him to give her daughter some extra attention. Seeing the way Lydia talked so much to Jared made Amy think that her good friend had feelings for him. It hurt, but at the same time, Amy couldn't fault Lydia if she was attracted to Jared. He would make any woman a good husband. The question was, did he return those feelings?

"What a busy day we had. I'm ever so glad it's over." Belinda joined Sylvia in the kitchen to finish cooking their supper.

"I assumed that's how it went since I heard cars and buggies coming and going most of the day when I wasn't busy taking care of the kinner."

Belinda rinsed a couple of tomatoes to slice. "It was nonstop at times. I'm a little surprised with that new place open on the other side of town that things haven't slowed down here."

"I think we get more tourists than the other greenhouse does. I saw a couple of vans loaded with people pull in at different times today." Sylvia rolled her eyes. "Some began taking pictures of our flowerbeds as soon as their feet hit the ground."

"Perhaps there's an appreciation on how well we did when a perfect stranger has to take home a picture. Of course, I'll not allow myself to get prideful regarding our gardening abilities."

Sylvia moved over and patted Belinda's arm. "You don't have to worry about that, Mom. You're not full of hochmut at all."

Belinda grabbed the potholders and drained the hot water from the potatoes. As she worked, thoughts about the conversation she'd had with Amy a few days ago floated through her head. Amy had mentioned that the owner of the new greenhouse in the area had come by, wanting to check out the competition. Belinda couldn't figure out why he would even care, because, from what she'd heard, his place of business was much bigger than hers. She wished she'd been there when he came by, so she could ask him a few questions, such as why did he feel the need to check out the competition.

Oh well, I suppose it really doesn't matter. He will go about his business, and we'll go about ours. We'll probably never see or hear from Mr. Perdue again.

Belinda had finished mashing the potatoes to go with the pot roast Sylvia had put in the oven for supper, when a knock sounded on the front door. "Would you please see who that is?" she asked her daughter.

"Sure, Mom."

A few minutes later, Sylvia returned to the kitchen with Monroe trailing behind her.

Belinda tried to conceal the shock she felt at that moment. Being tired from the hectic day she'd had, she wasn't running at full speed this evening. But she'd be pleasant to their guest, nonetheless, and she put a smile on her face for him.

"Good evening, Belinda. I hope I'm not interrupting." He glanced at the table, set for three people, and then his gaze landed on Allen's highchair. "I had hoped to catch you before you'd prepared your meal for this evening. Sorry for disturbing you."

"Today was quite busy in the greenhouse, and I thought that we'd get a later start fixing our meal. But this is our usual time for supper."

"I see." Monroe shifted from one foot to the other. "Well, I guess I'll just state what I came for and be on my way."

"What is the reason for your visit?" Sylvia asked before Belinda had a chance to say anything.

Monroe turned to face her. "I was heading to a restaurant in town for supper and thought I'd drop by and see if your mamm was free to join me."

A warm flush swept across Belinda's cheeks. "It's kind of you to think of me, but as you can see—"

"Jah, I can see and smell the wonderful aroma from the meal you've prepared." He tipped his head back and sniffed the air. "I'm betting you have a roast in the oven."

"You have a good sniffer." Belinda smiled despite her anxiety at him showing up this evening. Had Monroe really expected she would accept his invitation to go out with him for supper and with a last-minute invitation, no less? *Even if I did want to go, which I don't, I would have said no. If someone I know saw me out having a meal with Monroe, I can only imagine all the gossip that would run wild.*

Since Monroe seemed in no hurry to leave and because their meal was ready to eat, Belinda did the only thing she felt was polite. "Monroe, would you care to join us for supper?"

"Of course. Danki for asking."

Belinda looked at Sylvia and noticed her raised brows. Was she also questioning this man's motives?

"We'll all be seated as soon as my son comes inside." Belinda gestured to the table. "After you've washed up at the sink, you may as well take a seat."

Monroe nodded briefly. While he washed his hands, Belinda

opened the back door to call Henry.

"What do you want, Mom?" he shouted in return.

"Supper's ready and we have a guest. Please come inside now."

"Okay, I'll be there in a minute."

Sylvia set another place at the table. "I'll go see how the baby is doing and put Allen in his highchair."

Even though Belinda couldn't see where Henry was, she felt certain he was someplace in the yard trying to coax that noisy crow to eat from his hand. She'd caught him doing it this morning before breakfast.

She shook her head. *Silly boy. I doubt he will ever succeed in training that crow or making it a pet. But I guess if it makes him happy to try, it shouldn't be an issue.*

Belinda returned to the kitchen. As she dished up the potatoes, Henry came in. He stopped short when he saw Monroe sitting at the head of the table. Looking at Belinda, Henry pursed his lips. She could almost hear what her son was thinking. *Why is this man here?* Of course, even though Monroe had explained his reason, Belinda wondered that herself. *He has to realize I'm still in mourning. My black dress ought to be proof enough.*

Belinda instructed Henry to wash up, and once he'd finished, everyone took a seat. Silent prayer was said, and then the food got passed around.

During supper, Monroe seemed to be pleased with the meal, as he polished off his first helping of mashed potatoes and a slice of meat. "This is a very tender roast."

Belinda set her fork aside. "Thank you. Would you like some more?"

He smiled at her. "Jah, sure, I'd be delighted to have seconds." Monroe held out his plate as he waited to be served. After a few bites, he mentioned his concern for Belinda and her family. "You know, it's really not a good idea for you all to be alone without a man in the house."

Belinda merely shrugged and said, "We're getting along fine."

And they were—for the most part. At least they were still getting enough customers to keep sales going, and as far as she knew, no more vandalism had been done. With fall just a month away, many people, as they had in the past, would come into the greenhouse to buy fall flowers and plants. So for now, at least, Belinda wasn't worried about their safety or financial situation. As she'd reminded herself many times since the three men in their family died, *God will take care of us.* To which she added, *And we don't need any help from Monroe Esh.*

Jared felt slighted that Amy hadn't said much to him all evening. Truth was, it seemed as if she tried to avoid him. When Lydia's mother had called everyone to the tables, she'd indicated that Jared should sit beside her daughter. Once more, he'd been disappointed. If he could have been seated beside or even across from Amy, it would have given him a better chance to speak to her.

Throughout the meal, Darlene kept talking to Jared, asking him countless questions and complimenting him on how well their new roof had turned out. No one else, even Lydia, who sat beside Jared could get a word in. Jared was beginning to wish he had declined the invitation.

At eight thirty, Amy said she needed to leave the party, using the excuse that she had several things to do before going to bed. "Besides, tomorrow is church day, so I need to get to bed a little earlier than usual."

Jared jumped up and offered to get Amy's horse, but she declined. "Thanks anyway, but I can manage."

"No, I insist." He waited until she'd said goodbye to everyone then walked with her to the corral. After he took Buster out and hitched him to the buggy, Jared helped Amy into the driver's seat. "It was good seeing you. I only wish we'd had more time to talk."

Amy swallowed hard and fought against the tears pushing the

back of her eyes. "You'd best get back to the party. Lydia's there wait-ing." She gathered up the reins and backed up her horse. "Good night, Jared."

"Good night, Amy." She watched him walk back to the tables then guided Buster down the driveway and out onto the road.

"I should not have come to Lydia's party tonight." She spoke out loud, glad that no one was in the buggy with her and could see her tears. Amy was convinced that she'd lost Jared, which she'd known could happen when she broke things off with him. Nonetheless, it still hurt more than she would ever admit.

But taking care of Mom is my responsibility now, she reminded her-self. *I have no free time for courting, and becoming someone's wife is out of the question because I wouldn't have enough time to put into a marriage relationship anyway. So, I must come to grips with the choice I made con-cerning Jared. It's for the best, all the way around.*

Amy tightened her grips on the reins. *How much longer do I have to keep reminding myself?*

Chapter 33

Clymer

Ezekiel woke up in a cold sweat. He felt relieved to be awake and out of the dream he'd been trapped in. Something terrible had happened at his mom's house, but now he couldn't remember what it was. Lying there in the dark room, he pulled the sheet to one side. *That feels better. Now if there was just some fresh air blowing through the open window.*

He rolled over and sat on the edge of the bed, hoping he wouldn't disturb Michelle. *What happened in the dream that was so stressful it woke me up? Could the nightmare have been a warning or some impending doom? Are Mom and my siblings in some kind of trouble?*

Ezekiel pushed the button on top of his illuminated battery-operated alarm clock. It was 2:00 a.m.—too early for anyone at home to be up. He sat there a moment and reached for his glass of water, but it was empty.

Grabbing his flashlight in the other hand, Ezekiel headed to the kitchen for a refill. Once there, he checked the back door to be sure it was locked then got his water.

Heading to the living room, Ezekiel checked the front door too. *Guess after that dream, I'm feeling a bit paranoid. Everything's fine here. I need to get back to sleep because there's plenty of work waiting for me in my shop.*

After returning to the bedroom, Ezekiel set his glass on the nightstand and sat on the edge of the bed, not sure he if could get back to sleep. *Maybe I should have stayed in the kitchen and done some reading to make myself sleepy.*

There weren't many options for him at this hour, and it would be pointless to go out to the phone shed now. When he got up to get ready for work, he'd go out and leave a message saying he was just checking on them and asking Mom to give him a call. Ezekiel would also let her know that he and his family would definitely be coming there the first Saturday of September. Both he and Michelle looked forward to the trip, and so did Angela Mary. Someday when Vernon was older, he'd also be eager to see his relatives in Strasburg.

"Is everything all right? Why are you sitting on the edge of the bed?" Michelle's groggy-sounding voice caused Ezekiel to jump when she touched his arm.

He lay back down and pulled her close to his side. "It's nothing to worry about. I had an unpleasant dream and couldn't get back to sleep."

"What was it about?"

"I'm not sure. It was enough to wake me though, but I can't remember any of the details." Ezekiel didn't mention that he thought the dream was about his family in Strasburg or that he was concerned for their welfare. No point in giving his wife cause to worry. Besides, he was probably being paranoid. Mom and the rest of his family were no doubt sleeping comfortably in their beds.

Strasburg

That nasty wind is making a ruckus out there, and it's not helping me relax. Belinda tossed and turned, fluffing up her pillow and pushing it down. She'd gone to bed shortly before midnight and had lain awake ever since. So many thoughts swirled in her head. Even though some things had improved in her life, she had many problems to deal with yet—at the greenhouse as well as in her home.

Several orders had come in for chrysanthemums and other fall foliage. It was easy to get the areas needed in the greenhouse ready for the new stock because the more they sold, the more they had available.

They still had some varieties of summer flowers that hadn't yet sold. Belinda had already discounted many different types of plants, and they were fast disappearing. Whenever possible, she liked giving her customers a bargain.

Belinda would need her son's help moving heavier things and had the weekend for another sale circled on the calendar that hung in the greenhouse. A lot of what needed to be done from season to season was written on that date-keeper Vernon always kept.

Belinda shifted for more comfort and lay there, continuing to think about things. *I sure hope my youngest son will never again pull anything like what he did while I was away.*

Henry's punishment had ended, and since it had been the last Friday of August and summer would soon be over, she'd given him permission to go fishing with Seth at a nearby pond after they closed the greenhouse in the afternoon. Belinda liked fish and had hoped Henry would catch some they could have for supper.

I remember when my Vernon caught and brought home fish to fry. Belinda pictured her husband, all smiles, when he'd have a successful day at the pond. Sometimes he would go with Ezekiel, Abe, and Henry, and they'd have a nice time enjoying the peace and quiet near the water's edge. *If only I could go back and relive the good times, but unfortunately, that's not possible.*

When Henry had come back in time for supper, something about his demeanor hadn't seemed right to her. She'd also noticed a faint smell of what she thought was cigarette smoke on his clothes. When Belinda had asked Henry about it, he'd shrugged and said, "I don't smell anything."

Then Belinda had asked if he'd caught any fish, and her son's reply was, "A few, but they weren't very big, so I tossed 'em back in the water."

Maybe I'm overly suspicious, Belinda thought as she rolled onto her other side. *But I have a hunch my son may have been fibbing to me and didn't catch any fish at all. Why would he lie about that though?*

Belinda sat up in bed as another thought came to mind. *What if Henry didn't go fishing at all? Could he and Seth have gone somewhere that he doesn't want me to know about? How can I find out? Should I speak to Seth's mother and ask if she knows for sure where her son was today?* She shook her head. *Maybe it's best not to bring up the topic. Unless he does something out of the ordinary, I need to have a little faith in my boy.*

Belinda turned on the battery-operated light on her nightstand and picked up Vernon's Bible. Somehow it made her feel closer to him when she held it.

Opening the book to a place her husband had placed a marker, she saw that he'd underlined a few verses. One of them jumped right out at her. It was just the reminder she needed in this wee hour of the morning. *"The LORD is my strength and my shield; my heart trusted in him, and I am helped: therefore my heart greatly rejoiceth; and with my song will I praise him"* Psalm 28:7.

Tears clouded Belinda's vision. "Oh Vernon, how I still miss you. Thank you for being a godly man and a fine example to me, our family, and the entire community."

When Jared left the phone shack early Saturday morning and returned to the house, his mind replayed the message he'd received from a man who'd said his name was Earl Martin. Earl wanted to put a new roof on his detached garage. Jared noticed right away that the address the man gave was almost the same as the Kings' place—just a few numbers were different. He figured the Martins had to live across the road from Amy's family.

Jared's workload had lightened a bit, but with the weather changing, it would no doubt get busier. He'd returned Mr. Martin's call and set up a time to meet.

Jared entered the kitchen, where Mom was clearing the breakfast dishes. "How'd it go in the phone shed?" she asked. "Were there any messages?"

"Nothing on yours and Dad's line, but I had a few. One is a potential job near the Kings' place."

Her face seemed to tighten. "You're always so busy. Do you have time to work for a new customer?"

"I believe I can squeeze it in."

Mom offered him a brief smile. "I'm glad you had a good time at Lydia's the other night. When I saw Darlene a few days before the party, she seemed excited about throwing her daughter a nice birthday celebration."

"It turned out well, and there was plenty to eat."

"Lydia's a nice girl."

Jared nodded and grabbed his lunchbox. "I'd best get moving."

"All right, Son. I'll see you sometime this evening."

"Sure thing." *The only girl for me is Amy,* Jared thought as he walked out the door. *Why can't she see how much I want to be with her? Doesn't she realize a relationship with me is not impossible? If only there was something I could say or do to win her back.* Jared had revisited those thoughts many times since Amy broke up with him. Try as he may, he couldn't get Amy King out of his mind.

As Amy worked with her mother in the garden during the early morning hours, she noticed something and pointed. "What happened to that pumpkin plant? Looks like it's wilted, but I know it's been getting plenty of water."

"I bet we've got a beetle problem." Mom moved from what produce she'd already gathered and examined the base of the plant. "Jah, it's from beetles, all right. I'll need some straw to put around the plants." She discarded the bugs into the weed bucket.

Amy and her mother continued picking. They'd decided to get the chore done before it was time to open the greenhouse. And because the weather was cooler at this hour of the day, the work was easier.

Amy liked cucumbers, and there were plenty to pick from the rows. She wouldn't mind having some of them to eat with lunch or dinner. Their tomatoes were ripening nicely, and Amy thought about the neighbor across the road. She'd offered to let Virginia have more tomato plants when hers had died soon after planting them. Amy felt sorry for their new neighbor lady because she didn't know much about fertilizing properly.

"It's too bad I didn't give her some basic instructions on how to care for the new plants," Amy said as she pulled more weeds in the radish rows.

"What do you mean? Who are you talking about?" Mom asked.

"Guess I was speaking my thoughts out loud." Amy gave a self-conscious laugh. "I forgot to tell you about the neighbor's tomato plants. I talked to Virginia at the mailbox the other day, and she said they'd all died."

Mom swatted at a pesky gnat. "Does she know why?"

"Jah." Amy explained what had happened.

"That's too bad." Mom gestured to the nearest tomato plant that had already turned a nice red color. "It would be good to give her some fresh tomatoes, and we have plenty to share."

"I agree, but Virginia said she didn't want any—that she'll get what she needs at the grocery store or farmers' market." Amy moved away from the cucumber and cleaned the weeds crowding the tomato plants.

"She's a different person—not very friendly, that's for sure. But maybe there's a reason for it. We need to pray for her, Daughter."

"You're right, Mom." Amy glanced up from the weeds she'd been pulling and cleared her throat. "Would you look at that? Henry's got the crazy crow practically eating out of his hand. Now the noisy thing will probably never leave our yard."

Mom glanced in the direction Amy pointed and shook her head. "That bird may not be a pet, but Henry's succeeded in being able to get close to him. Sure didn't expect to see anything like that."

"I'd never have believed it if I hadn't witnessed it myself."

Amy returned to her chore until Henry's deep laughter rang out. It was good to hear this positive side of him. She looked up again to see what he found so humorous.

"Amy. . .Mom. . .look over there!" Henry pointed at Rachel's crib sheet hanging from a branch in a nearby tree. Sylvia stood below it, looking up and shaking her head.

Amy figured the breeze that had begun blowing a few minutes ago must have caught hold of the sheet while her sister had been trying to pin it to the line.

"Is that a new way to hang the laundry?" Henry laughed harder than Amy had heard him in a long time, but Sylvia wore a frown.

"It's not funny, little bruder. Now how am I going to get that down?"

"I'll get it for you, Sylvia. Just give me a few minutes." Henry jumped up, and the crow flew off as he darted for the barn.

Amy had to admit, seeing the small sheet dangling helplessly from the tree was quite funny. Mom must have thought so too, for her laughter brought forth an unladylike snort.

Amy giggled, and soon even Sylvia was laughing. It felt good to share in a little merriment—something they'd done so little of since their loved ones had been killed.

Henry came out of the barn carrying a ladder. He set it against the tree and began the upward climb.

"Be careful, Son," Mom called up to him. Her expression had suddenly turned sober.

Amy held her breath as Henry climbed higher. She released her breath when he had hold of the sheet and began his descent. His feet had no more than touched the ground when the crow flew into the same tree and let out several obnoxious screeches.

Amy covered her ears. She wished the crazy bird would fly far away from here and never come back.

Almost out of nowhere, a car sped up the driveway, turned into the greenhouse parking lot, and slammed into one corner of the building.

Amy and Mom jumped up at the same time, and they, as well as

Henry and Sylvia, dashed toward the vehicle. When they arrived, a middle-aged man with a nearly bald head got out and surveyed the damage.

"I'm so sorry, folks." His face was covered in perspiration. "A cat ran out in front of me, and I lost control trying to avoid hitting the critter."

Amy looked around but saw no sign of a cat. Of course, that didn't mean one hadn't been there. The poor animal had most likely been scared and run off.

The man stepped up to Mom. "I'll call my insurance agent right away, and in the meantime, I will go to the hardware store and get some heavy plastic to staple over the damaged area. That should help till it can be permanently fixed."

He and Mom talked for a few more minutes before he got into his car and drove off.

"He's going to the hardware store," Mom explained. Her voice quavered.

Amy felt shaky too. This event had been an accident, while the other things that had happened on their property seemed to have been done on purpose.

"You don't think that man hit the greenhouse intentionally, do you?" Sylvia asked their mother.

Mom shook her head. "No, of course not. Why would anyone do something like that on purpose?"

Caw! Caw! Caw! Caw! What a horrible screech.

Amy looked toward the tree where the crow had flown. Was that bird trying to tell them something?

Chapter 34

"See you both later. Have a good day." Sylvia watched her sister and their mother head for the greenhouse. She had a few things to finish before Ezekiel and his family arrived.

Sylvia closed the front door. The children had been fed and were settled in the living room. Allen pulled out a few toys from the box, and Rachel made baby sounds from her playpen. Sylvia looked at the bedding that needed to go on the guest bed upstairs. "I suppose there's no time like the present. Allen, please come with Mommy."

The little guy grabbed some toy figures and went with her. Sylvia had him sit in a chair in the room where she needed to work. Her pace quickened as she put the fresh sheets on the bed and placed a lightweight coverlet at the foot. She looked around the room to be sure everything was in order. Mom and Amy had cleaned in here yesterday evening, so Sylvia insisted that she make up the bed this morning. The space looked good and ready for Ezekiel and Michelle. Since it was the largest of the guest rooms, there was space for the cot Angela Mary would sleep on as well as a cradle for baby Vernon.

Sylvia tapped her son's shoulder. "I'm done now, so let's go back downstairs and check on your sister." As always, she spoke to the boy in the Pennsylvania Dutch language of her people. Although Allen knew a few English words, he wouldn't learn to speak it fluently until he started school.

When they entered the living room, the baby began to fuss, so Sylvia picked her up. Looking out the front window, Sylvia thought she saw someone out by the road. She watched longer, and sure enough, there was a person off by the shrubs. It was kind of weird and happened so fast, she wasn't sure if the person was a male or female.

She took a seat to tend to her little girl's needs. After Sylvia began nursing the baby, she kept watching out the window. Shortly thereafter, the person she'd seen moments ago came into full view. It was the poor lady who lived in the shanty not far from them. The woman walked up the driveway, while a horse and buggy approached the business ahead of her. Not long after, one of their ministers and his wife got out of the buggy and headed for the greenhouse.

Sylvia rocked and kept watching outside. *I see Maude is wearing a jacket this morning. Maybe it's a little chilly for her.*

Although Sylvia was absorbed with watching, she wondered where Henry might be. She hadn't seen him since breakfast and assumed he may have gone to the greenhouse to help Mom and Amy. At least she hoped he had and was not shirking his duties. *Of course, he might be checking on the bees,* she thought. *I believe during breakfast he said something about doing that this morning.*

Sylvia kept her eye on the gray-haired woman. She thought Maude would go into the greenhouse, but instead she veered off and headed toward the garden in their yard. *That's odd. I wonder what she's doing there.*

Soon, the bedraggled woman picked a couple of ripe tomatoes and popped them into her pockets. She moved over and picked a cucumber then hurried out of the yard and down the driveway.

Sylvia slowed the rocking chair, stroking the top of Rachel's head. *I think Mom and Amy will be interested in hearing about this. I feel sorry for Maude. She must really need food to be taking from us in broad daylight. Or maybe she can't stop herself from stealing.*

Ezekiel sat in the front of the van with their driver, while Michelle and the children were in the back. The day had finally come. Ezekiel looked over his shoulder. "I bet Mom will be surprised to see how much Vernon has grown." He couldn't help feeling pleased with his family, because after God, they were his world.

Michelle smiled and stroked the baby's head in the car seat where he sat strapped in beside her. In his sleep, the little guy seemed to be smiling at the attention his mom gave him.

"*Grossmammi!* Grossmammi!" Angela Mary kicked her small feet and shouted from the seat behind them.

"Shh. . .Jah, soon we'll see your grandma as well as your aunts and uncle." Michelle spoke quietly in Pennsylvania Dutch with her finger against her lips. "I know you're excited, but we don't want to wake your little brother."

"Okay." Angela Mary began to hum softly.

Ezekiel looked at their driver, Hank, and smiled. "In case you couldn't guess, we are all looking forward to seeing my family today."

Hank grinned. "That's how it should be, and you won't have to wait long because, as you can see, we are approaching Strasburg."

Soon, they turned onto a back-country road. A short time later, shouts of glee went up as the van drove up the Kings' driveway. Fond memories mixed with the sadness of his father, brother, and brother-in-law dying caused Ezekiel's throat to clog.

The vehicle stopped, and he jumped out and opened the door behind him. After helping his wife and children out of the van, Ezekiel paused to look around. Seeing no one in the yard, he figured they were either still in the greenhouse or in their home. They'd left Clymer a little over seven hours ago, which allowed for a few stops along the way. From his calculations, it would get them here by five o'clock, which was when the greenhouse closed each day.

Ezekiel was about to get their luggage from the back, when Mom and Amy came out of the greenhouse and rushed toward them with open arms.

"It's so good to see you." Mom hugged Ezekiel and Michelle then bent down and scooped Angela Mary into her arms. "How's my sweet *maedel* doing these days?"

"Gut, Grossmammi."

"I'm happy to hear you are good."

After Amy greeted everyone with a hug, she gazed with a longing expression at the baby in Michelle's arms. "And this must be my newest nephew. What a cutie he is." She leaned in and kissed little Vernon's forehead. "He's adorable. Ezekiel and Michelle, you must be so pleased."

"We are," they said in unison.

"Oh, my. . ." Mom stroked the infant's cheek. "I can hardly believe how much he's filled out since I was at your home."

"Bopplin grow so quickly. I bet you can still remember when I was a baby." Ezekiel winked at Mom.

With a chuckle, she poked his arm. "Of course I remember. You were such a character, I could never forget."

Everyone laughed. Then Ezekiel, with the help of his driver, removed their luggage.

"Where's the rest of your family?" Michelle asked.

"Sylvia's in the house with the kinner," Mom replied. "And I'm not sure where Henry is. He left the greenhouse the minute we put the CLOSED sign in the window, but I don't know where he went."

"He's probably somewhere with that irritating grapp." Amy wrinkled her nose.

"What crow?" Ezekiel raised his eyebrows and blinked a couple of times. "Why would my bruder be with a grapp?"

"Let's all go up to the house, and I'll fill you in." Amy picked up one of the suitcases and headed toward the front porch. Everyone but Ezekiel grabbed something and followed. He first had to pay their driver and set up a time for them to be picked up in five days. That was as long as Ezekiel felt he could be away from his job. Hopefully, it would be enough time to get caught up on how things had been going here with his family.

Amy sat quietly on the couch, holding baby Vernon, while Michelle visited with Mom and Sylvia. Angela Mary and Allen played happily together. After Ezekiel had come into the house and greeted Sylvia, he'd gone outside to look for Henry. Before he left, Amy had told him all about their brother's so-called pet crow. Ezekiel had laughed and said, "Now, this I've gotta see."

Amy smiled. She could only imagine what her older brother would think when he saw the crow and heard Henry carrying on about how he'd been trying to train the bird. *He will probably think our bruder is either quite strange or desperate for something to do besides work.*

Amy turned her full attention on Dad's little namesake. She hoped this child would grow up to be as kind and loving as her father had been. With Ezekiel and Michelle as parents, she didn't see how Vernon could grow up to be anything but well-behaved, loving, and kind toward others.

Holding the child and snuggling him close brought tears to Amy's eyes. *Will I ever experience the joy of becoming a mother, or will I spend the rest of my life unmarried and childless?*

Be careful, Amy, she told herself. *You are giving in to self-pity again, and that doesn't benefit anyone.*

"I hate to break up this wonderful time of visiting," Mom said, rising from her chair, "but we need to get supper made."

"That's not a problem," Sylvia spoke up. "I put a ham in the oven over an hour ago and cut up some vegetables from the garden to steam." She got up too. "I'll go to the kitchen now and check on things."

"And I'll join you," Michelle said. "After our long drive, I need to move around for a bit. And what better way than to set the table?" She smiled at Amy. "Feel free to stay here with the baby. He likes to be held and will probably fall asleep in your arms."

"Okay."

After the three women left the room, Amy moved over to the rocking chair with the baby. It was a treat to hold a younger baby. He smelled so nice of lotion and soap. The warmth he unknowingly provided Amy as she held him seemed to relax her. It wasn't long after she got it moving that little Vernon's eyelids closed. *I hope I don't fall asleep too.* Watching his slow, even breathing made her feel sleepy, but she kept her eyes open and focused on her niece and nephew playing with a set of building blocks across the room. They were so cute and got along well with each other. It was fun to observe them interact and sometimes entertaining to see the way they communicated despite their limited vocabulary.

Oh, to be young again, when life was so simple. Those two adorable children have no idea how easy they have it.

Ezekiel walked around the yard for a while, looking for Henry. *This is so weird. Where is that kid brother of mine? I hope he hasn't been pulling this trick on our mom very long.*

When he didn't find Henry in the yard, Ezekiel decided to check in the barn. Upon entering the building, he smelled the aroma of cigarette smoke. His fingers curled into the palms of his hands. *That boy had better not have taken up smoking.*

Ezekiel stood there a few minutes, looking around. He saw no sign of Henry and was about to call his name, when Henry came down the ladder that led to the hayloft.

"Oh, hey, Ezekiel. I'm glad you and your family made it okay. How was the trip?"

"It went well. We've been here awhile, and I've been looking for you."

"Well, ya didn't have to look far. I've been looking out the window of the loft, watchin' all the birds in our yard." He shook Ezekiel's hand as though they'd met for the first time. "It's good to see you. How ya doin'?"

"I'm fine, but I am not so sure about you."

Henry took a step back. "What do you mean?"

Ezekiel tipped his head back slightly and sniffed. "I smell cigarette *schmoke*. Have you been smoking, Brother?"

Henry shook his head vigorously. "Course not. I noticed the odor too when I came into the barn."

Ezekiel eyed his brother curiously. "If you're not the one who created the stink, then who?"

"Beats me. Maybe one of the people who came to the greenhouse today wandered in here and lit up a cigarette. I've smelled it in the barn before, so that's what I think must've happened."

Ezekiel reached up and rubbed the back of his neck. He had no proof that Henry had been smoking, but the kid kept shifting from one foot to another as though he might feel guilty about something. *Just to ease my own curiosity, I'd like to have a look up there in the hayloft later on.*

"I'm not saying I don't believe you, but if you have been smoking, you need to quit." Ezekiel looked into his young brother's eyes. "It's bad for your health, not to mention how Mom would react if she ever found you with a cigarette."

"She ain't gonna find me with no cigarette 'cause it's not true." Henry stuffed his hands in his pockets. "Now can we talk about something else?"

"Sure thing." Ezekiel pulled his brother into his arms and gave him a bear hug. "We can talk about why you gave me a handshake instead of a hug."

Henry wiped a trickle of sweat off his forehead. "Cause that's what men do when greeting each other—they shake hands."

Ezekiel was tempted to remind Henry that he wasn't a man yet but chose not to say anything that might rile the boy. Instead, he smiled and said, "I hear you've made a pet out of a crow. Why don't you tell me about it?"

Henry's eyes brightened as he stood to his full height. "Charlie's a beautiful crow, and he's gettin' more used to me all the time, and I've even gotten him to eat outta my hand for a while."

Ezekiel had to hold back a chortle. "So, you've even given the *voggel* a name, huh?"

"Jah. Not every bird deserves a people name, but my crow sure does." Henry's lips parted slightly as he looked right at Ezekiel.

"Wanna know something I've never told anyone else?"

"Sure, I'm all ears." Ezekiel leaned a little closer to his brother.

"I've decided to take up a new hobby."

"Oh, and what would that be?"

"Birding."

"You mean, as in watching for birds and writing things down about them in some sort of a journal?"

Henry gave a nod. "Exactly."

"Sounds like it could be a fun hobby."

"And I'll learn a lot too."

Ezekiel gave his brother's shoulder a squeeze. "Good for you, Henry. I like your idea."

"I haven't said anything about it to Mom, Amy, or Sylvia yet, so I'd appreciate it if you kept quiet and let me do the telling when I feel ready."

"No problem at all. I won't say a word."

"Do you wanna go outside with me now and see if Charlie's up in one of the trees or hanging out on a fence post?"

"We can do that, Henry, but it won't be long till we're called in for supper, so if the bird's not around, we can't linger. We'll need to go inside."

"No problem."

Ezekiel lifted a silent prayer to God. *Thank You for helping my brother find something to get excited about. And please, if Henry has been smoking, make him fall under conviction and admit what he's been doing.*

Chapter 35

Belinda had showered and picked out a clean dress. They'd all been invited to have supper tonight at Mary Ruth's house, where Lenore and her husband and children also lived. It felt good to do something fun for a change. *I need to make more of an attempt to move on with my life.*

Belinda got out her head covering and retrieved some white hairpins to pin it in place. *Ezekiel seems to be moving on with his life, and I couldn't be happier for him.*

This was Ezekiel and his family's second day in Strasburg, and the time was already going too fast. She appreciated the fact that Ezekiel had helped in the greenhouse part of the day while Michelle stayed in the house with Sylvia and their children. With her eldest son visiting, she found herself missing the days gone by, when he still lived at home. The extra pair of hands from the start of work today was a reminder of that, and it made things easier on her—especially given how busy it had been.

Ezekiel had pointed out the jars of honey that were being sold, along with jams, jellies, and other canned goods. He seemed impressed and stated his approval on it being a nice touch in the greenhouse. Belinda liked to hear the positive feedback, and in her heart she hoped Ezekiel would see that they were getting by okay. Of course, she had reminded him of the agreement they'd made back in April—that if she could prove they were doing fine on their own within four months' time, he would stay put at his place in Clymer.

It gave Belinda a feeling of security having Ezekiel and his family here, but she'd accepted the fact that in three days they would return to their own home. Having a taste of them here and enjoying their company made it tempting to ask Ezekiel to move back to Strasburg. But Belinda, still determined to make a go of things, had made up her mind months ago to do it all without her eldest son's help.

Belinda placed her head covering on and made an adjustment so it was squarely in place. Then she reached for a white hairpin to secure the kapp to her hair. *I'd better do a good job since we'll most likely eat outside. Don't want the wind taking my head covering off.*

Looking at herself in the mirror, Belinda gave a nod of approval. *Think I'm done getting ready. I just need to grab my comfy pair of shoes and then it's out the door for me.*

A knock sounded, and Belinda turned her head toward the bedroom door.

"Come in."

"Are you about ready, Mom?" Amy asked as she stepped into the room. "Our driver showed up with the largest of his vans, and everyone's in the living room, all set to go."

"I'm ready, and I'm glad our driver came in the van I requested yesterday." Belinda picked up her black purse and slipped the straps over her shoulder. "We don't want to be late for supper, and I'm sure Mary Ruth is eager to see Ezekiel and his family. She's missed them too—same as we have."

Amy nodded. "It's hard not to have all our family members living close by. We miss out on so much by not seeing them often—especially watching the kinner grow."

Belinda couldn't miss her daughter's wistful expression. *Did I make a mistake insisting that Ezekiel remain in New York when he offered to move back home?* She had asked herself this question many times since her husband and son's deaths. But each time, Belinda reminded herself that Ezekiel had his own life to live and that she wouldn't ask him to sacrifice the new life he'd made for himself and his family.

During supper last night, Ezekiel had sounded so enthusiastic as he talked about his work. And Michelle shared fondly what the family had been up to. Later, Ezekiel mentioned that he'd noticed the corner of the greenhouse near the parking lot and wondered why it looked new. Belinda filled him in on what had happened. He'd appeared surprised and then commented on how relieved he was that no one had been hurt and only a small portion of the building had suffered some damage. Ezekiel didn't know about all the other things that had gone wrong, and Belinda intended to keep it that way. After all, they were all fine and still managing to stay afloat financially despite the setbacks.

As she and Amy left her bedroom and headed down the hall, the sounds of cheerful voices emerged. *Now this is the pleasant noise I miss around here. I hope there will be lots more visits from Ezekiel and his family in the coming years.*

Belinda shook her thoughts aside and followed Amy into the living room, where the others waited. She was eager to go and have some fun. Sharing time with her loved ones meant a lot, and the memories made tonight would not soon be forgotten.

Belinda smiled as she turned to face her family. "All right, everyone, let's all pile into the van and be ready to spend the evening with some very dear friends."

When they arrived at Mary Ruth's house, Amy noticed a car parked in the driveway and a horse and buggy at the hitching rail, so she knew they had other company.

"Looks like it's gonna be a full house this evening," Ezekiel commented.

"That shouldn't be a problem," Michelle interjected. "There's plenty of room in Mary Ruth's house, and from the looks of it, I'd say we'll be eating outdoors." She pointed at the folding tables and chairs set out on the lawn.

With Michelle holding baby Vernon and Sylvia holding Rachel, everyone headed for the house. Mom held Allen's hand, and Amy guided Angela Mary up the front porch stairs, while Ezekiel and Henry brought up the rear.

When they entered the house, Mary Ruth gave them a warm greeting. "It's ever so good to see you." She slipped her arm around Michelle's waist while leaning down to kiss the baby's head. "And look at you, little miss." Mary Ruth lifted Angela Mary into her arms and gave her a kiss. The child giggled and squirmed a bit, but she didn't ask to get down.

Amy thought it was touching that Ezekiel and Michelle had chosen Angela Mary's middle name in honor of their friendship with Mary Ruth. Since Michelle had lived with Mary Ruth and her husband for several months before she joined the Amish church, she'd gotten to know them well. It was no wonder that Michelle wore a big smile this evening, as she answered the older woman's questions about the children, their new community, and how she liked being a minister's wife.

When they made it into the living room, Amy spotted Sara and Brad, along with Sara's father, Herschel. The three of them stepped forward, and the joyful greetings began all over again. Although Sara and Michelle had not always been friends, once they'd set their differences aside, a close friendship had ensued.

A few minutes later, Lenore and her husband, Jesse, entered the room with their daughter, Cindy, and baby boy, Noah. This brought another round of greeting and excited chatter.

After all the chaos subsided, Mary Ruth announced that it was time to eat. They all gathered in the kitchen for silent prayer, and then everyone who could grabbed a container with food in it and took it out to the tables.

The three babies, now asleep, were placed in a playpen Jesse had brought out and set in the shade of a leafy maple tree.

Amy thought it felt wonderful to spend an evening with the two families. *What a shame Dad, Abe, and Toby can't be here with us*, she thought as the food got passed around. *Maybe there's a window in heaven, where they can look down and see us all together. Even though we miss our loved ones very much, I'm sure it would please them to know we are carrying on with our lives the best we can.*

"Sara, have you told these good people your exciting news?" Herschel spoke up.

"Not yet, but I guess this is as good a time as any." Sara looked over at Brad. "Would you like to make the announcement?"

"Sure." He pushed back his chair and stood. "My dear wife and I would like you all to know that in about six months, we'll become parents."

A round of cheers went up, and everyone clapped.

Although Amy was happy for the couple, she felt a twinge of jealousy like she always did whenever she saw someone with a baby or heard that they were in a family way. *Will this great desire I have to be a wife and mother stay with me if I never get married?* she wondered. *Is my sister affected by this news too?* Sylvia had loved Toby so much and would probably never remarry and have more children.

"Will you continue working after the baby is born?" Sylvia's question cut into Amy's thoughts.

Sara shook her head. "I want to be at home with our child as a full-time mother."

"What about the flower shop?" This question came from Amy's mother.

"I'll either sell the place or hire someone who has a good business head to run the store."

"We're praying about the matter." Brad returned to his seat and reached for his glass of lemonade. "Prayer is essential in a Christian's life, and we feel sure that God will reveal His will for us about Sara's business."

Amy glanced at Sylvia, sitting beside her, and noticed her downturned eyes. She reached for her sister's hand under the table and gave her fingers a gentle squeeze. *I know our situations are different and we are hurting in separate ways, but I want to offer you comfort because that's what sisters should do for each other.*

Amy got a quick smile from Sylvia as she returned a soft clasp of her hand. Even so, Amy couldn't shake the helpless feeling in her heart. It wasn't easy to think about how broken her family still was. *I shouldn't be so impatient for us to rebound from something like what we've been through.*

She watched little Allen come to his mom and give a big hug. What a blessing that the Lord had given Sylvia two beautiful and healthy children to care for. *How can she not see the handiwork of our Maker who created them? Does she ever pray anymore and ask for God's direction in her life?* Even if her sister had given up praying, Amy was determined not to let her own prayer life slip. Not only did she need God's guidance, but the rest of her family did as well.

Sylvia felt uncomfortable listening to Brad talk about prayer and God revealing His will. Where had prayer gotten her, anyhow? Ever since she was a teenager and had joined the Amish church, Sylvia had prayed and read her Bible faithfully. But that all stopped the day Toby, Dad, and Abe were killed.

She pulled her hands into tight fists and placed them in her lap, where no one could see them. Sylvia wasn't sure she could ever let go of her bitterness and be able to trust God again.

She glanced across the table at Henry. As far as she could tell, he didn't put much stock in prayer anymore either. Like her, he was probably angry at God for taking three people he loved. So far, Henry didn't talk about the Bible, as he had done in the past. Sylvia remembered how Dad and Henry would chat about messages from the sermons given at church on Sundays. Other times, Henry would get into deep conversations with Abe about Revelations and what some of the things written in the last book of the Bible meant. She had to admit that listening in on some of those conversations had been interesting and sometimes funny with her brother's interpretation of things.

It was difficult for a young teenager to be without a father, and with Abe gone and Ezekiel living over six hours away, Henry had no male guidance—and it showed. An uncooperative son with a rebellious spirit was not what their father would have wanted. *If the accident hadn't happened and our daed was still alive, Henry's actions would be a disappointment. Of course, if Dad were still here, Henry probably wouldn't be acting so rebellious.*

Sylvia felt helpless when it came to dealing with her young brother. He didn't listen to anything she or Amy said. Most of the time, Henry carried on as if he had a chip on his shoulder. That certainly did nothing to help the situation. Even around Mom, Henry often acted like a spoiled boy. Yet Sylvia felt sure he wanted to be treated like an adult. Henry needed the right help to get his act together before something else went wrong.

But what would help? she asked herself. *If Mom got married again, would that make a difference in Henry's life? He'd have a stepfather, but he might resent someone other than a family member telling him what to do.*

Sylvia bit her lip so hard she tasted blood. *If Mom should ever marry again, I'd accept it if I thought it would make her happy. But for me, I'll never allow myself to fall in love or get remarried. Toby was the love of my life and always will be. There isn't a man in this world who could ever take his place.*

Chapter 36

Ezekiel couldn't believe how quickly their five days had gone, but tomorrow they would be making the journey back home. It felt bittersweet. Although he was eager to get back to Clymer and his growing business, he felt bad about leaving Mom and his siblings. *Sure wish I could talk my mamm into selling the greenhouse and moving close to us. But I guess she'll never consider that as long as her business is doing well and my siblings are willing to keep working there—at least until one of them gets married.* Ezekiel shook his head. *It seems like my mamm is becoming stronger and more confident. I'd say the Lord is at work in her life.*

He tugged his beard. *I wonder if Sylvia will ever remarry. Her children do need a father.*

Ezekiel got up from the couch, where he'd been reading his Bible, and looked out the front window. So many memories had been made here while he was growing up. Most were good, but he also remembered some bad.

"Course most of the bad things that happened were my fault," he said under his breath. *I was a stubborn, rebellious teenager who thought he wanted something other than what he already had.* Looking back on it, Ezekiel was glad he'd sold his truck and settled down to join the Amish church. That and marrying Michelle were the best decisions he'd ever made.

"What are you doing in here by yourself? I thought you'd be

outside with the rest of the family, watching the sun go down."

Ezekiel turned at the sound of his mother's voice. "Just wanted to sit awhile and do some thinking."

"Mind if I ask what you've been thinking about?" She joined him at the window.

He slipped his arm around her waist. "You and my brothers and sisters, mostly."

"You're not still worried about us, I hope."

"Concerned might be a better word for it."

"There's nothing to be concerned about."

"That's not what Henry told me this morning."

His mother's posture stiffened, and she let out a forceful breath. "What exactly did he tell you?"

"Said an old boyfriend of yours has been hanging around and that he even asked you to go out for supper with him."

She took a step back. "Well I didn't go, and if Monroe asks again, my answer will still be no."

Ezekiel closed his eyes briefly, releasing a quiet exhale. "Good to hear. It's too soon for you to be thinking about getting married again."

Her forehead wrinkled. "Now who said anything about getting remarried? Monroe Esh is just a friend from the past, nothing more."

Ezekiel didn't say anything further on the subject, but he felt a sense of relief knowing his mother had taken a stand. He'd never met this old beau of Mom's, but if and when he did, he'd make it clear to the man that Mom was still in love with Dad and hadn't gotten past the pain of losing him in such an unexpected way.

"I think Sylvia and the little ones have the right idea. I'm a little tuckered out, so I'll head off to bed too." Belinda rose from her chair.

"Good night," everyone else said.

"See you all in the morning." Belinda left the living room and went to the kitchen to fetch something to drink. After filling her glass with water, she made sure the back door was locked. The odd things that had occurred on their property made the uncertainty resurface more at night. Belinda tried to shrug it off, but since there'd been no identification of who had done those things yet, the unresolved situation was frightening to her. It was a comfort to have her eldest son here to give that sense of security.

It's funny how when my children were small, I protected them. Now there are times when it feels as though our roles have changed.

Belinda left the kitchen and walked down the hall to her bedroom. Upon entering the darkened room, she felt around and clicked on the battery-powered light by her bed. She took a drink of water and set the glass on the nightstand.

Tomorrow would be a day of goodbyes before Ezekiel and his family headed back to Clymer. She hoped anything Ezekiel had said to Henry while he was here had left an impression and would help in some way. Belinda wanted her youngest boy to have the right priorities.

She removed her head covering and placed it on the dresser before changing into her nightclothes. Next, she took out her hairpins from her bun, reached for her hairbrush, and brushed out the long, coiled strand. Once that was done, it felt good to climb under the cool sheets after an eventful day. Belinda then clicked off the light and closed her eyes.

As Belinda lay in bed, she reflected on the conversation she'd had with Ezekiel earlier this evening. It had been hard not to tell her eldest son about the problems they'd had over the last few months. If she'd said anything about the vandalism though, he would surely have decided to make the sacrifice and move back to Strasburg.

Belinda felt relieved that neither Henry nor his sisters had said anything to Ezekiel either. It was bad enough that her youngest son had told him about Monroe.

Belinda bunched the pillow in an attempt to find a more comfortable position for her head and neck. *Now my son has one more thing to worry about. Hopefully, I put his mind at ease concerning Monroe and his possible intentions toward me.*

Belinda stared into the darkened room and sighed. The house would sure seem quiet after Ezekiel and his family left in the morning. She dreaded saying goodbye but clung to the hope that they would return to Strasburg for Thanksgiving, which was only two and a half months from now. Last year they had stayed in Clymer and entertained Michelle's brothers, as they had done two years previous to that. Maybe this year Ernie and Jack would have other plans. If that were the case, then Belinda saw no reason Ezekiel, Michelle, and the children could not join them for the holiday meal.

Would it be selfish to pray for that? Belinda readjusted her pillow. *Guess I'd better try and get some sleep. Before I know it, the sun will rise and it'll be time to start breakfast.*

"Oh, look at the time." Mom turned away from the clock and frowned.

Amy could tell her mother felt overwhelmed, what with her brother and his family so close to leaving. Breakfast had been good, and visiting with one another had used up a lot of time.

Ezekiel sipped on his cup of coffee. "We tried to make sure everything we came here with is going back home with us."

"You could leave my grandchildren here, and I wouldn't mind." Mom chuckled.

Ezekiel winked. "One of these days, you'll get your wish."

"You movin' back?" Henry asked.

"No, little brother. I meant when the kinner are older and want to spend a week or so here without their parents." He poked Henry's arm. "You can put 'em to work helping you with chores."

Everyone laughed.

A few minutes later, Ezekiel's driver pulled in and honked his horn.

"Hank's here," Michelle announced from where she stood in front of the kitchen window, drying the last of the breakfast dishes.

"Why don't you invite him for a cup of kaffi?" Mom suggested.

"That's right," Amy agreed. "It'll be a few minutes before you're all ready to go."

Ezekiel shook his head. "I can offer, but if I know Hank, he will say that he'd rather wait in the van till we come out."

Amy looked at her mother, raising her eyebrows in question.

Mom merely shrugged and said, "We can send a thermos of coffee with you."

"That's really not necessary. We'll be stopping along the way, and Hank no doubt had breakfast and coffee before coming here this morning." Ezekiel stepped over to Michelle. "If you're fully packed, I'll start hauling suitcases out to the van."

Michelle nodded, and Amy saw tears in her sister-in-law's eyes. "All I need to do is change the baby's windel and we'll be ready to go."

A short time later, they were all on the front porch saying tearful goodbyes. Amy especially felt choked up at the moment, as she held little Vernon one last time and kissed his soft cheek. What an adorable baby he was, and the fact that he had been given such a special name made her feel even more emotional.

"Guess we'd better not keep Hank waiting. If we don't go out to the van soon, he'll be honking again."

Final hugs were given, and as the van drove out of the yard, Amy, Mom, and Sylvia waved goodbye.

When Rachel began to cry, Sylvia went into the house with Allen and the baby. Amy and Mom remained on the porch, waving until the van was clear out of sight.

Tears spilled out of Amy's eyes and rolled onto her cheeks.

"It's okay, Daughter." Mom patted Amy's back. "We'll see them again soon. If not for Thanksgiving then maybe Christmas."

Amy sniffed. "I will miss them terribly, but something else is bothering me."

Mom motioned to the porch swing. "Why don't we have a seat over there? You can tell me about it."

"Okay."

Mom seated herself on the swing, and Amy sat beside her.

"Whenever I have an opportunity to spend time with a boppli, I'm reminded that I'll probably never have any of my own."

"Why not, Amy? You're bound to get married someday."

Amy shook her head and wiped her eyes. "I'm still in love with Jared, and he is the only man I'll ever want to marry, but it's not meant for us to be together."

"Why would you say that?"

"If it was, that horrible accident would never have occurred."

Mom took hold of Amy's hand and gave it a squeeze. "I've told you this before, but you haven't been listening. Just because you're helping me in the greenhouse doesn't mean you can't have a relationship with Jared."

"But Mom, courting couples go places together, and I have no time for courting."

"You can make the time. I've never expected you to be chained to me, the greenhouse, or household chores. Sylvia does most things in the house, and Henry does chores around here too."

"I realize that, but—"

"There are no buts about it, Daughter. Instead of trying to do multiple chores every evening, sometimes you need to go and have a little fun with other unmarried young people—Jared included. Your life should not be only about working, and neither should Jared's."

Amy sighed, leaning her head against the back of the swing. "But it may be too late for us."

"Why's that?"

"I think he and Lydia might be courting, and if they're not, they probably will be soon. They sat with each other at Lydia's party and had their heads together most of the evening, talking whenever they could. Besides, I've seen them together and heard rumors that..."

"You won't know if he cares for Lydia unless you ask. If you find out that they're not courting, you need to speak up and tell Jared you still care for him and would like to resume your relationship." Mom spoke in strong sentences.

Amy's chin dipped slightly. "I'll give it some serious thought."

Virginia had said goodbye to Earl before he'd left for work but not before she'd complained about their yard again. Although he mowed the lawn once a week, she thought the place needed some sprucing up.

She'd been sitting out on the front porch looking at all the work that needed to be done. She certainly wasn't up to it, that was for sure. And with Earl so busy at his job, he'd probably never do much more than mow the lawn. All the bushes needed trimming, the grass should have been edged weeks ago, and a tangle of weeds had taken over most of the flowerbeds. Virginia had pulled some of the weeds, until her lower back began to hurt. Some days she felt worthless, especially when it came to doing strenuous tasks. Virginia's past mistakes had taken a physical toll on her.

Her thoughts changed course as she watched a passenger van pull out of the driveway across the street and onto the road. She'd seen from a distance a couple of new people she hadn't noticed before milling around the Kings' yard for the last few days and wondered if they had company. Maybe some relatives or close friends had come to visit.

Virginia leaned back in her chair and brushed her long bangs aside. She'd colored her hair yesterday with an auburn shade of henna, but her bangs still needed to be cut. The salon she'd gone to when they lived in Chicago had done a decent job with her hair, but she hadn't looked for anyplace here yet and wasn't sure which salon might be best.

Maybe I can cut my own bangs. Virginia got up and ambled into the house. She stood in front of the hall mirror and made pretend cuts on her bangs with two fingers. *Nope, it shouldn't be too hard at all.*

In the bathroom, Virginia located the pair of scissors Earl used to trim his moustache. Then, picking up her comb, she dampened it under the faucet, pulled the comb through the ends of her bangs, and cut. Virginia liked the bangs shorter and out of her eyes, but now they were crooked. *That shouldn't be a problem. I'll just trim away till they're straight.*

A few minutes ticked by along with more attempts at trying to make them look even. Her bangs were nearly dry, but they'd shrunk too. Virginia was in a panic. "I haven't had bangs this short since kindergarten! What am I going to do?"

She put the scissors and comb away and stood staring at herself in the mirror. "Wish I could glue the hair back on, but now, because of my stupidity, I'm stuck with how ridiculous I look. I will never cut my own hair again."

Virginia headed to the kitchen and poured herself some coffee. *I wonder what Earl will say when he sees my trim job. Sure hope he doesn't get mad.*

Chapter 37

After some serious prayer and Bible reading, Amy decided to approach Jared and see if he might be interested in courting her again. She wasn't sure yet when she might get the opportunity, but she thought perhaps after they had supper this evening, she might take a ride over to his place.

In need of some reassurance, Amy went to her sister to share the news. She found Sylvia in her bedroom changing the baby. "I know you're busy, but I wanted to talk to you about something."

Sylvia turned her head in Amy's direction. "Sure, come on in."

Amy entered the bedroom and took a seat on the edge of her sister's bed. "I've decided to talk to Jared and see if there's a possibility of us getting back together."

"Really? I thought you believed that you didn't have time for courting."

"It's true, but after Mom and I talked, she convinced me otherwise." Amy shifted her position on the bed. "I'm mostly concerned about whether Jared will want to start over, because I believe he and Lydia have been courting."

Sylvia slipped Rachel's little dress over her curly head. "It hasn't even been six months since you broke up with Jared. I can't imagine that he'd move on so quickly or forget about what the two of you had together. And if he were going to court someone else, I doubt it would be your best friend."

"So, you think I should go ahead and talk to him about it?"

"Jah."

"Okay, then it's settled. I'll talk to him soon." Feeling a bit more confident, Amy rose from the bed. "Right now though Mom asked me to go out before the greenhouse opens and check for phone messages, so I'd best get to it."

As Amy approached the phone shed, she glanced across the street and saw Jared in their neighbor's yard talking with Virginia's husband. His horse and buggy was in the driveway, and she noticed that Dandy had been secured to a fencepost. Seeing Jared made her heartbeat quicken. She remembered when the two of them had been seeing each other regularly and how she'd felt every time they were together. Amy had felt a connection with Jared and wanted to have that same bond again.

I wonder if he went over to the neighbors' to bid on a roofing job. I suppose he could have stopped by for some other reason.

Amy was tempted to walk over and talk to Jared but didn't want to interrupt their conversation. If he was in the middle of conducting business, which she suspected, an interruption would be rude, and he might not appreciate it.

So instead, Amy tried a different approach. She walked close to one of the shrubs and plucked some dead leaves off then waited a few minutes, hoping Jared might look her way. But he kept his attention focused on the English man.

This is so frustrating. If he would just glance over here, I could at least offer a friendly wave. Maybe then, once Jared's business was done, he'd come over and say hello.

Amy looked up at the crow flying overhead, emitting its irritating cry as it swooped through the air. "Probably after some poor bug," she mumbled. "Go away."

Amy stepped away from the shrub and brushed off her apron where some debris had stuck. She looked across the road again and realized that Jared and Virginia's husband had disappeared. They'd either gone into the house or around to the back of the home.

Amy figured it would be best if she went to the phone shed now, before any customers showed up at the greenhouse. It was disappointing not to have at least made eye contact with Jared. Perhaps by the time she came out, he would be finished with his business across the road and there might be another chance to get his attention.

As Amy approached the shed, she spotted Henry in the yard throwing a stick for his dog. *I do hope Henry will eventually get over his anger toward God and become a pleasant young man again.*

She entered the phone shed, and a short time later, holding a slip of paper with a list of messages, Amy stepped out of the building. Much to her dismay, Jared's horse and buggy were gone.

I suppose I should stick to my original plan and go over to his place this evening.

"Are you sure we can afford to get the garage roof redone?" Virginia asked after Earl came inside. "It seems like a waste of money to me."

His face tensed. "We can't afford not to reroof the garage, Virginia. It's in bad shape, and if we let it go, we'll probably have more than one leak to deal with." He pointed a finger at her. "Do you want that?"

"Of course not. I just thought. . ." She moved over to stand in front of the hallway mirror.

"You need to relax and let me do the thinking." He grabbed the lunch she'd prepared for him that morning. "I've got to go now or I'll be late for work." Earl paused and kissed her cheek. "I'll bring a pizza when I come home this evening. How's that sound?"

She smiled up at him and played with her tiny bangs. "That'd be nice. It'll save me from wracking my brain to come up with something to fix for tonight's supper."

"Exactly. And your hair looks fine, dear, so quit worrying so much. Those bangs look kinda cute so short in the front." Earl gave Virginia a thumbs-up and went out the door.

"Yeah, right." She left the mirror, picked up her cup of lukewarm coffee, and poured what was left of it in the sink. *That husband of mine always seems to know the right thing to say. And I'm thankful he's considerate of my needs. Even when I mess up on things here in the house or with myself, he's kind. Sure hope he stays that way.*

Amy was surprised when Lydia's mother came into the greenhouse that afternoon. She hadn't seen Darlene since Lydia's birthday party, and because she rarely came here for anything, Amy had to wonder what her reason was now.

Mom had gone into the house to get them more water and a snack, and Henry was busy loading plants into the back of a customer's van. That left Amy alone for a short while to wait on customers, so she smiled at Darlene and said, "May I help you with something?"

"I came for a few jars of honey," the woman replied. "I know where they're located, and I'll be back soon to pay for them."

Amy waited behind the counter until Darlene came up with the items she wanted. "How's your quilting business going?" she asked, wanting to be polite.

"It's doing well. We've had a lot of orders lately." Darlene fingered the jars of honey, sliding her thumb around the rim as though inspecting them. "Lydia's a big help to me. I'm hoping she'll keep quilting after she and Jared are married."

Amy's whole body felt numb. She breathed deeply through her nose, hoping she wouldn't faint. "I—I had no idea Jared had asked Lydia to marry him. She's made no mention of it to me."

"No, she wouldn't have. I only heard my daughter talking about it yesterday when her friend Nadine dropped by to pick up a quilted table runner for her mother."

Amy hardly knew what to say. She was aware that Lydia and Jared had been seen together, and the rumors going around all pointed to the fact that they might be courting. But Amy had no idea their relationship had progressed that quickly to a marriage proposal.

Her jaw clenched, despite her best efforts to appear relaxed. *For goodness' sakes. . .it hasn't even been six months since I broke things off with Jared. He sure managed to forget about me quickly. I should never have believed him when he said he loved me. No man who supposedly loves a woman should move on to another so quickly. Guess it's a good thing I found out what he's really like now.*

"Ah-hem!" Darlene cleared her throat. "Did you hear my question?"

Amy blinked a couple of times as her mind came back into focus. "Sorry. What was it you asked me about?"

"I wanted to know if you'll be closing the greenhouse for the season early this year."

"No, we'll be open through the week after Thanksgiving, as usual. We'll want to make our poinsettias available to customers who like to buy them before Christmas."

"I see. Well, I may come back sometime between now and then. I might buy some more honey or a plant to give my sister as a Christmas present this year."

Amy nodded, still reeling from the news that the man she loved would be marrying her best friend. She was tempted to ask if the wedding date had been set, but in all honesty, she didn't want to know.

"I saw your friend Amy today," Lydia's mother said as they stood in the kitchen, preparing supper.

"Oh? Did you visit the greenhouse or see her someplace in town?"

"At the greenhouse. I went there to get some hunnich."

Lydia smacked her lips. "Yum. I love their all-natural raw honey. It's super good on pancakes, and it goes well with peanut butter on toast or in a sandwich."

Mama nodded as she grabbed a potato peeler from the utensil drawer. "I've been meaning to say something to you all afternoon, but with customers coming and going to pick up quilted items, I never got a chance."

"What did you want to say?" Lydia asked as she chopped cabbage for a coleslaw.

"I just want you to know how pleased I am about you and Jared courting and even more so now that I know he's proposed marriage to you."

Lydia's brows shot up. "Where in the world did you get such an idea? Jared and I aren't courting much less planning to be married."

"Really? But I thought—"

"Where did you get such an idea, Mama?"

"I heard you talking to your friend Nadine. I couldn't be sure of everything you said, but I got some of the conversation—the important part that is."

"What did you think you heard me tell her?"

"That you and Jared are courting and that he proposed marriage."

Lydia's mouth gaped open. It seemed she'd been caught between a stone and a brick wall. It was time to tell her mother the truth.

"I have something to confess, Mama."

"Oh, and what is it?"

"I've been secretly seeing Rudy Zook."

"Did you say Rudy Zook, or are my *ohre* playing tricks on me right now?"

"No, your ears are not playing tricks. Rudy's a kind and gentle man, and I love him very much."

"You can't be *anscht*, Lydia."

"I am as serious as anyone can be." Lydia was aware that her parents, especially Mama, had never approved of Rudy because he worked in a general store and didn't make much money since he was not the owner. Mama had pointed out once that a man like that would be unable to support a wife and children properly, so the poor fellow would probably never find a woman willing to let him court her. In addition to that, Rudy stuttered, and Mama thought his speech impediment and crooked nose made him a less than desirable boyfriend. For these reasons, Lydia had kept her relationship with Rudy a secret, and whenever they'd gone anywhere together, it was someplace out of the area. If her parents had gotten wind of her feelings for Rudy, they'd do everything in their power to turn Lydia against the idea.

"But you've been seeing a lot of Jared since Amy broke up with him." Mama broke into Lydia's thoughts. "I was so sure. . ."

Lydia held up her hand. "Jared and I are just friends. The reason you've seen me with him so much is because we were talking about Amy—trying to figure out some way to get them back together. It also bought me some time to pray and decide how and when I should let you know the truth about Rudy and me."

Lydia's mother set the potato peeler aside and collapsed into a chair at the table. "Oh, dear. I'm afraid I've made a terrible mistake."

"You've changed your mind about Rudy?"

"No, not really, but if he's the man you love then I guess I have no choice but to give you my blessing. But I'll need time to prepare your daed for this news."

Lydia leaned down and gave her mother a hug. "Danki, Mama. I appreciate you paving the way with Dad. I can hardly wait to tell Rudy."

"Life can sure throw us a curve ball sometimes, and I've managed to swing and miss this time." Lydia's mother placed her elbows on the table and leaned forward, pressing her fingertips against her forehead. "The mistake I made was in telling Amy what I thought I heard you telling Nadine."

"About me and Rudy?"

"No, Daughter. I told Amy that I heard you telling Nadine that you and Jared were planning to get married."

"Oh, dear. Oh, dear." Lydia rocked back and forth with her arms crossed over her chest. "Amy must be so upset with me—and angry with Jared too. She no doubt feels that we've betrayed her." She moved quickly toward the back door.

"Where are you going, Lydia?"

"I need to go over to the Kings' house right away and talk to Amy. She needs to know the truth."

"I understand, but it will have to wait until tomorrow morning."

"How come?"

"The bishop and his wife are coming here for supper this evening. I can't believe you could have forgotten that."

"I remembered earlier, but the shock of what you said to Amy must have caused me to forget." Lydia placed a hand on her mother's shoulder. "Can I go as soon as we've finished eating supper?"

With a determined expression, Mama shook her head. "That would be impolite. You can go over to see Amy first thing in the morning."

"Okay." Lydia didn't feel that she had much choice in the matter. It was bad enough that she'd been deceiving her folks for the last several months by seeing Rudy on the sly. She didn't want to rile Mama any more by leaving the house this evening while their company was there.

Amy might not sleep very well tonight, but tomorrow when I go over to see her, she'll feel a lot better. Lydia rubbed her chin. *But then maybe hearing that Jared and I were planning to be married didn't upset my friend at all. She did, after all, break up with Jared, so perhaps she doesn't care about him anymore.*

Later that evening, Mom, Sylvia, and the children were settled in the living room after their meal. Henry said he was going outside to the barn.

Amy put away the last of their clean supper dishes and stepped outside to enjoy the setting sun. She stood on the porch, looking toward the west as the sky turned brilliant colors. The sight helped alleviate some of her depression after hearing about Jared and Lydia. *The Lord sure knows how to dress up the sky.*

She continued watching a little longer then headed to the barn. *Maybe Henry would enjoy seeing the gorgeous sunset too.*

Once inside the darkened building, instead of calling out to her brother, Amy used her flashlight to climb the ladder to the loft. She found him there, looking at a car magazine, with a battery-operated light, like they used for campouts.

"Hello."

Henry quickly laid the magazine aside. "What's up?"

"I came to find out if you'd like to see the sunset. It's really beautiful."

"Sure, let's go take a look." He followed her down the ladder.

When they stepped outside and looked toward the sky, it had turned an incredible pink.

Henry whistled. "Wow, that's gorgeous!"

Amy waited a minute, and then she spoke. "I noticed the magazine you were looking at."

"What about it?" His tone had become defensive.

"When did you get it?"

"Not long ago."

"You're not thinking about getting a car, are you?"

Henry stared straight ahead. "I'm only looking at it. The magazine belongs to Seth."

"Oh, that's good."

"I best go check on the horses' water before I get ready to go in the house. Thanks for showin' me the sunset." Her brother turned back toward the barn.

"You're welcome." Amy had misgivings about how honest her brother had been with her. *What if Seth has put some silly notion into Henry's head about getting a car when he's old enough to drive? It happened to Ezekiel when he went through his running-around years.*

Amy paused and looked up at the sky and the diminishing sunset. *Should I say something to Mom or let it go?*

Chapter 38

The next morning, when Amy entered the greenhouse still feeling depressed, she discovered that all their pots of fall flowers had died. She felt stunned. "How could something like this have happened?"

Amy raced out of the building and back to the house. "Where's Mom?" she asked Sylvia, who sat feeding the baby.

"I think she's still in the kitchen. She said she had a few things to do there before she joined you in the greenhouse."

"Something terrible has happened!"

Sylvia's eyes widened. "What is it? Has Henry been hurt?"

Amy shook her head. "I didn't see our bruder outside anywhere. So as far as I know, he's fine."

"What is it then?" Sylvia's chin quivered as she placed Rachel against her shoulder and began patting the baby's back.

"All the mums and other fall flowers are dead." Amy's body trembled with the pent-up anger she felt.

"Hasn't Henry been watering them?"

"I check every day to be sure, and none of them have appeared to be dried out. I just don't understand what happened." Amy tapped her chin. "I wonder if. . ." Her voice trailed off. "I'd better go tell Mom."

Belinda was removing a jug of cold tea from the refrigerator to take to the greenhouse when Amy burst into the room.

"I'm sorry to have to tell you this, Mom, but all our mums and other fall *blumme* are dead."

"What?" Belinda put down the jug. "But how can that be?"

Amy shrugged. "I—I don't know. I'm sure they've been getting enough water and fertilizer."

"Come on, Amy, we'd better go see if we can figure out what happened to those plants." Belinda tied a black scarf on her head and hurried out the back door.

When they entered the greenhouse and Belinda's eyes beheld the disaster, she brought a shaky hand up to her forehead. "This is worse than I imagined." She looked at Amy. "We have no more fall *blanse* left to sell."

Amy joined Belinda as they walked up and down the rows. "Do you think this could have been done on purpose?"

"Who would do such a thing, and how would they gain access to the greenhouse when we're not here?" Belinda pulled a tissue out from under her dress sleeve and blew her nose. "Where's your bruder?"

"I don't know. I haven't seen him since breakfast." Amy moved closer to Belinda. "You don't think Henry would do something so horrible, do you? I mean, he has to know that we were counting on the money we earned from the sale of these plants."

The tissue slipped from Belinda's hand, and she bent down to pick it up. In so doing, she noticed a bottle of weed killer under one of the wooden counters where this section of plants sat. "Oh, my!"

"What is it, Mom?"

When Amy leaned over, Belinda pointed.

"That's really odd. We never keep weed killer near the flowers, shrubs, or anything else it could damage or kill. I wonder how this got moved from the storage area where it's kept."

Belinda picked up the container and realized very quickly that it was almost empty. All of the weed killers they sold were completely full. "I am convinced that whoever did this used weed killer to destroy the plants, and then they set the near-empty bottle underneath this counter." She clasped her daughter's hand. "Oh Amy, what are we going to do?"

"The first thing I plan on doing is finding Henry and questioning him about this. He may be smiling more these days, thanks to that stupid crow he messes with, but I can tell by some of the things he says and does that his heart is still bitter."

Belinda stood up tall and pulled her shoulders back. If her boy was responsible for this, she would deal harshly with him. But if there was even a possibility of his innocence, she couldn't punish him. What they needed more than anything right now was something else they could sell that would bring in some money. "I'll handle Henry. Please go find your brother and let him know I need to see him."

Amy found Henry in the barn and said, "Mom needs you in the greenhouse."

"Tell her I'll be there in a few minutes. I still have a couple of chores to do."

"Please, Henry." Amy pointed in the direction of the greenhouse. "Mom needs to see you right now."

"Okay, okay." Henry ambled toward the greenhouse and Amy followed. Mom might need her help getting the truth out of him.

When they entered the building, Mom stood near the door with her hands on her hips and a stony expression. It was a good thing no customers had shown up yet, because it wouldn't be nice for anyone to hear this conversation or see all the dead plants. They would need to get them cleared out quickly before anyone arrived.

Amy waited quietly while Mom told Henry what had happened to the plants and about the weed killer she'd found. "Do you know anything about this, Son?"

A flush appeared on Henry's face and neck as he broke eye contact with Mom. "I hope ya don't think I would do such a terrible thing." He shuffled his feet. "I work here too, ya know, and I count on the money you pay me."

"Of course, but you've also complained about working here, and since you have access to the greenhouse with the new key Amy had made for you and eventually entrusted you with, I felt the need to question you."

His eyes narrowed. "Well, you can question me all ya want, and my answer will still be the same—I am not the one who destroyed the fall plants."

Amy wanted to believe her brother, but he'd lied to them before and snuck out of the house when he was supposed to be in bed. *He could be holding back the truth so he doesn't get in trouble.* Amy tapped her foot. *But if Henry is telling the truth, then someone has access to our greenhouse and must have come in during the night. That means they either had a copy of our key somehow or picked the lock on the door. Was it the same person who did the other things to our property? Does someone really dislike us that much, or could they be trying to make things difficult so we'll give up and close the greenhouse for good?*

"Standing here debating this matter is not accomplishing a thing." Mom broke into Amy's contemplations. "The three of us need to get busy hauling all the dead plants out behind the barn, where no one will see them."

"Who cares if anyone sees them or not?" Henry's voice grew louder with each word he said. "When people show up here today, they're gonna see that we have no fall flowers or plants to sell."

"We still have a few hanging baskets that Sylvia put together," Amy chimed in.

"But they're not specifically fall colors," Mom replied. "Also, what are we going to do about the orders Sara placed recently? She's expecting one of us to deliver them sometime this week."

"As soon as we finish hauling the dead plants out, I'll go to the phone shed and give her a call." Amy's heart thudded dully in her chest. "She'll probably end up ordering from the new greenhouse."

Mom gave a nod. "Be that as it may, we can't promise something we are unable to make good on."

Henry pulled his hat off and fingered the brim. "Here's somethin' else to think about. Once Sara sells her flower shop, the new owner might decide to buy from the other greenhouse. He or she could be more interested in dealin' with a place that's closer to town and is run by the English."

When Amy saw her mother's eyebrows draw together, she could have kicked her brother for saying that. Mom didn't need one more thing to worry about.

"It's just a shame we had to lose all those beautiful mums and other fall foliage." Amy stood near her mother next to one of the wagons filled with dead plants.

"Jah, but there's not much we can do about it now."

"I keep wondering who could have done this and why we're their target."

Mom looked at Amy and slowly shook her head. "This is really going to set us back."

Amy heaved a frustrated sigh. They'd hauled out about half of the ruined plants when a horse and buggy pulled into the parking lot. Amy stood in the doorway watching as Mary Ruth climbed down from her buggy and went to the hitching rail to secure her horse.

Amy waved as Mary Ruth headed their way. "Our first customer of the day is here," she called to Mom.

"What? Oh, no." Mom's facial features slackened. "I had hoped we could finish this job before anyone showed up. Is it someone we know?"

"Jah, it's Mary Ruth, and she's coming this way."

Wearing a cheerful smile and holding a toy wooden horse, Mary Ruth entered the greenhouse. "Guder mariye."

"Morning." Amy managed to smile in return.

"I believe this belongs to your nephew." Mary Ruth handed the toy to Amy. "I found it the day after you and your family came for supper at my place, but I kept forgetting to bring it over until now."

"No problem. Allen hasn't asked for it, so most likely he hasn't even missed the toy."

Mom came up to them, pulling a wagonload full of dead plants. "Good morning, Mary Ruth. I hope you're not here to buy any of our *harebscht* blanse, because we don't have any now."

Mary Ruth touched her parted lips as she looked at the pathetic plants with an incredulous stare. "What in the world happened to those?"

Mom explained, while Amy grabbed another wagon and piled on more dead plants.

"I'm sorry to hear about your autumn plants." Mary Ruth gestured to the two wagonloads waiting to be taken out. "I don't need any myself, but I'm sure you'll get lots of customers coming in for fall foliage."

"You're right, and we may as well put up a sign here at the front of store so people will know when they first come in that we have none to sell." Mom's shoulders slumped as she heaved a heavy sigh. "This is certainly not what we needed right now."

Amy hadn't seen her mother look this despondent since she'd returned from her visit to Ezekiel and Michelle's place. She wished she could say something to cheer Mom up, but she too felt the pain of this latest act of vandalism. It was a mystery to her that anyone would want to do this to them.

"I may be able to help with your problem," Mary Ruth spoke up. "Lenore and I planted more mums and dahlias than we know what to do with, so I'd be happy to let you have most of them to offer your customers."

Mom's eyes brightened a little. "That is a very generous offer, but don't you usually sell them at the farmers' market or set up a roadside stand in front of your place?"

"We've tried that a few times, but it's a lot of work. And with Lenore being so busy with two little ones, it's more than I can keep up with by myself." She touched Mom's arm. "Please, Belinda, I want you to have them. I'll just keep a few out for ourselves is all."

Mom nodded and gave Mary Ruth a hug. "All right then, but I insist on paying you. I'll send Henry over with our market wagon to get them as soon as he finishes disposing of the rest of the lifeless plants."

"If you sell a lot, you can give me a small payment, but I want you to be able to make a profit." Mary Ruth's big smile and light, bubbly voice indicated that she was more than willing to share from her abundance. It was kind and generous people like her who made the world a better place. It appeared that things might be looking up for them again.

Chapter 39

Later that morning, Lydia got out her scooter and headed to the greenhouse to talk to Amy. She needed to set her straight on how things were between her and Jared. She could only imagine what her friend must have thought when Mom told her that Lydia and Jared were talking about getting married. *Amy probably thinks I betrayed her. If I don't set things straight right away, it could be the end of our friendship.*

Lydia thought about Rudy and how she'd kept her relationship with him a secret even from her best friend. "I should have at least told Amy," she mumbled as she neared the Kings' place. "I'm sure she would have kept my secret, and she wouldn't have gotten the wrong idea about me and Jared."

When Lydia arrived outside the greenhouse, she parked her scooter near the building and went inside. She found Belinda sitting on a stool behind the counter, sorting through some papers.

"Guder mariye, Belinda." Lydia smiled. "Is Amy here? I need to speak with her about something important."

Amy's mother shook her head. "My daughter had a dental appointment. She hired a driver to take her there. I believe she may have had a few errands to run too, so she probably won't be back for several hours."

"Oh, I see." Lydia was tempted to tell Amy's mother the reason she had come over and ask her to give Amy the message, but she decided against that idea. It would be better if she talked to Amy herself. Perhaps she could put in a good word for Jared too, like she'd tried to do in the past. Only this time, maybe she could talk some sense into her friend.

Lydia pulled her shoulders back. *If Amy could take time out to attend my birthday gathering, she could certainly find the time for Jared to court her. I just need to make her see that and then act upon it.*

"Now that was sure strange." Belinda stroked her chin, watching as Lydia rode out of the parking lot on her scooter. *I wonder why she wouldn't give me a message for Amy. She didn't even ask me to let my daughter know she had stopped by here looking for her. Oh well, I guess she'll come back if it was anything important.*

Remembering the new watering cans she'd purchased to sell in the greenhouse and left outside the door, Belinda stepped out. Her forehead creased as she looked down at the spot where she'd placed them. There had been four cans earlier, but now there were only three.

I wonder if Henry thought they were for our personal needs and hauled one off to use somewhere.

She looked up toward their garden but saw no sign of her son. *Maybe he took it up to the house for Sylvia to use in the flowerbeds near the back door.* Belinda was tempted to walk up there and see but didn't want to leave the greenhouse unattended. *Guess it'll have to wait until Henry shows up.* She picked up two of the watering cans and brought them into the building then went back and got the third one.

Twenty minutes passed, and two customers had come in, but still Belinda saw no sign of Henry. *What could that boy be doing all this time? He was supposed to join me here as soon as Amy left for her dental appointment.*

Another ten minutes went by before Henry finally made an appearance. "Where have you been?" she asked. "There are people here who might need some assistance, and I can't do that and be up here at the checkout counter too." Belinda kept her voice down, hoping none of the patrons could hear her conversation with Henry.

This business of him showing up late for work and disappearing all the time was getting old. She'd need to have a talk with him about this, but it would have to wait until a more opportune time.

"I was lookin' for my crow. Haven't seen him in the yard for a few days, and I'm worried about him."

Belinda rolled her eyes. *Is that crow really so important?*

He shrugged and started walking toward the customers, but Belinda stopped him with one more question. "There were four brand-new watering cans outside the door, but now there are only three. Did you take one of them?"

He shook his head. "I never saw four cans, only three, and that was when I went lookin' for Charlie."

Belinda waved her hand. "All right then, go ahead and see if any of the customers have questions or need help with anything."

As her son headed down aisle 1, Belinda leaned forward with her elbows on the counter. *Am I losing my mind? Could I have purchased only three watering cans to sell and thought it was four?*

Clymer

"I wonder how things have been going for your mom and siblings," Michelle commented when Ezekiel came into the house to get his lunch. "Have you talked to any of them lately?"

He shook his head. "Guess it's been close to a week. I've been meaning to phone them and ask, but I've had so many orders to complete in my shop, I keep putting off making the call."

He combed his fingers through the ends of his beard. "Guess my priorities are mixed up right now. I'll stop at the phone shed and call before returning to my shop."

"Would you rather I do it for you?" Michelle offered. "I could do it right now while you're in the house or wait till the baby and Angela Mary are down for their naps."

Ezekiel shook his head. "No, that's okay, it's my responsibility to check on my family back home." He pulled Michelle into his arms and gave her a kiss. "You have enough to do taking care of the kinner as well as the house."

"I don't mind, really."

He kissed her again. "I know you don't. You're such a sweet and caring person. I feel *seelich* that you agreed to marry me."

She stroked his face. "I'm the one who is blessed."

He grinned at her and grabbed his lunchbox. "I'll see you later this afternoon."

"I look forward to it." Michelle's dimpled smile almost made Ezekiel change his mind about going back to work, but his responsibility to the customers who'd placed orders won out.

As he headed to the phone shed, Ezekiel thought about Henry and how he had suspected the boy might be smoking. He'd made good on his decision to climb into the hayloft while he and his family were there visiting and had been relieved when he didn't find anything except a pair of binoculars by the open window. Maybe Henry wasn't lying when he said he hadn't been smoking. Ezekiel hoped it was true.

Strasburg

Amy came away from her dental appointment feeling more depressed than ever. It turned out that the sensitive tooth she'd been dealing with for the last week—and hadn't told anyone about—was abscessed. The dentist had prescribed an antibiotic to deal with the infection and offered her two choices: a root canal, followed by a porcelain crown, or pulling the tooth. Due to the expense of the first procedure he'd offered, Amy had gone with the second option and scheduled an appointment for next week. The tooth in question was near the back of her mouth, so at least having it gone wouldn't be noticeable.

"Seems like there is always some kind of trouble," Amy mumbled as she approached the pharmacy, which was a block down the street from the dentist's office.

When she entered the building, she checked at the counter for her medicine, and they told her it wasn't quite ready, but Amy went ahead and paid for it. While she waited, she milled around the aisles, looking at things.

Amy looked up and saw their neighbor come in and walk up to the prescription counter. "I'm Virginia Martin, and I'm here to pick up a prescription for my hormones."

"All right, let me go check." The man stepped away.

"Amy King!" the other clerk called.

"Yes." She stepped up to the counter.

"Here's your antibiotic, and the receipt is in the bag."

"Thank you." Amy turned to her neighbor. "Hello, Virginia."

"Oh hi. So, you had to come in here too, huh?"

"Yes. I have a tooth that's giving me some trouble."

"That's too bad." Virginia looked at the pharmacist who had returned with her prescription.

"Here you go. Do you need anything else today?"

"Nope. That's all." She pulled out her checkbook.

"Well, have a good day, Virginia." Amy left the counter.

"You too." Virginia barely glanced her way.

Mom's right. She is a person of few words.

When Amy came out of the pharmacy with her prescription, Helen, one of their new drivers, was just pulling into the parking lot. After Amy approached the van, Helen rolled down her window and stuck her head out. "I'm sorry to have to tell you this, Amy, but I just got a frantic call from my mother. She said my dad was in a car accident and is being rushed to the hospital in Lancaster. She wants me to meet her there right away."

"I'm so sorry to hear about your father. I hope he'll be okay."

"So do I. Listen, would it be all right if I call a friend of mine and ask her to come and take you home?"

"That's okay. I'll walk."

"Are you sure? Your place is a good two miles from here."

"It'll be fine. I've walked that road before, and it wasn't too bad. Besides, the fresh air and exercise will do me some good."

"All right then. Thanks, Amy."

"Please give us a call later and let us know how your father is doing."

"I will."

Amy watched as Helen's van pulled out of the parking lot and onto the street. She knew all too well the agony of losing her father. Right then, Amy said a prayer that Helen's dad would be okay.

Before Amy started her trek toward home, she stopped at Strasburg Country Store on Main Street for a bottle of water. Despite the cooler weather they'd been having, the warmth of the sun beating down on her head caused Amy to wonder if she'd made a mistake telling her driver not to call someone else to take her home.

Well, it's too late to change my mind now. Amy trudged along and soon headed out of town and down the country road in the direction of home.

She'd gone a short way when a horse pulling a market buggy came up beside her. "Where ya headed?"

Amy turned and was surprised to see Jared in the driver's seat. "I'm going home." Her heartbeat picked up speed as he gave her a friendly smile. "Hop in. I'll give you a ride."

Common sense told Amy she should say no, but her heart won out. As much as it hurt, the only right thing to do was tell Jared that she wished him and Lydia all the best. She truly did want the best for her friends, but it would be impossible to say she was happy for them. Just a sincere "Well wishes to you both" would have to suffice.

Amy climbed into the passenger side of the buggy. "I appreciate the ride. I thought I was up to the two-mile walk, but I'm not feeling my best today."

Jared turned in his seat to face her. "I'm sorry to hear that. What's wrong?"

Amy explained about her tooth and what the dentist had said. "Guess it could have been worse." She touched her jaw. "The prescription I got should relieve the ache until the problem can be fixed." *If only there was something that could take away the pain I feel in my heart.*

"Are you going to get a root canal?" he asked, guiding his horse back onto the road.

She shook her head. "It would be too expensive, so I made an appointment to let the dentist pull my abscessed tooth."

"If it's about the money, I'd be happy to pay for it, Amy."

She shook her head so vigorously the ties on her kapp swished across her face. "Since there are marriage plans in your future, you'll need all the money you earn."

"Marriage plans?" Jared glanced at her and tipped his head.

"To Lydia."

His head flinched back slightly. "Where in the world did you get that idea?"

"Lydia's mamm told me that you and Lydia were courting and also talking of marriage."

"I have no idea where Darlene would have gotten that idea. Lydia and I aren't courting, much less planning to get married."

"You're not?" Jared's denial didn't make sense. Amy saw no reason that Lydia's mother would make up such a thing."

"Lydia has secretly been seeing Rudy because she knew her parents did not approve of him."

"Rudy Zook?"

"That's right."

"But. . .but you and Lydia have been seen together several times, and at her birthday party, you were with her most of the evening."

"Jah, thanks to her mamm. She kept pushing us together." Jared reached over and lightly touched Amy's arm. "The only reason Lydia and I have been together is because we were talking about you. She was trying to help me figure out some way to—"

A car with a couple of teenage boys inside came roaring up beside them. Amy recognized the blond-haired fellow sitting in the passenger's seat. She didn't know the boy's name, but he and his family lived down the road from them. Sometimes she had seen him mowing lawns or doing yard work for other people along their road.

Amy was preparing to wave, but before she could lift her hand, the young driver honked the horn and sped on by. She could hear the boys' laughter through their open windows.

All the noise must have spooked the horse, because Dandy took off like a shot as they neared a Y in the road. Amy wasn't sure they'd even be able to make the turn that veered to the right.

Her heart pounded erratically as she clung to the edge of her seat, and Jared's knuckles turned white as he clutched the reins and hollered, "Whoa, Dandy! Whoa!"

As if in a frenzy, the horse's hooves kept pummeling the road. Several times the gelding crossed over the white line, and then he would jerk back again.

Amy's mouth went dry when she saw a car coming from the opposite direction. All she could think about was that she'd lost her father, brother, and Sylvia's husband in a tragic accident less than six months ago. *Please, Lord, don't let anything happen to Jared or me. Our families would be devastated.*

Chapter 40

Amy hung on for dear life and kept praying as the vehicle approached. Jared pulled sharply on the reins, forcing Dandy to the lane they should be in. When the car passed, the driver shook his fist and blew the horn, which only riled the horse more. Amy was so scared, she couldn't speak. Didn't the man behind the wheel of that vehicle realize Jared had not directed his horse into the other lane on purpose?

It seemed that the more Jared hollered for his horse to stop, the faster Dandy galloped down the road. Amy feared if he didn't get the horse under control soon, they could end up in a ditch with the buggy toppling over. And if the horse kept moving into the opposite lane, they would most surely be involved in a head-on accident.

Sweat poured off Jared's forehead and ran down his face as he continued the struggle with his horse. Finally, when Amy felt sure the buggy would tip over, Reckless quit running and slowed to a trot.

"Whew, that's a relief. Are you okay, Amy?" Jared reached across the seat and touched her arm.

"I'm fine," she said, barely able to catch her breath. "That ordeal really shook me up."

"Same here." Jared guided Dandy to a wide stretch of the road where there was plenty of room to stop. "I think we need a little time to catch our breath and quit shaking."

Amy nodded her agreement.

Still holding tightly to the reins, Jared looked over at Amy with such a tender expression, tears flooded her eyes. He let go with one hand and reached over to wipe them away with his thumb. "I love you, Amy, and I always will. Please say that I can begin courting you again. I would do just about anything to get you back."

"What about Lydia? Did you come to care for her during the time you and I were apart?"

Jared pointed his finger at her. "Didn't you hear a word I said before Dandy started acting up?"

"Well, I wasn't sure..."

"It's you I love, Amy, not Lydia. Like I said, she's secretly been seeing Rudy, and the only reason Lydia and I have gotten together is to talk about what I could do to get you back." A muscle in Jared's right cheek twitched. "I think if you'll just listen to me, we can work things out."

Amy pressed a trembling hand to her chest. "Oh Jared, I've missed you so much, and I have been praying about our situation."

"Did you receive an answer?"

"I thought I had until I ran into Lydia's mamm and she mentioned that you and Lydia were talking about marriage."

He chuckled. "Oh, Lydia's talked about it all right, but it's not me she's eager to marry. Your good friend is eager to become Rudy's fraa." Jared lifted Amy's chin so she had no choice but to look right in his eyes, and then he leaned forward and gave her lips a sweet, gentle kiss. "And I'm eager for you to become my wife. After we have courted a respectable time, will you agree to become Mrs. Jared Riehl?"

Amy nodded slowly as a renewed sense of hope welled in her chest. They had a lot to talk about the rest of the way home.

When Belinda heard a horse and buggy pull into the parking lot, she opened the greenhouse door and looked out. *Are my eyes playing tricks on me?* Her mouth nearly fell open when she saw Jared helping Amy out of his market buggy at the hitching rail.

"What's going on? Where's Helen?" Belinda asked as Amy and

Jared approached the greenhouse. "I thought she was supposed to pick you up after your dental appointment."

"She met me outside the pharmacy where I went to get an antibiotic for my abscessed tooth."

"Your tooth is that bad?"

"Jah, but we can talk about it later."

Belinda listened with puckered brows as Amy told her about Helen's father.

"I'm so sorry to hear that. I'm sure she must be quite worried about him."

"Jah. I asked her to call and let us know how he's doing."

"So how is it that you ended up bringing my daughter home from town?" Belinda looked at Jared.

"When I saw her walking along the shoulder of the road, I stopped and asked if she'd like a ride." The grin on Jared's face looked like it might never come off.

"And what a ride it turned out to be." Amy glanced at Jared then back at Belinda.

"What do you mean? What kind of ride?" Belinda questioned.

"I'll let Jared explain."

As Jared told Belinda what had happened with the car that passed and his horse getting spooked when the driver of the vehicle blew the horn, Belinda stood speechless.

"But I finally got Dandy under control, and your daughter and I are both okay."

Belinda's tense muscles began to relax. "I'm ever so glad."

"So are we. It could have ended in disaster."

"Do you think that young fellow tooted the horn on purpose to see if he could scare the horse?"

Jared shrugged. "I don't know, but it's a definite possibility. Some teenagers, even those who are Amish, think it is fun to fool around and do mean or destructive things. Like the vandalism that's been done to you good folks."

Belinda met Amy's gaze. "You told him about it?"

"Jah, Mom, but he already knows some of the things because Henry blabbed it some time ago. I also explained how Henry's been acting and that we are concerned about him. I figured if Jared and I are going to begin courting again, there should be no secrets between us."

Belinda's eyes opened wide. "You're back together?"

"Yes, we are, and if you would kindly give us your blessing, Amy and I would like to be married next fall."

Belinda placed one hand on Jared's arm and the other one on Amy's. "You most assuredly have my blessing. Oh, how I wish Vernon, Abe, and Toby could've lived to hear this wunderbaar news." Her eyes misted.

Jared felt such relief when Belinda gave her approval, although to him next fall seemed like a long time to wait. But they would need about a year to plan for a proper wedding.

"There are still a lot of things that need to be worked out," Jared said in a confident tone. "But together, and with the Lord's help, we'll figure it all out."

Amy leaned heavily against him and sighed. "As our bishop said during the last church meeting, 'With God, all things are possible.'"

"That's for certain," Jared agreed. He wasn't 100 percent sure what all had caused Amy to change her mind about them being together, but he was ever so pleased that she had. With them courting, Jared would be coming around more, which would give him an opportunity to check on things and make sure the women and Henry were safe. *I hope I can help Henry in some way to have a better attitude and be there for support in case any more weird things should happen around their place.*

That evening, Amy sat at the kitchen table going over the books to see where they stood financially with the greenhouse. Thanks to the fall plants Mary Ruth had given them, they had remained in the black.

It was hard for Amy to concentrate with Jared on her mind. All she could think about right now was her future with him. Although the future of their family business might be uncertain and even though they still did not know who had vandalized their property, Amy felt confident that things would go better for them now. If Henry was the one behind the damage done to their property, she hoped he would stop doing it and own up to his misdeeds.

All she and the rest of her family needed to do was to put their faith and trust in God, asking Him with prayerful and humble requests to protect and provide for them.

Caw! Caw! Caw!

Amy tipped her head toward the kitchen window. This time the annoying crow's call didn't bother her at all. As long as Henry kept feeding the bird, it was bound to keep coming around, so she would have to get used to its noisy ruckus. Perhaps in some strange way, God had sent the crow to warn them of things to come. Or maybe it was just a coincidence that Charlie the Crow had appeared when he did.

In an hour or so, Jared would be here for supper and their courting days would resume.

Amy sighed and repeated Psalm 56:3, a verse she'd read in her Bible last night. "What time I am afraid, I will trust in thee."

Recipe for Amy's Vanishing Oatmeal Raisin Cookies

1 cup butter or margarine, softened
1 cup packed brown sugar
½ cup sugar
2 eggs
1 teaspoon vanilla

1½ cups flour
1 teaspoon baking soda
1 teaspoon cinnamon
½ teaspoon salt
3 cups quick-cooking oatmeal
1 cup raisins

Preheat oven to 350 degrees. Cream butter and both sugars in large bowl. Add eggs and vanilla. Beat well. Combine flour, baking soda, cinnamon, and salt in separate bowl. Add to butter mixture and mix well. Stir in oats and raisins. Drop by rounded tablespoons onto greased cookie sheet. Bake for 10 to 20 minutes or until golden brown. Cool for 1 minute on cookie sheet before removing to wire rack. Yields about 4 dozen cookies.

Discussion Questions

1. Have you ever suffered a catastrophic loss like the King family did? How did each of the main characters in this story cope with their loss? Which character do you think handled it the way you would?

2. Do you think Amy's refusing to continue a courtship with Jared was a reasonable way to handle things? Could she have continued the courtship and still worked at the greenhouse and helped at home?

3. Was there anything Jared could have done to win Amy back? Did it appear that he gave up too quickly?

4. Sylvia went into deep depression after her loss. Have you ever suffered from depression? What did you do to get better?

5. Henry became rebellious and uncooperative after his father and older brother died. Were you a disobedient teen? Do you have a rebellious teen at home? How can you help a defiant teen?

6. Why do you think the Kings' new neighbor, Virginia, was so unaccepting of the Amish way of life? Have you or someone you know dealt with people who are prejudiced?

7. Belinda was unsure of who was vandalizing them and wondered if it could be her own son acting out his frustrations. Do you trust your children? Can doubting them with no solid proof damage your relationship with them?

8. Ezekiel struggled with whether he should move back to Strasburg to help his family or remain in New York, where his home and growing business were located. What would you do if you were in a similar situation?

9. What would you do if a homeless person like Maude came and took vegetables out of your garden without asking? Would you be angry or offer to help them?

10. If someone caused vandalism on your property, what would you do? Would you get a watch dog, an alarm system, or call the sheriff? Do you think Belinda did right by not notifying law officials and not wanting anyone outside their immediate family to know about it?

11. Amy's friend Lydia kept a secret from her parents. Is there ever a time when keeping secrets is okay?

12. Did you learn anything new about the Amish way of life by reading this story? If so, what did it teach you? Were there any particular scriptures that spoke to your heart or helped with something you might be going through?

About the Author

New York Times bestselling and award-winning author Wanda E. Brunstetter is one of the founders of the Amish fiction genre. She has written more than 100 books translated in four languages. With over 11 million copies sold, Wanda's stories consistently earn spots on the nation's most prestigious bestseller lists and have received numerous awards.

Wanda's ancestors were part of the Anabaptist faith, and her novels are based on personal research intended to accurately portray the Amish way of life. Her books are well-read and trusted by many Amish, who credit her for giving readers a deeper understanding of the people and their customs.

When Wanda visits her Amish friends, she finds herself drawn to their peaceful lifestyle, sincerity, and close family ties. Wanda enjoys photography, ventriloquism, gardening, bird-watching, beachcombing, and spending time with her family. She and her husband, Richard, have been blessed with two grown children, six grandchildren, and two great-grandchildren.

To learn more about Wanda, visit her website at www.wanda brunstetter.com.